EYE OF THE
BEHOLDER

EYE OF THE BEHOLDER

EMMA BAMFORD

SCOUT PRESS

New York London Toronto Sydney New Delhi

Scout Press
An Imprint of Simon & Schuster, LLC
1230 Avenue of the Americas
New York, NY 10020

First Scout Press hardcover edition August 2024

SCOUT PRESS and colophon are registered trademarks of Simon & Schuster, LLC

Simon & Schuster: Celebrating 100 Years of Publishing in 2024

For information about special discounts for bulk purchases, please contact Simon & Schuster Special Sales at 1-866-506-1949 or business@simonandschuster.com.

The Simon & Schuster Speakers Bureau can bring authors to your live event. For more information or to book an event, contact the Simon & Schuster Speakers Bureau at 1-866-248-3049 or visit our website at www.simonspeakers.com.

Interior design by Hope Herr-Cardillo

Manufactured in the United States of America

10 9 8 7 6 5 4 3 2 1

Library of Congress Cataloging-in-Publication Data is available.

ISBN 978-1-9821-7039-4
ISBN 978-1-9821-7041-7 (ebook)

PART ONE

It's not what you look at that matters, it's what you see.

—Henry David Thoreau

AFTER

1

AT EMBANKMENT STATION, THE OVERHEAD LIGHTS CAST EVERY-thing in a sickly yellow glow. It's crowded in the passageway and a bit-ing wind blows in off the night-dark Thames, dragging with it a smell of exposed mud and rotting river weed and God knows what else. Beneath my feet the ground shakes as a Tube train rumbles through a tunnel and I think of the hollows gouged in the rock below, wonder how deep they go. How far, if the earth cracked open, I would fall.

I shove my fists into my parka pockets. Stop it, Maddy. Just focus on getting home. Stupid idea, going out. Should have stayed in the flat, on my own. Out of harm's way.

A pack of Chelsea FC fans exit the barriers and flood into the passage-way. They're as jubilant as if they'd played and won the game themselves, tossing war cries back and forth, their baying amplified in the enclosed space and echoing off the tiled walls. Hunkering further into my coat, I try to tune them out and push on, but there are so many people that we are bottlenecked, and I'm slowed to a shuffle, forced to a halt. I really don't need this right now. One supporter hollers particularly loudly and a man ahead of me turns to stare at the commotion.

It's him.

Shock explodes in my stomach. I reel back.

It can't be; I'm imagining it. It must be a trick, an illusion, like all the other times a flash of an orange scarf at a man's neck caught my eye or an American accent sparked hope of a miracle, only to plunge me back into pain.

I almost daren't look again. Yet I can't help myself. He has a beard now and wears a black knit hat and a shearling jacket I haven't seen before. But that's just window dressing. His height, his coloring, the way the jacket hangs from his shoulders, how he tilts his head to one side in curiosity—I'd recognize that movement anywhere. My heart pounds and there's a disjunction, as if I've stepped outside myself. It *is* him. I don't know how, but it is.

Before I know it, I'm calling out. "Scott!"

He doesn't hear me over the fans' hullabaloo. I try again. "Scott!"

Other people are looking. He isn't; he has turned away. He's with two guys and all three have their backs to me. I don't recognize them, but of course I wouldn't. I never met any of his friends other than Angela.

The Chelsea supporters are still blocking my path. I try to squeeze through but can't. There's a jangling in my ears, my breath is coming hard. "Excuse me," I say. "Let me through!"

One of the Blues holds his scarf aloft and chants beerily in my face, "Who are ya? Who are ya?"

I crane my head to see past. Scott and his friends are exiting into the street. The crowd closes and I lose sight of them in the jumble of heads. I've got to get out of here. I can't lose him all over again. I struggle against the press of bodies, but it's useless. I'm trapped. There's no choice but to move with the throng.

Finally I'm swept out of the station and dumped on the pavement. I scour the street, left, right, behind. There! Beneath Hungerford Bridge: a dark archway. A door, a bouncer, girls in thin heels and thinner dresses. The thud of music. He and his friends are going in.

They have paid and pushed through the turnstile by the time I get to the club, and the chipped inner door is closing behind them. I push past the bouncer to the front desk, reaching for my bag and credit card. My bag isn't there. Shit. I slap at my pockets wildly. Phone, money, keys, all gone. I should retrace my steps. But there's no time.

"Please," I plead with the woman selling tickets. "My bag's been stolen." She gives me a disbelieving look from under her fringe. Desperation helps me improvise. I point at the door. "My friends are inside. I can get them and they'll come back and pay for me."

"Sorry, hon." She pops her gum, already moving her attention to the next in line. People are backing up behind me, tuts and murmurs building.

The bouncer looms. "Stand aside."

No, no, no. This can't be happening. I step out of the line, mumbling an apology, which placates him. Think, quick. Through the gridded safety glass of the door I can make out three wobbly shadows walking down a corridor. Music and voices leak in beats around the edges of the frame. Any second now he'll be swallowed by the crowd and I'll never find him.

I can't take that chance. As soon as the doorman's attention is elsewhere, I press myself up against a girl who has just paid and piggyback through the turnstile.

"Hey!" calls the ticket clerk.

"Oi, you!" yells the bouncer.

But I'm in.

It's too much at once—heat and noise and light, reverberation and movement and smells. Green lasers sharding through darkness. Bodies corralled like cattle. Two hundred people? A thousand? A strobe light strafes, shattering reality into a series of movie stills. The music is so loud it drums in my chest, *DOOF DOOF DOOF DOOF*, overruling my heartbeat, making it race.

Where is he? I surge into the mass, pushing hard against the resistant friction of arms and torsos. Someone else's sweat streaks the back of my hand. I scan the faces near me. Blank, all strangers. Where is he? The music, the lights, fracture everything. I didn't stop to check my coat and I'm way too hot, panic-level hot. It's hard to think.

I whip my head around, trying to take in the room. Across the floor are two stages, one holding the DJ, the second more people dancing. The dancers' stage is raised maybe ten feet above the ground—from there I'd be able to see more. I drive on through the crowd.

Somehow, I make it to the stage. The side steps are rammed with people. I climb the first couple, but the final rise is too high and, like in the station tunnel, there's no space to move. Someone slams into me and I stagger. I can't do it. Tears burn. A young man on the stage looks down and sees me floundering. He gestures—*Coming up?*—and elbows a neighboring guy to help. I lift both arms. Strong hands grasp, there's a wrench, and then I'm standing on the top level.

The music is even louder up here, punching into my body. My eardrums jump. There's no time to thank my helpers. Where is he? I press toward the front of the stage until I'm right at the edge. Better: I can see maybe two-thirds of the dance floor.

I search left, right, close to the stage, farther away. Most faces are turned up to the DJ booth, a congregation exultant before a secular altar. That guy—in the center. Is that Scott? He turns between passes of the light. Not him.

The music reaches a tachycardic peak and my heart has no choice but to follow, hammering to a frenzy. A laser flares, searing my retinas. I'm momentarily blinded. I blink to clear my vision. A commotion breaks out behind me, but I ignore it. Where is he?

Toward the left-hand wall of the club is a pair of men who could be the friends I saw him with at the station. I widen my search to take in the people around them but don't see him anywhere.

And then I do.

He's at the edge of the dance floor, still wearing his knit hat, drinking from a water bottle, laughing with another man. A laser dips over and behind him, throwing him into silhouette, until he is only a green outline, a ghostly aura.

The laser shuts off. The room goes completely dark. There's a split second of silence. Then the beat drops, and everything is bleached with light, and in that moment he looks over at the stage, catches my eye, and stills. The strobe fires and there's that freeze-frame effect again, and with every flash he's Scott looking at me, as he did in the mirror. Scott looking at me, Scott looking at me. Scott looking at me.

Back from the dead.

BEFORE

2

VIBRATIONS FROM THE HELICOPTER FILL MY ENTIRE BODY, making me aware of the skeleton inside me. Everything thrums: heels and toes against insoles, elbows against armrests, lower teeth against upper, even my brain against the inside of my skull. Above, the rotor blades *tchk-tchk-tchk* and turbulent wind shudders the fuselage. The bitter scent of aviation fuel sits on the back of my tongue, so dense I can taste it. Although my seat is soft and plush, I shift, restless.

Next to me, the pilot consults a complicated bank of winking instruments. "You doing okay?"

I'm wearing a heavy headset that is too big and keeps sliding down my ears, and his voice comes through small, making him sound much farther away, as if he's speaking down a tunnel. I wipe my clammy palms on my jeans and nod. He turns to me. "First time?"

The foam-covered mouthpiece on the headset has sagged. I pinch it closer to my mouth. It smells sickly sweet—traces of previous passengers—and makes me feel slightly nauseous. "Yes."

The static coming through my earphones dims, indicating he's about to speak again. "Not quite what you were expecting, huh?"

For all my faked nonchalance when I boarded, he's seen right through me. I don't move in these kinds of circles, there's no place for me in a Venn diagram of wealth and power and influence, not with my little flat, the scrabbling around for work, and the fairly small, tame life I lead. Before this, the last time I flew was two years ago—no, make that three—on a budget airline city break to Amsterdam, that fateful last trip with my ex. It was great—bikes, beers, museums. Normal stuff, in my normal life—nothing wrong with that. Perhaps not exactly what I envisioned for myself when I was younger, but, well, things happen. They get real. No, if life were such a Venn diagram, I wouldn't be anywhere near the center; I'd be in the corner of the page, on the outside of the rings of power, looking in, observing, recording. And it's not such a bad place to be.

Because while the idea of a helicopter was exciting—*is* exciting—there's an edge to it; the reality feels raw, risky in a way a plane never did. Although the cabin's movement is smooth and the interior luxurious, I'm acutely conscious of how much lower we are flying, of the rotor blades above us cutting the air, the slicing motion carrying us forward, and of how fragile the fuselage feels.

"Do you get travel sick?" the pilot asks.

"No."

"Great." His eyes scan the empty sky, taking in everything and nothing at once. "What are you going up there for? Holiday?"

I lift the droopy mic again. "Work. And a kind of favor for a friend. I'm a writer and my friend knows someone who needs help."

We bank, and the earth tilts. After leveling off, he flicks a sideways look at me. Is he trying to work out whether I'm famous? Often people do that when I tell them what my job is. They think all writers are like J. K. Rowling.

"What kind of things do you write?" he asks. "Anything I've heard of?"

I dread this question. The simple answer is, if you're into obscure political memoirs you might well have heard of one of my early books. It did quite well, was long-listed for a minor award. But my name isn't on the cover, and contracts and lawyers and NDAs mean I can't even mention it. "I ghostwrite, mainly."

"As in books about poltergeists and haunted houses? I love that spooky stuff."

I smile. That he might believe in ghosts seems so at odds with the formality of his uniform, the conformity of his haircut, the precise science of his job. I'd had him down as ex-military, a pragmatist. "No—autobiographies, memoirs. I write other people's life stories for them."

"What kinds of people?"

"All kinds. Generally successful ones."

He nods, understanding my point, and I think, of course he does. They're the people he works for, too, although his passengers will be even more successful than my clients—people whose wealth allows them anything they want, even if that's just the opportunity of getting where they need to go faster.

Another scan of the air. "Must be fascinating. Hard, too, I bet."

"Says the helicopter pilot."

His lips twist. "Touché. But I only take folks places. Usually I'm not delving into their lives, trying to find out all their dirty little secrets."

If only. "They tend to keep that stuff to themselves."

"I bet they do." He consults an instrument on the panel. "Well, we've got about ninety minutes until we land. So relax and enjoy the experience. You'll be fine."

I look out of the side window at the sky, willing my muscles to soften and telling myself the helicopter must be safe—presumably Angela Reynolds does this all the time. Maybe for a doctor of her standing it's like hopping in an Uber. How much does a short-notice private helicopter flight from London to Scotland cost, anyway? I'd have been happy with the train—less intimidating, for a start—but from the little I've seen so far it doesn't seem that money is an issue for Reynolds RX. And if this job opens as many doors as Sacha promised it will, and the high-end ghosting work comes flooding in, perhaps this'll become my new normal. No, scratch that. I couldn't bear the carbon footprint.

After a while, I find the pilot is right and that, even if I'm not entirely relaxed, at least I've got used to the constant beat of the blades and can enjoy the scurry of the land below. Ours is such a green country when you see it from the air, once you're freed from the concrete and tarmac of the roads and cities. Beautiful. It reminds me I ought to get out of London more.

We pass over field after field, all stitched together like a giant emerald-acid-chartreuse quilt tucked tight over the earth, and the farther north we go, over forests and mountains, the bigger the gaps between clusters of roofs grow, until there are hardly any buildings. Imagining living like that, so far from other people, so disconnected, gives me . . . not the creeps, exactly, but a sense of preemptive loneliness. Fine for a couple of weeks or a holiday, but permanently? I'm happy in my own company, but only a certain kind of person could stick it out here full time, someone tough.

It surprises me that a doctor like Angela would choose a house in such a wild, empty place. Even though we haven't yet met, given the tone of her email, the Mayfair office address, and the game she's in—aesthetics so good, apparently, she can charge five figures for injectables and still have a two-year waiting list—I've pictured Angela as urbane. Sophisticated. Have I got her wrong? Is she going to be a robust outdoorsy type, all tweed hunting jackets and jolly hockey sticks bonhomie?

We fly over moorland, mile after mile of never-ending bracken. A herd of deer, startled by the helicopter's approach, take off, cantering so fast I imagine I can hear the flint-cracked thunder of their hooves. They continue running after we've overshot them, trying to get away from a danger they don't understand.

I lift my eyes to the horizon, which is smudged and bent to the curvature of the earth. We skim over a large inland body of water. I steady the headset on my ears. "Is that Loch Lomond?"

A tinny "Yep." The pilot dips his head. "And over there, at about ten o'clock, is Varaig."

I crane my neck to try to spot the loch and the house, hoping to gain a few clues into what Angela is like. Sacha told me so little, just assured me the commission was in the bag and said I'd be fine. I trust her, but even so the first-day nerves are jangling. I'm not a huge fan of going into a job blind.

There are three smaller pools in the distance, looking from this height like flat spills of mercury. I presume, comparing what I can see now with yesterday's recon on Google Maps, that Varaig is the one in the center. It grows as we approach, silver darkening to steel, reflecting the overcast November sky, and at one edge I spy a single white building, a small cottage perhaps, tumbled out alone like a lost die. Angela's place? But no—we loop back over empty, houseless heath and a few minutes later the pilot is circling over mown grass and then bringing us low. Landing is an impossible rush and upward buck of the ground, wind, vibrations, noise. I can't help but close my eyes for touchdown.

A woman's face appears in the helicopter window. The whine of the blades is too loud for speech, so she mouths "Hi!" through the glass and opens the door. I sense she's not Angela. More likely the assistant, Raphaela, the one who emailed me the flight details and directions to the heliport in London. She's a little younger than I am, immaculate in raincoat, silk blouse, and tailored trousers. I lift off my headset and unbuckle my seat belt. She reaches for the handles of my wheelie case and my rucksack.

"I can take those," I say, but she shakes her head and points at her ear—she can't hear me. She flashes a smile and hoicks my luggage onto the turf. After extending a hand to help me out, she puts her palm to the back of her head and mimes ducking.

I copy her beetle-backed posture as we scurry out of the danger zone. The downdraft fills my coat, whipping it around me. No sooner are we clear than the helicopter takes off again, the noise monstrous as it rises. We both stop and watch it grow small against the clouds, lights winking white. Where is the pilot off to next, I wonder. Home to his family? Or elsewhere, to the next job, a new place and another stranger willing to put their life in his hands?

"Right," the smart woman says when the thundering has faded. "Now that we can hear ourselves think, how about a proper introduction?" We shake hands. "Raphaela." Her hand is warm, the grip confident.

"I guessed so. Maddy."

"Welcome to Varaig."

Raphaela has the kind of smile you find in hotel receptionists, or front-of-house staff at good restaurants. I'm suddenly conscious of how the strap of my rucksack must be wrinkling her outfit and of how tatty my case is. I reach for the handle. "Here, let me take that."

But she's already picked it up and is making her way across the grass. "Honestly, it's fine. I'm used to it. And we're almost there."

"At the house? But I didn't . . ."

She's crunching onto gravel. A path. "You didn't see it from the air?" She smiles over her shoulder, wide-eyed. "Angela's little trick." She leads us on a sharp turn around some trees and suddenly ahead there's a house; more than a house—a complex. Two large buildings are set perpendicular to each other, the one on the left a traditional stone barn. This must have been a farm once. The barn looks original but carefully restored: the stone has been blasted clean, the rustic wooden doors are freshly painted. But the large building next to it is no working farmhouse. It is a paragon of modern minimalism, brutalist in design: three interlinked concrete blocks fronted with huge walls of glass. From this angle, the glass reflects the clouded sky, shrouding what is inside from view. Yep, money's definitely not an issue.

I look up. The roofs of the house and barn are carpeted with moss. Raphaela is a fast walker and I have to half trot to keep pace as she reaches the end of the house.

"That's why I couldn't see it from the air?" I ask. "The moss? It's like camouflage."

"That was Angela's idea. Makes it a kind of nice surprise, right? Of course, it helped with the planning permission, too." She skirts the side of the house, where there is a circular gravel driveway, and goes to a door. From this spot I can see that the whole building sits against rock. It's shady here, and a lot colder. I pull the edges of my coat together. Autumn is far chillier in Scotland than in London.

"Right then, one moment." Raphaela leans my case against the wall and rests my rucksack on top of it. She holds her phone to a small unit next to the doorframe. There's a beep, then the door unlocks. "I've emailed you the link to download the key app," she says, letting me past.

Stepping inside with a quick "thanks," I find myself in a combined mudroom and utility area bigger than my kitchen at home. A fully stocked floor-to-ceiling wine cabinet hums in a corner. Next to the door we came in through, waxed and waterproof jackets hang from pegs; below, walking boots and Wellingtons are ranked on a rack. They are all fastidiously clean. Makes sense for a doctor.

"Does Angela live here permanently?" I ask.

There's a clunk as Raphaela swings my luggage onto the rack. "She's not here often. She travels so much. And mainly she stays in London. But she comes here when she can. Calls it her sanctuary." She hangs her raincoat and straightens her blouse. "Feel free to look around. You should find everything you need but let me know if there are any amenities or foods you prefer and I'll get them sent over."

I open a door to a double-height atrium with a corner staircase spiraling up to a mezzanine. The ceiling and floor are honey-toned concrete, the walls white and hung with pictures. Apart from one old-fashioned watercolor landscape in a scalloped gilt frame, the art is contemporary, photos and abstracts, in keeping with the house. Tucked under the stairs, in the center of a Perspex console table, stands a small bronze sculpture, a rough molding of a human form standing supplicant. I step closer. It looks like an artist's manikin, one of those little wooden puppets with jointed limbs. But it is finished in a way that makes it seem as if its skin has been stripped off, leaving its crude metal muscles exposed. The effect is grotesque.

"Impressive, isn't it?" Raphaela is in the atrium behind me. She isn't talking about the manikin but the room, even the whole house.

I turn my back on the sculpture. For all I know of art, it could be worth millions. "She seems quite the collector."

"It's her hobby." She's tapping at her phone, making a call. "Excuse me while I . . ."

"Of course."

"Your room is upstairs. I can show you in a moment or you can make yourself at home."

I'm more than happy to look around on my own. It means I don't have to pretend to be cool when truthfully I'm blown away by this place. I tiptoe past her into a kitchen and dining area. Like the atrium, it is large and airy, birch and limestone. Tastefully anonymous. I open a cupboard. I've found the fridge. It's full, packed with fresh fruit and vegetables, meat and fish, high-end ready meals, eggs, cheese. The next cupboard, a pantry, is the same: unopened jams and condiments, two types of peanut butter, Marmite, vinegars, oils. All pristine. No moldy half-used marmalade here.

The end of the house is a living room, although the word "room" seems inadequate to describe it, suggesting something smaller. All the furniture—sofa, armchairs, inset fireplace, wood store—is minimalist, the colors natural and muted. It's a blank canvas with nothing to distract the eye, and when I look out I can see why. The view is everywhere, is everything. Lawn and the beginnings of leggy heather in the foreground, a long dip of moorland—maybe the Scots would call it a glen—fading to blurred woolliness in the distance, and then the loch and, beyond, mountains. It's late afternoon now and sunlight slats the glen, casting long shadows where it snags on gorse bushes, illuminating motes suspended in the air on the other side of the glass and faceting the water beyond like a jewel. So this is how the other half live.

Raphaela is still on her phone as I backtrack into the atrium. There's another door, which I missed earlier. It opens onto a corridor that runs the length of the back of the house. It's bunker-like here, being closed off from the view, and almost claustrophobic. Two doors stand ajar—empty bedrooms. A third is closed. As Raphaela said I've been put upstairs, I don't go in.

I can't help but catch a strand of her conversation as I climb up to the mezzanine: ". . . can't you keep him a while longer? Please? I have no choice . . ." Off the landing is a bedroom, the bed made up with crisp sheets. A jar of white roses rests on the nightstand. A card reads: *Madeleine. I hope you're comfortable. Call Raphaela if you need anything. Angela*. I examine the handwriting, which is looped, generous. Did she write this herself or get her assistant to do it? I wander into the bathroom, which has both a walk-in shower and an egg-shaped tub.

Beyond the en suite is an office, a glass desk dead center. It's like being in a spread from an architectural magazine, far more impressive than the cozy living rooms or golf clubhouses where I usually meet my clients. I sit in the chair and picture writing here. My pulse quickens. I could definitely get used to this. When you work for yourself there's no such thing as a promotion, but this feels like a step up. Maybe my words will come out as clean and perfect as the house.

A noise breaks the peace. It settles into the distinguishable *chudder* of a helicopter, getting louder every second. I cross to the window. Yes, there it is, hovering above the place it dropped me, already tilting its rails toward the ground like a giant black bird angling on its prey.

I clatter down the stairs. Raphaela looks up, her face the mask of a consummate professional.

"Angela's here."

3

ANGELA, WHEN SHE ENTERS THE HOUSE, HAS TWO TINY, CUTE dogs trailing her. She comes straight up to me, her heels and their claws clicking on the polished floor, and squeezes my hand.

"Madeleine. I'm so pleased to finally meet you."

Angela is what my mum would have called "well put together." Exceedingly so. She's classic-looking: slim but not bony-thin, average height like me, but with far more poise. Her eyes are pale, cool, assessing; her hair, that fashionable shade of West London blond, is held in a neat chignon. Her dress is the chicest I've ever seen. Seamless and hemless, it floats around her like a white cocoon. Just from looking at her, I know she is excellent at what she does.

"And you," I say. "Thanks again for the commission."

"My pleasure. Shall we?" She has a curious accent, transatlantic. It reminds me of the way Hollywood stars of the 1950s used to speak. Slow, considered, held in.

She indicates with her head that I'm to follow her through to the living room. The dogs come with us. They are spaniels, small as toys, one black and white with tan eyebrows, the other pure tan. Show dogs by the look of it. As we go, I retuck my shirt and unroll the sleeves. I'm wearing what I always wear when meeting clients—shirt, black skinnies. What I always wear full stop. But now I feel like I should have put on something smarter, a blazer maybe. At least these are my newest jeans.

In the living room I sit where directed on the sofa, and Angela takes an armchair. The dogs make to jump onto the chair, too, but Angela warns, "Rudy, Massimo," and they settle by her feet. To me she says, "Before we get into it, would you like something to drink? Coffee?"

"That'd be great, thanks."

"Of course. Raphaela?" As she speaks to her assistant, I scan Angela's face. Her skin looks so good that she must have had work done herself. Yet there's no telltale shiny tightness, no immobilized features: her eyebrows lift as she talks; her forehead puckers.

Raphaela bows out of the room. Sounds of a machine warming up come through from the kitchen.

Angela smooths the silk of her dress over her knees. "So you know Sacha from university?"

How much has Sacha told Angela about me? Will she have explained how she basically became my big sister after Mum died, how I completely fell apart? Man, I hope she kept it strictly professional. Yes, she must have done, or I wouldn't be here. "That's right, from day one," I say. "We had neighboring rooms in halls." So long ago. To think of us then is to think of two other people—barely more than kids but believing we were adults, blissfully clueless about what life would soon chuck at us. "She's a fantastic lawyer."

Angela raises her eyebrows and smiles tightly. Of course she already knows this. Embarrassment tingles my cheeks. I'm not normally anxious when I meet new clients or start a project. But the stakes feel higher than usual: we had no preliminary meeting to see whether we'd be a good fit; time is tighter, the money greater. "Have you been looking for a ghostwriter for a while?" I add.

She leans down to stroke the ears of the tan-colored dog. "I know Lord Malouf."

Malouf was my client who was offered a peerage. He has never publicly acknowledged me as his ghostwriter. Crap. If Malouf thinks I've blabbed about being his ghost, broken the terms of the NDA, I could be in big trouble.

She sees my panic. "Don't worry. Abdul knows you didn't tell. He's very proud of the book, you know. He has a copy of the cover, blown up and framed, in his cloakroom."

Raphaela comes back through with a coffee for me, water for both of us. If Angela has been in Malouf's downstairs bathroom, she must know him well. He never invited me into his home when we worked together. Are they friends? I can't imagine how their paths would cross. Unless he's a client of hers? I try not to laugh. Imagine!

"He was a pleasure to work with," I say neutrally, copying the word she used earlier.

"Abdul says the same. You come highly recommended."

I try to hide the warmth growing in my face—a happy glow, this time—by sipping some coffee. I need to play it cool. This woman seems all business and pretty shrewd.

"I was also impressed with how discreet you were about your previous clients when Sacha put us in touch," she says. "It's what piqued my interest. We're the same here. We're all about discretion."

"We?"

"Myself and my business partner, Scott De Luca."

Discretion. That's exactly the right word for Angela. In her composed manner and understated style, both in her dress and her house.

"And in answer to your question," Angela continues, "yes, I have been looking for a ghostwriter for my memoir for a while. I had one. He started, but sadly there were personal issues at his end. I don't like to go into detail"—her diction is studied, formal, like her unusual accent—"but there were difficulties with his family, an emergency, and he wasn't able to produce on time. My needs are precise, Madeleine, and I need someone who is a good fit. A safe pair of hands and a good pair of eyes. Someone who won't get distracted. I can't afford to get it wrong again."

"Well, I like to think I'm both reliable and perceptive." And she certainly doesn't have to worry about family emergencies with me.

"Perfect." She stands. The tan dog is immediately on his feet. The black-and-white one, Rudy, takes a couple of attempts to get up, staggering a little as he does so, as if caught unawares. "I'll show you the clinic so you can begin to get a feel for what we do."

"I'd like that." Sacha told me there was a clinic on site, for "convenience" for certain clients. It puzzled me how this remote place could be more convenient than London, until she mentioned Balmoral. The helicopter wasn't gone long, so Angela hasn't come far—has she just been to see a royal client?

In the kitchen, we pass Raphaela working at a laptop. Angela clicks a mechanism and slides open the huge glass window. "No, my loves," she says to the dogs. "Stay here." They do as told, but reluctantly, pacing circles on the kitchen floor, unsure why they aren't getting a walk.

The air outside is crisp. I've left my coat in the mudroom, and I don't want to waste Angela's time going back for it, so I fold my arms over my chest for warmth and follow her along the terrace to the barn, where she holds her phone to a reader by a side entrance. We go through a small vestibule and she flicks on the lights beyond.

All traces of the barn's former purpose have been erased. Now this section is a doctor's office, windowless, with a rank of medical machines arranged around an examination table. The air in here is still, rarefied. It smells sweet, of vanilla and jasmine and a hint of something medicinal: scented candles disguising disinfectant, perhaps. Angela is standing by a counter with a fridge and a cupboard both fitted with electronic locks like the one at the entrance. The room is reassuring in its neatness and array of high-tech equipment, and only the presence of the yellow sharps disposal box by the gleaming sink reminds me that this is a place where blood is shed.

I'm dying to know if this is where she tweaks duchesses—even princesses. "Do you see many clients here?"

"Only those who prefer not to come to London. Some clients I fly to see. I have identical treatment rooms set up in major cities around the world."

I nod, pretending the logic of this has naturally occurred to me. I hold up my phone. "Mind if I record this for my notes?"

"Of course."

I start the voice notes app. Angela crosses to the machines beyond the table, pointing to each in turn. "We have ablative and nonablative lasers for cell turnover, resurfacing, and collagen stimulation. LED phototherapy for strengthening, IPL and radiofrequency for rejuvenation, ultrasound and RF again for tightening. Freeze-sculpting."

I clutch at the only term I half understand. "Freeze-sculpting?"

"Cryolipolysis for nonsurgical targeting of localized fat."

Lipo, as in fat, and cryo . . . "Wait, you can freeze fat off?"

"No one does lipoplasty anymore if they can help it. You might be surprised at how effective this is." She takes a pair of latex gloves from a box before unhooking a gadget that looks like a small vacuum cleaner head. She hovers it beneath her jaw. "An hour at four degrees for four to six treatments. Zero downtime. It's very popular for double chins."

I lift my head and lengthen my neck. Next to Angela is something that looks like a handgun connected to a barista's espresso machine. "And that?"

She slots the freezing gadget back into its place and picks up the gun. "It's for mesotherapy." She holds out the tip for me to see. When she pulls the trigger a superfine needle shoots forward. "Subdermal micro-injections at up to three hundred fifty shots a minute. Hyaluronic acid, amino acids, minerals, and vitamins. A cocktail tailored to whatever the client needs."

Needs. "Does it hurt?"

She puts the gun back. "It depends on your pain threshold, of course, and your perception, but we do our best to keep our clients relaxed."

"And what about Botox and fillers?"

"Doing botulinum toxin or fillers on their own is more of a . . . high street approach. Here we're holistic. First I'll do a blood screen for a client, check their hormone levels, and prescribe bioidentical hormones to rebalance."

"And your partner, Scott? Is he a plastic surgeon, too?"

"No. He has a medical degree but is on the business side. And I'm a cosmetic surgeon, not plastic."

"I didn't realize there was a difference."

"The industry separates us. A plastic surgeon will tell you that theirs is essential work, perhaps to repair damage after trauma or illness or a congenital condition."

"Like breast reconstruction after mastectomy?" Mum had a brief dis-cussion with her doctor about that but hadn't opted for an implant, saying she'd prefer to stay wonky if it meant less surgery.

"Exactly. Or skin grafts after fire damage, correction of cleft palates. They tend to look down on the kind of work we do here as shallow, call it nonessential. But I'd argue that there's trauma in many of my clients' cases, too, just not the kind you can see on the outside. And I'm one hundred percent private practice, so there's no question of use of public funds. It's my clients' choice."

She indicates the machines. "So, to continue with your question, after endocrine balancing, typically I'll recommend some of the medical technologies and finally some injectables. Depending on the particular client's needs."

There's that word again. "Does anyone need any of this?" That came out sounding more critical than I intended. I add a little laugh to disperse any received cynicism.

Angela looks straight at me, so keenly that I feel weirdly exposed. "Again, that depends on your perception."

I consider the equipment, remembering how in demand she is. These machines are ugly, clunky, but, according to Sacha, they are basically a magician's toolkit. "I hear you have a two-year waiting list."

"Three, actually." She sounds more American as she says this. "I—that is, we—are very lucky. We can afford to be choosy with our clients. They're of a certain milieu. They don't tell anyone they've been to see me, they don't shout about it on social media. Most of them aren't even on social media. They don't tell their friends who their derm is because they're afraid they won't be able to get appointments if I'm too busy. My clients are the one percent of the one percent, and aging isn't a game to them, it's a very serious business."

"Of course." It looks it, with all this paraphernalia.

"I know how it might seem from the outside—like we're benefiting from other people's insecurities."

"I wouldn't say that exactly."

"You wouldn't be the first." She's testing me, daring me to say something wrong.

I'm up for the challenge. "So what would I need, for example?" I'm careful not to put any emphasis on "need." She levels those light eyes at me. "Go on. Tell me what you'd prescribe. It'll help me understand." I'm thirty-nine. I'm certainly no supermodel, and some things have started to slide, but how bad can it be?

She puts on a mask from a box near the gloves and cups my chin. "Well," she says, her voice slightly muffled, "you have a lot of sun damage." She hovers a fingertip, sketching the rim of my forehead, my nose. "Sooner or later there'll be hyperpigmentation here, broken capillaries there. You've already developed quite deep lateral canthal rhytids."

"Lateral . . . ?"

"Crow's-feet."

Ouch.

She angles my face this way and that, looking for more problems. I'm not used to being so closely examined. My scalp prickles and there's that feeling once more of exposure. It's bordering on vulnerability, as if she can see all my flaws, inside and out. She lets go and steps away, and with the distance I breathe easier.

"Well," she says, "I'd start with an LED facial and the removal of the solar lentigo. Cell renewal laser treatment to plump the skin." Her face mask comes off and is dropped into a bin. "Then hyaluronic injections here, here, here"—she touches the top of her own cheek, below her eye and near her mouth, in the place where a spot of ketchup might fall—"to redefine your zygoma—that's your cheekbones—fill out the tear trough, and lift the corners of the mouth. Botox in the forehead, of course, and around the eyes." She lifts her chin and makes an upward gesture with a hand to tell me to do the same. "You've still got a few years before middle age, but it wouldn't hurt to put a drop in the tip of the nose."

Middle age? That stings almost as much as the length of her prescription. "People get wrinkles in the tip of their nose?" I'm pretty sure I've never seen such a thing.

"No, but for some the tip does droop after a certain point."

My finger comes to the end of my nose. I press the cartilage, lift it minutely.

"The sooner you begin, the better the results, you know."

"I don't think I could afford you." And what would be the point? It's not like I'm a celebrity, constantly being photographed and having my appearance dissected. I'm free to slide into decrepitude, if I want to. Do I want to?

There's a snap as she pulls off her gloves. She tosses them after the mask. "You're lucky. As I say, you're relatively young, you have some time to think about it. And if you do decide to try, just ask."

The thing is, I think, once you start, how could you ever stop?

- - -

Back in the living room, the dogs having leapt joyfully at Angela's shins, we resume our seats. A coffee table book has been laid on the sofa, presumably by Raphaela. A woman's face in quarter profile curves across the cover, lips in the bottom corner, temple at the top. In the white space on the other side, the title is picked out in a Didot-style font, like the one *Vogue* uses, although slimmer and more refined: SKIN DEEP. That's the title of the book I'm here to write. So this is a mock-up, a dummy.

I open it and flick through the pages. The paper is thick and smooth under my fingers. Black-and-white close-up shots of faces, male and female and a variety of ethnicities, are interspersed with text. I choose a page at random. I'm conscious of Angela's eyes on me as I turn, of the paper making a scoring sound. The text has wide margins, a deep head and foot. It is *lorem ipsum*, the nonsense Latin used as placeholder copy by print designers. I flip the book on its side. On the spine, RRX, the logo of her company, Reynolds RX, is foiled in silver.

"Beautiful, isn't it?" she says.

It is—but it's also rather overorganized of her. I've never known a book to be designed before the words have been written. Things change so much during the process. Occasionally, depending on whether the client wants me to act as a kind of managing editor, I might get to see a printed proof before we start the full print run. But I don't get to handle the almost-finished article before I've even asked my client one question about themselves.

I reopen the book. The picture here is a headshot of a young woman, dewy and fresh. The model's eyes are closed and nearly all of her skin—her face, neck, the tops of her shoulders—is freckled. Only her eyelids are clear. In these days of flawless foundation and photo filters, to have freckles so unapologetically displayed is refreshing, even startling.

"That one was taken with a UV camera," Angela says. "It has a filter that only lets ultraviolet light through, showing the sun damage to the dermis. She'll regret not using sunscreen when she's older."

I reframe what I'm looking at. "I thought they were freckles."

"To the untrained eye. Freckles now, carcinoma later."

Cancer. It comes up everywhere, anytime. Even in a work meeting. I close the book and put it down.

Angela watches me. "I appreciate this may be an unorthodox way of working, in your industry. But it's how I'm used to doing everything. Preparation is key. And time is short." I haven't said anything about her approach, so she must have read my expression. It's not surprising that someone who works so closely with faces can read them so well.

"I see this book as being quite different from most, if not all, of the previous projects you've worked on," she says. "More of a mission statement." She bends to a large handbag by her feet that wasn't there when we left the room. Raphaela again, I guess. Out comes a paper folder. She opens it to show me. "In here you'll find all the details. Publication date. Word count. Deadline for the final text to go to the typesetters. I've also taken the liberty of including a list of topics I'd like to cover in the order I'd like to cover them."

As she lists each point she takes papers out of the folder and fans them on the sofa. "Of course, you're the expert here and that's why I'm hiring you. So if, when you get into it, you think things need reordering, feel free to play around and we can work it out between us."

I nod. She seems single-minded as well as organized, but I can't help admiring that. Presumably that kind of focus got her where she is in life.

She adds another sheet of paper. "Now, I have a very busy list, and I'm frequently out of the country, so here I've scheduled some slots for us to talk over video calling. I've marked which time zones I'll be in."

She taps a bullet-pointed section. It's a list of dates, times, and locations over the course of four weeks. Bahrain jumps out at me. New York, Cape Town. This is weird—Sacha told me I'd be staying in Scotland for a month. I thought Angela would be here for a few days at least.

"And obviously you'll be coming here as well?" I ask.

"No," she says. "On this next sheet you'll find instructions for joining the video conferencing system that I use to consult with clients. It's encrypted, much more secure than standard software, and it automatically records the calls. I've created an account for you. You don't need any special equipment—a laptop with camera or you can download the app to your phone."

Why get me to come to Varaig if she isn't even going to be here? I could have done this from London. On-screen is okay but talking in person is far better. I look for how much writing and approval time she's allowed after the interviews end. There doesn't seem to be any. I find the final deadline and my stomach drops. November 30! That month isn't just for research and initial interviews; it's for delivering the whole manuscript. No way. Not possible.

Angela is striding on, either not noticing or ignoring the consternation I'm now making no effort to hide. Yet more papers are added to the fan. "Raphaela has emailed you some information on our treatments. And I took the liberty of giving you basic background info, plus the draft so far and the transcripts of the interviews I did with your predecessor. I have everything for you in hard copy here, but also as electronic and audio files."

I'm flushing hot. The coffee, all the information, the micromanaging. This isn't how I work. I interview, digest, discuss. Collaborate. This is too much. Over the years I've developed a sixth sense for nightmare clients and normally I plead a full diary to avoid taking them on. So stupid to get into this situation, to have accepted the job before meeting the subject just because Sacha said I'd be doing her a huge favor. I definitely shouldn't have agreed to stay in this woman's house. Maybe I can back out gracefully and catch a train back to London. "Angela—"

"I'll get Raphaela to email it all over to you, along with the contract and the NDA."

"Angela—"

"They should be standard but let me know if there's anything you're not happy with, and I can get it redrafted."

I edge forward on my seat. "Dr. Reynolds—"

She holds up a hand. "I'm aware that it's a short deadline, Madeleine, and I'm sorry. It's nonnegotiable, I'm afraid—this is a critical time for the company, and the book has to come out this year. The printer is booked, and I've scheduled the launch. It's unfortunate we were delayed by the change of writer. But I'm confident you'll be able to meet it, especially up here with no interruptions. That's why I invited you to Varaig—we've taken care of everything, so all you need to do is focus on the book. Abdul says you did his in six weeks."

She's got me there—I did. But I was younger then, and hungrier. Different. And I'd done the interviewing and got a lot of background beforehand.

Before I can object further, she says, "Now, of course, your fee. I've outlined it here. I presume it'll suffice?"

She's pointing to the contract. The edge of her buffed nail underlines a figure. A figure far, far higher than the rate I quoted—more than enough to finally divest myself of my student loan and cover my mortgage payments right through to the end of next year. Jesus, is this what I should have been charging my clients all along? Am I actually worth that much? Screw the boring student loan and mortgage payments—with that amount of cash in the bank I could become a different person entirely.

"And, of course, I'll give you joint credit on the book," she adds.

My name on the cover, after all this time. I look at the SKIN DEEP dummy again. So beautiful. It would make one hell of a business card. This could be the break I've been waiting for, like Sacha said when she connected us. The chance to be noticed.

I flick through the pages, thinking fast. What is it, forty, fifty thousand words? I can make it work. Like she pointed out, I did it before and I can do it again. I'm here now anyway. One month of hard work, that's all. As Angela says, no distractions. And it's bound to be an interesting subject— this woman is absolutely at the top of her game. No more jobbing for peanuts, recording retirees' memories for the grandkids. I can start to make a name for myself.

"You had a question?" Angela says.

My voice sticks. I take a sip of water. "So many questions." I stretch a bright smile across my face. "Mainly about you. But you're busy, so it'll probably be best if I hone them and save them for our first interview on the . . ." I scan the list of dates. "On the fifth." In three days' time. "And I'll have reviewed all of this by then."

Her whole face lights up. "Great."

A knock, and Raphaela comes in. "Sorry to disturb, Dr. Reynolds. The pilot is anxious to depart if you're going to make your flight from Glasgow."

"Thank you, Raphaela." Angela rises and passes her assistant her bag. "Madeleine, you'll have to excuse me. Come on, Rudy-boy." She picks up the black-and-white dog with the eyebrows, pressing her cheek to the top of his head for a moment.

I just have time to shove all the paperwork back into its folder and stand before she's squeezing my fingers in a goodbye.

"I'll call you from Saudi," she says.

From the window, I watch her climb into the helicopter and settle in an accustomed way into the back seat. Raphaela passes up both dogs and gets in. The pilot closes the door. The helicopter fires up, noise ricocheting around the house, wind making cut blades of grass dance like fireflies in the air. Low sunlight winks on the windshield, obscuring the faces of those inside.

I watch them lift off. This is either going to be the best commission I've ever accepted, or the worst. Whichever it turns out to be, at least it'll be over in a month.

4

THE HOUSE IS UTTERLY SILENT AFTER THEY'VE GONE. I STAND in the atrium, listening. There's nothing, not even a ticking clock. After the constant hum of London traffic, it makes me aware of how alone I am here, on this empty moor, in a stranger's house. A stranger's darkening house. Only three thirty and the sun will soon be down.

To lessen the creepiness I switch on the lights and my attention is drawn to the bronze sculpture. An artist's manikin is meant to represent the ideal human proportions, the perfect body, albeit scaled down, and whenever I see one I'm always struck by how beautiful they are, how graceful in their symmetry and smoothness. But this statuette, with its gnarled, featureless face and flayed body, insides on display for all to see, is gruesome. I notice its joints are articulated, like a real artist's model, and I try raising one of its arms. When it holds in place I lift the other, too. Waving, the thing is marginally less unnerving.

I carry my case upstairs and unzip it. But when I slide open the wardrobe, there are clothes already hanging, pushed to one side to create space. So this is Angela's room. Why give it to me when there are three others? Maybe I should move my things downstairs.

I skim the wardrobe's contents. Pale colors, fine fabrics—silk, cashmere—the opposite of my adopted uniform. I stroke a gauzy sleeve and imagine what it would feel like to wear something so soft next to my skin every day. Seductive, I guess. And, like tweakments, habit-forming. Luxury ought to come with an addiction warning.

My eye lands on the welcome card on the nightstand. Angela did say she wants me to be comfortable. I look through the en suite doorway to that deep tub and picture myself enjoying a soak. Screw it—she's not going to be here anyway. If I'm alone in this house, why shouldn't I have the best room? There's no need to settle for less. I am earning this, after all.

I unpack my clothes and set up my laptop in the office. The submission date, marked in my calendar, seems perilously close, and I want to begin right away. If I work until midnight or so, I can get a good sense of the project before starting fresh in the morning.

First I make myself a sandwich. I eat it quickly in the kitchen and then brew tea. Getting milk from the fridge, I spot a bar of dark chocolate, eighty-five percent, the kind I love. I snap off a couple of squares, slide the remainder into its cardboard sleeve, and put it back. That'll make a nice treat for the long evenings ahead.

In the office I nibble on the chocolate as I go over the contract and the NDA. Both look fine so I e-sign them. Then I open the other ghostwriter's draft. Angela didn't tell me his name, but his initials are on the file: JP. I check the word count—thirty thousand. As long as JP asked the right questions, this'll help. I'm giving myself two weeks to get a first draft done, then a week each for the second and the third, final drafts. It's tight, but not impossible. I begin to read.

Oh crap. It's no good. There are so many gaps—gaps I'll have to fill. *Born on XX XX 19XX [insert: day, month, year] in XXX [town] to parents XXX and XXX [names].* He hasn't even got the basics. How did he even get hired by someone as meticulous as Angela? I need a good pair of eyes, she'd said—she must have known it needed a huge edit. I scroll through the document. It's heavy on medical jargon, full of complex statements like "I prefer spot-precision liquid nitrogen cryosurgery for the treatment of dermatofibromas and seborrheic keratosis." I have to hit Google four times before I understand that. Whole sections give detailed descriptions on how to perform certain procedures to maximum effect, yet there's no narrative through line, no sense at all of the person holding the surgeon's knife. If it goes to press as it is, the text won't live up to the beauty of the cover and inside layout. It really will be only skin deep, in a way Angela won't like. And it certainly won't be the career-changer I'm aiming for.

Remembering Angela's invitation to play around, I go through the first pages of JP's draft, adding comments to myself and highlights where the text would benefit from explanation—*What is "ptosis"? Dejargon this!!!*—or more color: *Were parents doctors? Include anecdote to show what sparked interest in aesthetics, e.g., Was she bullied at school? Or did she play dress-up as a kid? Been under the knife herself? Who has she worked on (big names)?*

I've been reading and annotating for several hours, long past sunset, when my phone buzzes with a message. Sacha. Spill! What's the house like?

I call her, relieved at the chance to take a quick break. "Pretty swish."

She snorts. "Of course it is. Turn on your camera and give me a tour."

I switch to video mode. The screen fills with her face and her hair— which is bright pink.

"Whoa, Sacha!"

She pulls away from the camera and turns her head one way, then the other, so I can get the full effect. It's short and sharp, shaved up the back, longer in the front.

"Fortieth birthday present to myself. If I'm going down, I'm going down fighting." She flashes the sides again. It's edgy, almost provocative, the rose shade balanced the right side of extreme.

"It's amazing." She looks like Rihanna, if Rihanna were a successful lawyer. And happy—happier than I've seen her look in a long time. I think of her boggle-eyed boss, conservative in his navy suits. I bet he practically imploded. "What did Theo say?"

She grins naughtily. "I told him perimenopause was making the hot flashes so bad I had to cut it short or risk barking at a client."

"I bet that shut him up."

"Yep."

Only Sacha could get away with such a comment. I think of my first, short-lived temp job out of university, receptionist at a finance firm in the City. In the joining instructions there'd been a page on "appropriate attire"—no trousers for women and heels mandatory. I'd borrowed money from Mum to buy shoes I could barely walk in. Then came her diagnosis and the heels got shoved to the back of my wardrobe as glamour gave way to practicalities.

Sacha twirls an impatient finger. "Come on then. Tour."

I flip to the rear camera and hold out my phone, panning across the office. In the bathroom, Sacha whistles at the egg-shaped tub. She has the same reaction when I show her my bedroom and downstairs.

In the living room I flop onto the sofa and flip the camera back around. "And the view is even better. I'll send you a photo tomorrow, when it's light."

"I told you the aesthetics sector was massive. In five years it'll be worth sixteen billion a year in the UK alone." She sips from a glass of red wine. "Some vanity project."

I laugh. "Yeah." The first time I was hired as a ghost, Sacha dismissed it as vanity publishing. So did I. Then somehow it became my career. "She's kind of fierce."

"Angela?"

"But I guess you know that."

"You can handle it."

"Thanks, Sacha."

"What for?"

"For tons of things. But, in this particular instance, for this gig."

She looks at something off camera. Contracts, probably. She often works in the evenings at home. Not usually with wine, though—she tends to be quite controlled about that. "Yeah, well, you scratch my back, I'll scratch yours."

"She's keeping you guys on, then?"

She grins, wide. "Yep!"

Maybe that's why Theo is okay with her pink hair, since they've retained Reynolds RX as a client. It was touch-and-go for a while. Something about a roadblock with a merger that even Sacha couldn't get past. I didn't ask for details. She's very discreet about her job—she and Angela must work well together. "That's brilliant. *You* are brilliant."

"I know." She raises her glass in a toast. "Note she's not bloody flying me up to her grade A place in the Highlands, though."

I can feel a draft. I tuck my feet underneath me on the sofa, pull my sleeves down over my hands. "You'd hate it here."

"Sure, I'd detest sitting on that sofa, sleeping in that bed, soaking in that tub."

"You'd be bored in five minutes. It's way too quiet for you. All this . . ." I look toward the view, but the window is black, "nature."

She shivers, pretending to be grossed out. The action makes me feel colder. Then she smiles, but not at me, at someone there with her off-screen. "One sec, Maddy." She gets up from her desk and I hear her telling whoever it is that there are spare towels in the cupboard under the sink. I glance away from my phone at the window frame. Are there really no blinds here, no way to shut out the night? I get goose bumps on my arm, from the cold, but also from thinking about the huge, dark moor. I rub, trying to get the pimples to go away.

"Sorry," she says when she comes back.

"Who was that?"

She grins into her wine. "That was Marco."

Ah. The colleague. "And how's it going with the . . . ?"

"You can say it, it's allowed. Divorce. How's it going with the divorce?" She tips back her head, yells at the ceiling. "Divorce!" More wine. "So Jada's fucking someone else. So what? Two can play at that game." She looks off camera again, but this time it's with sadness.

Eighteen-year-old me was mildly surprised when Sacha told me she was bi, but I quickly learned not to let anything about Sacha surprise me—although I couldn't help it when she announced she was marrying Jada; she didn't seem her type. And didn't that turn out to be the truth? "Just take care, okay?" I say. "Don't rush into anything."

She's distracted once more—Marco coming out of the shower, I guess. She plasters on a smile for him, then turns it on me. "Mads, I gotta go. We've tons to get through tonight."

"I bet!"

She smirks. "Work."

"Yeah, me too."

"And watch it, with Angela."

"What do you mean?" Is there something she hasn't told me?

"With the injectables. If she offers you a freebie, I promise not to laugh when your eyebrows are up beyond your hairline and every time you try to say a 'th' word you spray spit all over the table."

I blow her a raspberry in reply.

After I hang up, I go into the kitchen, coffee on my mind. If I'm going to get more done tonight, I'll need caffeine. I find the source of the draft—the huge window in here is ajar. I'd have put money on Raphaela closing it properly before she and Angela left, but apparently not. No wonder I got goose bumps. I go to the threshold and catch the smell of the night air, earthy, rich, and ancient.

As I start to slide the window shut, I hear a scream. It was faint, perhaps a way off. I listen hard, aware of my blood pulsing against my eardrums. Nothing. Could it have been the squeak of the window track mechanism, proximity making the noise seem louder than it was? I pull the handle again, and the glass grinds along its rail but doesn't squeak. It's almost all the way shut when I hear the scream again, this time identifiable as animal—although in the dark there's no way of telling what kind of animal, and whether the scream came from hunter or prey.

5

DESPITE THE SUPREME COMFORT OF ANGELA'S BED, MY NIGHT
is fitful and I sleep later than I intended to. Downstairs, while the coffee
brews, I unlatch the kitchen window to let in some fresh air. The weather
has brightened, the sky cleared, but a fog has crawled up from the loch,
veiling the moor, bringing with it a drawing-in feeling, a closing of the
landscape and a deadening of sound and sight. No wind, no planes, no
birds. Vapor begins to creep into the house. I shut the window.

As I turn to go back upstairs, drink in hand, I catch movement from
the corner of my eye. Someone or something is outside. I jump and coffee slops onto my sock. I stare into the white. There—movement again. A
hesitant creeping forward, then a pause. It's difficult to judge distance in
these conditions, but I think it's on the other side of the terrace. Angela
or Raphaela returned? Surely not at this hour. And I would have heard
the helicopter. I stare at one spot. The fog is shifting. There's something
more substantial behind it. An animal, a stray sheep? My eyes are starting
to hurt and I'm about to look away when there is movement again, in a
patch where the fog is thinner. A woman, kitted out in walking gear, a large
knapsack over her shoulders. Long hair, an artificial shade of red, emerges
from under a knitted hat.

It's a relief to see another person. I crack the window again and call.
"Hello?"

She starts, then stares right at me. She doesn't reply.

"Can I help you? Are you lost?"

She looks behind her, as if checking an escape route. But then she shakes her head, quickly, as if clearing her thoughts, and calls back, "Actually, yeah." She's young, possibly even a teenager. American or Canadian. "I think I am lost. I was hiking and . . ." She indicates the fog with a gloved hand. "I don't know the area very well. I'm sorry I ended up on . . . on your property."

"That's okay." I don't know why I don't correct her, tell her it's not my house. "Hopefully you won't have to wait too long."

Again she seems to startle. She peers behind me into the house, as if expecting to see someone else.

I point at the fog. "Until this burns off, I mean."

"Oh yeah." She backs away. "I'm sure you're right."

"Well, mind how you go."

She stops. "Excuse me?"

"Where you step. In this visibility."

"Oh," she says. "I will." And she's swallowed up again by the fog.

My first task of the day is photo research. There are lots of photographs in the SKIN DEEP dummy, but none of Angela herself. Often it's the responsibility of the ghostwriter to collate images of the subject, preferably taken at various points throughout their life, and sometimes to source them if they aren't already provided. I don't recall seeing any in the paper folder Angela gave me or in the digital files Raphaela sent through. Once I've drunk half my coffee and thrown a sweater over my pajamas, I sit at the desk and check both sets of files. I'm right. There's nothing. This totally should have been done by now, especially if we're printing in a few weeks and if this book is, like Angela said, important to the company's operation.

I switch to my browser. There are only three results when I search for "Angela Reynolds and cosmetic surgeon": the Reynolds RX website, her LinkedIn profile, and an entry in a list of registered practicing UK doctors. On the register, there is scant information: primary medical qualification (1993–2001, the University of Beaverbrook, Oregon), gender (female), and a General Medical Council registration date of 2006. Reynolds RX is cited as her designated body. LinkedIn holds even less: "Co-founder, Reynolds RX, 2005–present." She hasn't uploaded a profile picture and her avatar is the generic version, two semitransparent circles overlapping to create a vague human form.

I go to the RRX website. The animation begins, just as when I first visited the site last week, when Sacha broached the possibility of this gig: black pixels flying in toward the center, a silent explosion in reverse. They land at random, layering and bunching until they've formed a human eye. The white is filigreed with fine capillaries, the lashes curled, the socket fading into the otherwise plain black screen. The eye blinks, as slowly as a cat's kiss, and when the lid lifts again there's the RRX logo in the pupil. And that's it. No menu; no descriptions of procedures or prices or before-and-after testimonial pictures; no office location, team member bios, or social media icons; only an email address in the bottom left corner: enquiries@reynoldsrx.com. Last week I thought the lack of info seemed odd, but now that I've met Angela, and been in her minimalist house, the website makes perfect sense. In fact, the only thing that's out of keeping with her low-key style is this book, given how private she is. Because there's no way to write about Reynolds RX without writing about her.

People I've ghostwritten for tended to want memoirs for a couple of reasons: either for ego indulgence, a sense that they matter in the world, or, common in those approaching the end of their years, for posterity. Those clients want to live on—in words as well as memories. I wouldn't have put Angela in either camp, but I could have got her wrong. Maybe SKIN DEEP will have a very limited distribution, copies given to only the most loyal of clients. Or maybe she's tired of never being in the limelight. Whatever her reason, it's fine by me. I'm certainly benefiting from it.

I log in to the image library that I normally use for research and type in "Angela Reynolds and Reynolds RX" and then "RRX." No hits for either. I try her name on its own, knowing it's a silly idea, that there'll be too many results to process. Yep—the bane of having a common name. My screen is filled with shots of thousands of different people called Angela Reynolds, old to young, smiling to stern, white, Black, and Brown.

Next I try one of the smaller agency databases, working through a combination of search terms: "Angela Reynolds" and "surgeon." "Dr. Angela

Reynolds" and "US," "Angela Reynolds" and "aesthetic." I scroll down and down each time, waiting for more tiles to populate my screen; tiny glimpses into a myriad different lives but none of them the life I want.

It's when I try "Angela Reynolds" and "Beaverbrook University," where she went to med school, that I find something. I hadn't expected a hit because she was a student at a time when cameras still contained actual film, but an enterprising local photographer, probably hoping to earn a few bucks here and there, has digitized his archive and uploaded it to the agency. I click on the top thumbnail to enlarge it. It's a black-and-white reportage image from a social function. In the top left corner are a bunch of balloons and a sparkly banner, tuxedoed young men huddled beneath. Two young women are caught in conversation on the right. They're dressed in formal attire, in gowns with sweetheart necklines and pearls, their hair puffy, yet to become enslaved to straighteners. The caption reads: "Beaverbrook University Med Soc Valentine social, February 13, 1994. Students GiGi Libcewicz and Angela Reynolds. Contributor: Rex Harris Photography/Stock Photo."

Neither seems to be enjoying the party much. That year was only Angela's first in college, but maybe the pressure was already on. Both are in profile, the one on the left, GiGi Libcewicz, slightly blurred and eye-lids lowered, as if she'd moved just as the photographer's shutter closed. I switch to studying the woman on the right. Her mouth is open as she talks, but her attention is on something out of the frame. The agency's watermark is stamped across her face.

Is it my Angela Reynolds? The place and date are right, but she has the unformed features of youth, her forehead half obscured by a kinked fringe. The hair is darker, but good highlights would explain the difference now. I think it's her. It's not not her.

According to the menu, I can buy the high-res for a few pounds; for fifty I get a license to use it in a book or magazine. I scroll through the other results but this is the only one captioned Angela Reynolds, and I don't see the gown and pearls in any other images of the party. I screenshot the watermarked low-res and save it in a folder to send to Angela.

As an afterthought, I enter "Rex Harris," "GiGi Libcewicz," and "med school alumni Beaverbrook University" into the agency search field in case any other images pop up with Angela in them. I get one more result for GiGi Libcewicz from the same photographer, but the date in the caption under the thumbnail is wrong—1991, which was two years before Angela started at Beaverbrook—and even at this size it's obvious that the other people GiGi is pictured with are men so I don't bother enlarging it. Google gives me an outdated website for the photographer, all swirly fonts and tiny text. The most recent news and events entry is from four years ago. Judging by his profile pic, I'm guessing Rex Harris must be retired by now. I send an email anyway, attaching the screenshot, and asking whether he has any more on file that he hadn't got around to uploading. I cc Raphaela, so he knows I'm legit. On the Facebook page for the med school graduates, I post that I'm trying to get in touch with anyone who knew Angela Reynolds who graduated in 2001 and attach the same screenshot. Let's see what happens. I love the research part of my work—it makes me feel like a detective, chasing leads. I reckon I would have made a bloody good reporter. For a moment, I wonder where I might have ended up if that had worked out all those years ago. Then I mentally shake myself. No use dwelling. There's a perfectly decent job here that needs doing. And is worth doing well.

I turn to social media. Instagram is a fast-track education in cosmetic dermatology. @ReynoldsRX and @RRX yield no results so I search for things like #dermatologist and #fillers: #fillers has two million posts; #Botox eight million. A lot of the photos under #Botox are actually pictures of fillers—plumping not freezing; even in the short period I've been exposed to this world I've learned that much. The majority of those hashtagged #fillers are close-ups of lips wearing a post-injection bead of blood like a badge of honor. I remember the yellow sharps box in Angela's clinic.

I scroll on. Some of the doctors pictured are celebrities in their own right. Prominent is Dr. Singh, a New York practitioner with a sweep of thick hair and a strong chin. His own grid is populated with shots of him beaming alongside Hollywood and music industry stars. To my eye, his clients look strange. Eyebrows arched too high, mouths puffed, cheeks as full and round as babies'. Pillowy. All similar. Funny to think that a surgeon has a signature look, like a fashion designer. I wonder whether Angela does, too. Not having seen any examples of her work, I couldn't say. In a few posts Dr. Singh even appears on the red carpet himself. I bet he has an autobiography already; I bet he's got a whole series of them.

Next I create a new document, Skin Deep MS, and start to copy text over from JP's original and mold things my way. In my work I use this idea of life being like a photograph album, that it's a series of snapshotted memories—I try to write in a similar way, in curated scenes, linked by theme, to find examples of decisions made and actions taken that will reveal the subject's character to the reader. A life's story, not just a life. As I edit Angela's book, I can't help but think of a surgeon's knife paring excess flesh. As I weave together different strands of information into a narrative, I imagine a needle stitching it all together, suturing everything taut. In a way, editing is not unlike cosmetic surgery: you're choosing which parts to show and which to hide.

Despite all the gaps in JP's notes, after two days I have a chunk of manuscript to email to Angela. I've toned down the medical jargon so it makes sense to the layperson. By combining opinions I've gleaned from JP's notes with things Angela told me, such as taking a holistic approach and not going the "high street" way of only loading the skin with filler, I think I can make this book quite different in its field. To properly bring the manuscript to life I'll need biographical detail and some personal anecdotes, which I hope to get out of her in interviews. Coupled with those stunning pictures of the models, it could be a powerful manifesto on beauty and aging.

I send the excerpt that night ahead of our video call the next morning. Her checklist has her in Jeddah. I scan her list of our other appointments. Singapore, Monaco, Barcelona, all within a fortnight. Punishing for anyone.

When she dials in, she's in a suit, the blouse buttoned up to the chin. I tuck a strand of loose hair behind my ear. I'm wearing a new shirt, which is clean and not too wrinkled, and she can't see my lower half—but if anyone can tell that I've got jeans on, it's Angela.

Behind her is an elegant bed with a tall black frame and a pale chaise longue stretched under a netted window—none of the gilded furniture and jewel-colored fabrics I'd imagined for a Saudi Arabian hotel room. She could be anywhere.

I tell her I won't keep her long, as I know she must be busy.

"It's fine. My clients here like to rest in the day, get up in the evening, so I make the most of the free time for researching, catching up on paperwork, and run my clinic after dinner, starting around ten, until the early hours."

"Goodness!" Only a workaholic could cope with that kind of schedule, especially coupled with the travel, the jet lag. "That sounds exhausting."

"I'm used to it."

"But still . . ." It's about nine in the morning where she is now. That's a long day.

She takes a sip of water and looks at me expectantly. She doesn't appear tired at all. I take the hint—efficiency is key. She doesn't need my sympathy.

"I emailed you what I've done so far," I say. "I don't expect, if you were working late last night, that you've had a chance to read it yet?"

"I'm sorry, but I haven't."

Not surprising but not ideal, because having to allow her more review time will hold things up. The pressure dial twists a little higher. I take a breath. "Well, I hope, once you find the time, that you'll be happy with it. I've gone in a slightly different direction from your previous ghostwriter, but I'm excited about what this could be. Will be."

Another pause. Interviewing digitally is always harder than in person. It's as if all the nuance that can so easily be read when you're in a room with someone in real life gets lost, as if personality loses all depth in 2D. "There are a few points—facts—that I want to go through with you. Would you like to do that now or shall I email them over?"

"Now is fine."

"Great." I consult my notepad. "Your website is gorgeous," I say. "But I couldn't find anything about your history. Would you mind filling in some of the blanks for me?"

"Such as?"

"No biggies. Easy stuff." I give her my charming smile, the one I use to warm up clients that tends to do the trick. "Let's start with the basics. Where were you born, and what's your date of birth?"

She laughs, but it's a broken laugh, disbelieving. "What do you need to know that for?"

Maybe her age is a touchy subject, which would be ironic, given how she's made her name. If she started university in 1993 she must be forty-three or forty-four now—hardly an age to be ashamed of. I look up from my notebook to the screen. Digitized, her unusual eyes are almost colorless. They give nothing away. "Okay." I turn the page. "How about your parents. What are their names, and their occupations? Are or were they doctors, too?"

"I'd rather leave them out of it."

"Really? Most people like to mention their parents." Even if they weren't the most loving or supportive. It's as if knowing where you come from is a foundation for your sense of self. It's rare to completely disregard your roots.

"I'm quite sure."

"Right." A family feud? I readjust my plan of what to ask next. There's plenty to choose from. "How about you? Are you a parent yourself?"

"No."

"It'd be hard, I imagine, to work your travel schedule around a family."

"Yes."

"Are you married?"

"No."

"Have you ever been?"

"No."

Wow, this is hard. But often these parts of an interview feel clumsy; the flow comes when we start a conversation. "Sorry. I've got a couple of things to fact-check, then we can talk properly. You started med school at Beaverbrook in 1993 and graduated in 2001, correct?"

"Yes. That's in the notes. I included a list of all the places I studied and worked, dates of graduation and qualification."

"I've got it. But I like to double-check these things."

"They are correct. I typed them out myself."

"Okay." I make a show of crossing off the list of dates in my notes. "How about we try something else?" Something that's easier for both of us. "When was it that you decided you wanted to go into this field? Was there a particular moment you can recall, a flash of inspiration, that made you choose aesthetics?"

She sips from a glass of water, taking her time, thinking of how to answer. She puts down her drink. Great, here we go. This interview is being recorded but I ready my pen anyway.

"That was all so long ago," she says. "It's not relevant."

I stare at her image on the screen. Of course it's relevant. What could be more relevant in a book about her life's work? One thing always leads to the next and the next. If it was a book about my life, it'd have to include the fact that my father left before I was born; that I was an only child who compensated for loneliness by making friends through books; that that led me into a life based around stories, but that I lost the ability to finish reading a single novel while I was caring for Mum during her illness and it took a long, long time for my concentration and love for the written word to return, but when it did I found real sanctuary in it. I wouldn't be who I am today if those things hadn't happened.

I don't understand why she's making this so difficult. She wants this book to work out as much as I do—she made that clear. I've had other subjects who were reluctant to talk about themselves even though they commissioned the project, but this is an extreme version of that. Or maybe it's me and I'm approaching this wrongly.

I put on my most reassuring voice. "Angela, I can understand your reticence. I've come across it many times, with other clients. I promise I'll never put anything in the manuscript that you're not completely happy with, but often it helps me to understand, to write a better story, if I can fill in the blanks, even off the record."

"I get that. But I'm not one of your other clients."

This isn't working. There has to be a way. "What about your previous ghost, JP? I'm sorry, I don't know his actual name . . ." She leaves me hanging, so I push on. "If you could put me in touch with JP, maybe he can fill me in on this information, save wasting your time?"

"That won't be possible."

"Well, maybe Raphaela can—"

"That won't be possible either." Angela stares tightly into her webcam. "Madeleine, I already included, in the briefing notes, the background material I want you to use. As I said, this is to be a mission statement, forward-looking, focused on both now and the future."

How can you have a future, or even a present, without a past? "Okay, but—"

"So my family life, my childhood, aren't relevant." She breaks eye contact, drinks more water.

I let a few seconds pass. Maybe if I give her some space, she'll relent a little. "I don't need to probe your earliest memory or go into any trauma you might have experienced"—Is that what's happened? Have I unwittingly hit a nerve?—"and we can keep it right on topic. But surely we can include your date of birth, your parents' names, basic facts like that—"

She cuts me off. "Raphaela said you were looking for images of me."

It takes me a second to catch up with the switch in topic. "Yes. I couldn't find any in the folders, so I did a little digging."

"Digging?" She's verging on angry.

"Standard photo agency research. I do it for all my other . . ." I catch myself, adjust my words. "It's part of my service."

"But SKIN DEEP already has photographs in it. You have the dummy. I commissioned them especially."

"Yes and they're beautiful. Stunning. But there aren't any of you."

"No, because I want it to be about my work, not me."

"But aren't you part of your work?" Somehow we've circled back. "I'm not suggesting replacing any of the model images, only adding at least one of you." An idea comes. "Your business is anti-aging. What better advocate for your work than you? Pictures of you from years ago, others from now."

"I don't see . . ." She turns her head, distracted. "One moment." She goes to her hotel room door, opens it a fraction to speak to someone, widens it to let them in. It's a man. He's taller than she is and in a suit— too well-dressed to be room service. He crosses the room to the bedside table. At the same time she walks back to her laptop and the camera angle means her body blocks my view of him. He's collected whatever it is he was after and is exiting by the time Angela resumes her seat, so all I see is his back. There's something in the way they ignore each other's presence that suggests they're very familiar.

"Scott De Luca, my co-director," Angela says once he's left. "I'd have introduced you, but he has a flight to catch so you'll have to talk another time."

"Angela, to go back to what we were discussing, the photographs."

"Yes, I'm sure, Madeleine. The images stay as they are. I hired you for your words, and words is what I'd like you to stick to. Don't waste any more time on it, okay? We don't have long."

That much is true. And she is the boss. But it niggles, not being able to do my job properly. First the bio, now this.

Before I can raise another objection, she consults her watch. "I have to run."

"Angela, can't we at least—"

But she's already gone, her face and the room replaced with a typed message in a box: *The host has ended the meeting.*

My first instinct is to call Sacha. My client crap-o-meter has swung all the way into the danger zone, because if Angela is going to be this difficult about the basics, how bad is it going to get once we're further in? I pick up my mobile, but there's no signal. I take my phone through to the bedroom to see whether it's any better there. Nothing. I type an expletive-laden text to Sacha, but it fails to send. Frustrated, I toss the phone onto the bed.

What kind of a book is this going to be if it contains no information on its subject? And, assumed introversion and full-to-bursting work schedule aside, who on earth commissions an autobiography ghostwriter if they don't want to speak about their life?

6

I SPEND THE REST OF THE DAY AND THE NEXT MORNING FIDDLING
with the same small section of text, cutting a sentence, moving it, moving
it back again. A "redo," surgeons call it—rather flippantly, it seems to me,
when you're talking about someone's body. Although I bet they'd be less
flippant if they'd had to redo an operation as many times as I've unpicked
these words.

I click back to JP's manuscript. It occurs to me to check the review
settings. When I change the settings to show comments, a column opens
up at the right-hand edge. Now as I scroll through the document I can see
Angela's marks. Some are corrections to or clarifications of medical terms.
Infraorbital darkness, not intra and *Topical aminolaevulinic acid-photodynamic
therapy is a treatment involving light and acid designed to prevent actinic keratosis (sun-damaged skin) progressing to cancer.* But many are instructions
to delete: *Please remove. Not relevant. Delete.* I keep going down. Almost
all these comments appear where there are blanks in her life info. I can't
tell whether the *XXX*s were holding text written in by JP or whether the
information was redacted by Angela.

Down, down, down. Reynolds Angela: *Delete.* Reynolds Angela: *Delete.*
Reynolds Angela: *Delete.* It's like a repeat of the conversation she had
with me.

Then, suddenly, a comment box with a different name at the top.
Prosser Jonathan.

I sit up. I've met him. He was at a networking event. Avuncular, kept pushing his glasses up his nose, seemed pleased that I started talking to him, gave me some good tips. That's my predecessor? He's one of the best—I only got that Malouf job because he was double-booked. For the first time, I feel a fillip—Jon'll definitely have the info. I can write a brief history section for SKIN DEEP and I'm sure once Angela sees it in context, she'll agree it's the right thing to do.

Looking online, I see that Jon's back catalog is impressive but niche: former politicians, the odd judge. Ghostwriting for a cosmetic surgeon is quite the departure for him. Is that why his manuscript is so vague? His mobile number is on his site. I dial, but my phone beeps in my ear. No reception again. I drop him an email, explaining my problem, and try as best I can to get back to work.

- - -

By midafternoon I can no longer kid myself that I'm getting anything done. I need a change of scene. Down in the mudroom, I reach for my coat before remembering how chilly it was when I landed in the helicopter. I lift down one of Angela's thick wax jackets, weighty with padding, and slip it on. I go to put on my Converse, then have second thoughts and borrow a pair of boots as well. A size too big but I'll manage. There's a full-length mirror on the back of the door. I look quite the part.

Outside seems like a different place from the night I arrived, welcoming rather than foreboding. It is one of those fast-moving-sky days when the world seems to be in a hurry. I step off the terrace onto the long grass. It is trampled in places—footprints left by Angela, Raphaela, and me. And, I realize, by that lost backpacker, too. I wonder idly where she'd come from that morning—there are no other buildings in this V-shaped valley that I can see.

I fill my lungs and coldness pricks the back of my throat. The air feels clean, not clogged with thick countryside smells like those on childhood walks on school holidays, when Mum would bundle me into the car and drive us out of London. When she cranked down the windows I'd complain—"Mum, it stinks of cows"—and pinch my nose. "Isn't it wonderful?" she'd reply, sniffing until her chest lifted. She always missed the Dales, where she'd grown up. She was outside in our little square of inner-city garden every chance she got. Before she became ill, in those healthy years that we both took for granted, she'd be pulling weeds and turning over the soil. Toward the end, too weak to do those things any longer, she'd sit in her deck chair, trying to warm her thinning bones in the wedge of afternoon sun that fell between the back door and the fence. She would have loved it here. Not the property—"Far too grand for me, Maddy"—but everything else.

I don't know why I haven't left the house earlier. Four days cooped up isn't healthy. I've never felt a great pull of the outdoors before, but there's something about this place. I can see for miles. London has turned me myopic, never seeing beyond the building in front of me. Here the scale is too much to take in at once. It's easier to break it into thirds, to parcel and parse the perspectives. In the near distance are the terrace and the lawn and the beginning of the moorland. The lawn is bumpy, the grass wiry and tufted. The moor—glen, I'm still not sure—is wilder still. Long and broad, and muddled with rocks and boulders, it stretches down the valley to Loch Varaig. In the middle distance and on the other side of the loch are undulating hills, dark in patches firred with forest; lighter where the trees have been felled. And then, far off, way back beyond the hills, are the mountains, belted with cloud. They feel unreal. Dour and watchful, empty and huge. In comparison, I am tiny, humble. Part of nature, yet at its mercy, too, vulnerable should anything go wrong.

I strike out down the rough ground toward the loch, weaving between clumps of coppery bracken and heather and gorse bushes in autumn bloom, colors bursting and fading like fireworks. The slope steepens and I find myself almost trotting. I've had to ditch my normal gym routine in coming here, and it's great to let go, to use my body after all those hours of sitting. I look around—still not another person in sight—and all I can hear is myself, the regular beat of my footsteps and the quickening swish of my arms against the body of the coat.

Then the configuration of the ground changes, and perhaps it's a primeval instinct, but something about the way there's suddenly no plant cover but a lot of grit then exposed rock, angling up now instead of down, makes me slow. And thank God I do, because just like that the ground disappears and there's nothing but a sheer dead drop, a hundred feet or more straight down onto sharp, jagged stone.

My breath halts. My vision zooms in and tracks out at the same time, hard ground racing up to meet me. Heart hammering, I take one step back, two, four, until I feel safe. I slump onto the cold, wet earth.

I could have easily fallen. Simultaneously, flashes of memory come back to me: Mum, running in horror after I went over my handlebars when she was teaching me to ride a bike; my ex, helping me up from the ground after I twisted an ankle crossing the road; both of them, nearly thirty years apart, saying the same thing once they knew I was all right: "Maddy, you need to be more careful."

I look over my shoulder. The house is visible from here, its angular lines in stark contrast to the humpbacked hills all around, yet from the house I couldn't see the cliff. It must be an optical illusion, like a hidden dip in the road, an invisible break in reality. My pulse is still pounding. In Varaig there may be no one to distract me from my work, but there's no one to help me, either, should something go wrong.

I check my phone. As if to prove my point: no network. But there was a signal at some point because two messages have come through from Sacha.

The first is a response to my frustrated text from yesterday, which she must have just received, asking me whether everything is okay. The second is a follow-up: BTW, divorce papers came through.

Such a simple statement. That's not like Sacha at all—no attempt at self-deprecation, no onward-and-upward mentality. The words are plain, factual, but I know they're hiding her pain. After Patrick and I split I was up and down as well, even though we weren't married and I ended it. All that history, that connection, gone. I'd think I was fine, and then something would come along and fell me. I try to call her, but the phone beeps in my ear. I type a text, hoping the reply will reach her soon, telling her I'm here for her whenever she needs me.

Damp is seeping into my jeans, but I stay seated, feeling silly for yesterday's immature outburst. My woes are nothing in comparison to Sacha's. I touch the mauve flattop of a thistle sprouting from the granite nearby, soft as a paintbrush against my finger. Perhaps I'm the one with the problem, not Angela. Doing the same thing time after time, never changing, never innovating. Out of the two of us, she's the one with vision and success. She'd called SKIN DEEP "forward-looking," like her work. And if that's what her professional philosophy has been for the past thirteen years, her book should match that. She doesn't have to talk about her early years if she doesn't want to. After all, staving off the aging process is a way of reversing youthful mistakes: skin-damaging cigarettes, late nights, forgotten sunscreen. It's all about forgetting, or erasing, the past.

I get to my feet and decide to walk on a little farther in the direction of the loch. After a while, the path I've taken through broken bracken emerges onto heather and I realize I'm below and to the side of the cliff. The huge sheet of rock is slightly concave, the flayed surface a dark gray and fissured like old teeth. The effect is uncanny, as if I'm seeing something I shouldn't: the skeletal frame of the land, the usually secret substrata that hold up the plants and trees. It makes me think of a video I watched on YouTube the other night, a full face-lift in which the patient's face had been sliced around the hairline and peeled away from the muscle and bone before being stretched and stapled into place.

Then, above the cliff overhang, someone appears. A lone figure standing at the top, a man. He is dressed in a black city coat, long and woolen, the collar turned up against the wind, and seems out of place among all this wilderness, as if he's been yanked out of his normal life and deposited here like Dorothy in Oz. He's near the edge where I stood not long before, facing this way, a cutout against the damaged sky. The clouds behind him are racing so fast that I get a strange sense of motion, like being on a stationary train when the next one along pulls away. It makes me feel dizzy, so I glance down at the ground to steady myself, and when I look up again, he has disappeared.

Dusk is encroaching by the time I near the house. I must have left all the downstairs lights on, because the interior is brightly lit, and I can see everything inside: the sofa and armchair in the living room, the kitchen table with a dozen chairs tucked around it, the old landscape watercolor on the wall of the atrium. The house looks like it's waiting for me, makes me feel late for a party I didn't know I was invited to.

I hold my phone to the reader by the front door and wait for the beep as it unlocks. The mudroom isn't lit. And my mind is on other things:

Sacha's sadness, Angela's stubbornness, what I'm going to do about the manuscript. So I don't spot the man until I'm about to walk right into him.

He is silhouetted against the doorway to the atrium and I can't immediately take in much other than his height (tall) and his frame (wiry) and immediately I think: *Intruder*.

But before I can react, he says "Sorry" and switches on the light, and a little dog scampers up to my feet. I recognize it instantly—Angela's Rudy, with the brows. So the man is connected to her. My blood pressure calms. Sure enough, the dog's companion trots in.

"Rudy, Massimo, come," the man says, firmly yet affectionately. He is about my age and even-featured, with a straight nose and defined jaw, his body the good type of rangy. He wears his brown hair short and neat, parted on the left. His skin is a little flushed, as if he's been outside. He must be the guy I just saw on the moor. His dress is smart—a collared shirt under a V-neck sweater, work trousers—and the luxe quality reminds me of Angela. Of course he isn't a burglar—they don't dress as well as this, in getup more suited to Bond Street than the Scottish Highlands. I scan down. Burglars aren't usually barefoot, like they're right at home. The dogs, responding to his instruction, go to him. They sit and thump their tails against the tile. He rubs their heads.

I recover my voice. "You scared me."

"Sorry." He hooks a finger into the neck of his sweater and loosens it. Then he twists to open the wine cabinet. From this angle, there's something familiar about him. "You must be Madeleine." He talks into the cabinet. His accent is American and he accords all three syllables of my name equal weight. "She didn't tell you I was coming."

"Maddy." I take off the coat and boots and return them to the rack, feeling bad for taking what wasn't mine, hoping he hasn't noticed. A new coat is hanging on the pegs, long and woolen and dark. So I'm right—he was the man at the cliff. I add: "And no, she didn't."

He closes the cabinet without taking anything out and straightens. Despite the bare feet suggesting he's comfortable, there's a strained energy to him, as if he's on edge. "Well, I must apologize for that."

He opens a different cupboard. The fine wool of his sweater stretches across his shoulders as he takes out two dog bowls. Steel clangs as he pours kibble from a box. He closes the cupboard door and puts the bowls down for the dogs. Only once he has done that does he hold out a hand for me to shake.

"Scott De Luca."

It's a brief shake. He drops my hand quickly and folds his arms across his chest. That's why he looks familiar—he's the co-director, the one from the Saudi hotel room yesterday. He got here quickly. And quietly—no helicopter for him. He carries the smell of outdoors, peaty yet fresh.

"Good walk?" I ask.

"Pardon me?"

"To the cliff. It gave me quite the shock earlier. I nearly came a right cropper."

He sticks out his lower lip. "I'm not sure what you mean."

"The cliff. I saw you up there. Or down there, rather."

He shakes his head. "Not me, I'm afraid."

"Really?" I could've sworn it was.

He sees me checking out his hung-up coat. "Really. I've only just arrived."

The dogs crunch on the kibble.

"Sorry," I say. Everything seems tangled, starting from the way we introduced ourselves. Regardless, where he has or hasn't been and why he doesn't want to say is not my business. "Evidently I've been here on my own so long I'm hallucinating." And coming down with word vomit. "I'm also sorry for being startled. I didn't know anyone was coming."

He looks at me and quickly slides his gaze away. He's done that a couple of times now, as if he isn't very good at holding eye contact. "Don't worry, I'll stay out of your way. We've both got, ah, plenty to be getting on with. I'm down the other end of the house. You won't even know I'm here."

"No, please, this is more your house than mine." Actually, his being here could be a real bonus. "I know you're very busy yourself, but if I have any questions, about the business, I mean, can I ask you?"

"Of course. Yes, sure." Another tug of the collar. So nervous. I almost want to tell him I don't bite.

As if it's an afterthought, he reopens the wine cabinet and pulls out a bottle. He holds it first by the barrel and then changes his grip, looping his fingers around the neck so that it hangs down by his side. Holding it at arm's length or hiding it from view, I'm not sure.

"Well," he adds. "Good night." The dogs follow him out of the mud-room. Eventually, I hear a door click softly shut.

I've become so attached to this house that it's with reluctance that I email Raphaela: Mr. De Luca is here—perhaps I should head back to London? The reply comes from Angela herself: Not at all. The house is big enough for two. Please do stay.

Sacha's take on it is similar. I've got plenty to keep him busy and out of your hair, she messages. This merger of theirs is a big deal and there's a lot to get through. He'll be working hard on that—FINALLY! She sends two party-hat-wearing emojis, and I'm relieved she sounds more herself. So Scott was the roadblock to the deal that she mentioned a while back. Interesting. A second later, another text comes: BTW, the fact it's a merger is confidential. Don't let them know you know, ok? In my reply I agree, but it does surprise me that Angela is merging her company with another. She seems to value control and discretion so much, and joining forces with another firm would mean she'd have to relinquish at least some of that. Mind you, it does explain the short deadline on the book, if she needs it to woo investors or something.

By nine o'clock it's impossible to ignore my hunger any longer. I take my laptop downstairs and find a lasagna in the fridge. I put on the oven. Scott has made good on his promise—the house is completely silent. I can't even hear the dogs. Although it's that unsettling kind of silence where you can still sense someone's presence nearby. I find myself treading softly, closing drawers as unobtrusively as I can. I pull tomatoes from the crisper and slice them, add salt to macerate. I open a bottle of merlot and sip a glass in front of my laptop while the lasagna cooks. The wine's delicious but a single serving is my limit. Got to keep sharp.

There's easily enough food for two. When the smell of bubbling cheese fills the kitchen I go in search of Scott at the other end of the house. The first two rooms are empty but the final door is closed. I hesitate. He might be busy working. Muffled sounds come from the other side, a movie or

TV show—he's not working, then. I knock lightly. The sounds stop, but he doesn't come to the door. I wait in the silence, knock again, a bit louder. Muted scratching—a dog pawing the other side of the door. It stops. Evidently Scott doesn't want to be disturbed. Lowering my fist, I head back to the kitchen.

I eat, the scrape of knife against plate loud in the empty room. After dinner I fancy something sweet, but I can't find the chocolate anywhere. He must have eaten it. Never mind.

It's long past midnight when I stop fiddling with the manuscript. Before going to bed, I leave the rest of the lasagna and the salad bowl out on the counter, a clean plate and cutlery beside them.

The next day, the food has been eaten. As I take my morning coffee up to my office, I notice the statuette at the bottom of the stairs. Its arms have been adjusted, elbows bent out to either side and palms pressed together at its chest. In thanks, in prayer, or, it occurs to me, in a plea for help. The problem is, without a face, it's hard to tell.

7

MY INITIAL PLEASURE AT GETTING TO STAY ON IN THIS BEAUTI-
ful house cools over the next few days. Part of the reason is sharing with
someone I never see. Scott's presence registers only through the sounds of
a life: the soft tap of a closing door or the rush of water through the pipes
in the walls. He's so elusive that even when I hear the chink of dog kibble
being poured into a bowl and go down to the mudroom, seeking company
for a minute or two, it seems he and the dogs are already out for a walk or
back in his room. This merger sure is all-encompassing. I keep thinking he
might join me for dinner but he eats the leftovers after I've gone to bed. In
a way it's more lonely, being in a house with someone who is hiding—or
ignoring me, I'm not sure which—than if I actually were alone.

On the afternoon of the ninth day since I arrived at Varaig the weather
turns unseasonably warm and things, as they often do, seem brighter with
the sun. The day feels like a good omen and I slide the kitchen window
all the way open. I love how it removes the barrier and frees the house,
letting the outside in. Even though it's past Bonfire Night, the air brings
with it a feeling of spring-like unfurling, as if the seasons have been
swapped. In come noises, too: the ice-pick call of a territorial robin layered over the knock of a bumblebee roused too early from hibernation,
headbutting the windowpane in confusion, *tap-tap-tap*.

I pop back up to boot up my laptop, and when I return to the kitchen to make a quick sandwich to eat at my desk there are footprints on the floor trailing a path back and forth between the terrace and the atrium. Scott must have gone out, making the most of the sunshine—I can't believe I missed him again.

Upstairs, I work on understanding and explaining more of the technical and medical descriptions from the material I was given. I've got a running list, things like hyfrecation and autologous ADSC therapies. Who, apart from a cosmetic surgeon, knows what these are? The latter, I discover, are the next step up from a "vampire facial": cells are extracted from a patient's own fat, processed in a lab, and injected into the face for rejuvenation. Results can last up to five years, apparently. The cutting edge of science (without the cutting). I can't help thinking it sounds a bit medieval, not that far removed from leeches—which are, I'm surprised to learn, now available from the NHS. I leave references to "tissue banks" out of the manuscript, as no reader wants to know that the filler they may have been injected with, the one with the innocuous, clean-sounding brand name, and which is FDA- and MHRA-approved, is derived from processing the collagen fibers of a human cadaver.

I'm diving deep into medical, dermatological, and academic websites, trying to get my head around these and more, when the internet cuts out. I check my phone—the Wi-Fi symbol has gone. This happened before, but it seemed to come back by itself after a minute. I wait. Nothing. My chair scrapes as I push it back. I search the house for the router, hoping the old trick of switching it off and on again will solve the issue, but can't find it. It occurs to me as I search that there are no electronics in view other than the kitchen appliances—no television, radio, or even clocks. I open all the cupboards in the kitchen, rifle through those in the mudroom. I'm on my hands and knees, peering under the shoe rack, when the dogs scuttle in from the atrium, claws clicking on the tile, tongues lolling. They make me jump—I didn't realize Scott had returned; I hadn't heard the front door beep. He must have come in through the kitchen.

He follows. "Lost something?"

"Ah, no." I get to my feet, dust off my hands, even though they're not dirty. "Actually yes, I suppose I have. The Wi-Fi signal."

"And you thought you'd find it in a gum boot?"

The American term tickles me but I can't for the life of me think of a funny reply. He doesn't smile, but there's a glimmer of amusement in his eyes. He seems less guarded today: his arms are loose by his sides rather than folded across his chest. "Come on, I'll show you where she keeps the router. It's temperamental."

I tail him through the atrium. His hair is tousled, sticking up from the crown. He has good hair, thick. He must feel me looking, because he combs a hand through it, smoothing the loose strands back into place.

"Do you come up here a lot?" I mean it genuinely, but it sounds like a bad pickup line. Quickly I add, "For work, I mean."

"Sometimes. Not too often. It's really Angela's place." He leads me all the way to the living room, which I haven't spent much time in yet, and goes to a stack of logs at the edge of the broad hearth. Surely it's not among those? He pushes at a spot on the wall and a door springs open. Inside are several black boxes and a nest of wires. The router is among the boxes, a fixed red light on the front. Scott clicks a switch, waits, clicks again, and the light blinks blue. It flashes a few times, then changes to green.

"Should be good now," he says.

I check my phone. The Wi-Fi is back. "Thanks." He tucks a wire out of the way and closes the door. It's so cleverly engineered that there's only the most hairline of gaps. I say, "You'd have to already know that was there in order to find it."

He nods. "There's a sound system inside as well if you want to play some music."

I look around for evidence of speakers. I see nothing other than the fireplace, sofas and armchairs, rug and coffee table.

Scott is watching me, his lips tilted up on one side. "The speakers are built into the walls. Plastered right over. Clever, huh?"

Rudy and Massimo mosey into the room, sniffing a trail along the floor.

"You just get back from taking them out?" I ask.

"No, I was about to go."

"Oh." I thought, from those footprints, that they'd already been. But, now I come to think of it, those were only human, not canine. Scott must have nipped out on his own.

"Oh . . . ?" He's noticed my stalled question and is waiting for the rest of it.

I'm frowning; I release it. "Where will you go? Down to the loch?" A flashback comes, of my near miss at the cliff. I'm about to warn him to take care when I remember he's been there already.

"Probably not that far. Me, I'd hike all day if I could. But they're so small."

I pat my knees and call the dogs' names, trying to get them to come, but they ignore me, keeping their noses to the interesting scent.

Scott crouches to my level. "Angela trained them to only go to people they know." He taps the side of his thigh and immediately Rudy and Massimo come to heel. He fishes in his pocket and holds out two treats to me. "But if you bribe them, they're yours for life."

I take the treats. Immediately the dogs skip over, hope in their eyes. Rudy drops his biscuit and has to scoop it up from the floor, but Massimo is more precise in his manners. I ruffle his fur. His ears are silky. "What kind are they?" We never had pets.

"King Charles spaniels." He points to Rudy's snubbed snout. "Flitwick Rudy Tuesday and Flitwick Massimo Blue, to give them their full pedigree names. They're brothers."

"The names are bigger than the dogs."

He rolls his eyes. "I know, right."

I've noticed that his accent wavers, blunted, I suppose, by his time in the UK, but the way he says this is all-American. Rudy looks at Scott dotingly, trying for more snacks. Scott feeds him. He seems a natural with animals.

"Do you have a dog yourself?" I ask.

One beat too many passes and I think he's going to ignore the question. But eventually he says, "I did, when I was a kid."

"What kind?"

"A mutt. We never knew. Huck."

"As in Finn?"

"Yeah. My dad found him when he was a pup, hiding from a storm in our barn. Never did know how he got there. Tiny thing, not much bigger than this." He cups his hands together. "Dad brought him in, wrapped in a towel, gave him to me. He grew so big. Had this loping kind of run like he thought he was a wolf." He smiles at the memory. It's the first time I've seen him properly smile. Dimples bracket his mouth and he shows his teeth. One of the canines is slightly crooked, twisted a little in its bed. I like the effect—it takes the edge off the clean-cut-ness of him.

"You grew up on a farm?"

He blinks. "No, I grew up in Manhattan." He stands. "I meant we were on vacation at a place with a barn. Dad asked all over town, but no one was missing a pup so we took Huck back with us. To the city."

"Quite the souvenir."

"Yup." He adjusts his shirt at the throat as if he's making room to breathe. I can almost feel a shutter come down inside him. He stares out the window, along the valley, toward the hidden cliff. "So if you're all set?"

He heads for the door. I think back to what we were talking about. Maybe I got too personal, although it wasn't that personal. Innocuous stuff, little more than small talk. I ought to try to clear the air anyway, since we're sharing the same house. "Thanks again. There's no way I'd have found that."

He throws a reply over his shoulder. "No problem." Before he disappears he adds something else. "She likes to hide the ugly stuff away."

That comment stays with me as I return to the manuscript, taking my laptop to the office upstairs. All those *XXX*s in the text. I jump from one to the next. I told myself I'd let it go, but the knowledge I'm not doing a proper job itches like a wound that won't heal. Jon Prosser hasn't replied to my email. I send him a second.

Sacha messages. How's the dream gig going?

That's not an easy question to answer. I constantly feel slightly restricted, a bit like I've put on a shirt that's half a size too small.

Barking starts up outside, frantic and persistent. I go to the window. The tan-colored dog, Massimo, is on the terrace below, scampering along its length, yapping at the moor, a tiny guardian protecting his territory from an invisible enemy.

I lean against the glass as I reply to Sacha. Wouldn't call it a dream exactly.

I get the vibrating dots as she replies. Nightmare then? Sorry . . .

Not that either. I struggle to explain, even to myself, but it's as if every time I move I can feel this metaphorical too-small shirt rubbing against me in some new place. Probably homesick. TBH I'm kind of wondering why I'm here.

What do you mean? At the house?

Her questions help crystallize my own feelings. Yeah, partly. I could have done this from London—she's not even in Varaig and her business partner seems preoccupied.

Yeah, De Luca can be hard work.

That's not how I'd describe him. Quiet, maybe. Distracted. But not hard work. How so?

Massimo's barking becomes frenetic. I look again, but there's nothing out there that I can see. Then comes a whistle—Scott calling him back inside, three tones, up-down-up—and Massimo temporarily turns his attention to the house. Scott steps onto the terrace. He drops into a crouch at the dog's level and the way he does it is easy, agile, as if he spends time in the gym and is comfortable in his body, confident in its ability to hold him in a squat. I watch him extend a hand, trying to coax Massimo over.

My phone pings. Sacha says: Short fuse, you know the type. Between you and me, he's been a right thorn in our side. Screaming matches in her office, the works. Angela says all sorted now tho. I never warmed to him personally but he's a client, so . . . She adds a shrug emoji.

Down on the terrace Scott is patiently squatting, his arm still outstretched. I'm guessing there's a treat in his fingers, something to distract Massimo from whatever's bothering him. Massimo is still on the edge of the slabs, unsure, but at least he's stopped barking. Scott gives a tiny flick of the wrist, a flick that says "There's something for you here when you're ready, no rush."

He seems ok to me. Maybe a bit tense but kind, esp with the dogs.

Kind?! Are we talking about the same Scott De Luca? Asshole more like. All that country air must be doing weird things to you. You need to get back down here to reality.

I smile at her three crying-with-laughter emojis. It's not this place, or him, it's her. I can barely get a thing out of her, and there's nothing online either. I don't get it. I could write ten books about Dr. Singh without ever meeting him.

She replies: Just because she's successful doesn't mean she's automatically agreeing to be in the public domain. She has a right to privacy, rights in law. Get a lawyer involved and you'd be surprised how quickly things can disappear.

I text: Surely even your reach doesn't extend to Google? She sends a smiling devil face emoji, followed by a cheeky ghost.

Of course money can buy that kind of anonymity; the rest of us have to lump it—drunken pics from parties we attended years ago, unflattering angles and all, on the web for eternity.

I type: It seems weird to me. Sure, get the bad stuff off the internet, if you can, but the rest? Things that are good for business?

Well, she's the boss.

Below me, Massimo has approached Scott and is tentatively sniffing his hand for the treat. Reassured it's not a trick, he snaffles it up. Scott waits until the dog has eaten, then picks him up. He stands, as effortlessly as he squatted, and dips his head, speaking close to Massimo's ear as if to reassure him. They disappear from view. Shame—I was enjoying the show.

I move away from the window. Oh, I dunno, I type to Sacha. I can't blame this displaced feeling I have on Angela's opacity, Scott's aloofness, or even on living in this house. The job seems out of balance, somehow. I know you shouldn't look a gift horse, etc., but it seems mad. Why me? Shouldn't she have picked someone who knows more about this than I do? Someone with contacts, industry smarts?

There's no reply for a few minutes. I check my bank app and see Angela has paid me half already, rather than waiting for me to invoice at the end of the commission. I stare at the comma in the numbers, sitting in a place it never has before.

I wonder what Mum would have made of what I'm doing with my life—not just this book but ghostwriting as a whole. Proud, I think, but maybe a tiny bit sad that I didn't get to do what I really wanted. Or maybe that's me, projecting onto her. She wasn't a career professional; she had lots of different jobs over the years. Office admin, cleaner, teaching assistant at my old primary, whatever worked around school times. She was well liked, and she found satisfaction in whatever she did. "If a job's worth doing," she'd say, to encourage me whenever motivation waned, and I'd finish the phrase: "It's worth doing well." Sometimes I think you must get a far broader view of the world by mixing it up like she did. If you stay in the same job for too long, if you get used to thinking of and seeing yourself in a certain way, does that mean you start to narrow? Perhaps I should think of doing something else. Pick up that traineeship I had to quit when Mum got ill, if they'll still have me at my age. I wish I could ask her opinion.

Sacha comes back. Maybe Angela wanted a fresh pair of eyes. Mate, it's imposter syndrome. You need to value yourself more. Trust me, it's all fine. That's what it's like at the top. You get paid more to do less. The flunkies lower down the ladder do the hard work and you get to take all the credit.

I need to lighten up. I reply: I've been a flunky all my life. I knew it!

She sends a GIF of a woman looking at the sky, lit by a sunbeam, having an epiphany. Seriously, Mads, enjoy it. Sometimes you slog your guts out for peanuts and sometimes, well, you don't. Success is all about opportunity— you see what's there and you go for it. No looking back, no regrets. A decent payday AND your name on the cover? Laughing all the way to Harvey Nichols.

After she signs off with kisses, I pick up the dummy copy of the book. I stroke the cover in the blank spot where I hope my name will go. Inside, in the photographs, the models are fractured into body parts: a breast as perfect as a globe; an L-shaped jawline; a closed eye, upper lashes resting on the lower like the fan of a bird's wings. The dissected bodies are all young and firm, so far unmarked by life. I suspect the models haven't had any augmentation done but how, short of seeing the scars, would I ever know? And if there were scars or moles or uneven skin tone? Then good lighting, choice framing, and a bit of postproduction work would soon edit them out. In this age of documenting everything we do, perhaps we should think of ourselves as drafts, like a manuscript: the way we're born is the rough first draft; cosmetic and aesthetic work polishes us up to second; airbrushing and filters produce the final, most refined version of how we want to be seen.

I can't get Scott off my mind as I go back to work. Telling myself it's technically research, I look him up online. There's only one page of results. I'm seeing the RRX website, of course, and LinkedIn. As with Angela, the info on LinkedIn is scant—a bachelor of science degree at Salesian University in New York, graduating in 1997. That would make him older than I took him for by about five years. Maybe he gets RRX treatments as a perk of the job. Although I can't see it. He's too natural. Must have good genes. The first degree was followed by an MBA in healthcare management at Fontaine University in Massachusetts, from 2000 to 2002. A gap of three years, then he became co-founder of Reynolds RX. No mention of what he spent that time doing; I suppose when you run your own successful company you don't have to worry about blanks in your résumé. I've fudged my patchy CV to cover those years spent caring for Mum, because somehow it doesn't feel right to include personal challenges in a list of career achievements. It's as if we have to divide ourselves up: work is work and life is life, and to let these identities overlap is to risk being written off as unprofessional.

Unlike Angela's LinkedIn profile, Scott's has a photo, a three-quarter-length profile of him in a suit, one hand in a trouser pocket. He looks different, thinner maybe, although it's difficult to tell at this scale, because the image is about the size of a pound coin. Maybe it's an old pic. I haven't updated my LinkedIn photo in a decade. My reason is pure laziness, but I can easily imagine some people leave their profile shots unchanged so they get to be seen as younger—sort of like free Botox. Scott, though, despite the fancy clothes, doesn't strike me as vain like that.

For comparison, I google Dr. Singh. He has about a gazillion results. His website has the kind of details I want to know about Angela and her company: full bio, links to research papers, before-and-after pics, and price lists for the treatments he offers—his specialist face-lift costs a hundred thousand dollars. Christ. There's a tab for press that pulls up links to interviews, articles, and inclusions in "best cosmetic doctors" glossy mag listicles. In contrast, it strikes me how little there is about Reynolds RX online, considering it's so sought-after. Where are the *Wall Street Journal* features or the profiles in the *Sunday Times* or *Harper's Bazaar*, things that could help me get a feel for Angela and her company?

I email Raphaela to ask whether there are any press cuttings available, and her response, while prompt, is not helpful: Dr. Reynolds always declines interviews. Why, though? If you're as good at what you do as she is, wouldn't you want to celebrate that? Why hide your light under a bushel? Discreet she may be, but Angela doesn't strike me as overly modest. Maybe she's such a control freak that a book that's under her strict direction is as much publicity as she'll allow.

I check Facebook and see I have two messages from people I don't know. The first is from the Beaverbrook med school alumni group, signed off Marinda Stern, Admin. Great. Maybe she'll be able to fill in some of the blanks for me.

But no: Hi there. Whilst I'm afraid we can't hand out contact details of alumni, I can pass on a message, and the relevant person may be in touch if it so behooves them. Have a great day!

Data protection strikes again. Typical.

The second message starts in the same way: Hi there. I saw your post in the Beaverbrook group. You may well have found her by now but yes, I know Dr. Reynolds. An extremely competent physician. I came across her at Beaverbrook, although barely—we overlapped only very briefly, as I graduated in 1992. We were later employed at the same teaching hospital in Boston, Redleaf, where she was finishing out her clinical rotations—dermatology, as I recall. We were in different departments, and I didn't make the connection at first, as she was practicing as Dr. Reynolds, rather than under the name by which I knew her at Beaverbrook, but I expect she married. After Boston I understand Dr. Reynolds set up her own practice and moved to London, England, where I hear she has had immense success. I wish her all the best—she is obviously gifted in her field. I suggest you contact her through her business, Reynolds RX, if you need to know more. Best wishes, Dr. Michael Madrigal.

It reads like a very vague reference for a job. And tells me nothing I don't know, apart from Angela having been married. Is that true—she told me she hadn't been—or was it a supposition on Madrigal's part? *Ask Dr. Reynolds if you need to know more*—fat chance. Why is it so hard for me to do my job?

Irritated, I push my chair away from the desk and take my water glass through to the bathroom for a refill. Hovering in front of the sink, I drink a whole pint straight down, and half a second until my stomach is full. Keeping hydrated is one of the best things you can do for your skin, according to Angela in her interview transcripts. I know more about her bloody beauty tips than I do about her. I open the vanity cupboard. On the shelf is a hair dryer, the cord wound neatly around the handle, and a pair of matching wooden boxes with lids. I pull off the lids. Tampons, neatly lined up like glossy white bullets. She's so damn impenetrable that even her bathroom cupboard is immaculate.

Can I find anything else? In the bedroom, the nightstand drawers yield nothing. I open her side of the wardrobe but can't get beyond my initial sense of who she is: expensive, tasteful, and ordered. I pull out a dress on a hanger. The action releases her scent—detergent and a musky perfume. Parting the clothes to return the dress, I peer into the depths of the wardrobe. No surprises here, just varnished wood. Above the hanging rail is a high shelf. It appears empty, but when I stand on the bed I can see the top of a box at the back, labeled in marker pen: *Photos*. Success buzzes in my chest. I bring the office chair through, reach my whole arm in, and nudge the box to the front. It's a shoebox, Italian designer brand, and, judging from the near weightlessness, empty. I lift the lid anyway. Yep—nothing inside.

I don't know why I'm so disappointed. Even if I'd come across a birth certificate, a whole photo album, and her teenage diaries, enough to have filled in all the blanks, I wouldn't have been able to use the information because Angela has the final say over what goes in the manuscript anyway. Sheepishly, I return the box to its original position and the chair to the office. I smooth out the bedclothes, which are dented from where I stood on them, and slide the wardrobe closed.

I have to accept that I'm only going to know what she chooses to tell me. Dr. Angela Reynolds isn't a riddle to solve.

8

NEW DAY, NEW START. DETERMINED TO MAKE THE BEST OF MY second scheduled video call with Angela, I carry my laptop down to the kitchen, hoping the connection will hold if I'm closer to the router.

"I must apologize, but something's come up, and I can only spare a few minutes," she says when she appears online.

Right. Trying not to show my frustration, I make an effort to reframe the situation. A few minutes is better than nothing.

I have her down as being in Monaco. But the room behind her is identical to the one in Jeddah: a chaise, black four-poster, white sheets. "Did you get stuck in Saudi?"

"What? No. Why do you say that?"

"Your room."

She looks over her shoulder. "I didn't realize. Chain hotels. Globalization. Who knows?" I wouldn't have thought Angela was a chain hotel kind of person, but "chain" to her probably means Park Hyatt or Four Seasons. She turns back to me. "We'll have to reschedule, but I wanted to check in and make sure you're okay. How are you finding the house?"

"It's spectacular. Thank you."

"You have all you need? We've arranged for more food to be delivered in a few days."

"Yes, I'm all set, thanks."

"How are Rudy and Massimo?"

"Great. Happy." Angela visibly softens at this news and I decide to say a little more about her dogs. The stronger the connection I can forge with my clients, the more they tend to open up and the better their book becomes. "They seem to love going on walks with Scott."

"Wonderful." She looks off camera and adjusts something on her desk. "And you're getting along well with Scott?" She gives whatever has distracted her another nudge. "Have you spoken to him much?"

"No." We've been sharing the same house for three days now and I've only bumped into him twice. "Do you want me to set up an interview with him?"

"Not necessarily." Her attention returns to me. "As I said, he handles the business side of things, so won't have much to contribute of interest to SKIN DEEP. But I thought, since you're living in close proximity, that naturally you might, you know, talk."

"Well, we said hello when he got here. And he helped me reset the Wi-Fi yesterday."

"Good, that's good."

She's fiddling again. Is it me or is she less together than usual?

"Apart from that," I add, "he kind of keeps himself to himself."

"Yes. He's . . ." She looks away from the camera a second time as she chooses her words. "I wasn't sure whether to tell you this, Madeleine, but you have a right to know." Ah. This doesn't sound good. "I'm sorry he kind of sprung himself on you like that, but he needed to go somewhere quiet and I thought the house would be the best place. He's working through some things." From the way she says it, it's clear that in "working through" she doesn't mean the merger.

"I've known Scott for a long time," Angela says. "Since, oh, 2004? No, earlier—late 2003." I let the timeline anchor itself between us. She would have been at Redleaf then and he not long out of his MBA at Fontaine. "We were both living in Boston, and I met him at a party. He told me he had a business idea and gave me his card. He was persistent, kept calling, so I met him for coffee and he outlined a plan."

At last she's sharing some useful detail. I must have been going about it the wrong way, should have let her set her own pace. I grab my pen and start to take notes. "And Reynolds RX was that business?"

"Yes. Botox was taking off, major developments were being made with hyaluronic acids, the FDA had approved Restylane earlier that year. Medspas were becoming a thing, at least in California. Scott thought we could capitalize on that and offered to put up the initial investment. It made sense. I was on a dermatology rotation and enjoying it. He said he'd do the background work and we'd go out on our own in 2005, once I was licensed."

I'm not sure what happened to only having a few minutes, but now that we've finally got going, I'm not going to point this out. "Okay. And what was he doing before you decided to go into partnership? Did he already have experience in the industry?"

"No, this was the first time either of us had worked in aesthetics. He was, well, he was looking for a fresh start."

My attention is on what I'm writing. "A fresh start from?"

"Perhaps it's best not to write this next part down," Angela says. I glance up in surprise. She is serious. I cap my pen. She sips some water before continuing. "You see, Scott is a brilliant, brilliant man, but he suffers periodically from depression, which can make him erratic. Understandably. Obviously we got there in the end, because Reynolds RX is where it is today, but there have been some close calls and we very nearly didn't." From her tone, it's evident she thinks he was the reason. "And while we're on the subject, I should tell you he's spent time in rehab for addiction. A couple of times, while I was finishing up at Redleaf and we were setting up the company."

The missing years on his CV. She hasn't mentioned what he was addicted to, and it could be other things—purging, gambling, sex—but I can't help picturing the self-conscious way he took a bottle of wine from the cabinet the day he arrived. "I see." What on earth do you say when someone tells you another person's problems like this? God, the poor guy. I wonder at her choice of the past perfect tense, as if these issues are behind him. "And how is he now?"

"He's learned how to deal with it." She gives a small, sad smile. "But the stress of everything that's going on with the company makes me worry. So that's partly why I sent him up to Varaig. Asked him, I mean, if he'd like to use the house." Her normal eloquence is gone. It must be hard, watching someone you're close to go through all that. "It was all quite last-minute, and that's why you were unaware that he'd be joining you. I hope it's not a problem?"

It's not ideal, but what can I do? "Of course not."

"Thank you. I know you can be discreet." She signs off in a hurry, saying she'll send through a revised date for our interview. Immediately, my mailbox pings with the recording of the conversation. I notice that the end timestamp is from only a couple of seconds ago—Angela must have forgotten to cut it off when she asked me to stop taking notes. I'll have to ask her whether she wants me to delete the file.

I close my laptop. There are finger smudges on the aluminum case. I pull down the cuff of my shirt and try to polish them off. That word again: discreet. Angela used it at our very first meeting, when she mentioned Lord Malouf. Did she already know then that Scott would be coming here and was checking I could be relied on to keep quiet, worried that if word got out, rumors might damage their business? Does Sacha know about Scott's issues, or Raphaela? He seems a little reserved to me, but not like someone in the throes of a breakdown. "Working through" can mean all kinds of things. So maybe it's no big deal and Angela is just taking care of a friend.

My thumb catches on a scratch on the laptop case that is too deep to wipe away, more than surface damage. That information about Scott was so personal, and now I know more than I should about him. I'm no therapist, but I am used to people unburdening their mental health issues on me. It seems to go with the job of ghostwriter. However, usually clients speak about their own problems, not others' difficulties.

Why involve me?

Midafternoon, there's a knock on the office door and Scott sticks his head around. "Sorry to bother you."

He's not been up here before, not sought me out. "Oh, hi." I hear the question in my voice. "I mean, come in."

He half accepts, pushing the door all the way open but staying in the doorway, his phone in his hand. I can't help but look at him differently and I don't like having this knowledge; it makes me feel complicit. I don't even know whether Angela has told him what she's shared with me.

But Scott, if he is aware, shows no sign of it. "I came to ask a favor. The dogs are desperate to go out, but I'm due a call at"—he checks the time on his phone—"well, any minute, and I didn't want to let them wander on their own. So I wondered if you were planning on taking a break soon?"

He asks this smoothly, easily, as if we're neighbors who do each other little favors all the time. Maybe he's already dealt with whatever was stressing him out in London, or the fresh air up here is doing him good. Or perhaps he's putting on a front, using the fact that we don't know each other as an opportunity to be seen as he wants to be, rather than as "poor Scott"—at least that's how I felt after Mum died. Often it was easier to be in the company of strangers than friends; it allowed me to, if not forget my grief, at least try to pretend it wasn't there.

"Sure," I say. "A walk would be good—I've been slouched here too long."

"Great! Thank you." He fishes a packet of dog treats from his pocket and puts it on my desk. "A quick out and back will do fine. I wouldn't ask, I know you're swamped with the . . ." He catches sight of the SKIN DEEP dummy. "Hey, is that your book? Mind if I . . . ?"

I like how he said "your" book. He waits until I nod at him before picking it up and bouncing it in his hands, testing its weight. "And what you're writing now," he says, "your . . . ?"

"Manuscript."

"May I see?"

Straight to the point—so New York. But while sending Angela a rough draft is one thing, letting someone else read the manuscript feels exposing.

He notices my reluctance, and both hands rise in apology. He's still holding the dummy and light glints off the foiled typeface. "Oh, I'm sorry, that's rude of me."

"No, it's . . ." I can hardly refuse; it's his company paying the bill. "Of course you can." I rotate the laptop toward him. "Go ahead. This is the latest part. Just please bear in mind that it's a work in progress, not the final copy."

He puts the book and his phone down near the keyboard and plants both palms on the desk. He is close enough that I can smell his shampoo, menthol. In repose, his dimple has gone and in its place is a tiny curved line, no bigger than the impression a thumbnail might leave if pressed into the skin. His eyes move side to side as he reads. His proximity is heady, and I want to look at him more, but I've always found someone reading my words excruciating. I think of the manikin downstairs, flayed and exposed. I fixate on Scott's hands instead. Sacha jokes that I have a fetish for hands, but I maintain that they tell you a lot: what kind of a life someone lives, whether they look after themselves. They're one of the first parts to age, and you see older people, women usually, who have spent a fortune preserving their faces but whose hands give them away. I wonder whether Angela has a gadget for hands. Chemo made Mum's itch and she scratched at them constantly. Patrick's were rough; I could always feel the calluses in his palm when he touched my bare skin. Scott's hands are broad, the nails trimmed, the skin a light golden brown.

He has clicked down, is reading on. I'd been exploring the etymology of the word "beauty," interested in how it morphed from meaning "goodness" or "courtesy" in early Anglo-French into the definition we use today that denotes a physical, bodily attractiveness or seductiveness. I'd been attempting to argue that the modern words "beauty" and "beautiful" can still carry the original moral meaning, using the example of describing a piece of music as "beautiful." Music isn't visible and therefore can't have a physical beauty, but someone who finds a song "beautiful" finds it "good," not only judging it to be of merit but also seeing "goodness" in it, feeling uplifted. The word "uplifted" itself first meant "exalted" or moving closer to God, so, logically, to be judged beautiful is both to be exalted and to cause exaltation in others. I'd even found a quote from Edgar Allan Poe to back up my theory, although I was planning to paraphrase the first part to refer to all people, not only men: "When, indeed, men speak of Beauty, they mean, precisely, not a quality, as is supposed, but an effect—they refer, in short, just to that intense and pure elevation of soul."

Now I wonder whether I've gone too far, because by the time Scott finishes reading and nudges the laptop back toward me, his eyebrows are jacked right up. Definitely too far. Etymology, for God's sake. That's so basic, like something from an A-level essay. This guy has a medical degree; he deals in facts and precise measurements, not late-night "logic" brought on by panic, overthinking, and way too many coffees. I close the laptop lid. "It's very clunky. I probably won't even keep that part in."

"No," he says, "you really must." He is looking straight at me and his expression, as much as I can judge it, barely knowing him, seems earnest. "It's fascinating." He picks up the SKIN DEEP dummy again and leafs through slowly, taking his time looking at the photos. It's as if it's new to him.

"You haven't seen it before?"

He glances up. "What? No. Well, obviously yes." He shuts the book quickly and puts it back where it came from. "In concept, I mean, but not as an actual physical object. It's Angela's idea. I have little to do with it." He jams both hands into his pockets.

A phone buzzes—Scott's, on the desk. He checks the screen and holds it out to show me. *Angela Reynolds.* He pulls a funny apologetic face and leaves.

The idea that anyone could be close enough to Angela to be casual about her in that way makes me smile. She's so self-contained that she seems to invite seriousness—at least she does in me.

Before collecting the dogs I check the kitchen pantry. We seem to be low on canned goods—tuna and beans especially—but the bottle of merlot I opened is still in there, with just my glass's worth gone. Next I scan the wine cabinet. Only one other bottle is missing—the red Scott took when he arrived. I hate that I'm snooping, but it's reassuring all the same. One bottle of wine in three days is not a problem in my book.

Massimo skips a merry dance around my feet when I tell him it's time for a walk, although Rudy seems more hesitant. I borrow Angela's jacket again but I can't find boots that even half fit. They all seem much bigger than before; I must have been wearing thicker socks last time. Converse it is.

Massimo scampers ahead; Rudy follows more slowly, limping a little. Clouds have blown in, lidding the valley, their gray heaviness bringing a closed-in feeling. Autumn is almost at an end, and the dying season is encroaching, the land darkening as leaves turn brittle, sagging from their stalks like tanned hides. The needles on the larch trees down by the loch have changed, rusting and thinning, exposing branches bare as bones.

Before I get to the cliff I spot a path off to the left, more tramped than I would have expected considering how few people there are around, the undergrowth flattened and some bracken stems snapped in half. Maybe it's a deer trail. It leads us across and down the hill and deposits us on a narrow stony beach on the long side of the loch.

In the middle distance, near the loch's edge, is a small white building almost hidden behind trees—the place I saw from the helicopter that looked like a thrown die. I head in that direction, my feet crunching the pebbles on the beach, hoping for a pub or a shop. It'd be nice to have a change of scene. I miss that from home. I get out my phone to check the map and see whether I'm right, but there's no signal at all.

As I get closer, I see the building is quite run-down, possibly abandoned. The roof is mossy, the whitewash grayed, the windows foggy with dirt. Despite the moss, the roof slates are all in place and the windows are intact. Perhaps it's a bothy, a shelter for those hiking the valley. The dogs sniff the base of the wall. I put my hands to the grubby glass and try to peer in, but the shutters inside are closed. Stepping away, I dust off my hands on my jeans. Now I see a sign staked into the ground, its wooden face blotted with green. PRIVATE PROPERTY. NO TRESPASSING. Rudy cocks a defiant leg against its post.

A person moves among the trees, coming our way. I ready myself to apologize in case it's an irate landowner, but it's a girl I recognize: the backpacker from the foggy morning. Massimo, taken by surprise, starts to growl. He hunkers low and switches to barking. The girl freezes.

"Sorry," I call to her over the noise Massimo is making. To him I say, "Hey, it's all right." I crouch and offer him a treat as Scott had done. He looks from me to the stranger, barking, still unsure, but eventually he takes the biscuit. I drop a few on the ground to keep both him and his brother busy.

The girl seems wary, as if she might take flight at any moment. No backpack today. I reckon she's squatting here. She associates me with the big house—I did kind of let her believe that; maybe she thinks I own this cottage, too. I give her a friendly smile. "Hi again. It's all right. It's not my place."

There's a pause and then she eases out from behind a tree but stays close to the trunk, as if ready to hide at any moment. She watches me spoil the dogs with a few more treats. "I wasn't making any trouble."

The American accent strikes me. Three Americans, Angela, Scott, and this girl, all in this tiny part of the world. I stand. "I didn't think you were. It's okay. I was just nosing around."

I can see her far more clearly than I could the last time. I was right, she is young—late teens possibly, or early twenties. The older I get, the harder it is to tell younger people's ages. Her hair is an extraordinary color, dyed close to burgundy, the shade that the Boston ivy that Mum trained to grow up our back fence would turn in autumn. She's wearing a little cap, crocheted in a mustardy wool, and the contrast makes her hair gleam. Her khaki jacket is too thin for the weather, and her leggings seem similarly flimsy, but at least she's in proper, sensible walking boots—more sensible than I am today. She shifts shyly closer to the tree so her feet and half her body are hidden.

Rudy nudges my calf for more biscuits, but he's had enough. I tell him no. To her I say, "You decided to stick around, then?"

"Excuse me?"

I'm struck by her old-fashioned politeness. I'd noticed it the other day. Good manners. I curve a hand, indicating the loch, the wider valley. "To stay in the area. Gorgeous, isn't it?"

"Oh." She looks at the water as if only now noticing it. "Sure is. But I'm not sure how much longer I'll be here. I'll probably move on tomorrow."

There's a nervous tremor to her laugh and she's holding herself stiffly, anxious for me to leave. "Well," I say, smiling, backing away, making it clear I won't bother her any further. The dogs dart off in the direction of the moorland. "Enjoy your trip."

I've barely finished speaking before she's disappearing into the trees, as if she can't wait to get away.

9

WHEN I EMERGE ONTO THE LANDING THAT EVENING, THE SMELL of spices drifts up the staircase to meet me. I go down, following cooking sounds to the kitchen. Scott is at the stove, shirtsleeves rolled up to the elbow. The sight of him stops me in my tracks. I study his back as he works. He had a haircut recently—it is neat and straight at the nape of his neck. A few small moles right below his hairline disappear and reappear as the collar of his shirt bounces up and down when he jiggles a wok.

He notices me and I look away, embarrassed at being caught staring. But maybe I wasn't as obvious as I thought, as he gives me a wry, unself-conscious smile. "Thought it was probably my turn."

A curry is bubbling in a pan. There is a mass of sloughed skins on the chopping board: onion, lemongrass, shrimp. Impressive, making it from scratch. I should have made more of an effort these past days. "You're putting my reheating skills to shame," I say.

"You might not say that when you've tasted it. I'm a little rusty. Don't see the point in cooking for one, you know?"

For one. I store that little nugget away. "Oh, I know."

When I was with Patrick, I cooked quite often, ripping recipes out of Sunday supplements to try, shopping in farmers' markets for fennel and romanesco and black garlic. Since he left—since I pushed him to leave—it's been pasta or a precooked salmon fillet eaten at a space carved out of all the junk cluttering my kitchen table.

I don't want to mention Patrick though, so I just say, "Well, thank you. This is a real treat."

"My pleasure." His smile is full and warm; warming. "Say, do you know if we have peanut butter?"

"Crunchy or smooth? We've got both." He has his hands full at the stove so I go to the pantry. It's quite an intimate thing, cooking and eating together, and it could easily be awkward, sharing domestic duties like this, but for some reason I don't find it at all weird. To reach the pantry I have to skirt around Scott and he shifts a little to make room for me, as if we're dance partners, do-si-do-ing to a practiced routine.

"Smooth, please," he says.

Despite moving jars around, I can't find either. I think of the chocolate and his sweet tooth. "Did you finish them?"

"No."

I check again. They were right here, stacked one above the other, next to the Marmite.

He must read the doubt on my face because he adds, "Honestly, I haven't touched them. I only use peanut butter for cooking and obviously . . ." He waves his spoon around, emphasizing he hasn't been doing any of that.

I must have been seeing things. He has no reason to fib. "Sorry, I could've sworn we had lots, but obviously not. Must be thinking of my place. Is it crucial?"

"I'll manage. Afraid you're going to miss out on the full effect, though."

We slide out of each other's way again, bodies orbiting. Then the seal on the fridge door hisses as he opens it. He takes out a bottle of Chablis. "Want one? I ditched that red because it'd been open so long."

I hesitate. If it is alcohol he had a problem with, I don't want to be encouraging him to drink. "No, I think I'm okay."

He's already driving in a corkscrew. The tendons in his forearm lift rhythmically as he twists. "Sure? It's a good year. Angela has great taste in wine."

Two glasses are already standing side by side. He pours only a small amount into one glass, swirls it to release the aromas, and lifts it to his nose.

It's so unlike the way I'd expect an alcoholic to behave that it reassures me. "Go on then. Thanks."

He glugs wine into a second glass—a more generous serving for me. "Here you go." He hands it over. "Dinner won't be long. Pull up a pew." It's funny hearing such a British idiom in his accent. We must have rubbed off on him over the past dozen years.

I sit at the table, which he has already set. The dogs are in their beds by the window, dozing. Scott uses a spoon to test the sauce, picks up a tea towel to wipe a spill from the counter, and drapes it over his shoulder afterward, like a chef in a restaurant. He's obviously at home and enjoying himself as if, like me, he's relaxed into our being thrown together. Again, he is barefoot. He has elegant feet, for a man. Each toe orderly, descending in size, high arches, nails neat. Good feet, good hands . . .

A click as he switches off the extractor fan. Quickly, I pull myself together.

"Here," he says, coming over, carrying two plates, the cloth still over his shoulder. "Hope it's not too spicy for you." He hops back to the counter to retrieve his glass of wine and the rest of the bottle.

"Slàinte." He says it the Scottish way, *slan-ja.*

"Cheers."

The curry is delicious, fragrant and light.

"So how'd it go this afternoon?" he asks as we eat. "With your book, sorry, manuscript?"

He's remembered what I called it. "Okay, I think. At least . . ." I stop. I can hardly complain to him about it. But my face gives me away.

"I see," he says. "Angela's got you on a tight leash." He takes the cloth from his shoulder and uses it as a napkin to dab at his mouth. "That happens."

I chew, buying some time to think before replying. "It's understandable. She has a certain way of wanting to go about things, and that's"—*annoying,* but I shouldn't say that—"great. Look, I'm very new to aesthetics, and it's not exactly my forte . . ."

He refills my glass. "Nor mine."

He widens his eyes as he says this, using humor to make me feel more comfortable, and it works, because I laugh. "Yeah, right."

His eyes fall to his lap and he flushes. That's interesting. But then he sort of seems to shut down again. We eat for a while in silence and then I say, "Do you see many clients up here?"

"*I* don't see any clients," he says, emphasizing the *I*.

"That's all Angela?"

"Uh-huh."

I'm still curious about whether I was right about duchesses and other royalty. "And up here, they would be, what kind of person?"

If he knows what I'm fishing for, he doesn't take the bait. He laughs to himself. "I—I mean my brother—calls them the 'discreet elite.'" I notice the swift change of pronoun, wonder whether it's the equivalent of "asking for a friend," that he doesn't want to let on that this is his own opinion. "Sounds like high-class call girls, doesn't it?" he says. "But you can't get much further away from call girls than Reynolds clients. She's good at what she does, Angela. She's more like an artist than a doctor, working with light and shadows."

Although I'm yet to see confirmed evidence of her work, I can well imagine this is true. "How come you set up RRX in the UK, anyway, given that you're both American? That wasn't explained in my notes."

"There are notes?" The hint of jokey sarcasm is back.

I find myself wanting to match it. "Ohhh, yes."

He nods knowingly. "Of course there are notes."

He's right on the edge between making fun and being serious and I'm enjoying the banter, which might even be flirting. I wonder what he's like with Angela, whether he teases her in this way. Angela and repartee don't seem natural bedfellows to me, but maybe she warms up once she's known you a while. Then it occurs to me that maybe he's able to speak of her like this because they're extra close—maybe they have been, or even are, together, actual bedfellows? I wouldn't have thought so, because I haven't sensed anything and he said that thing about cooking for one, but he has got her dogs. I sink a little.

I reach for my wine, aiming for insouciance. "You've known each other a long time."

"Mm-hmm."

He's not going to bite. I backtrack. "So, then, why London?"

"I had . . . connections over here, thought it made sense." He finishes his dinner, lines up his knife and fork, and pushes the plate away. It seems he doesn't want to talk about that. "Have you always been a ghostwriter?"

"Pretty much. It wasn't the plan, but." Normally I'd leave it there, but from the way he's scraping his chair back a few inches from the table and angling it toward me, I sense he's one of those rare people who actually listens, who's interested in what I have to say. "My mum was ill and I had to care for her. And that caring"—I mean dying, but still find it hard to say that word out loud—"went on for a lot longer than either of us expected or hoped for." Oh God, that sounds wrong, like I hoped she'd die sooner. "I mean, of course I didn't want her to . . ." Although sometimes I think she might have.

He blinks—he understands. Three drawn-out years Mum clung on, getting smaller and weaker and less herself. I shake my head to clear the memories. "I had a graduate journalism placement once, but I couldn't take it up, because, well, obviously . . ." Because my mum was dying and I was already deep into loss before she'd even gone. "And after, a while after, I needed to earn money, fast. And so I kind of fell into a job, like a lot of people do. I signed up with an agency that sent me off with a Dictaphone and a list of questions to ask someone. I told myself ghosting was a kind of journalism, interviewing people, piecing together the facts, and knitting them into a life story." I twirl my wineglass on its base. "It seems to suit me. And to be something I'm not bad at." I don't want to look at him, because he'll be wearing that sympathetic expression people get when you talk about death, and I hate that because it tips the careful balance I've worked so hard to establish within myself.

"You must be better than 'not bad' if Angela hired you."

I'm not sure about that, given the way this Reynolds job is going so far. I lift my drink and huff, and the huff sounds louder in the bowl.

I can feel him watching me. "That must have been tough, though, with your mother," he says. "Was it just the two of you?"

"Yes." I twist the glass again.

A pause, a sinkhole of a pause that threatens to drag me down into too many sad memories. After a few seconds of quiet, there is a shift in the air as he stands. A clatter as he collects up the plates. Then the warmth of his hand on my shoulder, a slight pressure. It pulls me back into the present. "Oh God, let me do that."

"No need." He waves me back into my seat and loads the dishwasher.

I sip my Chablis. It has warmed and tastes like old pennies. "How about you? Any family?"

"My mom. Brother." He is quiet. "We lost my dad when I was young."

"Then you know."

"I do know." He gives a tiny nod, at the kinship to be found in pain. He's felt that grief, the kind that some days is—was . . . *is*—so raw and so deep your bones literally ache.

We seem to have progressed very quickly from small talk to deep this evening. "I'm sorry." I'm aware my words are weak. People used to say that to me all the time, if they said anything at all. *Sorry.* But what possible words are there that would measure up? Words can't fill a gap that big. Maybe it's better not to try, not to say anything at all.

He gives me a small smile. "Thanks."

"Do you see them much, your mum and brother?"

"Some."

I want to ask whether they're in the States, but he closes the dishwasher and the snap of its door feels like an end to the subject.

He comes back to the table, not to sit but to swoop away his half-drunk wine. I'm not ready for the evening to end, to go back to that lonely, thorny manuscript. Our couple of brief encounters aside, I haven't had a real-life conversation in days. But it's more than that—I like talking to him, being in his company. I like him. Maybe if I steer a course back to safer subjects, he'll stay. I mirror the question he asked me first. "How's it going with the . . ." Remembering Sacha's warning not to let on that I know there's a merger, I catch myself. "With whatever it is that brings you up here."

"That's one way of putting it. It's . . ." He contemplates his glass, then dumps the contents into the sink. "It's complicated."

"Right." He's silent. I suppose that's it, then. Back to work. I polish off my own drink and ready myself to stand, but then he speaks.

"I did a skydive once."

A story is coming. I feel an inner lifting at the realization he's not ready to go yet, either, that he's enjoying my conversation or even my company. Resettling, I shuck off a slipper and put my foot on the seat of my chair, hug my knee.

Scott stays where he is, across the kitchen, leaning against the counter. "On holiday one summer. My friends were hungover, sleeping late, so I took off for a hike and saw a poster and knew I had to try it. The next morning I was going up in this little plane, crammed in with a group of other wide-eyed tourists. You ever do it?"

I shake my head, wondering where this is going. Maybe he wants to tell a lighthearted anecdote to erase death from the room. "What was it like?"

He sucks his teeth. "Kinda hard to explain. Nothing like flying. I remember there was this huge blast of wind as my instructor edged us closer to the door. It was up to me to decide whether to let go or to chicken out and shuffle back inside the plane. The land below looked so unreal, like a model village. But at the same time it felt more real than anything I'd experienced before. It kinda sharpened my perception."

I think of the flight here in the helicopter, of those running deer. "Of what?"

"Of . . . it's hard to describe. Of life, I suppose. Like until that moment I'd been following this road. School, college, summer jobs. And there was a gap ahead. And I had this choice: turn back or take a leap of faith."

I snort.

"What?" he says. "Too cheesy?"

"Trust the American."

He laughs at that but then becomes still and I worry I might have punctured the mood. But he is happy to go on. "Not like a leap of faith in a religious way. Within my own life, I suppose. Knowing that I had a choice and accepting that it was my decision to make that choice, no one else's, and therefore being okay with the consequences."

There could have been some pretty dire consequences. I imagine myself in that plane, standing in the open doorway, wind beating in my ears, heart beating in my chest.

"It's funny," he says. "In that moment before you jump, you don't feel or think anything at all. I don't remember much about the free fall. I know there was this almighty jerk when the guy pulled the cord and I had bruises for weeks afterward. Oh God, and coming in to land, the speed the ground came rushing up. I couldn't make my legs move fast enough."

We stay still in silence for a while, one of us remembering, the other imagining. Our conversation has taken so many turns this evening that it's hard to get the measure of him, but there's a message in this story, I sense, a message for me, something cryptic that I'll have to puzzle out, or that will become clear if we spend more time together.

"Would you do it again?" I ask.

He purses his lips no. "It wouldn't be the same. You only get to experience a feeling like that once."

He pushes away from the counter and arches his back as if he's been still for too long. The bubble has burst; it's time to say good night. Reluctantly, I release my knee and search with my foot for my slipper, idly, slowly. Delaying.

Scott stops in the doorway to the atrium, lingering, too. "What about you, Maddy? Would you jump?"

My toes touch sheepskin. Was his story about consequences or about risk? Maybe it's a slanted way of trying to work out how adventurous I am, how brave. How confident in my own future. I could say yes, make him believe that I'm a certain kind of person, the daredevil kind who'd be happy to fling themselves out of planes at any opportunity. But I was honest with him earlier, and I don't want to switch now.

I slide my foot into my slipper and cross the kitchen. "I'd like to think so. But I can't be certain I would."

"Well, you know what they say."

"No, what do they say?" I pause to turn off the kitchen spots. Only the lights on the mezzanine are on, and, backlit, he is merely an outline.

"Never say never."

In the half-dark, his hand finds my shoulder again, soft pressure. The touch is brief, barely there. I carry the memory of it all the way up the stairs.

10

OVER THE NEXT COUPLE OF DAYS, THE OCCASIONAL SOUNDS OF
Scott moving around the house are welcome. It's amazing how quickly
you can adapt, how something that once was strange, disturbing even, can
soon shift into the familiar.

Angela next calls me from South Africa. This time she has applied a
filter to her background, blurring it out.

She opens with a compliment. "I've read the latest installment and I
have to say, I'm impressed. It's coming together brilliantly."

I was *not* expecting that. I followed Scott's advice and kept the etymology part in. My face heats with pleasure. "Thank you." Should I say
something back? I've never been very good at accepting praise. I clear my
throat. "Angela, I know we discussed images before . . ."

"Ye-es?"

She draws out the word and I know I'm not going to win her over on
this. And it seems bad manners to push after she's complimented my work.
I change tack. "I was hoping for some before-and-afters. For research, not
for inclusion. So I can get an idea of the results you generate. Also I was
wondering if you have any famous clients, people I've heard of? Actors,
maybe? I was looking at Dr. Singh's website—"

"Dr. Singh?" She is sharp. "Why do you mention him?"

"It's kind of hard to avoid him. He's everywhere. On his site there's
no end of glowing testimonials from big Hollywood names. I imagine your
client list is similar?"

Angela looks off to the side. "Tell me, Madeleine. I'd be curious to know—what did you think when you saw the pictures of the people he'd worked on?"

The question feels like a trap. I need to be careful. "I'm not sure it's something I'd choose for myself."

"Yes, that was apparent in my clinic." She gazes steadily into her webcam. I can't decide whether she's chiding or teasing.

"What I mean to say . . ." I slow down, try to choose my words diplomatically. "Is that . . . I'm, you know"—Mum pops into my head, Mum before cancer—"I'm more into the idea of aging gracefully. But of course it's everyone's right to decide."

"Aging gracefully."

I swear inwardly. I need a better poker face. And to learn when to keep my mouth shut.

She pours water from a bottle into a glass, the pitch rising like a musical scale. She screws the lid back on, slowly. "It's okay, Madeleine. If I'd wanted a sycophant I would have hired one." The bottle is returned to the desk. "I like that you know your own mind. As long as you're not closed-off—and I don't think you are, are you?"

I think she's praising me. "No."

"Dr. Singh is, as I'm sure you're aware, the most successful dermatologist in America. He made twenty million dollars last year from his product line alone. His work may not be to your taste—and yes, his approach is very different from mine—but the man is extremely successful. And that is for a very simple reason." She sips her water. "Think about it this way: the magazines you pick up, the billboard advertisements you pass every day. Where are the older people in those? What was the last movie you watched?"

The change of direction makes my mind go blank, then I remember catching the last half of *Pretty Woman* on a lazy Sunday afternoon. I can't admit to that. Instead, I name an arthouse film I haven't yet seen but that won a clutch of awards.

"And the actors in that would have been, what, in their twenties? Maybe the men in their thirties?" I nod, hoping that's right. "Okay, with movies, I grant you, there are certain older actors who are still working, and working well, but they are the exception that proves the rule. Consider them the ones we're 'allowed' "—she signs air quotes—"to see. Especially the women." Straightaway, I think of prominent examples: Judi Dench, Tina Fey, JLo. "Now, let's consider the advertising industry. We all know how powerful it is. Half of the population in the UK is over forty and a quarter is over sixty, yet in advertising, unless there's an age-specific product being sold—retirement homes or cruises—you don't see them. They're invisible. Why do you think that is? It's not due to lack of spending power—the over-forties have far more disposable income than the under-forties. I'll tell you why." She leans in to her camera. "Our culture hides them away because it values health and youth over age and experience. This is partly because our brains decode youth, which we see as beauty, as this person would make a good mate, a good co-parent to my children. You already know this. Most people do. But there's another element to it. Being young means you have your whole life ahead of you— you can dream, fantasize, plan. Aging means accepting there's likely more life behind you than ahead."

This is all great material for the book. I scribble down that last quote and mark it with an asterisk. What I miss I can transcribe from the recording later.

"And this philosophy," Angela continues, "is what I use in my work. What I do is maintenance. It's about preserving someone as they are. Not allowing the temple to hollow, the jawline to dissolve. Uplifting them mentally, emotionally, as well as physically. I don't accept anyone I assess as being vulnerable, and I don't have before-and-after pictures for clients to see because it's not like going to a hair salon and choosing from a magazine of styles and saying I want that one. When does that ever work, anyway?"

I laugh. "Never. At least not for me."

"Quite. Your hair and bone structure are unique, so obviously the cut will never work out the same as the model's."

She drinks more water. I'll give her this—she practices what she preaches. "My patients don't want to age. They want to look like themselves—the best version of themselves—for as long as they can. Because if every time they look in a mirror they can see themselves as not getting older, if what they were is what they still are, then they can forget there might be less road ahead of them than there is behind; they can forget time has marched them, as it marches us all, a little closer toward death."

Bingo! This is exactly what I need. She pauses, and I'm grateful for the chance to catch up. I shake my hand to relieve the aching muscles and look back at my screen. Angela is watching me. One eyebrow rises. "I hope that proves useful? I hope that now you see where I'm going with everything?"

"Yes." And I do, I really do.

"Great. Because that's my idea of aging gracefully. Withstanding, not giving in."

After we wrap up, confirming the date of our next interview and what I'll be sending her and when, once we've said our quick goodbyes and closed down the meeting, something strikes me.

Not once during our whole conversation did she ask after Scott.

A little while later I'm in the kitchen, scrolling through #aestheticsresults on Instagram, when I see the latest reel from @DrSingh: a young woman presenting one side of her face to the camera, then the other, played in a loop. She is round-faced, sweet-looking, quite different from the usual high-cheekboned, tiny-nosed influencer type. Text appears at the top of the video: "Another happy client. Dimpleplasty. In and out in less than thirty minutes. Doesn't she look cute?" There is a rosy-cheeked emoji.

Dimpleplasty? Surely not.

But yes—here it is online, on Dr. Singh's own website: "A simple procedure performed under local anesthetic, in which part of the muscle inside the cheek is removed and the incision sutured to create a permanent dimple effect. Patients can choose the depth and location of their dimples for a more youthful look. Call now to inquire."

I return to the reel. This time when the text appears, I'm struck by how the red dots on the cheeks of the emoji look like dimples. Dimples equaling happiness. How long must the pain last after that surgery? Does it feel like your face might rip whenever you smile?

Scott comes in. "Hey." He clicks on the coffee machine to warm it up.

"Hi."

"That's a hell of a frown. You okay? Whatcha looking at?"

"Dr. Singh's latest work."

"Who?"

"Dr. Singh." I add emphasis, to mean *that* Dr. Singh.

"Oh."

The machine hisses loudly with pressure and I raise my voice. "Have you met him?"

"Ah, no."

I turn my phone out to show him. "Angela was singing his praises, but I don't know what to make of it."

He peers at my screen and pulls a face of distaste. "Astonishing, what some people will do to themselves."

I laugh.

"What?" he says.

"Well, that's not what I was expecting from someone who makes his living from the aesthetics industry. You sound like my mum."

He colors, as if realizing he's let his professional guard down. "A healthy dose of skepticism is a good thing, right?"

"Well, yes. Of course." I'm flattered that he feels comfortable enough with me now to be himself. He doesn't necessarily have to believe in order to make his fortune from it.

"Well, I'd better . . ." He gestures with his coffee cup in the direction of his room. After a couple of paces, he turns back to me, head tipped to one side. "Out of interest, what would your mum have said?"

I like that he says mum, as I did, rather than mom. I can picture her so clearly. "She'd have done this"—I press my lips together and put one hand on my heart, pantomiming her—"and gone, 'Doesn't she know that that's never going to make her happy?'"

Scott's own dimple flashes for a moment. "And she would have been right."

I can see why Angela chose to build her office at the top of the house—it has the best view. The lateness of the afternoon has drained the valley of some of its color, and tendrils of mist are beginning to rise off the surface of the loch like steam off a bath—a false promise because in November the water must be bone-chillingly cold. I'm starting to learn the patterns of the moor and I know that there'll be a thick fog tonight, sliding in silently to cloak the house.

I've not long opened the manuscript when a notification pops up from Messenger, from an Angela Rodriguez.

Dear Madeleine, I've been informed by my old college that you're trying to get in touch with me. Can I ask what it's about? Best wishes, Angela Rodriguez (née Reynolds). The green dot shows she's online right now.

Née Reynolds. So I misidentified my Angela. Easily done: Angela Reynolds is a common enough name. And it's a moot issue now anyway, seeing as though there aren't to be any personal pics in SKIN DEEP. There's no need to write back to this Angela Rodriguez, but I'm not a fan of ghosting people and so I type a brief message, explaining I'm a writer who has been commissioned to research and produce a book, and that I was trying to get in touch with the woman in the photo. I end it: Evidently I made a mistake. I'm sorry to have wasted your time.

I soon get the vibrating dots that show she's replying.

No problem. Tell the truth, I was mighty surprised to see my face pop up on my screen like that! Where in heaven did you get that picture?

I explain about using an agency. I guess you're not the Dr. Angela Reynolds I'm looking for. Sorry for the mix-up.

She's still online. Like I say, no problem. I expect her to leave it at that, but she carries on, clearly a chatterbox. It's nice to see the picture. It was a Valentine dance the night that photo was taken. I remember, because that's the night I met my husband. That's him right in the corner there, beneath the balloons. And that's my roommate, GiGi. I wonder what ever happened to her. How cute we were! Lordy, I wish I could still fit into a dress like that. She signs off with a pair of laughing-face emojis.

I've just settled back into editing mode when I register the sound of a vehicle approaching. An unfamiliar chime echoes through the house, the ding-dong of a doorbell. I wait, expecting Scott to answer as his room is closest, but when there's no movement I save the manuscript and go down. Two men are outside the entrance, one older, one young, stacking crates of food and drink on the ground. On the drive behind them is a van painted with a logo for a deli.

"Afternoon," the older man says. "Delivery for Reynolds?"

Angela mentioned more supplies were coming for us. And we need them because a lot of things—crackers, cheese, bread—seem to have been used up, although not by me. Scott must be a secret midnight snacker, despite his protestations over the peanut butter. I wish I had his metabolism. "Great, thanks."

I go to lift a crate, but he swoops it up first. "No bother. We usually leave them outside, but as someone's here we'll take them through."

It's obvious he's itching to have a peek inside. I stand aside to let them in. The younger guy whistles when he enters the atrium, taking in the height of the space, the art, just as I had. "Nice place." They deposit the crates in the kitchen and wait while I cram everything into the fridge.

I trail them back to the front door. "Thanks very much."

I'm starting to close it when the older man calls, "There's more." He pulls another crate out of the back of the van. This one is nearly all bottles, wine and whiskey. Our wine cabinet is still nearly full.

"This can't be right," I say, instantly worried that Scott ordered this booze.

"You did say Reynolds?"

"Yes."

His colleague pulls a phone from his trouser pocket and scrolls down. "Aye, well, it's definitely all for Reynolds."

"But there's only two of us. Maybe there was a computer error, a duplicate order, something like that?"

He consults the screen again, taps it a few times. "Ah, sorry now, my mistake. Wrong address." Relief surges through me. He turns to his colleague. "It's all right, Willie, that one's for down the way there." He jerks his chin in the direction of the loch. The crate goes back into the van. So do the men, the older one behind the wheel. As they leave, he winds down the window and tells me, "You have yourself a nice day now, madam."

Madam. I know he's only being polite and I'm not in any way offended, but it always surprises me, being called madam. It feels too grown-up, too matronly, yet I'm too old these days to be *miss.* Like with Ms., there ought to be a neutral spoken address, one that doesn't assume or patronize. Men don't have this problem; they're always sir. The perception of who they are doesn't shift just because they age.

In the office, my laptop has gone to screen-saver mode. It's an old photo of me and Mum, taken when I was a toddler, grinning at each other in close-up. In this shot, which Mum's big hair and pastel blouse immediately date as the eighties, she is younger than I am now, must be twenty-six. A fan of tanning, she has the beginnings of laugh lines at the corners of her eyes. Laugh lines: so much kinder a term than crow's-feet.

Mum never got the chance to see how time would change her face beyond middle age, how it would lighten her hair and thicken her joints and fold memories into her skin. She wasn't vain; I think she'd have worn her years happily, gratefully. People say we turn into our parents. I have no idea whether this will be true in my case. I don't know my dad. And because my mum is gone, I have no template for what will happen to my face, my body, my character or temperament. I have no foreknowledge about the kind of person I will turn out to be.

She is radiant in this pic. When Mum was alive, I didn't necessarily think of her as "good-looking." I'm not sure I could strip out her humanity and judge her like that, like a gemologist grading a diamond. How could I ever get enough distance from the belly that grew me, the arms that comforted, the facial features that taught me how to read and express emotion, to be able to say "She is beautiful"? Beauty comes with perspective. Get too close to anything, anyone, and the eye can't focus.

Late in the night, I'm woken by sounds from downstairs, doors being opened and closed. Footsteps. I look at my phone clock: twenty past two. I haven't been asleep long.

I go to the bathroom and am on my way back to bed when I hear more noises: chinks and a muffled clatter. Are the dogs awake? Does one of them need to be let out to pee? I step out onto the mezzanine and peer over the balustrade. The kitchen and atrium are in darkness. The doors to the back corridor and mudroom are closed, but there is a dim light under the mudroom door. The noises seem to be coming from there. Maybe one of the dogs accidentally got shut in. I grab my dressing gown and turn on my bedside lamp and use the light from that to go downstairs, because I don't want to wake myself up fully with the big lights—it'll take me ages to get to sleep again if I do.

The stairs are smooth beneath my feet, the concrete of the atrium cool now that the underfloor heating is off. From the other side of the mudroom door comes a clunk and a roll and a scrabbling noise. God, they'd better not be making a mess.

When I open the door, it's Scott in there, not the dogs. He is squatting in the corner by the wine cabinet, hunched into himself. The cabinet is open and the light inside has come on—it's that which was shining under the door—and he is rummaging through the bottles and appears to have knocked one onto the floor. For some reason he's wearing his coat and shoes inside. His coat is torn, the sleeve coming away from the shoulder at the back—I can see the pale lining gleaming through the gash. He makes a kind of grunt as I come in.

"Oh," I say, reaching for the main light switch, "I thought you were the dogs."

"Don't!" He shouts it.

I jerk my hand away from the switch so fast I knock my knuckles against the wall. "Okay, sorry. Jeez." I know I don't like bright lights at night, but I'm not sure I'd have roared like that.

He slams the cabinet door shut and the light goes out, dropping us into complete darkness.

"Scott, what are you doing?"

He must press a button on his phone, because there's a brief flare of blue-white and he is lit from underneath like someone playing the ghoul at Halloween, features mutated by the angle of the light. Is he making a joke? Frankly, it's not funny considering it's nighttime and I'm alone with him in this house and we don't know each other well at all. I get the same spike of adrenaline as when I first bumped into him here, coupled with a hot flush of confusion, because I'd have thought, from what I've learned of him so far, that he might recognize that I could feel unnerved. But he doesn't seem to care. He's muttering under his breath. Swaying on his feet.

"Scott?"

"What?" he barks.

I recoil. "Are you all r—"

"Fine."

"What's going on?"

I move toward him and immediately he shuffles away, his shoes making a scuffing sound on the tiles. He never wears shoes indoors. Has he just come in? The light skitters away from his face. A clatter. He's dropped his phone. It has landed face up and I can see the screen saver, the illuminated eye from the RRX website. Automatically, I bend to retrieve the phone. He does, too, and our skulls collide.

"Shit!" I back off, bringing a hand to my head. He doesn't apologize, doesn't even seem to register any pain. Instead he grabs his phone and the bottle of wine on the floor and wrenches open the door to outside, to a blast of cold, damp air.

"Where are you going?" I ask.

I hear his feet skid on gravel. "Leave me alone!"

I'm so shocked and my head is throbbing so much that I don't know what to say, and I don't get a chance anyway because he reels off around the side of the house, into the fog, and I'm left standing there in the mudroom, in the dark, wondering what the hell just happened.

11

FIRST THING IN THE MORNING, I RAISE IT WITH SACHA.

She replies: Told you. Tricky.

I chew on my cheek. I know you said that, but I don't see it. We've had dinner together and he was completely normal.

Wait. Dinner?

Just in the house.

Mads!

What?! He was cooking, we're sharing this space. It'd be rude not to.

I suppose. If you say so. A delay, then four eggplant emojis.

She's incorrigible. No! Not like that. Well, maybe a tiny bit like that. At least, until last night.

She sends a sweat-on-the-brow emoji.

I type: But what do you think? I realize that could be taken two ways, so add: About last night?

You were definitely awake? Didn't dream it?

No. Think he was sleepwalking?

A zombie emoji. No, Mads. I think he's an ass, like I told you before. Or the sight of you in your nightie and bed socks freaked him out. Or he's pissed off at Angela and took it out on you. She emailed me at 3am. I swear the woman never sleeps.

I ping her the female vampire.

Sacha replies: Would explain the obsession with eternal youthfulness! Keep your distance. Write the bloody book, forget about De Luca.

She's right, I should. That's the annoying thing about Sacha—she always is right. I send her the blowy kiss.

The wind has almost dissipated the fog, and I decide a brisk walk might clear away the effects of my disturbed night. In the mudroom, I still can't find the boots, but my jacket, as I've come to think of it, is on the hook where I left it. I glance quickly at the wine cabinet. There doesn't seem to be anything out of order.

I walk down to the loch, careful to skirt the cliff, but before I reach the water the weather begins to turn, the sky darkening, overburdened. Around me, tufts of long grass rustle in the gathering wind. I turn to head back, and when I get onto the rough ground above the cliff I see Scott not far ahead, watching a bird circling. Rudy and Massimo are with him.

I hang back, hoping he'll carry on without noticing me, but he must feel me looking, because he glances down the slope and waves. I dither. To walk away now would seem rude, but what was he to me last night if not rude? It feels mean, but Sacha was right. I don't need any complications in my life right now.

Then Rudy and Massimo catch my scent and race toward me, bounding black, white, and tan over heather and rocks, their excited yaps carrying on the air. I bend to ruffle their fur. Scott is still looking in my direction, waiting. He doesn't wave again but the stillness of his body seems an invitation. He is so changed from last night, more his normal self, relaxed, one foot propped on a lichen-furred boulder, not a trace of anger. I feel I have no choice but to start toward him. Massimo is happy to run on but Rudy gives me big eyes, asking to be carried. I scoop him up.

"Morning," Scott says when he judges I'm within earshot. "Sleep well?"

Still picking my way warily across the heather, I offer a noncommittal "Not really."

If he understands my reference, he doesn't show it. Instead he comes the last few yards to meet me. "Look at this." He points at the sky, at the bird he was watching. "Pretty amazing, huh?" I scan his features, but can't see any sign of repentance at last night's outburst. When I don't reply, he turns to me. "Are you okay?"

Is this his way of apologizing? "Are *you*?"

"Yeah. Not bad." He returns his attention to the bird. "So cool."

This is weird. I must be missing something. I put down the dog. "Look, about last night."

"Last night?"

"In the mudroom." He looks at me blankly, so I continue. "I heard noises and went down and you were in there."

"Do you mean when I was giving these guys their dinner?" At "dinner," Rudy and Massimo prick up their ears.

"No, later. Much later. After two."

He shakes his head. "I'm sorry, Maddy, I don't know what you're talking about. I was in bed then."

I watch him closely. He looks guileless, sounds adamant. "You're sure?"

"Yes, of course."

Why deny it? Unless he's embarrassed at being caught raiding the drinks stock and is dissembling. If that's the case, I don't want him to think I'm judging him. Better to forget about it and, like Sacha advised, keep my distance. "Never mind," I say. "Anyway, I'm heading back."

"Wait!" He catches my sleeve to stop me. He points at the sky, excited. "You've got to see this first."

In terms of mood swings, this is a definite one-eighty. Reluctantly, I follow his eyeline. At first I presume the bird he's indicating is a crow, but as I track its movements I realize the feathers are lighter in color, the undersides flecked with white, its tail fan broader. Once I get a handle on the perspective I can tell it's bigger, too. Huge, in fact. The bird flaps its wings and there's immense power in the movement, a drawing in from the chest followed by a ripple of energy all the way out to the wingtips.

I can't help but be struck by its majesty. "What is it?"

"Golden eagle."

"No!"

He meets my side-flicked glance and there's a lightness to his whole being that I haven't seen before. It's hard to be chary in the face of such delight. "Uh-huh. Look." The eagle soars for a few seconds, then flaps again in that muscular way, five, six times. This is an animal built for speed, for hunting. A smaller bird enters its fly zone—definitely a crow this time, wing feathers splayed like ink-dipped fingers raking the air. It edges toward the eagle. The eagle moves away and the crow follows.

"What are they doing? Playing?"

He's silent for a moment as he tracks the sky. "No," he says, rapt. "Fighting. Probably competing for food. There'll be a juicy rabbit or something down there, in their territory. Oh, incoming." He nudges my arm with his elbow. "Check this out."

His enthusiasm melts away what remains of my circumspection. A second crow flies in, determination evident in its unwavering course. The corvids are loud, cawing as they feint toward the eagle, which remains silent as it flaps out of reach. Every time it flies somewhere, trying to outmaneuver them, the crows are at it, like war planes on the attack, wheeling, diving, circling back.

"Cocky, taking on an eagle," I say. "I'd have thought it'd tear them to shreds." We're talking without looking at each other, standing side by side, focused on the battle in the sky.

"Given the right circumstances, and one-on-one, I imagine it could."

As he says that, the eagle finally accepts defeat. It makes a sharp turn down the valley and flaps to gain speed. The crows start their pursuit, but the eagle is faster. It keeps to a straight line, shooting ahead, until finally it is gone. The crows cackle in victory.

Scott claps their bravery. "Goes to show, there really is strength in numbers." His grin is even wider than when he told me about hiking with his own dog.

The David and Goliath battle has stirred something in me, too, something akin to the memory of youthful conviction when you'd fight for what you wanted because you hadn't yet accepted that the expectations, beliefs, and rules of life were already decided. When being young meant caring less about the consequences and how you looked and more about what you wanted and the way things felt, about how they lit you up inside.

If this is his way of saying sorry, I'll take it.

The dogs have wandered off. Scott whistles for them in that way he has, up-down-up. "Shall we head?" He angles toward the house.

As he turns I notice his coat sleeve has already been expertly reattached. He must have kept up his old medical school suturing skills. "Nice job on the rip," I say.

"What rip?"

I don't want to go into last night again, not now that we're back on an even keel. "Sorry," I add, "my mistake," and let it drop. We walk up together.

Once we're back at the house and he's taken the dogs through to the kitchen for a drink, I lift his coat, still warm with his body heat, off the peg. I examine the seam where the arm meets the shoulder. There's no sign of damage or repair to the wool and inside the lining is perfect. As I hang it up again, I think about what Sacha said, about whether I could have imagined the whole incident last night. I rub my eyes, which are hot with tiredness. Maybe she's right and I did. It's the most logical explanation.

- - -

Upstairs, I have a new message from Angela Rodriguez. Say, could you tell me again where you got that photograph from? It's my wedding anniversary coming up and I would love to get a copy for my husband Jorge.

Sure, I reply, and google the agency and copy and paste the URL for the home page.

She comes online pretty quickly. Thanking you. Y'all have a nice day!

I turn my phone face down and silence all notifications on my laptop so I can't be distracted and return to work. So it's a while before I see her next message.

Sorry to bother you again, but I can't for the life of me find it.

As if I don't have enough to do. I could ignore her, but actually it's sweet, wanting to give someone you've been married to for ages a picture of the night you met, so I go back into the agency's search and type in, like before, Angela Reynolds Beaverbrook University.

No results found.

That's odd. I check my typing—yep, it's spelled correctly. Adding quote marks around the words yields the same result. I try "Beaverbrook University" and the name of that other girl in the caption, GiGi Lib-something. I can't remember how to spell her surname, but GiGi should do it.

No results found.

I go back to the screenshot I took of Angela and GiGi and do a reverse image search on Google. The picture's not there.

That's strange. Even if the agency was having a cleanup and ditched some of its listings, the photo should still appear on Google for a while. I was looking at it just days ago. Yet now it's completely vanished, erased.

I write back to Angela Rodriguez. The agency seems to have removed it. Such a shame. But happy anniversary!

Shoot! she replies. Oh well, it was worth a shot. Anyhoo, back to plan A: buying him a chair.

I can't resist asking. Why a chair?

For 17 years, the gift is furniture, to symbolize stability!!! I like her over-enthusiastic use of exclamation marks—I can tell what she'd be like in real life if we ever met. I saw an armchair in the thrift store that he might like. A bit of a stain on one arm. I guess I could get it recovered, but it's leather. Antique, tan, all cozy from being worn in, y'know? And I quite like that it's not perfect—one of those things that get better with age. Probably what my Jorge would say about me!!!

Later, when I'm on LinkedIn, checking some dates, I notice something else. The timing must be a coincidence, because what possible connection could there be, but Scott's profile photo has gone, too.

12

I MISS LUNCH, SO MIDAFTERNOON I GO DOWN TO GET A SNACK and on my way I dally in the atrium, taking in the art. I haven't looked closely at Angela's collection up to now. It's mainly abstracts, all swirls of acrylic, and oversized photographs of beautiful people cropped to show faces without bodies and bodies without heads. Some of the shots I recognize from SKIN DEEP. One is the freckled girl, blown up to twice real size. I hear Angela's voice in my head, pointing out the photoaging, the risk of cancer, and wonder why she chose to hang such an image in her house. A warning to guests of the dangers ahead if you don't take care? That wouldn't surprise me.

My eye is drawn to the rural landscape, because it's a real outlier, so different with its washy watercolors and ornate scalloped frame from the rest of the modern, clean-lined artworks. To my untrained eye it's a fairly crude painting but what would I know? In the foreground is a simple wooden house, a small brown dog not unlike Massimo lying on the grass in front. A path snakes through tree-dotted gold-green land toward distant hills where there is also the grayish-blue suggestion of water, a river or a lake. Above, sunlit clouds puff across a docile sky. We had a not dissimilar landscape, although a print, hanging in our living room when I was growing up—so did almost everyone I knew. There's nothing in this scene to date or place it, so it's impossible to know when it was painted, or where.

Footsteps, then a tightening of the air, a hint of cologne. Scott appears and stands by me as if we're in a gallery. The silence of our contemplation stretches on, and in every moment I'm increasingly aware of the height of him, of the distance between his upper arm and mine, of how little space there is between us. The dogs mosey in from the corridor and take themselves through to the kitchen.

"Do you like it?" I ask.

He tilts his head and pushes out his lips noncommittally. "It's not bad."

"Do you know who it's by?"

"Not a clue." He goes up to the painting and immediately I wish I hadn't spoken, so that he'd stayed where he was. He runs a finger along the frame. I watch his shoulder blade protract, the inside edge pressing against the fabric of his sweater. His finger stops at the frame's bottom right-hand corner. "Might be a signature here, but it's mostly covered by the wood. You can just see the top of three letters."

He straightens and quickly I return my attention to the painting. He stands back, giving me room to look at the signature. The first two letters have a vertical downstroke, so an *I* or a *J* or an *L* or even a *K*; the third also has the peak of a loop. *P*? *R* or *B* or *D*? "It's hard to tell."

I move closer to him again. Now that I can see the whole picture I notice a detail I'd missed before: a cow grazing in a distant field.

"I listened to this philosophy professor the other night," I say, "on the evolution of beauty. I guess you already know that stuff, doing what you do." Scott shakes his head but seems interested enough for me to go on. I skip to the point, hoping he doesn't think I'm too boring. "Well, this guy, Dutton, talked about paintings like this, why we find them beautiful." I gesture at the painted fields. "You've got fertile land for agriculture." The house, then the river. "Shelter, a source of water. Trees like these, with low-hanging branches, so you can climb up into them if a predator comes along. And there's usually some form of animal life, like a bird or a cow, to represent food." I glance at him. He's nodding. "And one thing he said, which struck me, was that he reckons these kinds of landscape images are idolized even in cultures where no such savanna landscapes naturally exist. We've inherited this idea of beauty from ancient ancestors, and it's been passed down, like a genetic memory, because we equate beauty with safety or, rather, with life." I sound like a right geek. I stop. "Anyway," I add.

"I thought it might be useful for Angela's book, but I can't find a way to work it in."

Scott inclines his head toward the view and the gesture tightens his skin against his jawline, sharpening it further. "She's clever, Angela. Building the house to frame all that out there." He puts thumbs to opposite forefingers and looks through the rectangle. "It's like what you're saying, about the savanna, about this painting." He goes up to the glass. The window gives a border to the view, like the gilt frame on the watercolor, and I see what he means: the distant mountains, the loch far down, the path our feet have worn into the lawn. There are a couple of sheep on one of the hillsides; a pigeon trails the sky like a fat-bellied plane. "Maybe that's why I love places like this," he says. "Wild, unspoiled places. Maybe they're speaking to us in a way that goes so deep we react instinctively."

I join him by the window and together we look out. They say money can't buy you happiness, yet it can get you somewhere like this. Money and beauty—they're both about buying into the promise of something better.

There's something missing, I realize. "No trees," I say. "I mean, you've got larches down by the loch and way off on the hills, but nothing up here, nothing to offer safety."

I feel Scott's eyes on the side of my face. I have my hair up and I'm conscious of the skin of my throat, of the exposed length of my neck, but when I turn, he is already studying the valley again. The sun breaks through intermittently, casting cloud shadows that darken and warp the land, appearing and disappearing so quickly as the sky races on that it's as if someone has pressed fast-forward on time.

"Do you know, we're practically standing on the equator right now?" he asks.

It's such a random comment to make, like when he told me his skydive story. Then again, I'm not one to talk, after my little speech.

"Seriously," he says, going with his non sequitur. "Scotland used to be in the Southern Hemisphere." He swings an arm wide. "All this was desert. None of that green, just dirt and dust. Tens, no, must have been hundreds of millions of years ago. No savanna then."

I keep my expression neutral. I don't want to set myself up as the butt of a joke, but nor do I, if what he's saying is true, want to look like a fool.

He's into his stride, enthusiasm at sharing this knowledge—or theory, or shaggy-dog tale, whatever it is—spilling over. He holds out his hands, hovering one over the other, as if holding a ball. "We were down here"—he jiggles his lower hand—"and then there were these massive collisions of tectonic plates." He checks to see that I understand.

The sounds of claws scrabbling in the kitchen distracts me. One of the dogs must want to be let out. I begin to crab my way across the room, keeping my body angled toward Scott so he knows I'm listening. "I know what tectonic plates are. Go on."

"Well, I guess it juddered things around a lot and"—he rotates his invisible globe, so that his bottom hand is on top and his top hand on the bottom—"and now we're here. Crazy, huh?" He spins his hands back to their original position, rotates them again. "The south is now the north. Basically, we're antipodeans. G'day, mate." He's a good mimic. He switches from Australian back to American. "Seriously, though, apparently that's one of the reasons there are so many bens around here."

At the kitchen doorway I check for the dogs. Rudy is lying on his side on the floor. "Bens?"

"Mountains." Scott closes the distance between us, making his hands into fists that he bumps against each other. When he reaches me he allows the fists to stay connected and then he slides the right knuckles higher than the left, ridge against trough. "Plates smashing together, forcing the rock up. Changing the land, what you would have seen from here, completely."

I look from his hands to his eyes, which are bright, to his dimple, etched deep, and lastly out to the far-off mountains, which look not un-like knobbly fists of stone. This isn't the kind of thing that happens to me often—ever, in fact—but I don't think I'm imagining it, this connection between us. Still, I sense I should tread carefully. I consider the glaciers that would have followed this desert of his, and of how, when you walk on ice, you need to first test the strength of it before committing your whole weight. I adopt the half-jokey manner he used at dinner, feeling my way across what may be fragile ground. "You know a lot about Scotland, for an American. Where'd you learn this stuff?"

He releases his fists and scratches his nose. "What?"

"Geology, the birds."

He shrugs. "School?"

"Some school!" I know little of his background, but from his mention of Manhattan, the business he's in, the way he presents himself, I imagine he had a preppy upbringing. Who knows—maybe top schools in America teach worldwide tectonic plate theory and ornithology?

He shoves his hands into his pockets in that way I saw him do in my office. "I don't remember. I guess it interested me."

I make a globe of my own and copy the movement of north heading south and south heading north, the flipping of the world, the merging of continents. I hold out my invisible earth, an invitation. Touch me. "Where were the States during all this?"

"What?"

"You know—the birthplace of your forefathers. Land of the brave and home of the free?" I know, once I've said it, that I got the phrases mixed up.

He doesn't correct me. "Right. Umm . . ." He dips his head to peer at my hand. He touches the thumb of my bottom hand, brushing the skin beneath the nail, lightly, tentative.

I laugh. "You don't know, do you?"

He scrapes his teeth against his lower lip. It blanches, then flushes red. "I must have skipped that class."

The scrabbling noise has started up again, and I turn toward the kitchen. Rudy's legs are skittering and at first I think he's dreaming, but then I realize he's awake and his leg is violently tremoring. Something is wrong.

"Scott! Rudy's . . ." Before I can say more, he's across the kitchen, then on his knees. His hands hover in the air above Rudy, his eyes scan the dog's body. Both of Rudy's back legs are shaking, kicking out, the nails catching the concrete with every jerk. His eyes are open but fixed, his jaw clamped.

"Scott, what's happening?"

"Get me a pillow," he says.

I run to the living room. Massimo is in there, nose to the window glass. As I dash back to the kitchen he comes with me. He stops a way off and drops into a crouch, unsure. I pass Scott the cushion, and he slips it under Rudy's head. Drool seeps onto the fabric, tingeing it pink.

"I think it's a fit of some kind," he says. "Can you look up a number for the closest vet?" Again, Scott's hands hover over the dog, but it seems he dare not touch.

I spin, looking for my phone. A flicker at the edge of my vision distracts me. Outside: movement farther down the moorland, going away, into the bracken. A wave of vegetation as it envelops whatever caused the disturbance.

I pull back into the room, scramble for my phone on the table. Thank God the Wi-Fi is working. "There is a vet, but it's miles away. And it could take hours to get a taxi."

Scott gets to his feet, Rudy cradled to his chest. "Don't worry about that. Just get your bag, bring Massimo, and I'll meet you on the drive."

It turns out that Scott has a car here, parked in a rear section of the barn the whole time. It's a beaten-up Golf, one door panel a different color from the rest of the bodywork. It's not at all the kind of car I'd imagine him driving, but at this point I'm grateful that he has a car at all.

I let Massimo in the back, next to where Rudy is lying. We'll need to take him in case he's ill, too, in case they've both somehow eaten something they shouldn't have. I climb in beside him and Scott lifts Rudy gently across my legs. The fit has stopped, thank God.

The vet is twenty-five minutes away, twenty-five minutes of nauseating bends and abrupt braking at passing places. When we get there, Massimo keeps whining and barking and pulling at his lead, so I stay in the waiting area with him and let Scott go with Rudy and the vet. Being medically trained, he's bound to understand more than I would. A nurse gives Massimo a biscuit and it calms him a little. Across the room, a woman waits. She has a cat carrier with her, but inside is a chicken, not a cat.

The vet comes out, Scott following with Rudy in his arms. I can't work out from Scott's expression how bad the diagnosis is. I go to them and stroke the dog's head. Please get better. He perks up and squirms in Scott's grasp, wanting to come to me. I take him, glad he's well enough to lick my fingers. "He's okay?"

"He's fine," the vet says in a Scottish burr. She has a name tag on her scrubs—Indira—and is carrying a clipboard. "It was a seizure, probably due to syringomyelia, caused as a consequence of abnormal cerebrospinal fluid movement through the foramen magnum."

"I'm sorry, I don't understand." I look to Scott to translate. "What does that mean?"

"It's, well, it means . . . I'm sure the expert here can explain it far better than I can." He crouches to Massimo and makes a fuss of him. "Come here, you."

The vet looks from me to Scott and back again. "It's a case of Rudy's brain being too big for his skull. Part of it is being pushed into his spine. That's why he has trouble walking sometimes."

I think of his limp, of his asking to be carried. We should have realized something was the matter.

"Will it happen again? Will it—" A bell chimes as the front door opens and a man comes in with a frisky springer on a lead. I move out of his way. "Will it kill him?"

"I've given him prednisone and gabapentin. It's an antiseizure medication used in epileptics, but it's also a painkiller. It'll calm him down."

Doctors—they never talk in certainties. Not this one, nor Mum's, nor, come to think of it, Angela, either. "But will it fix him?"

Behind her, the nurse ushers the chicken owner into a second consulting room. Indira glances at the wall clock and signs some paperwork on her clipboard.

"It's a hereditary condition, usually caused by overbreeding. We see it fairly often in pedigrees like these. Also in Maltese terriers, Pomeranians, wee toy breeds. Is your other dog related?"

Scott clears his throat and stands. "They're brothers."

"Then you should get them both checked out by your regular practice. Push for an MRI, agree on a treatment plan. If it's managed well, they could live a near-normal life span. Rudy'll probably be tired tonight and tomorrow, that's normal. Try not to let him overexert himself—exhaustion doesn't help." Scott's face falls—he's blaming himself for all the walks. "And do call us if it happens again before you get to see your usual vet." She puts the clipboard on the front desk for the receptionist. She's done with us, is on to the next job. For some reason, I think of Angela and all those clients on her three-year waiting list.

13

WHEN WE GET BACK, SCOTT LAYS RUDY ON THE SOFA. RUDY immediately jumps down. Scott picks him up and returns him to his place. Rudy thuds his tail against the seat, wondering what game they're playing, as he's not normally allowed on the sofa. Massimo, sensing an opportunity, joins him and they cuddle up together. I stay with them, Rudy's chin sneaking onto my knee, while Scott calls Angela. He leaves the room to make the call. He must go into his bedroom and shut the door, because I can't hear anything.

Rudy's head is heavy on my leg, his skull bumpy beneath my fingers. Is this particular bump above his eyebrow the problem, or is it his whole skull? I stop stroking, worrying it might be too tender, but he scrunches up his eyebrows to ask why I stopped so I start again, the rhythm working to soothe me as much as it does him. Poor Rudy, and Massimo, and other dogs like them, bred, for beauty's sake, into pain.

Massimo sits up so suddenly I fear he's about to have a seizure, too. He's stock-still, at attention, long ears cocked so that the tips lift away from his shoulders. He growls under his breath at something beyond the window. It's dark now and the lights are on so I can't see out. Massimo yips and jumps off the sofa. Rudy lifts his head, interested, but is too tired to follow. Massimo scurries to the glass. He yips, runs along its length, yips again.

I slide gingerly from underneath Rudy. "What is it?"

Massimo barks, looks at me, looks back outside. My scalp crawls. My reflection grows as I approach the window, its outline blurred. I cup my hands around my eyes. The glass is cold against the tip of my nose and smells petrichoric, as bitter as the air after a storm. Outside, the darkness is so complete that all depth of perception is lost and there's no terrace, no moorland, no world even, just two kinds of black: dense below and a paler, less substantial layer above, the sky. Then, in the distance—at least I think it's in the distance, because without perspective it's difficult to know—I see white light, two headlights, puncturing the darkness, a vehicle down by the loch. It's the first time I've seen a car there; I didn't even know there was a road. I think about the squatting backpacker, wonder whether she's still at the cottage, whether she's about to get busted by the property owner. The loch and cottage are too far away to be causing Massimo to growl. He must have caught a scent closer to the house—a pheasant, a rabbit? No way will I risk letting him out there to chase whatever it is. Coming close to losing one of Angela's dogs is enough for one night.

"Come on," I say, picking him up and carrying him back to the sofa. He wriggles but then relents and licks the back of my hand with a tongue soft as butter.

We've both resettled by the time Scott returns with a bottle of wine and two glasses. I'm grateful after the stress of the day so I don't question it.

"Raphaela's driving up here to collect the wee guys." He speaks quietly, as if trying not to wake a baby. Or a patient. The tone reminds me of long nights on the ward with Mum.

"How long will it take her?"

"This time of night? Fastest I've done it's eight hours and that's only to Glasgow." He says Glasgow like a local, with a long *a*, short *o*, as if Indira's Highlands lilt has rubbed off on him, not just the *wee*, but the way he pronounces his words, too. Maybe he's spent a lot of time up here. "Then she's got that extra section to Varaig to do."

"Christ." I rub my eyes. "Was Angela angry?"

"Worried, more than anything. But she's going to get them the best care. She knows someone. A specialist."

He passes me some wine. It's jewel red and smells of toast and spice. I taste. Strong, too.

He takes his to the window. His back is to me and in the glass his face is reflected, outlined, and then traced faintly again in the double glazing so that his cheek forms a parenthesis around itself. He brings a palm to his forehead and drags it slowly past his eyes, his nose, his mouth. The effect is like a mime artist's act or a sad clown's: the motion scrapes away the blankness and replaces it with down-mouthed anguish.

"You okay?" I ask.

The hand rubs up quickly, erasing the grimace, and he snaps to. "Yeah. Just tired."

He lowers himself onto the sofa, keeping the dogs between us, but he's near enough that I could touch him. He feels much closer emotionally now than he has before, as if what happened with Rudy has united us somehow. We're no longer two strangers just inhabiting the same space. He leans right back and lets the cushion take the weight of his head. He closes his eyes, allows his jaw to slacken. He breathes deeply and the cotton of his shirt rustles as his chest expands. The curve of his neck leaves his Adam's apple pronounced. Two more deep breaths, then he rolls his head on the sofa, opens his eyes, looks at me. He seems troubled. I wonder what else Angela said to him, whether she admitted she'd told me he was having difficulties. He was on the phone a long time. I still don't fully understand why he's here. He never mentions his work.

I copy his position, letting the side of my head rest against the sofa back. "You sure?"

He sighs deeply, a full-body sigh, and it makes me think that maybe he's decided to tell me about his past, about his time in rehab.

I've learned, through years of difficult interviews, particularly when clients have wanted to reveal a trauma, that side by side can be easier than face-to-face, because it allows the person to feel partly hidden. I break eye contact and look instead at the black window. It has started to rain, peppering the glass with drops. "Do you want to talk about it?"

I sip wine and wait. When I'm listening to clients—although he isn't my client—there's often a moment like this, a finding of inner strength before they can admit to something they believe is shameful.

"Maddy." He pronounces my name similarly to how he did Glasgow, drawled, with a long, deep *a*, a short *dy*. I roll my head again and he's looking at me. "There's something I need to tell you."

We hold eye contact for a long time. A sensation spreads through me, a quickening, heating and tightening my skin, making me aware of how near we are to each other and of the edges of my body, of my feet tucked up underneath me, of the grain of the sofa upholstery against the heel of my hand. At the same time, it's a kind of unfurling within, a peeling back of layers. It's intimate, strange. After infancy, when do you ever stare at someone or accept someone's stare for that long? Only with a lover.

Maybe it's too strange, too intimate for him, because he breaks away. I reach a hand across the gap between us and touch his upper arm, feeling soft wool and warm muscle beneath. "Scott . . ."

As I say his name he flinches, as if my kindness hurts. He gets to his feet, clearing his face with his hand again. There's resolve in his features now. Whatever confession he was going to make is not coming tonight.

"Hey," I say. "I'm listening, whenever you want to talk. This is my job, letting people feel comfortable to open up." Christ, why did I say that? Make him feel that this is work, rather than what it truly is: a connection, his life, even mine?

A tired smile. "You're good at it," he says. "Night. Sleep well."

I go up not long after, leaving the dogs snoozing on the sofa, Massimo spooned protectively around his brother as if he knows something is wrong. The shield of family love. In the atrium, I catch sight of the manikin. I haven't paid any attention to it for a few days. It is facing into the room, hands covering its eyes, or at least the space where its eyes would be if it had them, hiding or shy. I'm moved that Scott and I share this little quirk, the desire to manipulate the sculpture. Only as I reach the mezzanine does it occur to me that there could be another interpretation to the posture: a warning.

See No Evil.

I work beyond midnight to make up for lost time and the blue-lit hours at the screen coupled with the lingering unsettled mood of earlier in the evening leave me wired. Sleep takes a long time to come and it feels as if I've only just drifted off when the unfamiliar growl of a diesel engine wakes me a little after six. It must be Raphaela; she must have driven through the night. It's still dark. I get up, grab my robe, and go down to meet her, clicking on the lights and blinking in the glare. Before I get all the way down to the atrium, the latch lifts and she comes in. She sees me at the bottom of the stairs and jumps, bringing a hand to her throat.

"Sorry," she says. "I wasn't expecting you to be up." The tapping of her heels as she walks is loud and feels out of place. I've become so used to it being me and Scott. She goes into the kitchen and puts her handbag on the table.

I follow her through and press the button to heat up the coffee machine. "You must be shattered."

She smiles wryly. "Trust me, when you have a baby you get used to it. I haven't had a straight night's sleep in nearly a year."

Just like when I flew here, she's in tailored trousers and a blouse. How can she look so pulled together at this time in the morning after an overnight drive? I pull out two cups, take down a third. Scott will no doubt have heard us and be through in a minute.

"Oh," she says, going to her bag. She fishes out a travel mug. "Here—use this."

I stare at her. "You can't be heading straight back? Raphaela, that's madness."

The dogs, recognizing her voice, her scent, come through from the living room and compete for her attention, tails wagging. She bends to them and they push their snouts into her palm. It's obvious they adore her.

She straightens, gives me a thin smile. "Angela wants them to be seen as soon as possible. She's booked them in with the vet this afternoon." She heads off my objections. "It's important they're taken care of."

Well, yes—but so is her safety. "You've been on the road all night already. Look, why don't you change the appointment, get at least a little sleep here?

She shakes her head. "I can't. Angela called in a favor to get them treated so quickly. And besides, I have things to be getting on with at work and I can't be too late home tonight. My partner's got a night shift and the babysitter won't work past seven." She goes into the mudroom and comes back with the dogs' leads.

The light on the machine has stopped blinking, indicating it's ready to go. I look toward Scott's room, wishing he was here to back me up. Where is he?

"The spare beds are already made," I say.

"It's fine." She looks pointedly at her travel mug. Sighing, I press the option to make her coffee extra strong.

I walk with her to the car, carrying the dogs' beds. The stones on the driveway bite icily into the soles of my bare feet. At least it's stopped raining. There's a feeling of lifting in the sky, the beginnings of predawn. The car is a new Mercedes, black and slick, and huge next to Scott's Golf.

"Whose car is that?" Raphaela asks.

"Scott's."

She pulls in her chin. "Oh. Where's his Tesla?"

The dogs hop happily into the trunk of the Merc and stand there panting. They think they're being taken for a walk.

I lean in to give them each a final stroke. I pull my fingers down Rudy's velvet ear, then feel again the bony lumps on his head. How do you give a dog an MRI? How do you even begin to heal an animal whose brain is too big for its skull?

As soon as I move away, there's an automated whir and the trunk shuts. Raphaela is already climbing into the front seat. "Thanks for the coffee," she says as she pulls the door shut. Moments later, the red rear lights wink around the corner.

The kitchen seems extra empty without the dogs. I put away the milk and turn off the lights, desperate to get back to bed. I'm partway across the atrium when I hear a chink behind me, of something hard against stone. It came from the living room.

There are no lights on and Scott is so still that at first I don't see him. He's slumped in an armchair, staring at the window. There's a settled-in feeling to the room, a solidity to the air that suggests he's been there some time.

"Couldn't sleep?" I ask. He doesn't answer, continuing to look intently out, his shoes planted on the floor and his arms along either armrest. I follow his gaze to see what's so interesting, but there's nothing of note. It's so early that the edges of things are only just discernible.

"You missed saying goodbye to the dogs," I say, wondering why he didn't come through earlier. It's so out of character—he loves those guys. "Raphaela wouldn't stay," I continue. "She drove up through the night and she's driving straight back down again. That's got to be eight hundred miles." I'm babbling, in tiredness and also because I'm aware of a heaviness between us that wasn't there a few hours ago. I want him to snap out of this mood and be like he was before, either the Scott I joked with or the Scott who opened up to me. I drop onto the sofa. If I stay with him, he might come back.

I can smell overoxidized alcohol—we must have forgotten to clear away our wine last night. I prop up my elbow and lay my cheek in my hand. Scott is wearing his coat, even though it's not cold. One knee jigs, a restless movement. I can hear his breathing—there's a sharp edge to it, a growing raggedness. He's not looking out, he's listening to something inside his head. Something that is making him increasingly uncomfortable. The waft of alcohol is coming from him, that and a kind of sour, unwashed smell that wasn't there earlier. Now that my eyes are more used to the low light I spot a whiskey bottle and tumbler by his feet.

"How about I make us a cup of tea?" I ask. By us I mean him.

He breathes out through his nose. "You Brits think a cup of tea will solve everything." His voice sounds odd: cracked, unused.

"Sco—"

He's up and out of his chair in less time than it takes me to say his name. The switch, like in the mudroom last night, is so sudden it pins me to my seat. He's gone from the room. I hear the staccato slap of shoes on the floor, the front door beep, then slam, stones crunch. Then I see him through the window, stalking toward the moor, stooped over, sort of folded into himself, as if he wants to shut out the world. He is rendered black and white by the weak light and framed, in turn, by each of the three sheets of glass, first close to the house, then smaller beyond the terrace, and finally, smaller still, disappearing in the direction of the cliff. He doesn't look back.

14

I TRY TO GET A LITTLE MORE REST, BUT I'M TOO JITTERY. AS I LIE there, listening in vain for sounds of Scott returning to the house, I keep replaying fragments of what Angela told me, that the stress of the merger might be getting to him. Is that what I saw last night? The beginning of a crack?

Accepting that sleep is not going to come, I try to distract myself at the laptop, hoping that filling my head with words means there'll be no room left for thoughts of him.

Although heavy with tiredness, I manage to finish a first draft of the manuscript. The word limit is forty thousand, a lot of which was given to me, and it's a very rough draft, still full of holes and not what I want it to be, but I've been working like a demon for the two weeks I've been here and so it feels like an achievement. Like potter's clay, a first draft gives me something to work with. The rest of the time will be spent reshaping, polishing, perfecting, filling in the gaps. I email it to Angela.

I message Sacha to tell her the good news. I'm not expecting a quick response, but she replies almost immediately. I must have caught her in a quiet moment. Amazing! Knew you could do it, superstar!

I send a blushing emoji. A least one thing has gone kind of right. How are things your end? How's Marco?

Marco who? She pings me a sweat-on-brow face.

You all right with that?

Yeah. Completely my decision. She told me, after Jada walked out, that the worst part was that she'd lost all control. She described it as being in free fall. Another message blinks through. Wish I'd made as much progress as you. There's a bit of a blockage. Your friend . . .

Angela?

No, Scott. I consider that. Is Scott a friend?

Sacha is typing again. We are almost there with closing this deal. Basically we just need Scott's signature. There's some delay, I don't know why. He's ignoring my calls and emails. Look, do me a favor. Next time you see him, get him to reply to me, would you?

He's out now. But I can ask him later. Hopefully he'll be in a talking mood then. I remember what Sacha first said about him. But those two odd incidents aside, I still wouldn't call him hard work.

Thanks, Sacha writes. Anyway, enough job talk. You succumbed yet?

At first, I think she means succumbed to Scott. To???

She sends a row of needles.

I reply: No. Angela's not been here.

All the research you've been doing, not tempted to nip into the office, give yourself a couple of tweakments?

In the UK a person can get a certificate for administering fillers in a couple of days. They don't need to be a doctor or even to have a license. They only need a doctor to sign the prescriptions for the injectables. That, I guess, is why Angela looks down on high street practitioners, because how can you do a proper, safe job when you haven't studied medicine or anatomy? There are horror stories out there about needles hitting a nerve or causing paralysis. I may know a lot about the theory of aesthetics now, but no way would I pick up a needle myself.

I send Sacha a couple of scream emojis. Speaking of research, here's a fun fact for you: did you know the first recorded use of the term crow's-feet was by Chaucer? I studied Chaucer at uni. She used to flick through my books and then, exasperated, throw them across my room in halls.

You're such a nerd.

I know. Old habits. Even in the fourteenth century people were pissed off by the aging process.

What do you reckon they did about it? Froze their foreheads with toxin of toad?

It's a relief that her sense of humor has held and she hasn't sunk back into the low mood that hit her after she got her divorce papers. I hated to think of her being so down, so not herself. I send a crying-with-laughter face. That'll probs be the next thing.

Course. Organic, innit?

When Sacha goes—Duty calls—crow's-feet are on my mind. I wander into the bathroom and look at my face in the mirror, *really* look at it. I trace a fingertip along the fine lines that fan from the outside corner of my eye, then down along the grooves that steadfastly shadow my mouth no matter how much moisturizer I use. I fake smile, watching the lines deepen. I can't remember not having them, so I guess they developed on the sly. My first gray hair, in my late twenties, was different, a shock; it seemed to have grown overnight. In horror, I'd wound the shaft around my finger and yanked, pulling the hair from my scalp. Up close, it wasn't gray at all but translucent white, and the root had come free with it, looking like the point at the end of an exclamation mark: *Surprise!* I'd wrapped the hair in tissue and chucked it in the bin, then made an appointment for highlights.

I place two fingers to each temple, as if about to massage away a headache, and lift my skin up and back. The tension dissolves the frown line between my brows and widens my eyes, giving them a look of innocence. Moving my fingers to where my cheekbones approach my hairline, I pull again. This time the grooves near my mouth, my nasolabial folds as I now know to call them, vanish. I switch, so my thumbs are at my cheekbones, first and second fingers above. My fingertips slide perhaps a half inch along bone, erasing all the lines at once. Oh, there she is! The me I know, the me of my mind's eye. I ease my grip and let the skin fall, then tighten it again. If my face has moved this much by the age of thirty-nine, how far will it drop by forty-nine, by sixty? How will I feel about myself when I look in the mirror then? Tightening and releasing, over and over, I begin to truly understand why people come to Angela. It's not vanity. It's more that they can't face losing themselves.

At a bit of a loose end for the first time since I got to Varaig, I go down for tea for something to do. While the kettle boils I pace the empty rooms. The house is as silent as it was in those initial days here on my own and for a moment I wonder whether Scott has gone back to London. I stick my head out the front door. His car is still in the driveway. It's an odd choice for a man who must be a multimillionaire. Raphaela mentioned a Tesla, so why wouldn't he be using that? Although, in a way, it suits him, this banger; it's so down to earth. I don't know why he hasn't parked it back in the barn. Or why he put it in there in the first place. Was he ashamed? In the atrium the manikin has changed again, hands brought to either side of the head in a mouthless, Munchian scream. If there's a message there for me, I'm too shattered to decipher it.

In the living room I spy our used wineglasses on the coffee table and Scott's abandoned tumbler on the floor. When I pick up the tumbler the outside is sticky. Whiskey fumes rise to my nose. The bottle is two-thirds empty. I try not to jump to conclusions. It might not have been full when he poured himself a drink, although he must have drunk a lot to smell so strongly of alcohol.

The sun is winter-low and as I turn to leave the living room the rays hit the glass in such a way that it shows the dirt. About a foot above the floor are smudgy nose and paw marks, set a spaniel's width apart. Above are more smears and a complete handprint, palm and splayed fingers. Judging by the size, I think it must be mine. Close to the edge of the window frame, I find another. On the kitchen window, two more, imprinted at head height and shaped like a *c* and a reverse *c*, from when I cupped my eyes to look out last night. In Angela's unsullied house, the smears feel like an insult.

Mum always said "Clean house, clean mind," especially when I was a teenager keeping a messy, drawn-curtain bedroom while I unsuccessfully tried on emo for size. That phase didn't last long—it didn't suit my personality, although it might explain my lasting fondness for skinny black jeans. I dig out paper towels and glass cleaner from under Angela's sink. The marks in the living room come off easily, but the curved prints in the kitchen won't budge. I scrub and the action is cathartic, almost a promise that if I can make the glass perfect again, I can save this day that seems to be running fast downhill.

I rub and rub, Lady Macbeth vanishing her damn spot, but the impression remains. My mind is clogged with lack of sleep, as if its gears have seized. Then the paper squeaks against clean glass and my brain finally catches, like an engine starting. I wasn't here in the kitchen when I looked out to see what Massimo was barking at, I was in the living room. And what's more, I can't remove these marks because they've been left on the outside. By someone coming right up to the house and looking in. Watching us.

I leap away from the glass. My pulse accelerates. The skin on my neck prickles, the hairs rising. I scan the moorland, fast, but can't see a soul.

A noise, inside the house. I stop dead. Listen. It came from the back. Scott? No, he's still out. Shit—someone else?

I creep through the rooms to the corridor, heart pumping. Gray light filters down from the skylights. The sky above is heavy, laden with damp. At the end of the corridor Scott's door is an inch ajar. Music comes from within. Has it been playing all night? I didn't hear anything, but the door to this back part of the house was closed. I move toward his room and peer through the gap but can't see anyone. I push the door wider. The bed is unmade, the duvet flung back as if he's not long crawled out of it. The music is playing on a laptop on a desk. The bathroom door is closed. On the other side a tap is running and there is cheerful whistling. So Scott *is* in the house. How can he be? I've been awake since he left and I haven't heard the front door beep to open.

I edge inside his room. Apart from the bed, the rest of the room is tidy, with only a glass of water and a stack of novels on the nightstand. Light from a bedside lamp spills onto the floor, diffusing onto the rug. The wardrobe is open. Inside, everything is on hangers, arranged in groups: trousers, collared shirts, sweaters in merino and cashmere, tasteful colors, all complementary, all new-looking. Aside from the laptop, the desk is clear. I thought there might be reams of paperwork, contracts and documents related to the merger, but there's not a single scrap of paper. Open my laptop and the first thing you'll see is the manuscript, but Scott's is running a playlist on Spotify. If I came in here looking for signs there was something amiss, an explanation for why he's sometimes so changeable, even for evidence of secret drinking, I've hit a blank. This all looks perfectly normal. I was being an idiot earlier, frazzled into paranoia by all the uncertainties. A small wheelie case leans against a wall next to where I'm standing, a scarf folded over the handle, a checkered kaffiyeh in burnt orange. It seems at odds with his other belongings, the bright color standing out against his uniform of blues, blacks, and grays. I reach out a hand to touch it. The cotton is soft from repeated wash and wear, the tassels frayed.

The tap is turned off, and I back out of the room fast before he finds me poking around. I'm halfway down the corridor, partly relieved at what I saw, partly ashamed for snooping, when I hear my laptop upstairs chiming. Odd—I don't have a video call scheduled with Angela today. Oh God—is there a problem with the manuscript? I break into a jog.

She hangs up just as I reach my desk so I call her back. Behind her, the background is blurred out again.

"I was between meetings," she says, "and thought I'd take the opportunity to check in. Is everything okay? No worries?"

"Worries?" I'm a little breathless from the sneaking and the dashing up here.

"About the house. Or the manuscript. Or, well, anything?"

"No."

"You look well."

That throws me. "Do I?"

"Yes. You've got a healthy glow."

"I've, ah . . ." I can't admit to what I was doing. "I've been walking." I thought there must be something urgent if she was calling me out of the blue, but it doesn't appear so. Why is she making an impromptu call to chitchat with me? This is not like her.

She smiles—one of the few times I've seen her do it. It changes her face completely, almost as if she's letting her guard down, allowing the real Angela to show through. "I love walking there with Rudy and Massimo." She takes a sip of something in a heavy glass with ice. It doesn't look like her customary skin-saving water. Is that vodka? She's in Singapore, it's early evening there. Still.

I use politeness to cover my surprise. "How are the dogs?"

"They're well, Raphaela says. I'll ask the specialist to adjust their medication, and it should lead to fewer fits. I'm sorry you had to deal with that. They'd been doing great and I thought we'd managed to stabilize their condition."

They. So Massimo is suffering as well. Poor little mite. I can't think how to follow that, so I jump to work. "I sent you a full draft."

"Yes, thank you. I've read it."

Already? I only just emailed it. That's some speed-reading.

She thumbs through some papers off-screen. "I've only skimmed it so far, but it's almost exactly what I want. Good work, Maddy." Blimey, if this is what Angela is like on vodka, she ought to start having cocktail hour every day. She's never called me Maddy before, always Madeleine. We could almost be two friends, having a virtual catch-up. "I'll get my thoughts to you as soon as possible," she adds.

"Great. In the meantime, I'll crack on with the next draft, start tightening it up." Funny that we use that word for editing, as well as in aesthetics. You get "baggy middles" and "flabby" text. It's as if lean prose is as desirable as a six-pack.

She sits back in her chair. "How's Scott?"

How to answer that? Distant but close, familiar but strange, hard to keep a grasp on. In my thoughts far more than he should be.

She reads something different into the pause. "Oh God, he's worse, isn't he? The depression's worse?"

We're back on this again? It feels disloyal to be talking about him. I picture the way he looked at me last night on the sofa, before Raphaela came, and how that made me feel: twisted inside, desired. "He seems mostly fine to me."

"Are you certain?"

"Please, Angela, I'm not comfortable . . ."

She isn't listening to me. "I don't want to distract you, or disturb you from your work, but you should know that Scott has been low in the past. And I mean very low."

"Okay, but . . ." I trail off, then think of his more lighthearted moments, his whistling in the bathroom, the manikin. "He makes jokes." Confusing ones, but still jokes.

"Yes, he can be like that. It's like waves—lifts him up, but then crashes him back down again, even deeper than before. And he's good at putting on a brave face. Sometimes he seems like a different person entirely."

A brave face—I can't believe that's all he's been showing me. This growing connection between us seemed—seems—real. Feels real.

"Has he been drinking?" she asks.

How does she know? It's almost as if she can see what's going on. For a mad moment I think of the handprints on the kitchen window, but that makes no sense. "Not really . . ."

"He can be good at hiding it. Drugs?"

"What? No!"

She nods to herself. "I'm glad you're there, keeping an eye on him. Promise me you'll call me if he has a bad turn."

Bad turn? Am I missing something? I'm starting to think I must be. "What do you mean?"

"Just, you know, if you think there's anything to be worried about."

That's pretty vague. "Such as?" I could mention the strange interactions, or mood swings or whatever they were, but I'm not sure I should. They were both late at night, probably my fault, no doubt I'm misinterpreting things. He's been okay every other time.

Angela swallows hard, as if she's nervous. "Like I say, if something gives you cause for concern. You'll do that, won't you? Call me?"

I feel the tugging of a thread. Or, rather, two threads: responsibility to her and to Scott, responsibilities I didn't ask for and don't fully understand. I'm a marionette, jangling at the end of its strings.

"Maddy?"

"Of course, Angela."

"Straightaway?"

I sigh. Nod. "Straightaway." I don't want to talk about this any longer; it's not right. To get her off topic, I say, "Oh, by the way, I've had an idea for SKIN DEEP."

"Yes?"

"I heard from someone who knew you at Beaverbrook, Dr. . . ." I check my notepad. "Dr. Michael Madrigal? He said he knew you at college in '92." She doesn't reply. "Angela?"

She blinks. "There must be some mistake. I wasn't at college in '92. I didn't start until the following fall."

"Oh right, of course. You don't know him, then?"

"Well, I didn't say that. We both worked at Redleaf in Boston for a time."

"So there is a link. Great! Because I was thinking"—Angela tries to interrupt, but I keep going, because a bit of flattery never did any harm, and he did say she was gifted—"that because he had *such* kind things to say about you it might be worth chatting to him, get another perspective on your work. Maybe several other perspectives, if there's anyone else you can recommend, especially other cosmetic surgeons?"

"I don't think so."

"Why not? We could get endorsement quotes from him, and others, for the cover." I'm into this idea now; it's a good one.

She snatches up her drink. "No."

"If you're worried about time, I don't think it would hold us up."

"No."

"Angela, come on. Surely this—"

"I said no, Madeleine!" She slams her glass on the desk so hard that liquid shoots up. "Christ, I thought I was hiring a professional!"

Her composure has utterly gone. Her skin has mottled, her nostrils are flared. She stares at me, a clear challenge, defying me to make a wrong move. Fuck this. I'm tempted to snatch up the gauntlet and walk away. I chose this job, but I didn't choose to be treated like this.

I look at the SKIN DEEP dummy on her—my—desk. But to walk away would be to admit defeat. I want something out of this deal as much as she does and I can be stubborn as hell, can dig my claws in just as deeply when my sights are set. I'm not scared of a challenge.

Conscious that I'm on camera, that how I look will carry as much weight as what I say, I bite back my anger and smile. "You *have* hired a professional." Deep breaths. Don't kick off, don't prove her point. "Of course it's your decision."

"That's right, it is."

My apparent capitulation must work, because she relaxes slightly. Not enough to erase all the stiffness, but enough to make her clear her throat. "I'm sorry—I have a lot on, with Scott, with . . ." She stops, starts again. "Carry on as you were, please. I'll call you on Tuesday." She signs off.

Freed from the camera, I want to scream, like that statue downstairs. Everything is so frustrating and confusing. I'm halfway through the month now, yet it feels as if I've slipped right back to where I started. I'm being blanked at every turn. And every time I think I'm getting closer, I'm being pushed further away. Why is Angela still being difficult about the book, praising then insulting me? How come I feel as if I barely know her, despite working on this project for nigh on all my waking hours for a whole fortnight? And why did Scott spend time with me, start to get close, if he was going to sever things again? Blank faces, blank spaces, blank after blank after blank.

15

THERE IS SOMEONE WHO MIGHT BE ABLE TO HELP, AT LEAST with Angela.

I grab my phone and punch through my contacts for Jon Prosser, the ghostwriter before me. I jab the button to call but get a broken sound. Typical—the signal is too weak. I'll have to go out and search for a stronger patch. In the mudroom, I jam on my shoes and borrow the jacket. My phone is in the kitchen, so I exit the house that way, sliding the window almost all the way closed, apart from an inch. As Scott's inside, I can leave it like that.

The sun has risen higher, and the smudged Cs on the window have disappeared. Like the skin damage on that freckled model in the photograph, they're invisible unless revealed by a particular kind of light. Why does nothing seem to stay in its place here? Why is everything so slippery, so hard to keep hold of?

There's a bluster to the air, mizzle, too. Wind helixes my hair. I pull the jacket tight. Its wax coating feels clammy against my fingers.

My phone has only half a bar of signal so I head down the slope. Dirty clouds obscure the tops of the mountains, hanging low, like cigarette smoke trapped against a ceiling. Around my legs the long grasses droop, rain-laden. I keep checking the signal. Halfway to the cliff, I get three bars, enough to try again. Jon doesn't answer. I cut off the call twice before it gets to voice mail and eventually, on the third try, he answers.

I turn my back to the wind and press a finger against my free ear to hear better. I try not to rush as we go through the hellos.

"What can I do for you, Maddy?"

I like that he's direct. Ex-journo. No messing around. But did he not see my emails? "I've picked up a new client. Reynolds RX."

"Ri-ight . . ." There's a question in his reply and something else.

It starts to spit and I pull up my hood. "I know you were working for Angela Reynolds before."

"How?"

"Your name was in the comments."

"And?" He's tight, cautious, wants to know where this is going.

"Basically, there are some blanks I'm trying to fill." It'd be unprofessional of me to bad-mouth a client, even if he might understand, even if seeking consolation is one of the main drivers for calling him. "Obviously Dr. Reynolds is a very busy woman and I thought it might save time if I got the answers from you." He is quiet on the other end, so I keep going. "It's mainly bio stuff. I noticed—"

He cuts me off. "I'm sorry, Maddy, but I can't help you."

I haven't even asked him anything yet, but he has turned prickly, defensive. Possibly annoyed by the fact I got the gig—and paycheck—he lost? I try to find a way around. "I was sorry to hear about your family situation. I hope everything has been sorted now."

"What?"

"Angela told me you'd parted ways because of a family emergency."

"I haven't had a family emergency." The wariness has gone and he sounds genuinely perplexed.

"Oh."

He pauses so long I'm not sure whether I've lost the connection. I check my phone—the call log is still clicking on.

"The truth is, Maddy," he says eventually, "she fired me."

"What? Why?" I can't imagine anyone firing Jon. He's an experienced ghostwriter, diligent. Clients like him because he does most of the background work himself, which means there's more time to draw out the good stuff in interviews. Which is what I'm trying to do with Angela. And failing.

"You tell me," he says. "I certainly can't tell you."

"What do you mean?"

He blows into the phone. "You signed an NDA?"

"Yes."

"Well, after she fired me, she hit me with an injunction. Had to hand over my notes, everything—not that I'd got much down. I didn't have a chance to get further than some preprepared jargon-filled technical passages she gave to me. When I was at the paper, I never would have handed over my notes. Ever. But you know this industry—it's people's life stories, sometimes powerful people. In fact, I'm not even supposed to mention the injunction. I shouldn't even be speaking to you at all. I should go."

NDAs are standard in this line of work, but an injunction is a step beyond. "Jon, why would she—"

"Maddy, if she finds out we've spoken, well, I'm fucked. If I'm caught breaking the injunction I could go to prison." His breathing is fast, panicked.

Prison? Oh God, what have I done? The wind snatches off my hood. "I won't say anything, I promise. But I—"

"Look." I sense him returning to that kind man I met before. "Keep your head down, ignore any inconsistencies, give her what she wants, take the money, and get out."

"Inconsistencies? Jon, I still don't understand. Why—"

Beeping. Either the signal has failed or he's hung up. I check the phone. Three bars. Hung up.

An injunction—or a gag order, in other words—is a massive undertaking. They're usually the preserve of the superrich—the very private superrich, or the guilty with a secret to hide. It seems like overkill in this situation. Is Jon mistaken? Or perhaps he's making it up, the result of sour grapes for having been fired. I did think his manuscript was a bit shoddy, although that's understandable, if Angela wrote the text herself. He sounded sincerely worried, though. I think of how Angela shuts me down every time I ask her a question. Is issuing an injunction an extreme extension of that? I dither on the spot, trying to decide: call Sacha and ask her whether she knows anything about a gag, or keep quiet, because if Jon is telling the truth, I could cause a lot of problems by mentioning the order? Something feels off, and I need to think it through.

Movement catches my attention. Way down the moor, Scott is striding along. He must have left the house after me. But then how did he get ahead? As I call his name the rain comes in properly, changing within seconds from a light drizzle to a real Highlands onslaught. Icy cold. I need to get back to the house. I wrestle my hood back on and it is pummeled in a deafening thrum. Instantly the rocks and boulders that stud the ground are dark and rain is running off the bracken, the heather. It's as if the groundwater is rushing up to meet the precipitation coming down from the sky, it's that wet. My shoes are soaked through, and my jeans chafe my legs with every slow, slippery step toward the house.

Finding the kitchen window closed against the rain, I trudge around to the front door, glad I have my phone to open the lock. Rain streams off the coat as I put it back on its hook. My trainers are going to take ages to dry. In damp socks I slap into the atrium, leaving imprints behind.

Just then Scott comes through from the corridor. "Jeez, you're drookit!"

He says it in a Scottish accent and I laugh at the joke. He is himself again, not the strange, tortured person I found sitting in the dark. There is no trace of booze on him. I wonder whether I'm the one losing her grip. I'm glad to see him and equally glad for the lightness he brings to this miserable day. I try to reciprocate. "Och, aye!" I expect him to return the laugh but he doesn't. He crosses his arms.

I sniff—my nose is running. I dab at it with the back of a damp hand. The wet ends of my hair are sticking to my neck and cheek. Scott's hair is damp, but his skin is dry and he's dressed in a dry T-shirt and jogging bottoms. Not only did he get back before me, he got back in time to change. And I didn't see him overtake me, either, when I first set out or on the walk back. "Is there another way up?" I say.

"What's that?"

"Another track that's quicker?" A full-body chill overtakes me. "Oh, I forgot," I add. "Sacha says can you call her?"

"Who?"

Is he kidding? "Sacha. You know—your lawyer."

"Oh yeah, sure, sure," he says briskly, in his normal voice. His brow wrinkles in concern. "Maddy, your lips are turning blue. I think you probably need to warm up. Dry off."

I shiver again. The hems of my jeans are leaking water onto Angela's unblemished floors.

He flicks the back of his hand, ushering me away. "Go upstairs, get changed. Doctor's orders."

In the bathroom I strip, towel-dry my hair, and do a fast rubdown of my limbs, friction pinking my skin as circulation returns. I copy Scott, pulling on joggers and a T-shirt, and rifle through the wardrobe for my thick woolly. Not there. Ah, I know exactly where it is—in the top drawer of my dresser at home. The request to fly up here came so quickly I packed in a rush, badly, and must have forgotten to put it in my case. The door rumbles on its tracks as I pull it across, hiding my clothes and exposing Angela's. A cream wrap cardigan looks tempting, but what would Scott say if he recognized it? Might he tell her I was wearing her clothes? I finger the soft cuff, considering chancing it, and the whole thing slips off its hanger onto the floor. As I pick it up to rehang it, my fingers close on something hard in a pocket. I dig it out—a lipstick.

The cap comes off with a noise—*pock!*—and I twist the base to extend the bullet. A dark pinkish red. I read the label on the end. Cardinal Kiss. Who makes up these names? I never wear lipstick—it makes me feel like a sham.

I start to screw the lipstick down again, but then hesitate—why not try something different for once? I go into the bathroom, lean into the mirror, and paint it on.

I'm so close to the glass that red lips are pretty much all I can see. Pulling back, I turn my head from side to side, presenting one angle then its counterpart, considering my whole face. I think the shade works against my skin tone, but does it suit who I am? Could I be the kind of person who nonchalantly wears red lipstick? I'm not so sure. It draws a lot of attention to my mouth. Too much.

I open the drawer to get a tissue to wipe it off. When I straighten and look at my reflection again, Scott is there, watching me in the mirror.

My breath hitches. My hand flies to my chest. He's the last person I'd want to catch me playing dress-up like a kid.

"Sorry." He has a mug in his hand. "I thought you could do with a hot drink." He extends the mug toward me. The liquid inside is pale, partway between cloudy and clear. I assume it's some kind of herbal tea until alcohol vapors rise up with the steam. "Hot toddy."

I'm still clutching the tissue. "I . . . thanks. I was . . ." I wipe my lips. "I'll just be a minute." I rub harder.

He puts the drink on the vanity. "Don't," he says, reaching out to stay my hand. "I like it on you." I stop rubbing and meet his eyes in the glass. They are steady, reassuring. "Seriously. It suits you."

There's something otherworldly about looking at another person in a mirror. An eyebrow on the left is slightly higher instead of the one on the right, a smile twists the wrong way, a blemish has moved. Flipping the face draws attention to flaws you never notice normally because you've grown so used to them, and it never quite feels as if the likeness in the mirror is the person you know in real life. There's a reason it was a looking glass Alice stepped through into an altered reality.

I like it on you.

I feel the agreement inside me, a soft caving in. I uncap the lipstick and lean toward the mirror. He watches me. My heart is beating faster than normal, my hand is even shaking slightly. I feel nervous, as if I'm walking along a high diving board, edging closer to the point of plunge. I trace the edges of my top lip, slowly because of the shaking, from the center of the Cupid's bow to one corner and the same on the other side, then the bottom, scooping down, aware his eyes are following the movement.

Oddly, instead of embarrassment that he's caught me pretending to be someone I'm not, I feel as if he's seeing me for who I really am. Straightening my shoulders, I allow my reflected gaze to meet his.

"See?" He inches behind me, and our reflections overlap. As he moves, the bathroom door swings away, until its mirror lines up with the one over the sink, and this causes a fairground effect, a series of the two of us, side by side, Scott looking at me, and me looking at Scott, projected endlessly on, backward and forward, into the past and into the future.

16

WHEN HE LEAVES, I FINISH DRESSING. I PUT ON MY OLD SWEAT-
shirt, the one I've had since university. Sacha and I bought matching ones,
although I don't think she still has hers. There can't be many people who
keep a piece of clothing for eighteen years. It's faded and frayed but I love
it. Time has layered it with memories, which bring as much comfort as the
way the material has molded to the shape of my body.

Downstairs, I find Scott crouched by the fireplace, having finished
building a pyramid of kindling and logs. I'm in socked feet, and he doesn't
hear me enter the room. Because he's in a T-shirt rather than his usual collared shirt I can see that cluster of moles on the back of his neck, although
it's half eclipsed now that his hair has grown a little. The T-shirt pulls taut
across his upper back as he adds a log, strikes a match. He pauses, so lost
in thought that he's forgotten the still-burning match between his fingers.

I put my empty mug on the coffee table and at the noise he looks up,
his face in the moment clear, open. Coupled with the casual clothes he
seems altered, softer.

Blinking, he shakes out the match before it burns all the way down.
He lights another and holds it to a fire starter. The kindling catches, going
up quickly with a crackle and hiss, throwing light onto his cheek.

"Hey," he says, standing. "Better?"

"Yes, thanks."

"Let me get you a refill." He swoops up my mug before I can answer
and slips away. Maybe it's the effects of the hot toddy, but I don't even

care that he's making us drinks in the middle of the afternoon. I bloody need to relax, need to take a break from this job that's driving me insane. Regain some equilibrium now that Scott is his usual self.

By the fire I let the heat scorch my shins as I watch the way the flames grow and recede, never forming the same shape twice. My lips have an unfamiliar waxy slip to them. I run the tip of my tongue over my front teeth, checking for lipstick smudges, feeling the smooth enamel. From the kitchen the seal of the fridge door hisses as Scott opens it; a knife blade whacks against a board as he slices a lemon. I wait. I've been doing a lot of waiting since I arrived here. Waiting for him to answer a knock at his door, waiting to hear his confession. Waiting for, I don't know—something more. I think of how he held that match, of the flame charring the stick and creeping closer to his skin. What was he thinking about? Is he waiting for something, too?

He comes back with a drink for each of us, and I wrap my fingers around the warm mug. A drop of alcohol to relax, lemon and honey to lift. It's a mix that feels fitting for today and for this situation as a whole.

He opens the secret cupboard and clicks a switch inside, picks up his phone. Music fills the room. It comes from everywhere, all at once, emanating from those speakers hidden in each wall but the one made of glass.

"This okay?" He means both the volume and the choice of music. It's electronica, something cool, Nordic-sounding, an edge to it, a woman singing about falling in love. *Baby, we rose so high*. Something between us has shifted again, like it did when he made dinner, and when Rudy fell ill. The tension I've been carrying around, the responsibility Angela saddled me with, has gone, evaporated in the heat of the fire. Right now he's the one looking out for me.

"Take a seat," he says. "No, wait a second. Watch this." He slides a hand under the back of the sofa and fiddles around, searching as though trying to find the release latch on the bonnet of a car. There's a click, and then he's arcing the entire backrest up and over and slotting it into a new position with a clunk. Now the sofa is facing the fire, rather than the window, and you'd never know it hadn't always been positioned that way. "Neat, huh?" It's a clever trick: two views for the price of one.

Even though we're flipped around, we still take our habitual positions on the sofa—with him at the end closest to the wall, and me nearer the door. I've been here a fortnight, and already I think of this end of the sofa as mine. I sink back against the cushions.

He raises his mug. "Sláinte." The Scottish pronunciation I'd noticed before, the same mimicry. With him dressed like that, in his T-shirt and sweatpants, his hair dried into spikes from the rain and his feet bare, I'm struck again by how changeable he is, how he can seem down or angry one day and fine, chilled, the next. The hot toddy seems be working on him, too—his movements are languorous but still controlled. I'm not sure he's eaten anything today. I haven't.

"Are you hungry?" I ask.

He shrugs, not dismissively but as a signal that he's comfortable here, that he doesn't want to leave the room. Or want me to leave. He feeds the fire. I watch him do it, watch his hands. They're muscular, as if he uses them a lot—unusual for the hands of someone who probably spends most of his day at a desk. A few veins are visible; tendons flex as he pulls a log out of the pile.

He resettles and we sit in silence, listening to one track then a second, overlaid with the percussive cracks of burning wood and the patter of rain against the glass behind us. It's a comfortable silence, mellow. He has his eyes closed, moving his head in time to the music. Unguarded—that's the word I wanted for how he seemed earlier, for how he still is now.

I tell him, "You seem so at home here."

Lazily, he opens one eye. "What do you mean? This isn't my place."

"I don't mean in this house. I guess I mean here in a bigger sense. The moorland, Scotland. Among all this nature. I mean, it's hard for me to picture you in the city, being some big businessman, some hencho."

He snuffs a laugh. "Hencho? Is that a word?"

I double-check my interior dictionary. Honcho. Christ, how much whiskey is in this drink? "Head honcho—hencho."

"Well, you're the writer. You make the words." His eyes crease.

Fire-heat heaviness makes me speak without filtering. "If I think of you as a little boy—"

"I hope you don't!"

He's teasing; I can, too. "*If*," I say, overemphasizing the conditionality of it, "*if* I were to think of you as a little boy, I'd picture you playing in the woods, with Huck, climbing trees, staying out till all hours, worrying your mother."

"That's not far from the truth."

"So you see? How did that country boy morph into this city business-man? The Mayfair office, the fancy clientele, the jet-setting? Sometimes I can't get a handle on you."

"What can I say? Hidden depths."

"Fathomless." I'm joking, but I'm also taken by this idea of his child-hood, because I suspect it has something to do with his changeability. I want to know more. "What's your brother like?"

"What?" He sort of pulls back into himself. "Why do you ask?"

"I'm an only child. Indulge me." I prop my head on my hand. "Are you similar?"

"Ah . . . he." He pauses. Then he laughs, and I glimpse that crooked tooth. "He's okay. Different from me. Way more outdoorsy."

"Not possible."

"Yeah, well. I'm usually in London. But him . . . he's always loved wild places. Nature. It gives . . . gives him strength, I suppose." He scratches his jaw, and I think he's going to stop there, but after a pause he continues, as if he's reconsidered. "We had very different lives, growing up—my dad had two marriages, on opposite sides of the pond, and we only met once our whole childhoods. Then we reconnected as adults and even though we were very different, it was . . . he is . . . family, you know?" Scott con-sults the dregs of his drink, as if trying to read his future. "It binds you. There are probably more similarities than I think." For reasons I don't understand, he looks sheepish, smiling a tight, pained kind of smile. It makes me want to reach over, to peel his fingers away from his cup and take his hand.

He sees me looking and discards his mug. "Can I ask you something?"

Is this to be the confession I felt coming the other night? Is he relaxed enough with me now that he can tell me about his depression himself? "Sure."

"What you said about me earlier. Don't you think it's normal for people to be complex, made up of lots of layers? Like, there's one side to you that you might show to the world and another you keep inside? No one's one-dimensional."

I worry I've offended him with my comment about his fancy lifestyle. I push up the sleeves of my sweatshirt, the one that's so interwoven with traces of the past versions of me. "I don't think you're one-dimensional. Far from it. I mean, you're totally different now from . . ." I shouldn't bring up last night. "From when I first saw you."

"Why, what did you think of me when you first saw me?"

God, I can't tell him that. Either my initial assessment or the fact that I found him attractive. Not so boldly. Embarrassment adds to the warmth in my face from the fire.

He senses he's hit on something. "Uh-oh! What was it?"

"Nothing."

"You must have thought something."

"Nope." I alter my position, bringing my feet up to tuck beneath me. I've really backed myself into a corner here.

"Of course you did," he says, but gently, not critically. "Everyone judges, pigeonholes. It's human nature. In a second you'd weighed me up. Less than that—a tenth of a second. The blink of an eye. Come on, Maddy, I know you thought something." His tone is still soft, encouraging, his head resting now against the sofa, as it had the other night we were in here, when he felt close. Maybe he does want to know.

In the pause, the fire gun-cracks. Okay. I drain my drink. "A burglar."

"What?"

"I thought you were a burglar."

His eyebrows rise. "I did not expect you to say that." He grins and the crooked tooth appears again. "What gave it away? My swag bag? Panty-hose on my head?"

Thank God he finds it funny. I extend a leg along the sofa and nudge him playfully with a toe.

"Seriously," he says, "they're great at smoothing out the wrinkles, pulling everything tight." He brings his hands to his temples and stretches the skin so taut his lips part. "Angie's looking into it as a new treatment."

"Angie?!" I can't imagine she'd let anyone call her that. I laugh, partly in relief. If he's joking, if he's bantering with me, he must be fine. Angela's wrong—this can't be a wave of depression or behavior that's cause for concern. I nudge him again. "Your turn." He grabs my foot, whether to stop me prodding or as an excuse to touch me, I can't yet tell. "What did you think of me in that instant?" I ask. A risky question. I may well get an answer I don't like. But there's also a chance it might be something I want to hear. I adopt a fake petulance. "*I* told you."

He squeezes my toes lightly, once, twice. "You told me you thought I was a burglar."

"Well, it's the truth. I did." I sound like an idiot. Yet, embarrassed as I am, I can't drop it now. From the way that tiny curve on his cheek has deepened, I guess his appraisal of me was good. I want to hear him say it. "Come on," I prompt. "I can handle it. I think I'm fairly self-aware. I'm not usually putting on a front, at least I don't think I am. I'm pretty much always just me."

His smile falters and he looks at me hard, as if I've said something profound. Profound and sobering. He releases his grip on my foot and stops the music, and I know that this connection between us is about to break.

Maybe it's the lipstick that emboldens me. The fire and the rustle of fabric are the only sounds I hear over the pulsing of my blood in this silent house. I kneel on the sofa and inch toward him, closing the space between us, until we are side by side, forming an S shape on the seat.

I lay my hand on his thigh. His skin, through his joggers, is warm. A thumping starts up in my chest. I risk glancing at his face. He is looking down, at the point where I am touching him. Carefully he takes my hand and circles my wrist with his thumb and middle finger, binding it. He is still not looking at me, and I see a tiny flicker on his brow. He pulls on his lower lip with his teeth, as if debating, and I wonder if I've read the mood—read him—all wrong. He releases the bind and begins to stroke the skin of my inner arm, three, four, five tiny, featherlight touches. I daren't move or say anything, barely breathing in case it extinguishes the moment. Then he lifts his head and levels his gaze at me, and I know he's made his decision.

He pulls me onto his lap. I rest my palms against his chest. I can feel the hard ledge of his collarbones, the push of his pecs and his heartbeat racing like mine, only faster. In this position, I'm higher than he is and he drops his head onto the sofa back so he can look up at me. He swallows, hard, and I hear it and feel the slight buck of his body between my thighs. I take his face in my hands and with my thumbs I trace the lower edges of his bottom lip toward the very corners where the shaved skin smoothens. He looks at my mouth, at my red lips, and my pulse starts to thrum there. I lean all the way down, my hair falling like a veil around us, and kiss him.

It is a light to a touch paper. As he opens his mouth and deepens the kiss, as he tightens his hold on my hips and presses me harder against him, as his breath grows ragged and he slides his hands under my sweatshirt, there is no confusion anymore, only clarity. And I am aflame.

17

A BEEP SOUNDS, THE DISTINCT BEEP OF THE FRONT DOOR, THE noise it makes when you open it from the inside, going out. We both freeze.

Someone's in the house.

I meet Scott's eye in shock. It can't be Angela—she's in South Africa. And we both instinctively know it isn't Raphaela, either. He sits up and I strain to listen. There—the door being closed, softly. A gritty noise in its wake—someone trying to tread lightly on gravel.

We jump up and I scramble back into my sweatshirt. Scott makes it first to the living room entrance. He holds out a hand for me and wordlessly we cross the kitchen and atrium, going as quietly as we can. The mudroom door is ajar—that's why we were able to hear the electronic lock. At the front door Scott lets go of me and depresses the handle sharply. There's that beep as the bolt releases and then a wave of cold air as he wrenches open the door. Whoever it was is already gone. Scott's car is there, tucked to one side, but apart from that the darkening driveway is empty, the only sign of any presence the grooves dug into the gravel days ago by the tires of Raphaela's Mercedes.

He closes the door. It beeps again as the lock engages. "I'll check the rest of the house."

"You think someone's still in here?" I wrap my arms around myself, cold with shock. Oh God, who? How? What do they want?

"I don't think so, but that's why I need to look."

The handprints, the feeling of being watched. "Scott, it might not be safe. And what will you do, if there is someone . . . ?"

He takes my shoulders. "There won't be. We heard them going out. But we need to be sure."

"Then I'll come with you."

"No. You stay here. I'll be as quick as I can. Okay?"

I don't want him to have to do this, to risk getting hurt, but what choice do we have? I'd be no use against an intruder. "Okay."

He stands straight, as tall as possible, and heads for the corridor. I back up against the wall, so that no one can come up behind me, and try to focus on what Scott said: We heard them going out. *Out.* Whatever it was they wanted, they must have found it. They're gone.

I'm hit by a sudden panic. My computer.

I fly up the stairs, only thinking once I've already raced through the bedroom and bathroom that the intruder might be up here. But I can see the office is empty and my laptop is still on the desk, untouched, the manuscript safe.

From below, I hear Scott saying, "It's all clear," then raising his voice to a shout, panicking when he sees I'm not where he left me. "Maddy? Maddy!"

I rush back to the landing. Below, Scott is spinning around, looking for me. "Up here," I call.

He follows my voice, and his frenzied expression dissolves into relief. He bends at the waist and lets out a huge breath. "Man, you scared me." He kind of swings on his heel, and I feel it too, a lightheadedness at the fact we're both all right, the start of the comedown from the adrenaline, but then he stops swinging, stops completely still. I follow his stare to the wall, to a hook—and an empty white space. One of the paintings is missing.

I know immediately which has gone: the watercolor. That's why someone was in the house. Then a second realization. "Oh God. I left the kitchen window open when I went out. That must be how they got in." I pat my pockets for my phone. "I need to call Angela. Was it valuable? Don't tell me it's a Cézanne or something."

"I don't know."

The phone's not on me. "We're in the middle of nowhere. They must have planned it."

Where is my phone? Have they stolen that, too? Then I recall seeing it on the desk when I was just in the office. I start up the stairs. "I'm calling Angela."

Scott nods briskly. "While you do that, I'm going to check all the locks."

For once my call connects. Angela answers with a half-swallowed word that I could swear is an expletive, followed quickly by a gruff, rushed "Yes? What is it?" I'm taken aback—I've never heard her curse. "Has something happened?" she says, as if she knows there's a problem. "Has Scott . . . ?"

Now I'm really lost, until I remember she said to call her immediately if he took a "bad turn." That discussion feels years ago. "There's been an incident."

"What do you mean?" She says this so fast, the words slide together.

"I'm so, so sorry, but one of your artworks appears to have gone missing."

"One second." The background noises are muffled, as if she's put a hand over the receiver. I hear what could be a car door, then a loud drumming noise. Rain on a roof? It's hard to tell over the noise, but I think she says "Show me."

"Pardon?"

"Your phone camera. Show me."

I go downstairs. Scott is at the kitchen window, rattling it to make sure it's properly locked. It's twilight now, and I switch on the lights, turn on my camera, and point it at the wall, panning left and right so Angela can see.

She hasn't turned on her own video. She has to raise her voice to be heard over the background hiss at her end. "That's enough."

The floor swings dizzily on my screen as I bring the phone closer to my mouth. "What do you want us to do? Call the police?"

"Stay there!" Because she's speaking at volume, over the drumming, it sounds as if she's barking an order. "I'll be there as soon as I can."

"How soon will that be?" I register Scott is trying to slip from the room. I gesture at him, but he either doesn't see or ignores me. I'm sure she won't be able to get here from Cape Town until tomorrow at the earliest—what are we supposed to do until then? Surely a delay will affect any evidence? "Angela, when—" But she's already hung up.

It's only when I'm alone with that accusatory white space that I realize that I hadn't got the overseas ringback tone when I called her.

Scott stays in his room and something tells me to give him space. Maybe he did know the painting is valuable; maybe he's on the phone to the insurance company or the police right now. I hope we don't get asked what we were doing while the house was being burgled.

I scour my memory for any signs that this was going to happen. The only people I've seen were that backpacking girl weeks ago and the men from the grocer's. One of those delivery guys did comment on the art, but it makes no sense to sneak in while the house is occupied when they could break in anytime it's empty. In a way, I almost wish it was them. Because if it wasn't, then it could have been anyone watching us, out there, unseen. Anyone at all.

Twenty minutes later I hear a car slosh on the drive. Police? But the doorbell doesn't chime and when I go down and open the front door, I find a black four-by-four sitting empty in the rain, RRX on the license plate. It must be Raphaela, she must have already been in the area and Angela sent her. Yes, there she is—the back of her raincoat, an umbrella shielding her head—rounding the corner of the house.

I call her name, but she doesn't hear me so I put on the still-damp wax jacket and my cold, soggy shoes to go and find her. As I step out into the dark, anxiety bubbles up my throat. Should I go and get Scott? But surely the thief is long gone by now. All the same, I glance over my shoulder. I'm alone.

From the corner I can see the lights are on in the barn clinic. I hurry past the empty lit rooms of the house, aware again of how open they are, how on display, and how anyone can see straight in, see absolutely everything, day or night. Especially at night.

The clinic's door is pushed right back on its hinges, as if opened in a hurry. A wet Reynolds-branded umbrella lies discarded just inside.

"Raphaela?"

But it isn't Raphaela. It's Angela. She has her back to me as she takes a box and a couple of vials of medication out of a cupboard. At the sound of my voice she startles and the vials chink against each other in her hand. "Lord!"

I'm almost as shocked to see her as she is to see me. She's meant to be overseas. What's she doing here?

"I didn't hear you come in," she says. She puts the medication down, shuts the cupboard, and locks it with her phone. Another mobile rests on the counter by the sink. She snatches it up and drops both into her raincoat pocket, her movements fast, nervy. Anyone would think she was the one who'd been in the house with an intruder.

I take another step into the room. "Are you okay?"

"What? Yes." She shoves the medication into her handbag. The zip growls shut.

"I didn't expect you so soon. I thought you were in Cape Town."

"My schedule changed." Before I can ask where she's come from she's making for the exit. "Let's go." The clinic door beeps as we leave, indicating it has locked, but she jiggles the handle anyway to make sure.

As we reenter the house, I pray that I've been mistaken, that there might be some way Scott was playing a prank or that Angela herself took down the painting to have it reframed. But I know that makes no sense, and he is waiting in the atrium near the corridor entrance, looking as stressed as I am, and it's clear from the way she blinks tightly that the watercolor has been stolen.

I edge off, as if I can distance myself from blame. "Is it insured?"

"No."

Crap. I look at Scott for an indication of how to handle this situation because he knows her so much better than I do. He avoids my eye.

Angela runs her hands over the bare plaster, as if feeling for clues. "When was it taken?"

"Sometime today," Scott says. "We think this afternoon." I notice the "we."

She goes to the window, looking left and right, as if expecting to catch the thief right there. Then she scans the blank wall opposite and the atrium floor, eyes tracing a search pattern across the blank concrete. There's an energy to her I haven't seen before.

"Is it very valuable?" I ask.

"Not this one."

Thank God. What an incompetent thief, to pick the worthless piece from a whole roomful of valuable art.

Angela touches the empty brackets. "But it has enormous sentimental . . ." Her eyes land on the manikin. Scott has messed with it again at some point, and now its back is curved, its knees and arms tucked right in, curled into a fetal position. She picks it up and stares at it for a long time.

Shame floods me. It's a piece of art, not a toy. "I'm so sorry, Angela. We shouldn't have played about with it."

I look to Scott, but he's not contrite; he's confused. "We? I never touched it."

Is he trying to lay the blame on me? "Yes you—"

Angela shushes us. Carefully, she adjusts the sculpture to its original standing pose and puts it back. She opens an app on her phone, tapping with such vehemence that her finger makes a *puck* noise against the screen. "What time did you last see the painting?"

"I don't know—about one?" I say. "I went out, and I can't believe I was so stupid, but I left the kitchen window open because I thought Scott was in the house."

"I was," he says.

"Well, then you were, but later you went out."

"I didn't."

Am I misremembering all these things? My mind reels as I try to work out the order of what happened. Was the painting missing when I came back from my walk? Surely I'd have noticed. Then again, I was distracted by being soaked, concentrating more on the floor where I was making puddles than I was on the wall, and by Scott having overtaken me on the moor. That's right—he *was* out there. "But I saw you . . ."

He is frowning. "Maddy, hang on, let me think a sec." To Angela he says, "I closed the window when it started to rain. Maybe around one fifteen, or one thirty."

"One to one thirty." She puts a finger on her phone and drags it along the screen, as if rewinding a video. In her haste, her finger slips. Sucking in her breath, she tries again.

"Is there anything we can do?" I take out my own mobile. "I can call the police, unless Scott's already done that?"

She speaks sharply, without looking up. "No." Her eyes flicker, following movement on her phone. Again I get the impression she's looking at a video. Is it CCTV? Have cameras been watching us, recording us, all along? Are they doing so right now? I scan the room: the ceilings, the corners, the tops of the walls. I can't see any cameras, but the speakers in the living room are hidden and Scott said she likes to disguise ugly things.

Angela must find what she's searching for because she taps once—to pause?—then moves her fingers in a zooming-in motion. She blinks. Shit, that means that it was that time—and that it definitely was my fault.

I hold up my own phone, desperate to make amends. "Really, I can report it for you, save you the trouble. I know how busy you are."

She hits the button to shut down her screen. "There's no need."

"But—"

Finally she makes eye contact. Her attention slides down to my mouth, to what remains of the lipstick. *Her* lipstick. Is there a camera in the living room, too—has she just seen us on CCTV? Even if not, she might wonder why I've put on makeup to work on her book, why I'm all mussed up. A flashback comes, of Scott's hands in my hair. I press my lips together to hide them.

She gives me a tight smile. "I'll handle it." Picking up her bag, she turns to Scott. He is raking his own hair back into its usual neat style, parted on the left. At his bare feet, his tracksuit bottoms, her eyes narrow. "Before I go, I'd like a word."

He drops his chin, more like an employee about to be reprimanded than a business equal. "Of course."

They go through to the back of the house, closing the corridor door behind them. I stay sitting on the stairs, staring at the wall, thinking of Massimo grumbling at the glass, barking. Has someone been scoping us out all this time, waiting for the perfect moment? Often I didn't bother locking the window, because Scott and I were in the house. The footprints—on the terrace, through the kitchen. All that missing food. God, has someone been inside more than once?

Insects, crawling on my skin. Moving swiftly, I go right up to the window and do what Angela did, pressing my face against the cold glass, craning my head left and right. Nightfall has chewed up the land, swallowing the details. Black moorland, black mountains, black loch, black sky. I stare for so long my vision swims.

After Angela has gone, with a curt goodbye, I wait for Scott to reappear, but he doesn't. I don't want to push things, especially if she has seen us together. And I'm sure there must be an explanation for why he said what he said. We can talk about it later.

Although I saw him check the kitchen window earlier, I do it again anyway. I daren't touch the handle, because of fingerprints. I turn off the lights and stand shrouded in darkness. Once my eyes have adapted and I can see enough to move—the edge of the doorframe, the glimmer of the stairwell—I make my way through to the atrium. The manikin glints in the scant moonlight and I'm relieved to note, as I start up the stairs, that it stands supplicant still.

18

MY SLEEP IS DISTURBED, MY DREAMS TROUBLED. THE ECHOEY
screech of an owl rips me awake, gasping, my pajama top clinging to me
with sweat. After that I can't relax, and I fidget in Angela's bed, soaking
in angst over the kitchen window, straining to hear strangers in the house
or Scott moving about, then wondering if Scott will come up to me,
worrying what it means that he hasn't; fretting about whether I should
call the police myself in the morning and if I should go down to Scott, or
worrying that that's a bad idea because he might have changed his mind,
and what if Angela has said something to him, warned him off fraterniz-
ing with the hired help and he agreed, and what might have happened
between us if there hadn't been an intruder, and why did he deny being
out on the moor or does it even matter anyway, seeing as though it was
my fault the thieves got in in the first place—spiraling on and on like this
as the room gradually lightens. As it does on most mornings now, thick
mist appears with the dawn and seeps over the moor. I don't like how it
hides everything; I can't know what or who is out there. I go downstairs,
without turning on any lights, so I'll be less easily seen by anyone outside. The house is so still that even from the stairs I can hear the fridge
churning away. The rest of the artworks remain in place, the manikin is
untouched. An armchair and footstool have been carried into the kitchen
from elsewhere and a blanket added to create a makeshift bed. Scott must
have dozed here during the night, making sure the intruder didn't come
back. I examine the kitchen window lock, which is secure, and as I search

for new handprints on the glass I'm sure I see movement on the lawn, a darting glimpse of red-brown. Without thinking, I grapple with the lock and jerk the window open.

"Hey!" Icy cold bites my soles as I leap out onto the terrace. "What are you doing here? What do you want?"

A flurry of limbs. I'm about to call out again when I register the clack of hooves. The mist moves, and I see a deer at the boundary where lawn changes to rougher ground. It is small and bareheaded, female or a young buck. No threat to me at all. Ashamed, I stay where I am, allowing the cold to seep further up into my feet, letting the burn be punishment for my overreaction and for possibly destroying evidence to boot. Tempted by the grass, the deer takes a few cautious steps toward the house, close enough for me to be able to make out its breath steaming in the numbing cold. We lock eyes. All of a sudden it turns, tail high, and scampers into the white.

Secured inside again, I make my breakfast, even though I have little appetite. Scott doesn't emerge from his room. I think about taking him a coffee and slipping in beside him, safe and protected. I take down a second cup but return it to the shelf. He couldn't have got much sleep in that chair, I should leave him be. I check the window once more.

Upstairs, an email is waiting from Angela with the subject "Change to schedule."

My brain starts to thump as I read. She's bringing the deadline forward. To now. She wants to run with the first draft.

As surely as if she'd yanked me, I rise from my chair and grab for my phone, pull up her number, hover my finger over the call button. My mouth is dry. We can't go with the first draft, we just can't. I hit call.

There's a delay connecting, and I worry the phone signal is down. I check the bars—two, which should be enough. She answers on the third ring. "Madeleine, I—"

I cut her off. "Angela, I don't understand what's going on. We can't publish the first draft. That's not how it works. It's not right, it's not finished." My voice is rising. I pace back and forth, to the window, to the wardrobe. This is my big break—it can't get ruined like this.

"I'm sorry for the alteration," she says. She sounds firm. "But it's unavoidable."

"Why?"

"Business reasons. I'm afraid I can't go into them with you."

"But"—my anxiety manifests in a laugh—"but *we* have a business deal. You and I."

"Yes," she says, "but things have changed."

"Is this because I screwed up with the window?"

"No."

I'm not sure I believe her. "You gave me a month." I'm in the bathroom now. I stop by the sink. "There are more than two weeks left of that. The contract—"

"As I say, I apologize, but I need to escalate . . ." A ringing has started in my ears, and I have to concentrate in order to hear what she's saying. ". . . And what you've sent me is great."

I pinch the bridge of my nose to try to relieve the pressure building there. "But it's not great. It's only a first draft. We need three at least."

"Three?" Now she's the one scoffing a laugh. "There's no way. If it's about the money, I can assure you I'll pay you the full fee."

I can't believe she thinks cash is my main motivator. "It's not the money." There must be a way of appealing to her. I glance in the mirror at my tired, pale face and see all the things that are wrong with it. "Look, Angela. You're thorough in your own work. You know what it is to take pride in a job done well." I will myself not to think of my mother, because if I do, it might tip me over the edge. "See it from my side. Reconsider, please. Give me more time. Not necessarily the whole month. Just something."

"Really, Madeleine, the book is fine as it is."

"It . . ." I've got to stop before anger overtakes me. I breathe out, hot, through my nose. "Fine isn't good enough. For me or for you."

She's quiet on the other end of the phone, and as I strain to hear I sense that something is changing, that I'm winning her over. Before she can say anything, I get in first. "I've already started the second draft. Give me that, at least. Give me a week."

A pause, then: "The launch date is moving up, too."

This all seems very rushed and disorganized for her. "To when?"

"The twenty-ninth."

"Of December?" It was meant to be mid-January.

"November."

It's the fourteenth now, Wednesday. I stare at the drain as if I can see my future swirling right down it. The book needs to be typeset, proof-read, printed, bound. . . . "It's not possible. You can't produce a book that quickly."

"I assure you it is."

I clamp my teeth together, hard, biting back the urge to tell her she's being unreasonable. "Two days. Give me until Friday, Angela, and I can have a second draft ready for you."

I can hear my nervous breathing as I wait.

She sighs down the line. "Okay. Leave it with me."

I know I need to start immediately, but I'm paralyzed by the enormity of the task I've just set myself. All I can think, as I stand there, squeezing my phone so hard the edges dig into my hand, is *Move, you fool, get going, you're wasting time*, but it's as if my body won't follow the command.

"Maddy?" Scott is in the doorway. He probably heard my raised voice. "Are you all right?"

Am I? I'm not entirely sure. I think I've taken too much on, there are so many things happening, and all too fast, no brakes, and none of it's any good, apart from him, but I can't even—there's not enough time to—

"Hey," he says. He approaches me cautiously, taking gentle hold of my shoulders. "Hey," he repeats, making me look up at him. He steers me backward and sits me on the edge of the bathtub.

"What happened?" he asks.

"Fucking Angela." Instantly, I regret it. "Sorry," I say, sheepish. "But she's dumped on me massively, moved up the deadline on the job and I'm not sure if I can do it."

"I see." He sounds judgment-free. "And there's no wiggle room?"

I snort. "What do you reckon?"

"Ah, no, I guess not."

A thought occurs to me. "Do you, I mean, could you possibly have a word? Buy me a little more time?"

I know his answer before he says it, from the way his face falls. "I wish I could, but I'm sorry, I have no sway on this. It's . . . it's Angela's baby, not mine."

There is a pain behind my eyes. I rub them. Scott crouches in front of me, putting a hand on my leg. "But anything else I can do, I will. I'll bring you food, load you with coffee, stay out of your way, whatever you need." It's an echo of what he said to me the very first time we met. "Okay?"

I nod. I don't know whether it will be okay, but at least he's pulled me out of my panic spiral.

My phone pings in my hand. Angela. What now? Part of me is perversely hoping she's turning down my plea for an extension—at least then I wouldn't have to face this mammoth task. But what a shame it would be to not at least try. I open her message. She's sent me the cover. It's a big file size, and I have to scroll down to see it all, the action not unlike a movie camera panning a starlet's face, revealing the model's temple, her eyes, her lips. The bottom section comes into view, with the curve of the woman's throat. In the right-hand corner, a name in fine gold: Angela Reynolds. I keep scrolling. Underneath: With. Then, finally: Madeleine Wight.

I don't gasp but it's as if I have, a feeling of everything in the room rushing in toward my core and freezing. There's a beat when nothing happens, when it's just me, looking at my name in print, set in gleaming Garamond, Madeleine Wight. And then everything melts, flooding me with heat—my cheeks, the tips of my ears, the ends of my toes. The culmination of fifteen years of striving, a decade and a half of being pushed into the background. My name on the cover. Recognition. I'm no longer invisible.

I show Scott my phone, suddenly shy. "Never had my name on a cover before."

He takes the phone to look properly. "It looks amazing. Beautiful. And you've worked so hard. You should be proud." He passes back the phone. "Truly." He lays his hand for a moment on my upper arm, then stands.

At the door he looks super serious. His reflection is caught in the mirror, so I get two views of him at once, head-on in real life and from the side in the glass. "Maddy, I hope you get what you want out of this."

It's an odd thing to say. "What do you mean?"

"Just that it matters to me, a lot, that you're happy." He pats the doorframe and leaves.

I take a deep breath and get to work.

Somehow, I hit the deadline. Two days—two days in which I don't sleep, I don't wash, I barely eat the food that Scott brings up to me. He stays only long enough to smile quickly before leaving with the previous meal's cold, congealed remains. There's no time to worry about intruders, stolen paintings, missing food, or injunctions. Sacha calls and I ignore the phone. She texts and I ignore those, too. I'll get back to her when this is done. Raphaela emails: she's booked me onto the afternoon train to London on Saturday. It seems as soon as I have done my job I am out of here—it's a message from Angela, reinforcing my deadline. I try not to think about it. Nerves and caffeine keep me going and I maybe it's the fear, but I seem to have gone up a gear. Angela messages to say she's got the typesetter on call.

At two minutes to twelve on Friday night, sixty-three basically non-stop hours after starting on Wednesday, I email her the second version. My eyes are stinging so much from the screen I can barely see through the smarting tears, my lower back has seized up, my mouse hand has locked into a claw, and I'm trembling so much from the constant coffees that I can no longer type. I hate that it's so rushed, that I have no control over anything, and that it isn't what I originally envisioned. I should be taking the time to redraft again, looking at page proofs, checking each word two, three times, making sure everything is perfect.

I'm aware that I'm so exhausted that it's impossible to judge dispassionately, that my usual artistic self-doubt is now sky-high, but part of me thinks that maybe the manuscript hasn't turned out too badly. It is definitely closer now to being that manifesto on beauty, because of all the work I'd done weaving in psychology and sociology and art theory, but I can feel where the weak spots are and I know it's lacking in context because of the information I couldn't find, everything Angela kept private. If she'd allowed me to get close to her, I think it could have soared. I still don't understand why she wouldn't let me in, am no clearer on why she wanted a biography ghostwriter if a life story wasn't what she wanted to tell. I think about what she said in one of our interviews, about a person's bone structure being unique to them and that that's why a one-size-fits-all approach to beauty won't work. It's the same with ghostwriting. It's almost like an X-ray—first you have to see the very core of a person and only once you've done that can you start to flesh them out. Then again, I tend to be my own worst critic, and maybe readers will only see what's there and won't realize what's missing. There's no such thing as the perfect book, just as there can be no perfect face.

Too wired to sleep, I refresh my email feed obsessively. I daren't leave my screen. At sixteen minutes past midnight I get a read receipt. At one fifteen a short reply, as if it's a small matter to be checked off her to-do list for the day: Thanks. Good work. Have sent on. She could only have skimmed it. But it's way more than mere procedure to me. I pray to God, after nearly breaking myself, it will be worth it.

Brushing my teeth feels amazing; showering, even better. But even though I've missed two full nights of sleep and was already exhausted before that, I'm too chock-full of energy, too amped up on adrenaline, to want to go to bed. At least not alone.

I tiptoe down the stairs, guiding the way with my phone. Scott's door is ajar, and I take it as an invitation. The light is off, and I leave it that way. I untie my robe in the dark and let it puddle on the floor, then lift the duvet and slip into sheets at first cool, then warmer from his body heat. I rest a hand on the side of his waist. The bone of his hip is solid against the inside of my wrist. He stirs, sighing in half-sleep, and tips onto his back. I slide my fingers across his belly, his chest, up to his shoulder, feeling the dips and planes, the changes from smooth skin to hair to smoothness again as I go, until my whole arm is wrapped around him. I shift my hips and knit the front of my body with the length of his.

The pillow and sheets rustle as he turns to face me. "Hey," he whispers.

"Hi," I reply.

And then we pick up where we left off.

19

AFTERWARD, I SLEEP, PLUNGING HARD INTO UNCONSCIOUSNESS.
At one point, early in the morning, I wake and he is there with me; later, once I've drifted off and woken again, his side of the bed is empty. There's a fresh glass of water on the nightstand, put there by Scott. As I drink it, I glance at my phone clock: 11:29 a.m. God—the taxi is coming to take me to the station at two o'clock and I need to pack. And eat. Reluctantly, I get up.

Scott isn't in the kitchen, but I see him through the window, outside. He's on the grass beyond the terrace, staring into space, his body utterly motionless, as if he set out on a walk but only made it beyond the lawn before forgetting what he was doing, or as if the urgency of a thought has stopped him in his tracks. What is he thinking about? I've noticed before how he does this, shuts down absolutely all movement. I'd be scratching an itch after a second or altering my stance. But he seems to have this amazing capacity for stillness when lost in thought. It makes him difficult to read sometimes. I tap on the glass but I don't think he hears me. After a moment he walks on down the moorland. The wind is gusting across the valley, shaking the bony heather stalks and rippling the grass in muddy waves. He carries his head low, his upper back bowed like a lone mariner on deck, pitting himself against a storm.

My legs start to shake. My blood sugar is too low. There's plenty of food in the fridge, but the thought of it turns my stomach. I need to sit down. As I pull out a chair, my mobile rings. Sacha. I answer and put her on speaker because I don't trust myself not to drop the phone.

"Where are you?" She's got her mother-hen voice on. "Are you all right? I've been worried."

"Sorry, I had this insane deadline and . . ." God, I feel like I've got the queen of all hangovers. It must be from the stress draining away. Not just the past two days, but the burglary and all the weird little things, and basically my whole time here. I can see myself reflected in the oven door—I look withered, the lines on my face deeper than before.

"Mads?"

I rub my forehead. I might be getting a migraine. "Yeah?"

"You stopped talking."

"Sorry, sorry."

"You don't sound like you. *Are* you all right?"

"Yeah, fine." A white lie, because I will be soon. "It's a bad line, that's all. You know how the reception is out here. And I'm tired. I had this insane deadline." I'm restless, itchy, yet I don't know what it is I need.

"You already said that. Are you done now? I thought you had a month?"

"Yeah, well, so did I."

"Are you still at Varaig?"

I pinch my nose to try to ease my headache. "Uh-huh."

"I think you should come home. There's nothing keeping you there now, is there?"

Someone is. I don't want to leave, but I have no choice about staying. I catch sight of the time on the oven clock—11:45. Barely any time left. I stare out the window. While I was working winter arrived and scoured the valley, stripping what little color remained, leaving it bare and bleak, uninviting.

Sacha takes my silence for agreement. "So come home. Please. Chill out, get ready for the launch. Your big night. Your name on the cover. Your triumph. And there's bound to be loads of well-connected people going."

London. It seems months ago that I was last there. "I'm getting a train in a bit." Even speaking is an effort; my words drop heavily from my mouth.

"Oh, Mads." Her voice is tilted with sympathy. "I thought you'd be

happier with this job. You should be. You should be bloody proud of yourself, you know."

That's what Scott said, too. "Yeah. I am. Or I will be. Sorry, Sach, it's
just . . ."

"Just what?"

I bottle it. I don't want to tell her about him. Not when he's her client
and she's not exactly his biggest fan, and it's all so early between us, in that
fragile spider-silk stage. I fall back on my earlier excuse. "Nothing. Just tired."

"Okay, I'll let you go. But do me a favor?"

I stifle a yawn. "What?"

"When you're all rested up, take some of those nice earnings, go down
to the shops, and treat yourself. And I'm not talking about yet another pair
of black jeans, all right? Something nice. Expensive. You've worked hard.
You deserve it."

It takes me three attempts to pack. Even though I don't have a lot of stuff,
every time I zip up my case I find something I've forgotten to put inside—
my hairbrush, my phone charger—and I have to try again to get it all to
fit. In the bathroom I make a final check of the vanity unit. All good. As I
open the drawer, the red lipstick rolls to the front. I fish it out, intending to
put it back where I found it in the pocket of Angela's cardigan, but when I
get to the bedroom I change my mind. She won't miss it. But if she does,
she can consider it payment for slogging my guts out.

I dump my bags on the mudroom rack and find my own coat, which
I haven't put on for the two and a half weeks I've been here. After the
weight of the wax jacket it feels flimsy. I slip my hands into the pockets—
an old tissue, a used ticket I no longer need. I scrunch them into a ball and
go to the kitchen waste bin, which is—of course—hidden in a cupboard.
When I slide it out it is three-quarters full. Resting on top is a pill bottle,
standard-issue, in semitransparent brown with rounded corners and a white,
childproof cap. I lift it out by the lid. No label. Empty.

Drugs? she'd asked.

Light from the window makes the bottle glow amber, a warning.
But this could be anything. Aspirin, for a headache. He's absolutely fine.

Wouldn't I know by now if he wasn't? I drop it back in the bin. Where is he? There's less than an hour until the taxi is due—still, enough time to go and find him.

It's windy out, gusts alternately pushing me forward and holding me back, and my hair is all over the place, whipping my cheeks, getting in my eyes and blinding me. There's no sign of him. I'm thinking I've made a mistake, he's gone somewhere else, taken that other track down to the loch that I never found, when I drag my hair yet again from my forehead and see the approach to the cliff ahead and he is there. In my tiredness I've forgotten to factor in the hidden dip. He's quite close to the edge, staring out over the valley, and the wind is flogging his jacket out behind him like an out-of-control sail.

"Scott!"

He turns slowly, his feet planted. His expression is oddly blank, as if he doesn't know where he is. It's disconcerting, makes me think of Mum toward the end, when the pain was so bad she'd lose track of what she was doing while she was still in the middle of doing it, when confusion would wipe comprehension from her face, settle her features into a strange mask.

I creep forward. The rock is slippery underfoot, an alien, treacherous ground. My legs are wobbly and I skid.

Life floods back into his face. "Stop, Maddy! Wait there."

Gingerly he picks his way across, watching his step. When he reaches me he takes my elbow and maneuvers me onto safer ground. "What are you doing out here? It's dangerous."

"Looking for you." He seems exhausted, in a way I haven't seen before: rings under his eyes, his skin drawn, stubble shading his jaw. Worn-out from taking care of me, from dealing with this merger he never speaks of?

"Did you sleep?" he asks.

"God, yeah. Did you? You look shattered." I don't want these last minutes between us to be serious so I shoulder-bump him. "Hope that's not my fault."

He puts an arm around me and tugs me to his side. "Come on." He turns toward the house. "Let's head up."

Halfway back, he stops and faces me. "Maddy, hang on a sec." He looks away, as if searching for something to cling to, to hold us to the earth. Instead he fastens on a crow, flying low and jagged toward the loch, beating its wings in a steady, insistent rhythm. It is alone.

The levity of earlier is gone. I think back to the other times when he was like this and I felt he was going to confess something. Maybe it'll come out now. "Tell me what it is, what's wrong. You can talk to me. You know that."

He examines the valley for the longest time, at first following the crow but then, when it disappears into the trees by the cottage, keeping his face toward the water. His irises flicker, flitting left to right, as if he's listening to voices arguing in his head.

He brings a hand to his face, wipes it down and back up in that same movement I've seen before, attempting to slough off tiredness. He takes a deep breath, as if gearing up to say something important. "Man . . . it's . . . it's all too . . ."

"Oh God, you're married."

"No!"

"'It's not you, it's me, this has been fun but . . .'"

"Not that either."

"Then what?"

Finally he looks at me and his eyes are clouded, as somber as the contused sky all around us. "I don't know what to tell you. Just believe me when I say that I'm sorry."

"Sorry about what?" His eyes are on mine, flickering again, but this time he's trying to read me, tell how I'm going to react. "Scott?"

At his name, he breathes out through his nose, long and final. "Nothing. Forget it." He kisses my forehead.

We're silent on the way back. I sneak the odd sideways look at him but can't work out what he's thinking, or guess what might have been said had our conversation not been left unfinished. Occasionally our eyes meet and he gives me a little smile. Up ahead, the house peers out from under its veil of moss. So many things here are unfinished, unsettled, unseen.

The taxi is already waiting on the drive, stealing what remains of our time together.

"I'll be a few minutes," I say to the driver.

"No bother. I'm a wee bit early. I wasn't sure where the place was."

Scott waits with the driver while I go in to retrieve my bags. I take a last long look around the rooms, at the clean, neat impressiveness of them. And at the view, which seems less breathtaking and expansive now in its winter desolation and more confining, forbidding. Stay indoors, it says, there's nothing for you here. Keep warm, keep safe.

Outside, the taxi driver takes my bag for me. "And these?" he asks, pointing to a pair of walking boots protruding from one of the shrubs by the front door.

Is that where I left them? "They're not mine." I return them to the mudroom rack.

The driver gets into the car and Scott and I stand facing each other, the silence heavy between us. My heartbeat quickens with nerves. Although he hasn't said anything, I can only assume that this awkwardness is a sign of regret.

"So," I say. "I guess I'd better . . ."

Wordlessly, he steps in and puts his arms around me. This is no so-long-and-thanks-for-all-the-memories hug. There's strength and passion in it. He grips me tightly, his chest pressed against mine, the side of his neck against my temple, and I feel his pulse pounding in his throat.

When he finally releases me I check the driver, to see whether he's impatient to be off, but he's tapping away at his phone and doesn't seem to be in any hurry. Scott still has hold of my waist. I put my palms on the lapels of his coat, maintaining contact for as long as possible. It's hard to know what to say. "You'll be okay here on your own? Not too lonely?"

"I won't be here much longer anyway." I'm relieved to find his eyes have cleared since earlier.

"Will you be at the book launch?"

"I . . ." He rubs the back of his neck. "There's a lot going on, you know? I wouldn't want to promise."

I nod. "Of course. But you'll be back in London soon? I'll see you then?"

Instead of answering, he kisses me with more feeling than ever.

Then the driver starts the engine, and there's air between Scott and me and Scott's opening the car door. His hand is at the small of my back as he guides me in.

He stays on the driveway as the taxi pulls away. I watch him in the sideview mirror, getting smaller and smaller, until we turn and he is lost.

20

IN LONDON I FEEL MORE MYSELF AGAIN. WHEN THE TRAIN
reaches King's Cross, I switch into local mode, picking up the pace to my
usual city march and ignoring the hostile glares of homebound commut-
ers furious I've deigned to bring a wheelie case *and* a bag with me at the
height of rush hour. This station used to be so dingy. But on the heels of
the Eurostar came millions in investment, and the whole area has had
something of a makeover, although the hustle and bustle are the same.
Renovating buildings, renovating faces—both involve injecting new life into
what was once old, tired. Yet even in the right hands, it can never lead to
complete transfiguration—something will always remain of the original.

After the space and luxury of Varaig, my flat feels cramped and drab. I
spend the next couple of days alternating between sleeping and cleaning.
I bet Angela never mops her own floors. I've messaged Scott a couple of
times, but I presume the Wi-Fi is down again, because I can see he hasn't
opened my texts. I try not to read too much into it.

Sacha is too busy to meet me—her turn for an insane deadline—and
so I potter about the flat, go to the gym, take time to enjoy not working.

Angela calls. She asks about my journey, whether it's good to be home.

"All fine, thanks. How did things go with the printers?"

"Really well. They couriered me a proof and it looks wonderful."

Well, at least that's something, although I'm still annoyed. I can't help a bit of a dig. "You're lucky that they managed to change your slot. They're normally booked for months ahead." I know full well there was no luck involved, just money talking.

"One moment, Maddy." She must place a palm over the receiver to speak to someone else briefly, because her voice deadens. *Maddy*—not long ago she was banging her glass down, shouting about how unprofessional I was. Forget what Sacha said; Angela's the one with the temper here, not Scott.

She comes back. "And how was Scott when you left him?"

Why is she still on at me about him? They've known each other for years, so can't she ask Scott herself? "Fine," I say.

"That's great." She pauses, and in the pause I suddenly wonder whether that was a loaded question, if she has watched us on CCTV. I feel my cheeks grow mottled. But if she was inferring that we'd been together, she doesn't follow up. "Glad to hear it. Let's hope it continues that way."

I think of that last kiss and can't help being happy at the thought I'm having a positive effect on his life. I wish I could get hold of him. But if Sacha is tied up with the deal, it makes sense that he is, too. I ignored my phone completely while I was on deadline. Although Angela seems to have time to gossip.

I change the subject. "How's the launch looking? Anything I can help with?"

"Raphaela has everything in hand." I bet she does. "Actually, I've moved it up. To Wednesday."

Today is Monday—how the hell is she managing this? "And the book will be delivered by then?"

She doesn't answer that and moves on. "I was wondering if you could stop by that morning?"

Wednesday is November 21, Mum's birthday, and I plan to visit her, like I have every year for the past fourteen. The crematorium is miles away from Mayfair, where Angela's office is. Maybe she reads something into my hesitancy, because she says, "It won't take long. I doubt we'll have a chance to talk at the party. You know what these things are like."

I don't. I've been to launches, but, ironically, none of my previous clients have invited me to the celebration of the book I wrote for them. Once my work was done, they wanted to keep me invisible so they could act the author in front of their assembled friends and family. I think again of Angela's generosity, of how she's included me, how we'll be there on an almost equal footing. And maybe Scott will be at the office. He said he wasn't staying long in Varaig. "What time?"

"Eleven."

"Okay." That's a dreadful time, but I'll make it work. Get to the florist as it opens, take the Tube across town, stop in at Angela's office on the way home, then get ready for the launch.

"Great. See you then."

After she hangs up, I call Scott. A prerecorded voice tells me the number is not available. Maybe I can't get hold of him because he's driving down from Scotland. I consider my detergent-cracked hands. They're not going to cut it at any party Angela throws. And if there's a chance of seeing Scott, the rest of my body could do with some TLC, too. Neither are ever going to be ten out of ten, but I can have a damn good go at trying.

At this time on a weekday, the crematorium is quiet. A worn-out new mother wheels a pram along the path toward me. Her step is slow, her eye sockets shadowed, her skin pallid. The pram is draped in a muslin cloth to keep off the light in a bid to get the baby to sleep. I think of Instagram. Sometimes those rosy images of maternal joy can take my breath away with longing and lack, both for my own mum and for the child or children I haven't had. Yet this before me is the unfiltered, raw reality of motherhood: trudging the path of the cemetery at nine on a Wednesday morning in yesterday's milk-stained clothes.

Mum's memorial plaque is the last in a row. The acacia tree next to it, which was knee-high when they dug the hole for her ashes, is now tall enough to reach my shoulder. Acacias were one of her favorites. "Look, Maddy," she'd say, if we passed one dressed in its autumn finery. "Isn't it beautiful? Doesn't it make your heart sing?"

"Hi, Mum," I say to the plaque.

The first time I came to the cemetery, I didn't know what to do with myself, how to stand, where to put my hands. I'd wanted to leave almost as soon as I arrived. Even though she was cremated, I kept picturing her lying full length in a coffin beneath the grass and I couldn't bear to be there. Gradually, over the weeks that followed, I learned to think of her in our old garden instead, sitting in her deck chair, happy, healthy. I found I was able to stay longer and then I decided to try speaking out loud to her. I'd wondered whether it'd be embarrassing, if people would stare. I don't do it if other mourners are close by—I like to respect their peace—and I don't say a lot, but if I'm alone it feels more natural to talk to her rather than to stand in silence, staring. That wasn't us at all.

"Sixty-two," I say to the plaque. That's how old she'd be today, if the cancer hadn't forced its way into her bones, but the stonemason fixed her eternally at forty-eight. There's a grim irony there, that Mum achieved what Angela's clients strive for. No aging for her. In nine more years I'll have outlived her.

I squat in front of her plaque and lift the empty vase out of the way. Then I take a bottle of water and tissue from my bag. "I did it, Mum. I know it took some time, but I got my name on a book." I wet the tissue and wipe the London pollution off the gravestone. The paper comes away black. I fold it, dampen a clean section, wipe again. "You'd laugh—it's about beauty. I had to do *a lot* of research." I unwrap the orange roses—another of her favorites—and arrange the stems in the vase. "And . . . and I'm not sure, it's very early days, but I might have met someone. I think you'd like him. He loves the countryside." I don't know what else to tell her. The vase goes back in its place. There—much better.

It's time to go. I stand. "Anyway, I miss you, but I'm happy. It feels as if things are finally coming together." It's true—even though I'm standing at my mother's grave, I am happy. "Happy birthday, Mum."

The London public transport system being what it is, I'm late for my meeting with Angela. I've walked so quickly from the Tube that I'm filmed with sweat by the time I reach the building. RRX is headquartered near Berkeley Square, with Chanel around the corner and a dozen top-tier hedge funds within finger-clicking distance. Angela's office is a redbrick town house with checkerboard steps. As I climb the first, the door opens and two men come out. One, the older of the two, looks familiar, but I can't place him. Asian, with ungrayed hair, smooth skin, well-cut suit. I wonder vaguely whether he's an actor, if I'm doing that thing where you think you know someone but it turns out they're just a familiar face from a screen. They pass me and a woman exits the town house. This time it is a face—and hair—I really do recognize. "Sacha!"

"Hi!" We kiss hello. She has her arms full of files. "Sorry I've not been able to come around. Are you feeling better? You look better than you sounded."

Embarrassed about the state I got myself into those last couple of days in Varaig, I laugh. "Yeah. Much, thanks. I've come from the crematorium."

"Of course, it's your mum's birthday. You okay?"

I nod. "Is Scott in the office?"

"No, and I can't get through to him either." She glances at the two waiting men, eager to get on. "Why?"

"Oh, nothing, just wondered. I think I left something in Varaig." I feel bad for not being honest with her. I will. Soon. "I shouldn't keep you. I'll see you tonight at the launch?"

"Definitely." Sacha walks backward as she talks. In real life, the pink of her hair is even more vibrant. "Can't wait to celebrate with you, superstar." She winks. "Catch up properly later, yeah?"

Inside, I enter a hallway decorated elegantly with more black and white tiles and a low table holding a huge urn of hydrangeas. Ahead is a broad staircase with a polished banister. When I push the front door closed the clamor of London traffic is sealed off.

Raphaela appears from a room to the side, her usual unruffled self. "Hi, Maddy. This came for you." She passes me an envelope. It was sent from the States, from that photographer I contacted, addressed care of Reynolds RX. I remember copying in Raphaela on my email to him—I guess he got the office address from her. Before I can open the letter she shows me upstairs, her heels hushed by a thick runner. She knocks on a door and swings it wide for me at Angela's "Come in." Beyond is a room is filled with light, a large fireplace, silk drapes at sash windows, a chandelier. Comfortable, five-star style—naturally. I slip the envelope into my bag.

"Maddy!" Angela puts an exclamation point on the end of my name as if it's a pleasant surprise to run into me here, in her office, at an appointment she requested. She comes over, both hands outstretched. Automatically I offer her mine, and she pulls me in, kisses me on both cheeks, fast, her skin not quite making contact, as if she's rushing.

She indicates a sofa that is identical to the one in her Varaig house. A flashback hits, of the last time I was on that one. I push it aside—now is not the time.

"You look well." She smiles but closed-lipped and it seems perfunctory. One of her eyelids twitches, as if she's nervous. Anxious about the launch, or is she preparing to say something difficult to me?

"Thank you," I say, lowering myself cautiously to the seat. "You too." There it is again, that twitch of the eyelid. She brings her ring finger to her eye as if she can make it stop. Seconds tick by. She doesn't seem to be able to instigate conversation. I speak first. "So . . . ?"

"So?" she echoes.

"I'm guessing you have a copy of SKIN DEEP for me?" Over the past few days I've been alternating between thinking the manuscript isn't too bad and knowing it's rubbish. It'd be good to see it for real so I can view it with a bit more objective distance than I had when I emailed it in.

"Oh." She brings a hand to her chest girlishly, not something I've seen her do before. "I'm so silly. Among all the prep, I didn't think to keep one here." I'm reminded of my first impression of her, of a golden-age actress, all congeniality and grace.

If she didn't want to show me the book, give me a copy, why did she call this meeting? I look around her office, but the desk is empty. Angela picks at a piece of lint on her dress. Again it's on me to restart the conversation. "Any news?"

Another press of the eyelid. "Of?"

What is up with her? "What did the police say?"

"Police?" She seems confused, almost alarmed.

"About the painting." I've expecting the police to show up, ask questions, but they never have.

"Oh." She looks away. "You know what it's like. They're very busy, it's unlikely they'll find who took it."

I could well imagine the police in London saying that—but not sleepy Varaig. She sounds flippant, which wasn't at all how she acted when she came to the house. She was verging on heartbroken then. I bet she never called them. But why travel all the way to Varaig that night to do nothing?

She stares absently at me, as if once more she's forgotten what we're meant to be talking about. Then she seems to snap to. She twists in her seat and lifts a wrapped gift from the sofa beside her, a black box tied with a white bow. She hands it to me. I throw her a questioning look.

"Open it." This is the more commanding Angela I recognize.

The ribbon is silky. I pull the bow free, lift the lid of the box. Inside is an envelope. Inside that a card, and another envelope.

The card is made of rich cream paper and one-sided, like an invitation. A message, in precise black ink, reads: *Dearest Maddy, thank you for making this possible. All my best, Angela.* Dearest! I glance up to see her waiting for my reaction. All I can manage is a confused half smile. I put down the note and open the second envelope. Inside is a slip of paper. I pull it out. It's a check. For ten thousand pounds. Made out to me.

"What's this?" The final installment of my fee hit my account yesterday.

"I know, checks are so old-fashioned. But I always think it's much nicer to get a bonus in this way rather than a bank transfer."

"A bonus? For what?"

"For what bonuses are always for—doing a good job."

I'm confused. She's already paid me more than I've ever been paid before. This is unnecessary. And now I feel bad for stealing her lipstick. I put the check in front of her on the coffee table. "Thank you, Angela, but this is too much." I squirm at how naive I sound—that kind of money is probably a morning's work to her. Yet to me, coupled with what she's already paid me, it's more than a year's salary.

"Nonsense." She slides it back. "I've had some good news and I wanted to share, that's all." She tucks the check back into its envelope, returns it and the card to the box, slips the ribbon around it, and passes it back to me. With her eyes on me like that, I have no choice but to take it.

As soon as it leaves her hands she stands and smooths out the lap of her dress. "I'm afraid I've got to get on, but I look forward to seeing you later."

I follow her to the door. As I descend the stairs, the box feels heavier in my hands than it should, as if unduly weighted with significance.

Back in the street, I check the time. The meeting was super short. I don't know why she called me in in the first place—she could have given me the check at the launch, or afterward. Next week, even. Today must be hectic for her. I rearrange the rest of my day in my head. I certainly don't mind getting extra time to myself. I'll have a long bath, shave my legs again with particular care, use the fancy, rich-scented body lotion Sacha gave me for Christmas that I save for special occasions.

As I walk down the street, box clamped under my arm, the display in the window of a posh boutique catches my eye. I pause and take in the dummy on the other side of the glass. It's clad in a stunning dress, a power dress in impractical cream. Not at all the kind of thing I'd wear—it's more of a cross between what Angela might choose and what Sacha would go for if she wanted to impress. Elegant, sleek, the right amount of sexy. There's a zip in the front, the kind you can pull all the way down until the fabric drops to the floor.

There are a million reasons not to buy it. Chiefly that I don't tend to have cheesy Bond-girl fantasies. And look at the price. But there's a ten-grand bonus practically vibrating against my inner arm and Sacha said I should treat myself. When would I ever wear it again, after the launch? Who cares? I probably wouldn't be able to breathe in it. But breathing is overrated.

I'm still running through the arguments and counterarguments in my head when I push open the boutique door and go inside.

21

PEOPLE TALK ABOUT THE GROUND SHIFTING UNDER THEIR FEET,
but sometimes things can change around you without your even noticing.
The elevator at the hotel where the launch is being held is one of those that
goes so fast, so silently that I don't register I'm moving until my ears pop.
A ding—top floor. The lobby is overly air-conditioned and immediately,
with bare arms, I'm freezing. None of my jackets or cardigans looked right
with the dress, so I decided to go without and brave the winter chill for
the few steps from my flat to an Uber and the Uber to the hotel.

Chamber music and low chatter drift from a wide doorway at the end
of the lobby. I check my phone to see if Sacha is on her way. She's sent a
message telling me she's delayed but will absolutely be there soon.

I duck into the ladies' room and find it empty. I lean in to a mirror and
reapply the lipstick I took from Varaig, my guilt at its theft gone. *I like it
on you.* I really hope he's here tonight. I rub my lips together, apply again.
Blot on a piece of tissue and drop the kiss into the bin. From the corner
of my eye I catch sight of another woman bending over the vanity, but as
I straighten up, she straightens, too, and I realize it's a trick of the alignment of the mirrors. I stand back from the glass, dissolving the trick, and
smooth down my dress. Turning from side to side, I examine my reflection.
No wonder I mistook myself for someone else. I don't look like me. The
heels change the curve of my spine, lift my head higher; the constrictions
of the dress make me move differently, with deliberation.

Raphaela is on duty at the entrance to the party, standing guard in front of a table covered in rows of beribboned black gift bags, which I presume contain the finished copies of SKIN DEEP. Of course Angela is far too discreet to have them displayed on tables. It's not as if she needs to sell loads of copies—this isn't about the money for her. In fact, this event doesn't look much like your standard book launch—at least, I've never been to one with a real-life string quartet. Glossy poster-sized versions of the book's photographs hang from the ceiling on invisible wires. In the center of the room stands a light installation, the cover model's profile rendered in pink neon tubes eight feet tall. She was already beautiful, but taking away most of her face and leaving only the outline, like a Matisse sketch or Warhol's Marilyn, has elevated her beyond mere beauty, made her iconic.

Raphaela nods in greeting. She doesn't have anything so crass as a guest list—it'll all be held in her head.

"Hi." I lift a flute of champagne from the stand at her side. "Good turnout."

"Hi. And yes, isn't it? Angela's so pleased."

She watches her boss across the room. There are maybe a hundred people here already, grouped in threes and fours. It's hard not to examine their faces for signs of work. Angela is on the far side, listening and nodding to a Middle Eastern man and a woman in a headscarf. Rudy and Massimo are by her feet, sniffing for canape crumbs. I catch Rudy's eye and he comes running, his brother on his tail. I put down my glass temporarily while I gather him into my arms. He licks my face. "Nice to see you, too," I say, and land him carefully back on his feet.

I scan the crowd for Scott but can't see him. He couldn't promise to be here, but still . . . Raphaela will know.

I arrange my features into a mask of neutrality. "Is Mr. De Luca here yet?"

She looks at me questioningly but is too polite to ask. She knows we shared a house for two weeks so it's not a strange inquiry to make. "Not yet."

Not yet. So he is on his way. I press my lips together and nod, as if his presence, or lack of, doesn't mean anything to me anyway. "I just wondered," I add needlessly. Heat is creeping into my face, so I make my excuses to move away.

"Enjoy the party," Raphaela says, her attention back on Angela in case she should call for anything.

Compared to the lobby, it is very hot in here. I decide to head for the open-air balcony. As I navigate through, a waiter offers me a blini piled with salmon and glossy black caviar. My mouth waters but I shake my head. No way could I eat a thing right now—the dress is too tight. Maybe this is how the rich stay thin. Besides, I'm starting to feel sick with anticipation at seeing the book, at the reception it'll receive.

The fresh air helps the nausea a little. I spot a man about Scott's height, with his back to me, and my stomach flips, but the hair is wrong. I turn away and blow air up my face, press the champagne flute against my heated cheeks.

"Madeleine?" a male voice says. Lord Malouf is there, smiling at me. "I didn't recognize you."

I take his proffered hand. "Lord Malouf." As we shake, I can't help scanning his face, searching for evidence of Angela's scalpel, her needles. Can't tell a thing—she's a genius. "You're looking well, as ever."

"Abdul, please." All those months we worked together, he never invited me to use his given name. "And you." He swirls the air in front of me. "You must be so pleased."

Stupidly, from the way he's staring at me, I think, *With what—the dress?* Then I realize he's referring to the book. "I should thank you," I say, "for the recommendation."

He gives a little pshaw. "It was the least I could do."

Another man comes to join us, older, Asian, and in a suit, too, like Malouf.

"Ranjit," Malouf says, "this is Madeleine Wight, who helped Angela with her book." The man nods in recognition. "Maddy," Malouf says, "this is my good friend Ranjit Choudhery. He has an interesting life story. I'll let him explain."

By the time Sacha arrives, I have four business cards in my clutch bag and a much clearer understanding of how networking operates in the higher echelons of society. The rich are their own club and it's not enough to be good at what you do—you must be validated by a member to get through the door. In the more recent past, I've scrabbled for work, had to go via agencies that take a considerable cut of the fee and leave me on not much more than minimum wage, with the balance of my unpaid student loans growing ever bigger with interest. Now Angela has cut me a set of the club's keys.

"You were so right," I tell Sacha when she rushes over, still in her work clothes, mouthing "sorry" at me on her approach.

"Obviously," she says, taking my drink out of my hand and swallowing half in one go. "About what, though?"

"About this opening doors for me." I show her the business cards.

"Great, but I don't want to talk about that right now. I want to talk about *this*." She draws a circle with the champagne flute, and this time I know it's definitely about the dress. "Sexy!"

I laugh and turn my flushing face away. Look back, laugh again. "Stop it!"

"Who's this in aid of?"

"Does it need to be in aid of anyone?"

She scans the crowd, trying to find somebody I might have my eye on. Then Sacha's face falls and I know she's worked it out. "Not De Luca. God, Mads, he's my client."

"I know, I know. I'm sorry."

"Man, I should have known this was going to happen." She polishes off the rest of the glass. "Well," she adds. "My feelings aside, clearly he's doing you a lot of good because I've never seen you look like this before. And I don't mean the dress. Although . . ." She gives a low whistle.

I take that to mean she's going to be cool with it. I bounce my upper arm off hers. "You seen him today? In the office? Or here?"

"Nope. AWOL."

A waiter passes bearing more drinks. I stop him and take two glasses, passing one to Sacha. "Thanks," she says. "I need this. Between you and me"—she lowers her voice, jokily conspiratorial—"our boss is a hell of a taskmaster."

I've positioned myself so I can keep an eye on the entrance for Scott. So that's why I see her before anyone else—the backpacker from Varaig. With that red hair, she's unmistakable. What is she doing here? From the doorway, she scans the room nervously. She's wearing a dress but even from this distance I can tell she's not one of Angela's crowd. The material is thin and clingy, a bra strap on show, and her shoes are too high, too obvious, more suited to a nightclub. She looks even younger than she did before. She takes an unsteady step in.

Raphaela is immediately there, a fixed smile on her face, barring the way with politeness. I can't hear what is said, but it's clear from the tilt of her head, from the way she holds out a hand, that she's explaining this is a private function. I see the painted lips of the red-haired girl—young woman, really, but she seems so unsure of herself—form Angela's name. Raphaela shakes her head, again holds out that hand. She's sorry, but she can't let her in.

Beside me, Sacha has succeeded in flagging down some canapes.

"Sacha?" I say.

She pops a blini in her mouth. "Mmm?"

"Do you know her?" I tip my head and she follows my gaze. *No*, Sacha's expression says.

A *ting, ting, ting*. Something hard against glass. The crowd quiets, bodies swiveling to locate the source. Angela is in the middle of the room, tapping a caviar spoon against her flute. The guests shuffle to form a circle around her so she's the pupil at the center of an eye.

"Welcome, everyone," she says, rotating to take in the whole group. She finds the position from which she can address the most people and stills. "Thank you so much for coming to celebrate my launch. I've long thought of this as my baby, but unlike most expectant mothers, I didn't have to consult the baby name lists."

It's weird, hearing Angela crack a joke. I imagine her practicing it in her office before coming here. There's a movement at the entrance—the girl staggering back, even though Raphaela isn't close enough to have touched her.

Angela, unaware, soaks up the polite laughs. "I knew from the start what I wanted to call this. And as you receive your gift"—she indicates waiters moving through the crowd, distributing bags—"I hope you'll agree it was an apt choice. Skin Deep."

Sacha accepts a bag but the waiter is empty-handed by the time he gets to me. I try to grab the attention of another server.

"So many of my loyal clients here will understand this," Angela continues. "Critics of practices such as mine"—there are some interruptions here as people protest, tell her that there's no one like her, she's unique—"thank you, you're too kind." She pauses, surveys her crowd again. "Critics say beauty is only skin deep; it's what's inside that counts. Of course what's inside counts. But only the delusional would disregard that what's outside counts, too. There is no separating inside from outside. A person is made from both together, and true beauty is what happens when these align." She takes a deep breath, gives a satisfied sigh. "And alignment is, as you know, what I'm all about. So I hope you'll forgive me when I tell you that we're not here today to launch a book, as you might have been expecting, but to celebrate something else."

What? I look at Sacha, who seems as surprised as I am. What has happened? Did the printer not deliver in time? Why didn't Angela tell me? I try to catch Angela's eye, but she's distracted by a phone ringing. The guests laugh good-naturedly. Who forgot to switch to silent for the speech? Angela slaps herself on the forehead, a gesture that I would never have envisaged her making. "Sorry, it's me. Raphaela, would you?" Raphaela leaves the girl, grabs the ringing phone from the entrance table, and steps into the lobby, one finger already at her other ear. Angela, satisfied, addresses the crowd again. "If you'll all open your gift bags?"

Murmurs and exclamations ripple through the room. Sacha draws away the ribbon that's tying her bag shut. Her hand goes in and comes out with a small cream-colored box. It slides open like a box of matches. She hands me the outer sleeve. It's debossed with an emblem: the same outlined face as the neon light installation, copied from the book. On the back of the sleeve is the eye from the Reynolds RX website. Sacha slips a glass vial from the inner case and holds it up. The same logos are etched into the glass.

"I wanted you all to be the first to try it," Angela says. "The Skin Deep Elixir. Youth in a bottle. It works like nothing else on the market, I can assure you. It's an absolute passion project of mine and I couldn't have done it without this wonderful man at my side."

My ears prick up. Angela motions at someone I can't see, encouraging them to come forward. I stand even straighter in my dress.

But it isn't Scott who enters her circle. It's an older man, dark-haired, dark skin, Savile Row smart, the man from the office.

"My good friend and, I'm delighted to be able to formally announce as of this afternoon, my new partner in launching SRX products and clinics across the globe. Ladies and gentlemen, Dr. Perry Singh."

Singh? How could they possibly work together, with his approach to aesthetics so different from hers, his celebrity acolytes endlessly name-dropping him on social media, his frequent appearances on TV, on podcasts, in magazines? Then I remember Sacha telling me that the aesthetics market in the UK alone is growing into the billions; Angela explaining that Dr. Singh's product line is worth millions a year. Now I see: she wants an even bigger piece of it. This merger is going to be huge, a billion-dollar business deal with a household name. The guests are clapping. So, too, is Sacha. "You knew about this?" I ask.

"Of course." When she sees my face, she adds: "Not about the book, obviously. Maybe she listened to you about another draft?"

That's bullshit; it's been scrapped, I can feel it. All that work for nothing. Vanished. And what's worse, the arguments Angela made for the work she does, the arguments I copied down and refined until her words sang on the page so clearly that even I'd begun to believe—well, they don't mean anything now. My book is gone, shouldered aside to make way for snake oil in an overpriced jar.

"Dr. Singh," Angela is saying, "needs no introduction. As soon as I met him and saw what we could be capable of creating together, I knew what I had to do." She smiles at him with real fondness. It's a far cry from her reaction when he came up in our conversation. Now I see she was trying not to give the game away. She switches her attention from Singh to Raphaela, who has worked her way to the front of the crowd with Angela's mobile. It's clear from the expression on Raphaela's face that this is some kind of emergency.

Angela's own smile fades. "I'm so sorry, everyone, Perry. Please bear with me a moment." With a pat on Dr. Singh's arm, she leaves him. Raphaela says nothing, just hands her the phone. We can all hear as Angela says, "Yes, this is she." When the person on the other end of the line starts talking, she clamps a hand to her stomach and her skin blanches paler than anyone's I've ever seen. She looks around wildly.

"Shit," Sacha says. "Don't tell me we've hit a compliance issue." She downs her drink without waiting for the toast. "That's the end of my evening."

The crowd is shuffling forward, trying to get a better idea of what's going on. Through a gap I see Angela looking as if she might collapse—this can't be a business hiccup. A woman I don't know has taken hold of her elbow. Someone is droning *no, no, no, no, no*. "Angela," I hear the woman say. "Tell me what's wrong." The guests are crowding in, blocking Angela, Raphaela, and Singh from my view. No one talks.

A scream, quick, sharp, like a stone dropped into the silence, and then murmurs ripple outward. I crane my neck, but I can't see anything. A man next to me gasps and covers his mouth.

"What is it?" I ask him. "What's happened?"

"The other director," he says.

"Scott?"

"Yes." His eyes are wide with shock. "He's dead."

PART TWO

My camera was in itself a desiring thing. It was a little bit like a detective, floating through my stories, looking for something, maybe a sparkle, a glint in the eye.

—*My Name Is Alfred Hitchcock*,
written and directed by Mark Cousins

AFTER

22

THE TREADMILL REBOUNDS BENEATH ME. I CHECK THE METRICS
on the screen—not far enough, not fast enough. I turn up the volume on
my music and dial the belt speed even higher, until my feet are pounding.
Hurting now. Better. A white dot, the remains of a sticker, whips around
on the belt every few seconds, *blit, blit, blit,* reminding me of the frightened
deer that I saw on my way to Varaig, galloping away from the helicopter,
tails flashing.

Stop it—don't think about Varaig.

I ramp the treadmill even faster, silencing thought, until all I am is
the pain in my legs. I'm going so hard that I grunt and a man pumping
iron glances over. That's right, buddy, a woman grunting with effort. It
happens. Get over it.

The song ends and a new track begins. Before more than two bars
have come through my headphones, I recognize it: the one Scott played
in the living room that evening. Shit—I can't listen to this. I jab at my
phone, trying to skip the music on, but I'm running so fast that my aim is
off and my finger is skidding on the glass and the singer is starting, *Baby,
we rose so high.*

No, no, please.

I punch the treadmill's emergency stop button, but it takes too long to
decelerate, and the lyrics are streaming into my ears, into my brain: *Stop me
from falling. Be there to catch me. You're my safety net.* Too late the machine
grinds to a stop and I rip the earphones from my ears and double over,

hands braced on thighs, lungs bellowing. Stupid, stupid woman. Why did you have it on shuffle? Why didn't you check you'd deleted that track?

More people are looking. Fine, let them look. Let them wonder: What's she running from? What's she running to? The answer is nothing. I like the treadmill because it keeps me in one place. Not everyone wants to move forward. Especially when moving forward means leaving something behind.

As I exit the changing room, Sacha calls.

"Let me guess," I say. "Just checking in?" She's been "just checking in" for what feels like forever.

"Where are you?" she asks.

"At the gym."

"Again?"

"Yeah, well." I don't want to get into it. "Hoping it'll help me sleep."

"Still no joy then?"

"Not much." My answer covers both meanings of her question. No sleep and not much happiness, either.

She sighs down the phone. "Maddy . . ."

"I know. Look, I'm doing all the things—working out to feel tired, avoiding caffeine after noon, no screens two hours before bed, warm baths, damn lavender pillow spray..." I stop—Sacha gave me that spray.

"And that other thing we talked about?"

She hates the chart. I say nothing. I promised I'd take it down, but I haven't followed through and I don't want to lie to her. I know she's worried about me, but she doesn't understand that sometimes that chart feels like the only thing I've got. I spend hours each day staring at it, looking for patterns, for a reason.

Sacha sighs again. "Mads . . ."

I give her something I know she'll want to hear. "I had an email from Choudhery about ghosting his memoir."

"You did? Brilliant! Getting stuck into work will be good for you. Distraction, you know?"

It's my turn to sigh. She's doing the best she can to help, but what works for her doesn't work for me. I need immersion, not distraction. Answers. I need to understand what happened at Varaig, because even now, a quarter of the way through a new year, I don't.

I rub my face, feeling the hollow between my temple and eye socket. The sphenoid bone, I recall, a part of the face where aging first starts to show. A part of the skull that can easily be smashed in a fall. From a cliff. Onto rocks. My brain, my thoughts—they press against the bone so hard it hurts.

"I'm trying," I say to Sacha.

"That's all I'm asking, Mads. That you try."

Outside, it is one of those bleak March days when it feels as if spring will never come. I tug down my beanie to cover my ears. This grimy, treeless stretch of road between Balham and Tooting is one of the last parts of the area to be regentrified. Half a mile southwest or northeast it's all organic delis, prep schools, and elegant town houses, but it's as if the money hasn't seeped this far, so there's still the sewing machine store, the halal butcher, and a newsagent's that's been displaying For Sale and Wanted postcards in the window for so long the ink has nearly vanished. I like that this little section of London is holding out against the advance of the chichi, that it's still largely how it was when Mum was alive, although it's only a matter of time. An estate agent's opened up a few weeks back, so perhaps the change has already begun.

I push open the door to the greasy spoon. It's that quieter part of the afternoon when most people are off doing something better—meetings at the office, picking up kids—and only a couple of tables are occupied. At the counter, I pull off my hat and order a coffee—no lattes here. The server nods and wipes his hands on his apron.

"Oh wait," I add, thinking of my vow to Sacha that I'm trying to get better, and that feeling better starts with sleep, "can you make that a decaf?"

He's slow, so I head for my usual table, the one in the corner with chips in the Formica and a wobbly chair. Sitting, I pull my phone from my gym bag and open my email.

I wasn't lying to Sacha about Ranjit Choudhery, the man Malouf introduced me to at Angela's launch. I have had an email from him—two, actually, over the past four months. The latest follows much the same form as the first, written as if there must have been a mix-up, an email gone astray, because why else wouldn't I have replied? Dear Ms. Wight. We met at Angela Reynolds' launch in November—on November 21, to be precise. How can I ever forget that date?—and exchanged cards. I mentioned at the time—six hours after paramedics retrieved Scott's body from the bottom of the cliff; eleven hours and four minutes after the police received a call from a dog walker saying she'd seen a person jump—that I might be interested in hiring a ghostwriter. If your schedule allows, I would love to meet to discuss the possibility of working together.

My schedule would totally allow—technically, it has been empty ever since my police statement was done, once I'd told the officer yes, I'd been made aware of Scott's history of depression; no, I hadn't known him long; yes, I'd witnessed his drinking; yes, he was familiar with the cliff. She wrote down my caveats—we got to know each other quickly and became quite close; he mostly drank no more than I did, as far as I was aware; I assumed his depression was in the past—but on reading them back they came across as weak excuses, added with hindsight by a person in denial.

The man behind the counter calls, "Decaf."

I fetch my drink and sit again. "And did you have any indication," the officer had asked, "that he might try to take his own life?" A euphemism, avoiding the word "suicide." Her pen was poised over her notepad, ready to take down my yes-or-no answer like before.

I'd leaned in, making sure she listened to me properly, aware that I needed to get this exactly right for the record. "Absolutely not. Scott De Luca was not suicidal. There must be another explanation for what happened."

"Such as?"

I'd stared hard at her. Why was it my job to point out the obvious? Weren't the police supposed to be doing the investigating? "Accident, of course, or . . ."

"Or?"

"Or . . . something else." I couldn't bring myself to say it out loud: foul play, homicide. Murder. It was too melodramatic. Things like that didn't happen in real life, certainly in my life people didn't die in that way. They became ill, got a diagnosis, tried treatment, worsened. They didn't care for me, make love to me, and then . . . do what the police, Angela, and Sacha all say Scott did. So there had to be another explanation.

The café door opens and there's a blast of cold air as a young woman comes in. She has that look: tilted eyes, glassy skin, pencil-thin nose, full lips with a proud Cupid's bow. One legacy of finishing Angela's damned manuscript is that I can spot an augmentation from a hundred paces: lash extensions, dermaplaning, nose job, lip filler, chin filler. Individually, each of her features is nearly perfect, but the sum of the parts is ethereal, almost too beautiful to comprehend, as if an anime character has come to life. The lips look tender, right-out-of-the-clinic fresh.

She pays for a bottle of juice, tosses a plait over her shoulder, and opens the door to leave. A man coming in lets her pass, gawking. Through the window I see other pedestrians watching her, too. Can they tell what she's had done, or do they assume she's always been that way, born lucky? Good looks used to be rare, considered good fortune—that's why it's called winning the genetic lottery—but these days, when anyone with a few hundred quid to spare can get an enhancement, this connection between luck and beauty is dissolving. When every other person is technically "beautiful," it follows that the currency beauty carries will lessen. In the future, if everyone looks like that young woman, will people such as the man at the door still find her attractive? Will all that she has done to herself be worth it? If beauty is truth and truth beauty, does that mean faking good looks—lying, effectively—is ugly?

The man sees me looking. I drop my gaze to my phone. I probably ought to reply to Choudhery, accept the job or at least arrange to meet him. Angela's money is going to run out at some point.

But not yet. I go through my other emails, hoping for something important. Nothing from the procurator fiscal's office. No surprise there.

On Instagram Sacha is pressed up tight against Monique, the two of them bundled in layers and beaming on a snowy Prague street. I'd forgotten she was away. When she called earlier I should have asked her how the trip was going. It's a big deal, the first overseas weekend with a new love. I'll ask next time. I'll make an effort to remember.

I scroll through my feed, which mainly consists of people posing: in new outfits, in mirror selfies, in yoga asanas. Like that girl, it's all so fake. I flick onto one of Singh's clients, pouting into the lens. Her huge eyes are flat and expressionless. They're preternaturally violet, like a doll I had when I was small. You tipped it back and its eyelids dropped shut, supposedly like a real baby going to sleep, tipped it forward and they opened again. Even aged four I knew it couldn't really see anything. Scroll. Someone from university feeding the ducks with her toddler. Scroll. A beauty influencer raving about the SRX Skin Deep Elixir, one of hundreds of stories posted since Angela went into partnership with Singh, even though the product isn't on sale yet. Under the table my leg jigs, the nervous twitch of an addict looking for a hit. I take a swig of coffee, trying to distract myself, but there's no use pretending—I already know I'm going to do it. I type in Scott's username and click on his profile.

His grid I know by heart: pictures of light filtering through the leaves of a tree, waves breaking on a beach, the elongated shadow cast by a sea wall. They're all snapshots of places he'd been, of things he'd seen. There are no photos of Scott himself. Even his profile picture is a repeat of the leafy tree image.

I didn't take any photos while we were at Angela's house. I didn't know then that I needed to capture him, trap him in the moment—I thought there would be so many more chances. So now I must make do with going through his Instagram and seeing things as he saw them. Attempting to put myself where he had been, as a way of feeling close to him.

"Hi."

A man is by my table, the one who was giving the surgery girl the eye. He has a takeout cup in one hand, my beanie in the other. He holds it out to me. "Is this yours?" I look at the hat, then at him, trying to pull myself out of the past and into the present. "Because I thought I recognized it as yours," he says. "You left it at the counter."

How could he recognize it? "It's a plain black beanie."

"Yeah." He laughs, shifting from foot to foot. "I mean I recognize you. You're in here most days, right? I'm Shawn."

So it was a line, an excuse to come over. He's still holding my hat, a shy, hopeful smile on his face. He's probably a nice guy. There's no reason not to take the hat, to start a conversation. I weigh him up: decent height, sweet-looking, about my age, maybe a little younger, probably lives or works locally if he comes here often, no ring, the logo on his sweatshirt is for a band I like.

We all judge, pigeonhole; it's human nature. A tenth of a second. The blink of an eye.

"Sorry," I say, jamming my phone into my bag and standing. "It's not mine."

I'm out the door before he can try again.

\-\-\-

At home, I ditch my gym stuff in the kitchen and go into the bedroom, which is in semidarkness because I've neglected to open my curtains again. I turn on the light, go up to the wall, and take in the chart.

What started out as a page in my notebook and spread to my kitchen table has since grown to bloom right across the wall, a jumbled mind map of sticky notes and web page printouts and my own scribbled theories, all tacked or taped together. The giant eye from the RRX website. Maps and satellite images of Varaig and the nearby terrain. A calendar for November. An article from a Scottish newspaper reporting that a man from London was found dead near Loch Varaig on November 21. I zero in on the words "no suspicious circumstances"—reporters' code, I've since worked out, for suicide. How would they know? They're guessing. I skip on. Here's an eighty-word story from the *Times*, and a similar one from an aesthetics industry magazine. A statement that RRX—now SRX—put out: "We are devastated over the loss of our dear friend and co-founder. We would like to extend our thanks to the Kolbe Care Clinic in Hertfordshire for everything they did and ask for privacy at this difficult time." Kolbe, I've learned, is an addiction rehabilitation center.

I've positioned myself, as I always do, in front of the only photo of Scott. Pinned at eye level, it's a grainy yearbook headshot from his college alumni newsletter, only about an inch or so in size. It accompanies a short report that a funeral was held in Syracuse, New York, for Scott De Luca, class of '97, who is survived by his mother, Marianne De Luca, and his brother. I brush his image with my fingertip. Scott looks quite different here from how I remember him, even factoring in the fluffier nineties hair—he's thinner and more serious, but also kind of hollow, somehow. I think hard, seeing the screw of his eyebrows when he laughed, the carved dimple, the crooked tooth. But these pieces of him in my mind's eye won't match up to the reality of what I'm seeing in this image on my wall. Oh God, don't let my recollection of him be fading already, don't let time be starting to rub him out in my memory. I couldn't bear it—it'd be like losing him twice over. I grab the nearest piece of paper, unpin it, and restick it over the photo. Instantly I feel calmer. With the photo hidden I can hold on to him without doubting myself.

The paper I've moved is a grainy satellite image of the half a mile of land between Angela's house and the cliff. I didn't mean to choose that one in particular, but now my attention is drawn to a small gray patch toward the right-hand edge, which I know is the area where the rocks smooth out right before that sheer, deadly drop. Unbidden, Angela's words come to me. *Oh God, he's worse, isn't he? Promise you'll call me if he has a bad turn.*

I rip the printout off the wall. The downdraft of my movement lifts the article from the Scottish newspaper. I snatch that one away, too, and drop them both. They land, crumpled, by my feet. Why do people keep saying it was suicide? No one who'd spent that time with Scott, who knew what we talked about, how he seemed, how he acted, would think so. He was warm, kind, funny, a bit nerdy. Distracted occasionally, yes, but not someone with a death wish.

In my imagination I see the person who got into the house and stole the painting returning, trying to take something else, and Scott chasing them out into the morning mist. In this film that plays inside my head a hundred times a day, so often it's more familiar than reality, he gains on the intruder and they grapple in the gritty, skiddy spot right at the edge of the cliff.

I snatch up my phone and scroll through recent calls, find Sonia Nabil, the police family liaison officer, and hit dial. It rings and rings, goes to voice mail. I hang up, call again. And again. And again.

Finally, she answers. "Ms. Wight. Please. I've told you—you've got to stop calling me. You know I can't help you further."

I ignore her exasperation. "I just want to know about the investigation."

"We've been over this, too. There isn't an ongoing investigation because there's nothing more to investigate."

"Right. Unless the coroner—"

"Procurator fiscal."

Potato, tomato. "Sorry, unless the *procurator fiscal* decides differently. You've said." She's not the only one who's weary. But why can't she listen? Listen and do something? If she listened, then there *would* be an investigation.

The mind movie starts up again. The intruder is always facing away from me because I'm not sure who I should be picturing. The backpacker? Was she lost that morning by the terrace? Why was she hanging around in such a barren place anyway, so far off the tourist track? And why was she at Angela's launch party? But she was just a girl. She couldn't have fought with him. Who, then? The outline of the back of the intruder broadens, becomes more masculine. One of those two delivery drivers? The man I saw at the cliff the day Scott arrived? No—that was Scott, I'm getting muddled.

"Look," I say to Nabil. "About the intruder." She tuts, but I don't give her a chance to interrupt. Because I've changed my mind since I gave my police statement. It couldn't have been an accident. Scott was familiar with the ground, having walked it so many times. He wouldn't have been careless enough to be near the drop-off without good reason. "If someone pushed him, to end a fight, then that's m—"

"Ms. Wight." This time she is teacher-firm. "There is no evidence of any intruder, or of manslaughter, or murder. And if there was, we would be handling it. Yes, I know you claim someone was in the house, but there was no complaint from Dr. Reynolds."

At the name, I feel a spark. Don't they say most murderers are someone the victim knew? Scott's assailant morphs into a woman with light hair, pale eyes. "Angela!" I tell Nabil. "She and Scott could have had a falling-out over RRX. Maybe that's why he was in Varaig. Sacha said there was all this tension, shouting . . ."

As abruptly as it lit, inspiration dies. Angela was in London on November 21. I saw her myself, twice. And in those video calls to me—calls that have been handed to the police—Angela was concerned for Scott's welfare, so . . . the intruder becomes nameless, faceless once more.

I've overstepped the mark. Nabil won't answer my phone calls again.

Technically, she never had to anyway—she's the family liaison officer, and I'm not family. I need to be quick if I'm going to get anything out of her. It's my last chance.

I try for a moderate tone, hoping that if I sound collected she'll treat me as such. "Well, can I ask about the fiscal? Any news about a hearing?" If they do decide to hold an inquiry, I want to go up there and give my evidence in person. I need to make sure they understand who Scott was. Before Nabil can shut me down again, I add, "Because a date's a matter of public record, right? You'd be able to tell me that?"

She speaks more gently this time. "You need to ask them."

"I would—if they hadn't stopped replying to my emails." Tears well; frustration stoppers my throat.

Nabil takes my silence as an opportunity to wind up the call. "You know, Ms. Wight," she says, sympathy in her voice, "I have some experience in cases like these, and I know how hard they can be for loved ones left behind. But sometimes people can seem like they're fine, when on the inside they're not. You take care now." She hangs up.

She was talking about Scott, but she also meant me. Drained, I drop onto the bed, turning onto my side so my back is to the mess on the wall and my face is to the window. Nabil's words aren't a million miles away from Sacha's when she discovered the chart: "Mads, this isn't right. You need some proper help. Let me find you a therapist, okay?" I'd had to tell her after the launch exactly what had happened between Scott and me, how much I'd felt for him, because I was such a mess then and in the days that followed. Still am. She thinks I've been driven mad, from lack of sleep, from compound grief, Scott on top of Mum, and from guilt. I'd tried to explain to her that the chart was helping me, that it was all too much to hold in my head and I needed to get it out. But maybe she and Nabil are right and I do need therapy. Maybe then I could begin to accept what everyone else seems to have already decided is the truth.

Through the gap in my bedroom curtains, I see the streetlight outside my flat come on. Now that we're approaching British Summer Time, the days are longer. I glance at my phone screen: half past five.

Suddenly, it's as if a switch has been pressed in my mind. Why haven't I thought of this before? In the early days, before her patience evaporated,

Nabil confirmed that a woman, a dog walker—the emergency call operator didn't get a name—dialed 999 a little after seven on the morning of November 21 to report seeing a man jump. Given how patchy the reception always was for me, it's a miracle the woman was able to get a signal but evidently she did, because police went out there not long after.

Sitting up, I open the browser on my phone. I type in "Time of sunrise November 21 Varaig Scotland." A table of sunrise and sunset times for the whole year appears. I click on the correct date. That day, the sun rose at 08:08. But that makes no sense—because if it was seven in the morning when the dog walker called in, then it was still dark, or nearly—so how could she have seen a man jump?

All of my nerves fire, alert. Because if the police have got that much wrong, what else have they missed? They need to resume the investigation. Energized, I call Nabil. She doesn't answer. But that's okay—I'll find another way to get to her.

Renewed conviction surges through me. No amount of therapy could talk me into believing something different from what I feel at my core. Because the man I knew, however briefly, would not have ended his own life. I've never been so sure of anything.

I retrieve the crumpled pages from the floor, smooth them flat, and pin them to the wall. And then I start to go through it all once more.

23

THE WEDDING INVITATION HAS BEEN STUCK TO MY FRIDGE FOR three months. Sacha put it there. She also replied on my behalf to Simon, our mutual friend from university, and assured me I'd feel better by now, that it'd do me good to have something to look forward to. "We can be each other's date. It'll be fun, like old times. Two single ladies, out on the prowl." Except now she's met Monique, and Monique is her date, and I'll have to go it alone. "Nonsense," Sacha said. "We'll all go together."

I'm trawling through the Facebook groups for the towns and villages around Varaig, hoping to find mention of a woman who walks her dog in the area and who might have recounted seeing someone at the cliff—two people, even, factoring in the intruder—when the flat buzzer goes. The video entry shows Sacha and Monique are downstairs. I beep them in and steel myself before I open my door, readying my excuses not to go.

"You're not dressed yet?" Sacha asks after I've kissed them both hello. "We don't want to miss the food—it's the best part." The wedding service was for family only and our invitations are to the evening reception party, which starts at eight. It's past seven now and I'm still in my jeans. They've pulled out all the stops with their party finery, the jewel colors and cuts of their dresses and coats complementing each other so they truly look like a pair. The clothes match the energy they bring into the room—high on fun, on love.

I open my mouth to explain why I can't come—a migraine; I'd be a gooseberry; I've got other stuff to do—but Sacha holds up a finger. "No, you don't. Come on." She bustles me toward my bedroom. Whenever she's visited in the past few weeks I've managed to keep her in the living room, but before I can protest she's through the door, seeing the chart. Stopping.

"Mate, you promised." She makes a face like she's in pain, looking from me to the chart to the unmade bed and back again. Tears fill her eyes. "Something happened to you in that house, Mads." Maddy, Mads, mad. "I know it's awful, that a man died, that you liked him, but this is . . ." She dabs at her eye with her knuckle and it hurts that I can't pull myself together for her.

"I know I did. And I will take it down. Soon."

"But not yet."

No. Not yet.

Sacha must sense my unvoiced answer, because she turns her back on both me and the chart. "Right," she says, opening the wardrobe, her voice too bright. "Let's see what we've got. They call them glad rags for a reason." She pulls out a couple of dresses, holds them up to me, hangs them back on the rod. Flicks to the end, pulls out another. "How about this one?"

It's the dress from the launch. "I don't think so."

She hooks the hanger over the inside of the door. "I'll leave you to choose while I order an Uber. Don't be too long."

When she's gone, I pick up the dress. How full of hope I'd been when I nipped into that boutique, how happy. I could sorely do with some of that now. I take hold of the zip and pull it all the way down until it parts. So easy to slip off. I'd lived in that dress for thirty-six hours, until the straps cut red welts into my shoulders. I gave my contact details to the police in it, wandered the street looking for a taxi in it, lay in bed, tossing and turning, in it. In the cold early hours I'd thrown my old sweatshirt over the top and stared, stared, stared out the window into the dawn, into the afternoon, into nighttime again, trying to hold on to something that was gone. Because to change clothes was to end the day, and to end the day was to acknowledge what had happened.

Might putting the dress on again feel like going back in time? Will it give me the same confidence, or at least help me fake it? I take off my sweater, undo my jeans, and push them down around my ankles. Lifting the dress off the hanger, I slip through one arm, then the other. It's like putting on a life jacket, and I'm taken by the idea that this dress is something that might keep me afloat. I catch the two bottom corners, bring them together, pull the zip all the way up. Step back and look at my reflection.

I've lost weight and the dress hangs sack-like from my shoulders, drooping as if it is heartbroken, too. Sad rags, not glad rags. I pull the whole thing off over my head and sling it onto the bed. Damn it. I breathe hard against my palms.

In the end I stay in my black jeans and throw an old blouse over the top. Tie back my hair. No makeup. What's the point in dolling myself up? Isn't that a form of pretense, of covering up the truth? Simon won't care. Surely I'm allowed to look exactly as I feel?

Neither Sacha nor Monique says anything about my choice. I think Sacha knows that it's enough that I'm willing to come. She puts an arm around me and squeezes my shoulder. "Well done." That's the thing about family, even family you choose, like Sacha—you can be yourself around them. There's none of this pressure to curate your identity like there is on social media, at work, or even around a new partner, to always seem like you're on top. Family see you at your ugliest, both physically and emotionally, and they love you anyway.

"Ready?" Monique asks, shooting me a steadying smile. I barely know her yet, but so far I like what I see. She seems stable, a good fit for Sacha after the melodrama of Jada. She loops an arm through mine. Sacha takes the other. As a threesome, we go down to the street.

The hotel is in Covent Garden. Once we're out of the Uber, approaching the entrance, we have to divert around a family that has stopped to stare at a pair of living statues, street performers who have painted themselves bronze from head to toe and are standing absolutely, perfectly still.

"Ugh," Sacha says. "They creep me out. It's like they're halfway between the living and the dead."

Right, I think, as she and Monique lead me up the steps and into the hotel. I know exactly how that feels.

"But Maddy, it's early," Sacha protests when I tell her I want to leave. We've been here less than two hours.

"I know, but . . ." I can't admit I want to get back to the Facebook groups. Also, it's disconcerting seeing people from university, looking the same but changed, eighteen more years of life written on their faces and bodies. Sacha and Monique have been happily circulating, all air kisses, smiles, and hugs, but no one has approached me at my stationary spot at the bar. My all-black getup was an error. I thought I'd feel more comfortable, that I might be able to fade into the background, but it's having the opposite effect, making me stand out, causing my skin to itch beneath the stares and whispers.

Sacha puts down her drink and the stiff silk of her dress rustles against her arm. "We'll come with you. Let me just sign the guest book."

Monique tries to but can't quite hide her disappointment. They're newly in love; she has every right to want to enjoy herself, to create memories with Sacha. And I want that for them, too.

"No," I say, "you don't need to." It's hard to separate the consonants. I haven't been *out* out since Angela's launch, and my alcohol tolerance has gone way down. Three glasses of fizz and I'm drunk. "You guys stay. Please. Dance, have fun. Do the things couples at weddings do."

My gesticulations are too wild. Monique looks from me to the disco. Sacha, forced to choose, caves in. "All right. But message when you get home, yeah?" She hugs me and the hug feels like nothing.

I'm partway to the exit when I call back over my shoulder, "Give Simon my love, won't you? Tell him . . . tell him anything you want. That I'm ill." Sometimes I wonder if I am. She nods.

Outside, the cold air bites. I decide to walk part of the way home to sober up—walking might also help me sleep, and God knows I need that. Covent Garden is overwhelming, stuffed with people, so I cross the Strand and slip around the back of the Savoy into that neglected mesh of streets where tourists don't venture. Instantly it is quiet and dark and I sigh a cloud into the peace, my breath blooming in the frigid air, the invisible made visible. Already I can detect the briny green riverscent of the Thames. Not far now to the station. The ground here on the service side of the hotel is dirty and studded with old gum, a far cry from the pristine slabs out front. Above my head a net is suspended across the road. It has been hung to keep pigeons off, but for one terrible moment I think it's there to catch people who have fallen, and a ball of alarm detonates in my stomach.

Don't think about it. Don't think at all. Just get home.

I press on. Three men emerge from a pub, laughing. They don't notice me as I fall into step a few yards behind them. One of them wears a woolly hat. They chat as they walk, all three abreast like I was with Sacha and Monique when we left my flat, and their easy familiarity touches me. Maybe I should have stayed at the wedding, made more of an effort. Practice makes perfect, Mum used to say. Maybe with enough practice I could make myself happy again.

Embankment station, like Covent Garden, is too much: shoppers, day-trippers, Chelsea fans, all shouting, crowding together. I'm caught in the melee, can't get free.

Then the man in the hat turns. It's him.

He doesn't hear me calling his name over the soccer chants, so I follow him to a club under the arches, heart galloping. I've lost my bag, left it at the wedding reception. I gate-crash the club, diving into the crowd to escape the security men. I don't belong here, I'm too old, too lost. It's too packed, too hot. Too strange.

Where is he? I make it to the stage. Green lasers shard. Strobes explode. Finally, I see him, and he sees me.

And then a rough hand grabs my shoulder and shoves.

24

I STAGGER. THE BOUNCER HAS FOUND ME. I STRUGGLE AGAINST his grip but he's at least a foot taller and eight times the muscle and it's no use. Below, at the edge of the club crowd, Scott sees what's happening and steps toward the stage. I yell against the music, even though he's too far away to hear me. "Scott!"

The bouncer, on the lookout for trouble, shouts into his lapel mic, guiding another security guard toward Scott. Then I'm dragged away and marched back to the entrance. My ears ring, there's a sour taste in my mouth, and the bouncer's hold on my shoulder is painful. The people in the line are gawking. I tune them out and focus solely on the chipped door, waiting for it to open, for him to come through. Nothing else matters, not even whether I'm going to be arrested or cautioned. Because I found him.

Then the door opens and there he is. Scott. Here. Alive. How? I fix my eyes on him, not daring to blink, looking so hard it hurts. That watchful gaze, that flushed skin; that line, a furrow of focus, between his brows. He stops and shoves his hands characteristically into his pockets, the motion pushing his shoulders up toward his ears like it did in Varaig. He's wearing a knit hat and he's grown a beard. A beard! Laughter, relief, sheer radiant light—I am a bubble of joy. I reach out. I want to touch him, to feel the solidity of him, to confirm what I'm seeing.

The bouncer holds me back. "You know her?" he says.

Scott shakes his head no at the same time I say yes. It's as if I've been slapped. "Scott?"

The bouncer frowns. "She seems to know you."

I flail against his grip. "Scott," I plead.

"I'm sorry." There's something wrong with him. He presses his lips together and scratches his beard. He looks away, at the floor, at the barrier rope by the line, at the ticket desk. Anywhere but at me. "Ye've mistaken me for someone else."

His accent. It's wrong, Glaswegian, swallowing the vowels in "you've," nipping the word shut. He pulls his hat lower, stoops so he's no longer so tall. Now I see a piece of metal that glints in his eyebrow. A tattoo flashes on the inside of his wrist. Fuck. Not again. Embarrassment floods in and I stop squirming. The bouncer, perhaps anticipating a trick, pincers his fingertips harder. The booze in my system makes me brave. "You're hurting me."

Not-Scott steps forward. "Come on, mate, ease up."

"She didn't pay." The bouncer eases the pressure but keeps hold.

"I lost my bag," I tell him. "Or someone stole it."

"Lost? Stole? Which is it?"

"I don't know. I was at a wedding and I left and—"

"I don't care. You can't come in here without paying. Twenty quid."

"But I told you, I don't have it."

"Phone?"

"That's gone, too." The full force of my predicament hits me. "How am I going to get home?" It's miles back to my flat. Sacha and Monique will have left the reception by now and I don't know where they're going next.

"Not my problem." The bouncer releases my shoulder and pushes me toward the street. It's not hard, but I'm not expecting it and I trip and land on all fours on the pavement. Grit needles my palms.

"Hey!" Not-Scott says. He helps me to my feet. "Are you all right?"

I'm close to tears. All I want is to get out of here. More people are looking, and this time I feel the full sting of their criticism, because it's obvious what they see. A dirty-haired, drawn-faced woman in black, down on her luck. Another crazy.

"Come on," Not-Scott says, cupping my shoulder with his hand, his touch gentle where the bouncer's had been rough. He angles me toward the street.

One of his friends says, "Con?"

"You go back in. I'll not be long," he calls back. The bouncer sucks his teeth in self-righteousness as we leave.

On the street this man, this stranger, steps to the curb and hails a black cab. When one stops, he opens the door and guides me in with a hand light at my back. I think of how Scott did that when I got into the taxi at Angela's house and a lump concretes in my throat, a boulder that cuts off my words.

"Where to?" asks the cabbie.

"Where do you live?" Not-Scott asks me.

I manage to tell them, croaking out the road, the area. He hands the cabbie some notes.

The cabbie isn't happy. "What if it's more? Traffic this time on a Saturday. And what if she pukes?"

Oh God. I make a move to get out.

"It's all right." Not-Scott gestures at me to stay inside. "She's not gonna puke." He pats his pockets, produces a pen and a slip of paper from the inside of his jacket. Even the jacket—a well-worn leather and sheepskin aviator type—is wrong. How could I have been so stupid? He writes something on the paper. Hands it to the cabbie. "I gave you enough. But here's my number. Call me if it's more and I'll pay by card."

The cabbie considers. Concedes. "I was headed home south anyway."

The door closes. I finally find my voice. "Wait . . ."

I'm too late. We're doing a U-turn. Already he's merely a shadow. My shoulder burns.

The journey is long enough for the alcohol to wear off. The neighborhoods of London file past the window, the mansion blocks of Millbank, the tower blocks of Vauxhall, the terraces and town houses of Battersea and Clapham. Rich shifts quickly into poor, working-class into aspirational middle and back again to rich. It's easy to lose your bearings in this city. Turn a corner and it's as if you've been transported somewhere else entirely. Easy to lose yourself, too.

The heating is on in the cab, but I'm cold. I pull my coat tighter, sink my head into the collar. When we pull to a stop, it takes me a while to register we're outside my block. I must have dozed off. All those months of anti-insomnia prep and I nod off in the back of a taxi.

The cabbie makes eye contact via the rearview mirror. "You all right, love? You look like you've seen a ghost."

Seen a ghost—it's one of those things people say, and particularly that men say to women, along with *Cheer up, it might never happen* and *A smile doesn't cost anything,* and all the other unasked-for bullshit we have to put up with. You're supposed to perk up when a man says that to you. You're supposed to laugh and maybe toss your hair and act like it hasn't bothered you that they've intruded, unasked, on your private hopes or shame. I don't perk up. I don't laugh. I crumple.

"Do you have enough?" I ask, meaning the fare.

He checks the meter, shrugs. "A quid or so short, but that's all right."

The tiny act of kindness defrosts me. "Thank you." I wrap my fingers around the door handle.

"Bit of a funny one, your mate," the cabbie says, as if he's trying to fill in the story of what happened between me and Not-Scott before he put me in a taxi and paid up front. "Didn't even say goodbye."

A thought occurs to me. "Can you give me his number?"

"Don't you have it?"

I don't want him thinking I'm some desperate woman snubbed by a date. "I lost my phone. All my numbers are in it. He . . . Scott . . ."—I have no other name for him—"he'd want me to let him know I got home safely."

"Yeah, who remembers any phone numbers anymore? Ask me our number for the house I lived in when I was a kid and I could recite it for you even now." He's still talking to me via the mirror, so his eyes are all I can see of his face. "Remember when they changed them? Doubt you're old enough. Big fuss at the time, but we got used to the new ones quick, forgot we'd ever had something different." He produces the slip of paper from his shirt pocket. "Here."

After he drives off, I press my neighbor's buzzer. We each hold the other's spare key. Luckily she's home, and awake.

Once in my flat, I open my laptop. Sacha sent a message over an hour ago: I've got your bag. We're worried—why haven't you come back to the hotel to get it? Contact me when you get this so I know you're all right x

I email: I'm home.

She must have notifications enabled, because she replies straightaway. Thank God. How?

My fingers find the slip of paper in my pocket. *Ye've mistaken me for someone else.* A stranger lent me the money for a cab.

She sends a starry-eyed emoji. Some good people in this city after all. Okay if we drop your bag round in the morning?

Sure.

Take some aspirin. Get to bed. Have a SLEEP x

Okay. Night x

From Sacha's repeated use of "we"—"we're worried," "if we drop your bag round"—I gather that Prague definitely went well. I think of the way he looked at me in the club, before the bouncer came, and it's as if the strobe has branded his flash-frozen image into my brain. That wasn't the look of a stranger.

The flat is so quiet I can hear the freezer's thermostat click and the cycle kick in. In my pocket, the paper almost seems to vibrate. I take it out and examine the writing. No name, only a mobile number scribbled so fast that the last digit, eight, runs off the edge.

It's the witching hour, and maybe I am bewitched, because I open Skype on my laptop. My account is linked to my mobile. I key in the number from the paper.

It rings. Goes to voice mail. "You've reached Connor. Leave a message. Cheers."

The accent, and especially the cheers—so Scottish—disorients me. What am I even doing? I should hang up. "Hi . . . Connor." Stressing his name is good—it feels important to let him know I know he isn't the person I mistook him for. "This is Maddy." Oh, but he doesn't know my name. "We . . . You just put me in a taxi . . ." I clear my throat. "I'd like to pay you back. Could you call me when convenient, please?" I recite my number. "Okay, then, have a good evening. And thanks again." Not the most articulate of messages, but it'll do.

I pin his number to the fridge with a magnet for safekeeping. I don't know whether it's the draining away of the tension from the encounter with the bouncer, the aftereffects of sobering up, or the aspirin I take on Sacha's command, but I'm suddenly very, very tired. I go to bed and, for the first time in ages, I sleep.

25

SACHA COMES OVER MIDMORNING, MONIQUE IN TOW, AND THEY stay for coffee. They're so loved-up, always touching each other, a hand on a knee, a head dipping to a shoulder, as if their bodies are magnetized. I don't remember Sacha being this tactile with anyone else, not even Jada. Love—so powerful it can change the way you act, who you are, without your even being aware of it.

As soon as they've gone, I retrieve my phone from my bag and check for missed calls or messages from Connor. Nothing. I dial his number and once more it goes through to voice mail. I don't leave a message.

All Sunday, I keep checking, but he doesn't get in touch. I can't call him again—I've already done so twice. Any more is verging on harassment. Midafternoon I send a text: Hi Connor. Not sure if you got my voice mail? I'd like to repay you for the taxi. Please let me know how. Succinct and non-stalkerish. I can see he's read it, but still I get no response.

At the gym I put in an hour on the treadmill, running until my clothes are soaked through. My workout feels different—powerful—my toes catching the front of the machine as I easily outpace the belt, and unusually, I get a runner's high afterward. I put it down to a good night's sleep.

When I still haven't heard from him by lunchtime the next day, it occurs to me that maybe I misdialed, left messages for a complete stranger, someone even more of a stranger to me than Connor is. I take the piece of paper off the fridge and double-check the numbers against what I have in my phone. They match. Maybe he's not interested in money. Maybe he's loaded like Angela and fifty pounds means nothing to him.

Meaningless or not, I feel a duty to repay him and thank him properly. Not many people would have done what he did. I turn over the paper. It's a receipt from a café in Dalston, dated last Friday. A solo coffee order. The address of the café is printed at the bottom. Again, I get a flash of standing on the stage in the club, of seeing him, and of his seeing me.

I grab my bag.

Two lattes, a brownie, a panini, a bottle of water, and a peppermint tea later, the café door opens and I'm rewarded for my persistence.

There have been a few false starts—in this part of town, almost every second man has a hipster beard—so I take my time checking whether it is Connor. Tucked in a corner of the coffee shop, I'm able to observe him as he takes off his coat and hangs it on a peg. I'm pretty certain he's the guy from the club: beard, black hat, chocolate-brown leather jacket trimmed in sheepskin. Underneath, he's in jeans and a winter-weight flannel shirt, a chunky scarf wrapped around his neck. He's a little more substantial than Scott, and his chest and arms fill out his shirt. Looks like he hits the gym regularly. He unhooks the scarf and loops it over the same peg as his coat. Lastly, he pulls off his hat and stuffs it into a pocket of the jacket. His hair is longish, messy, almost down to his collar at the back. He rubs a hand through it, mussing. When he greets the barista—"Hi, Niall. How's it going?"—and I hear the Scottish accent, I'm sure I'm right.

I can see why I mistook him for Scott—there's definitely a strong archetypal resemblance, even in the way he lifts his chin when he says hello—but in the sober, bright lights of a Monday afternoon it's the differences, rather than the similarities, that stand out. I'll do what I came to do and move on.

I'm getting to my feet, ready to catch him after he orders, when he slips through a gap in the counter, weaves between the barista and the big espresso machine, and disappears. For a moment, I think it's to do with me—that he's seen me, he's running away, he's slipped out of the kitchen door and is sprinting down the street. Then he comes back, knotting an apron behind his waist. He works here. I'm being ridiculous, letting my nerves, embarrassment, or whatever it is that's making me feel jumpy get the better of me.

Niall is quick to leave. A pat on the shoulder, a dumping of his own apron, and he's lifting his coat off the pegs. I glance at the other customers. Two teens are over by the flower-garlanded selfie wall, pouting come-hitherly into a phone lens and sucking on their straws, too young to fully understand the suggestive implications. A storm-faced mother feeding pieces of cookie to a small child is ignoring the girls so steadfastly she can only be vowing her own daughter will never be allowed on social media. No one is paying any attention to me. I should go and talk to Connor now.

Instead, I watch him. He has almost a dancer's precision as he moves around the small space behind the counter. He wipes a menu item off the blackboard, throws the towel over his shoulder, and chalks up a new special. Rolls up the cuffs of his shirt, exposing the end of a tattoo on his inner arm, I can't tell of what. Fetches a bottle of cleaning fluid from a cupboard, sprays the surfaces. He's familiar with this café, comfortable here.

Eventually, I rise. He is wiping down the machine and has his back to the room as I approach the counter. Blood rushes to my head, making me sway on my feet. I clear my throat. He must see a reflection in the chrome, because without breaking off from what he's doing he asks my order. "What can I get you?"

"Latte, please." Ah, no—I can't drink another one. It came out automatically.

"Medium?"

I pause. "Actually . . ."

He glances over his shoulder and gives me the well-worn, casual look of most people in the service industry, those who see hundreds of different faces a day, who have learned how to be polite without fully engaging. Then his polishing hand stills as he recognizes me.

I feel ridiculously on edge, as if I've been caught out. "It's, it's Connor, isn't it?"

He turns fully face forward and I get an uncanny flash of Scott, but out of kilter, changed. The eyes are so similar, the posture, the skin tone—but the beard, the longer hair, the fuller cheeks . . . His expression is fixed, present yet absent, as if he's zipping through scenarios in his mind as to why I'm here: Obsessive? Mere coincidence? About to cause another scene?

"I was just passing," I say, before remembering he heard me give my address to the cabdriver, and Dalston is on the other side of London from Tooting. "Work, you know?" Doubt fills his eyes. "Client meeting . . ." I try to keep going, telling myself I've nothing to be ashamed of. "Small world, hey?"

A lift of the pierced brow. "You've got that right." He grabs the spray bottle, gives the counter a dousing, starts to rub it vigorously.

"Look," I say. "I want to thank you for the other night and pay you back."

He concentrates on a stubborn spot. "There's no need."

"Seriously. I felt so bad, causing such a scene, dragging you away from your friends."

"Och," he says. "Don't worry about it. I found them again."

"All the same." I'd taken out some cash earlier. I pull the money from the back pocket of my jeans. If he works in a café, I'm guessing fifty pounds is not an insignificant sum to him, maybe a whole shift's worth of pay. It was a decent amount to me before I met Angela. I put the money on the counter. "I mean, I'd offer to buy you a cup of coffee, too, but, you know . . ." I hold out my arms to indicate the café surroundings, add an overexaggerated shrug.

I get a laugh this time and, even better, eye contact, long enough for me to feel a connection. This, I think. *This* is what I remember. It cuts through the differences and frees me, like a knife releasing bonds. *You only get to experience a feeling like that once.* Or could it possibly happen twice?

I slide the money toward him. "Please."

He slides it back. "It's not every day I get to do my knight-in-shining-armor act. You can't be taking that away from a chap." When he straightens, he looks me up and down, checking me out. He's subtle about it, but I catch it all the same and my body reacts with a sort of drawing up, a readying.

"Well then, how about I buy you dinner instead?" He looks away. Have I gone too far, is he shy? After all, I don't know him.

"I don't think that's a good idea."

"Why not? You won't accept my cash. And even knights have got to eat." I raise my hands, the picture of innocence. "Okay then, a drink. No strings attached."

He stares out the window, jittering his jaw. Thinking of what—his partner? He looks back, almost but not quite meeting my eye, clearly not sure. "Give me a minute." He pulls his phone from his apron pocket. "Sorry, I . . ."

"No problem."

He goes into the back room. Feeling too exposed, even though the mother and the teens have paid me no heed, I return to my table. I unlock my own phone and message Sacha. I just asked a guy out. I put down the phone then pick it up again, using it as cover while concentrating on this new feeling: a rosy pleased-with-myself glow, coupled with an inner, stomachy panic. I check the counter—Connor is still in the back room.

Sacha replies instantly. What??? What did he say?

Nothing yet. He had to make a call.

To who? Did you check for rings?

Yep. None.

OK, well that's good. Maybe. Where are you, anyway?

Dalston.

Exploding head emoji, because she knows this is all well out of my comfort zone.

The front door opens and a new customer enters, a man and a dachshund, bringing with them the damp air. Connor comes out of the back room, tucking his phone into his apron pocket. He throws me a glance, but I can't tell what it means. He serves the customer and makes a fuss of the dog, giving it a treat from a jar on the counter.

What's happening? Sacha texts.

The café fills with the pressurized *crr* of the coffee machine.

Waiting for his answer. I keep my eyes on my phone, on my lap. Tell myself that the worst outcome is he says no to a drink and still refuses to take my money. If that happens, I guess I'll have to leave. At least I'll know I tried.

God, the suspense is killing me, Sacha writes.

Me too.

At the sound of a ceramic chink, I look up.

Connor. Putting a latte in front of me. A strand of hair swings in front of his face, tickling his cheekbone. He tucks it behind his ear. "I finish at six."

Once the other customers have left Connor stacks the chairs on the tables and mops the floors, then he leads me to a pub around the corner. It's a new London boozer, fitted out to look like an old London boozer—stripped floors, shiny brass footrail, hearth tiled in green. I like the return to this cozy, traditional style of decorating.

The pub is fairly busy and Connor and I stand side by side at the bar, waiting to be served. As I glance up at him, I get a momentary sense of dislocation, because he's exactly the same height as Scott. I knew from the club and café that he was tall, but I hadn't realized quite how tall, and now that we're close it's evident. The coincidence makes my head spin.

Maybe he picks up on my reaction to his proximity, because he backs away a fraction.

"What would you like?" I ask.

"I'll have a Coke, please."

"Sure you don't want a beer?" A memory, of forearms flexing and a cork being drawn from a bottle. "Wine?"

"Coke's fine. I . . ." He scratches the back of his neck. "I don't really drink."

I relay the order to the bartender, getting myself a large Malbec. We carry our drinks over to a table, take off our coats, fold and pile them on the spare seats, sit, smile, look around, smile again. "You found your bag, then?" he asks.

"Yeah. I'd been at a wedding. Someone handed it in."

"Lucky."

I take a sip of wine. "You worked at the café long?"

"Few years. I part own it."

"Oh." More wine. "You enjoy it?"

"Aye." His Coke is a third gone already. "It's not too bad. Pays the bills."

God, this is awkward.

"What is it you do?" he asks.

Not much, truth be told. "I'm a writer."

"A journalist? Newspapers and that?"

I had a journalism placement. "No, not quite. I write books."

"What kind of books?"

"Biographies. Memoir. I'm a ghostwriter."

He takes another gulp of Coke. "Can't say I've ever met one of those before. You like it?" He drinks so fast I hear the ice chink as it passes his teeth. He's regretting having said yes. He'll be gone within ten minutes.

I shrug. "It's not too bad. Pays the bills."

Somehow my crap joke makes him laugh, but he's got his mouth full and he can't laugh and swallow at the same time. His shoulders convulse, his cheeks bulge, and he bugs out his eyes, fighting not to spray all over the table. Finally he manages to swallow. He gasps in air.

"Wow." I pass him a napkin. "You ought to lay off the Coke. It's bad for your health."

"Aye," he says, wiping his eyes. "I think you may be right."

It gets easier after that. We talk. Then he asks whether I want another drink, and I find my glass is empty. He waves me off when I try to pay. "My round."

While Connor's at the bar I have a chance to study him again. In my head I airbrush him, shaving the beard, cutting the hair, sharpening the jawline, changing the clothes—Scott's were never as casual as this. Physically it's a close match. But his manner. Scott, once I got to know him, was looser, fluid, apart from those late-night times. I don't like to remember those. Connor is self-contained, holding himself in. Kind of more like Angela.

As he carries the drinks back over, he catches me watching.

"Sorry," I say, hiding behind the action of taking my glass from him. "It's just you look like someone I used to know."

"The person you mentioned at the club?"

I nod.

He stirs the slice of lemon in his drink with a finger. "It's funny. I get that a lot. I guess I have one of those faces."

We talk again. Nothing deep or revealing. He seems interested in what I do, and so I let him ask, and as I answer, keeping the conversation away from my final commission, I steal glances at different parts of him, drinking him in in small sips. The eyes—they're chameleon-like, as Scott's were, the kind that change to reflect their surroundings. I know that if Sacha asks me, *What color were his eyes?* I won't be able to answer. All colors, none. Right now, in the dimly lit pub, they're muddy, shaded. But when I made those silly jokes they sparked. There's a small steel ring hooked through his right eyebrow. The beard fascinates me. When I was at school, my physics teacher had a beard, until one day he didn't, and it was such a shock seeing his naked face, as though he was a different person. Connor wears his full, and it's threaded through in places with silver. Would it feel rough or soft to touch? I find myself focusing on his mouth, trying to glimpse his canine. When he laughs, it's there, perfectly straight. And as we talk, he's laughing a lot.

Across from our table, on the chimney breast above the bottle-green hearth, hangs a mirror, reflecting an image of the two of us. In the mirror I can see my face, but only the back of him, so the differences, the beard and eyebrow ring, are hidden. I am flushed, more alive than I've been since Scott died. It's rare, for me, this kind of intense chemistry. And to find it again . . .

His forearms are resting on the table. They are more muscular. But, tattoo aside, these strong, capable-seeming hands could easily be Scott's.

"Have dinner with me," I say again.

"Why? Because you think you owe me?"

"No, because I want to have dinner with you."

"Now?"

"Yes."

His face takes on that unsure look, the one from the café. His attention goes to the bar.

"Are you married?" I ask. "Is that it?"

"No."

"Girlfriend?"

"No."

"Boyfriend?"

"No."

The negatives hover between us. This isn't like me. But there's a thrill in being this direct. "Have dinner with me." I brush my fingertips across his knuckles with the lightest of touches. His hand twitches. "Connor."

There's been a sense of inevitability in the air ever since he put the coffee on my table. When I say his name, he meets my eye and I know what he's going to say.

"Yes."

26

JUST OVER A WEEK LATER, I'M IN THE SUPERMARKET WHEN MY mobile rings. I fish around in my bag, my hand closing around the phone right as the ringing stops. I check recent calls, hoping for Connor. Angela Reynolds. I stare at the screen. Angela hasn't contacted me for months, not since a single email shortly after Scott died. The phone rings again and I nearly drop it. Composing myself, I slide to answer. "Angela."

"Maddy, hi. I thought I'd call to check in, see how you are, how you've been."

How I've been? Broken, lost. "Oh, you know," I say carefully, not sure what she wants, or therefore how to respond. "Okay."

"Good."

"And you?"

"I've been great." And then, as if remembering herself, she adds, deepening her voice: "Of course, it's been a difficult time."

"Yes."

"But I've managed to keep myself busy. Distraction, you know, that's the key. Dr. Singh and I have been working all hours to get the Elixir out."

Given the number of excited videos popping up all over social media and the mentions in the press, it doesn't seem as if she's been struggling, more like it's been all guns blazing. "I see it's getting rave reviews."

"Thankfully! Ah . . ." Again she seems to pull herself in, back into that moneyed old-Hollywood persona that I noticed when we met, tightening into discretion. "A limited-release campaign, so far, to select influencers.

We're planning the full launch for next year. It'll coincide with the first of the clinics opening."

"Right." Bully for her, but not so much for me, after all that work I did got canned.

There's a slight delay on the line, the kind you get phoning from abroad, and I wonder where in the world she's calling me from. Clearly she hasn't curtailed her jet-setting. After a beat of silence too long, she comes in with polite chitchat. "Ranjit mentioned he spoke to you at the launch about ghosting his memoir."

"Yes."

"That's great. You'd do a fantastic job."

I can't think of a suitable response. The email from Ranjit Choudhery is still flagged in my inbox, but I haven't replied.

"And you've been well, you say?" she asks.

"Yes." We've already covered this. What does she want? We're not friends; surely she doesn't care this much about my welfare?

"Good, wonderful! Okay then. It's been good to catch up." Although we haven't caught up at all. "Take care, Maddy."

Take care with what, though? At last I remember my manners. "Yes. You too, Angela."

One time, about a fortnight after Scott died, I went to her office. I'm not sure what I was seeking—solace from someone suffering as much as I was, I suppose. I was no longer party to her schedule, didn't know if she was even in the country, but I'd walked through Mayfair anyway, along kempt streets, past parked limos and gilded brasseries, hoping to find her at her office. The lacquered black door was solidly closed, the buzzer unanswered. Leaving, I noticed recycling bagged up by the road, four or five blush-pink sacks waiting for collection. The tops were knotted, too tightly to untie, but the plastic was semitransparent, and I could easily make out the contents: copy after copy of SKIN DEEP. Off to be pulped.

I clawed open the side of one of the bags and yanked out a book. As I had on the day I arrived at Angela's house in Varaig, I thumbed the pages. The words—my words—jumped about, blurring and running together, making as little sense as the original *lorem ipsum*. On the cover, the embossing on my name had lost its sheen. I shoved the book back into the bag.

The recycling truck, which was rumbling along the street, stopped ahead of me, hazard lights flashing, loading gear jagged like teeth. A man in high-vis clothing and heavy black boots jumped off a running board and jogged to the curb. Without a care for the contents he swung the first two bags into the truck's gaping maw. I didn't stay to watch him toss the others.

I'd walked at least a block before I registered a sticky feeling on my fingers. When I looked at my hand, I saw a deep cut on the middle knuckle of my ring finger. The gummy feeling was blood, which had oozed out and trickled almost to my palm. On top of the cut itself, a clot had formed in a perfect sphere, not unlike on those newly fillered lips on Instagram. I put my stained fingers in my mouth to suck away the blood. As is often the case with paper cuts, it was a while before I registered any pain.

Not long after that, Angela emailed to say she was officially axing the book.

Connor and I see each other two more times within a week. After the pub, we go for pasta in a cozy, Mamma Mia–type Italian. He eats a lot—"Been lifting." Two days later I invite him for coffee and a walk through Green Park. Then on Sunday night I make reservations for cocktails (for me—water for him) and a Hitchcock at the BFI. I haven't kissed him yet and I'm not sure when I will. God knows I'm drawn to him, and a sense of promise keeps me asking him out, keeps making him accept, keeps propelling both of us forward. Yet at the same time something is holding me back.

The morning of our fourth date, I go to the gym but not to run. I'm dialing back on that now that I'm sleeping okay. Instead I head for the mats for a routine of planks, side planks, dolphins, clams. A young woman next to me is doing endless squats with a barbell across her shoulders, trying to bulk her glutes. She glances at me for a millisecond, then returns to her counting. She is wearing cycling shorts that expose lengths of smooth thigh. Not a crinkle of cellulite nor a single spider vein. I can't get away with wearing shorts like that anymore. This is where it differs from the male version, the female gaze: yes, there can be desire in it, and objectification, but there's also comparison and even a turning in of the gaze onto the self, especially when looking at another woman. How do I measure up, it asks, next to her? What do I lack; where do I stand? And there's empathy in it, too, alliance. I see you; I see how you feel. I feel how you see me.

My lower back muscles complain as I move into another plank and I compensate by squeezing my abs until they quiver and burn. They do say it takes pain to be beautiful. When I was a teenager, working out wasn't so much of a thing. We didn't have the energy after half starving ourselves, desperate to ape the hollow-cheeked, flat-chested heroin-chic models who were on the catwalks then and in all the magazines. Today it's all about owning your curves, which I suppose is healthier—Brazilian butt lifts aside. I start a set of push-ups. The girl next to me is still squatting. She is slender-hipped, fighting against her natural body type, and I think of Mum putting a plate of delicious-smelling cheese on toast under my fourteen-year-old nose, tempting me to eat. I'd caved, but vowed afterward to redouble my efforts to look like Kate Moss. Luckily I didn't have the staying power to see it through. And then fashions changed and I was shopping for push-up bras and chicken-fillet pop-ins. I like to think I've lived long enough to understand that body shape trends will change as quickly as the width of jeans, that I've wised up to chasing impossible ideals and accepted myself as I am. Yet I'm here anyway, on toes and bended arms, lactic acid screaming in my triceps, shaking my way through another circuit because I want to look good when I see Connor tonight. Once more beauty's siren call has sucked me in with the promise that if I'm just that little bit tighter, more toned, sculpted, I will get everything I want.

Going down the stairs from the gym to the street, I'm scrolling through emails on my phone when Scott's name pops up in my inbox. Ages ago I set up an alert for his name and there it is: Scott De Luca.

I stop so suddenly that a guy slams into the back of me. "Watch it!" he says, pointing two fingers in a V shape at his own eyes, then at mine, as if he thinks I'm incapable of understanding.

I barely acknowledge him as I move to one side. Clicking on the link in the alert takes me to the website of the Inner West London coroner's court, to a diary—a calendar of times, names, and dates of death. Next to each is a label: hearing or inquest. Scott De Luca is assigned as inquest. What's going on? The police told me the authorities in Scotland would handle any inquiry into his death, so why is there an inquest in London?

I double-check the date: March 26—today. My mouth dries. Nine thirty. Oh my God, I've missed it. How? I search my email for the word "inquest" and get a hit for my junk folder. There are other email alerts in there, all relating to today, sent a couple of weeks ago. Since I met Connor I've been thinking about my chart less, happy now to be distracted, but this is important, my chance to hear the details about what happened, to get answers, to say my piece. Why didn't I think to check my junk? Why didn't Sonia Nabil tell me? She must have known, the last time we spoke. Why haven't I been asked to appear and tell what I know? Fuck, this can't be happening.

I click back on the coroner's court website. So many people, eight listed today alone. Eight lives, eight tragedies, reduced to a single stark line in an order of business. All but one are scheduled for nine thirty. Hang on—what if they're all scheduled together and the coroner works through them one by one? Scott's name is toward the bottom. Hope rising in my throat, I check the time. Coming up to noon. If they call the hearings in the order they appear here, there's a chance that they haven't got to him yet.

I know where the court is, not far from Victoria station. Clamping my hand around my phone, I begin to run.

- - -

I sprint all the way from the Tube platform to Horseferry Road, but even as I'm racing up the street I can tell that I'm too late. People are filing out of a grand old redbrick building, men and women in office clothes, police in uniform. A woman is in the process of locking the building's ancient double doors. She has already bolted the one labeled "Coroner" into place and is swinging the other, marked "Court," shut. It connects with a clang.

"I'm sorry," she says briskly when I run up. "We're closing for the day." She is middle-aged, dressed in a skirt suit and low heels. Given the fact she has the keys to the building in her hand, I'm guessing she's a court employee.

I brace my hands on my knees, acid burning the back of my throat. It takes me a moment to find my voice. "Scott," I pant. "Scott De Luca. Did they hold that?"

The keys rattle on their chain as she slips one into the keyhole. "The referral from Scotland? Yes, it was the third one we heard."

Shit. "Can you . . ." It's hard to breathe. "Can you tell me—"

She draws herself up and in. "If you're a reporter, you can contact the clerk in the usual way."

"I'm not a reporter. I'm . . ."

"Family?" I nod. She's still curtly professional, but there's sympathy now as well. "I'm sorry, but it was a quick hearing. Procedural mainly, because the fiscal in Scotland did most of the work."

"Can I ask, what was the determination?" Scott lived in London; that must be why they referred it down here. I haven't done any research into the English inquest system. I know there's a determination made in Scotland, a formal listing of the facts of what happened. I presume it's the same here.

"You mean the verdict? Suicide."

A hole opens inside me and the world rushes in. Dizzy, I grip the stone wall. I want to tell her that's impossible, that he . . . I can't speak, can't think.

"The coroner was satisfied, given the evidence and witness reports attesting to his state of mind in the days prior, that even though there was no note, Mr. De Luca intended to take his own life. Given his history, and the fact that the amounts of alcohol and sedatives in his system were very high and the injuries were consistent with a fall from height—"

"Sedatives? What witness reports?"

"His business partner, and another colleague."

She means me. The hole inside deepens, a vortex from my brain right down to my feet. "But—"

"Their police statements and video transcripts were quite clear that he had relapsed." She tucks her keys into her bag and clasps the handle, ready to leave. "I really am sorry." Sorry for cutting me off; sorry for my loss—it's all the same to a person who deals with death every day.

Her heels tap against stone as she makes her way into the street. I can't move. At the railing she pauses, waiting for me to leave the court grounds. I have no choice but to obey. When I reach the street she looks at me not unkindly. "There's a garden of remembrance around the corner there." She points to the side of the building. "If you need a minute." The heels tap away.

A minute. How could anyone think that that would ever be enough? Nevertheless, I do as she suggests, walking on autopilot into a classically designed courtyard. It is a peaceful spot, quiet and calming. Against the far wall a limestone portico represents a gateway to another realm. The space between its pillars is solid. None shall pass. At least, none living. I lower myself to sit on a ledge. Cold from the stone seeps into my body, chilling me right through to my bones.

There was no fight with an intruder. There was no fucking murder. There was just a man who was good at hiding how much he was struggling. Hadn't he told me himself? *I won't be here much longer anyway. Believe me when I say that I'm sorry.*

All those theories, that "evidence" I was accumulating in that stupid, stupid chart—they were excuses for what I refused to acknowledge; I plastered those things to my wall to try to cover up my own failings.

Knowing I had a choice and accepting it was my decision to make, no one else's.

I saw him drinking. Angela told me he was good at concealing it; she asked me to call her if he deteriorated. I found that pill bottle, that *empty* pill bottle. They must have been sedatives. I should have said something, I should have done *some*thing.

What about you, Maddy? Would you jump?

I should have opened my eyes to what was happening in front of me. Should have acted. And yet I did nothing. It didn't seem like a big enough issue to be a problem. I glossed over it because I didn't want to believe.

Suicide. Seven letters, steeped in so much pain, sorrow, and guilt.

With shaking hands, I take out my phone and call Connor to cancel our date. "Sorry to bail, but can we make it next week instead?" I don't want to go into what's happened—I haven't told him about Scott yet. Early on in relationships everyone keeps secrets; no one wants to reveal their true self right from the get-go.

"Yeah, sure." His voice is heavy, distracted. "Bit of a rough day here, too, and I was about to ask you the same. I'll call you."

The final thing is to let Sacha know. Need me to come over after work? she texts.

I tell her no, that I'd rather be on my own for a bit, and she sends me a row of hearts in every color of the rainbow and it helps a little, all that love.

At home, in my bedroom, I grab fistfuls of paper and wrench them off the wall. Damn you, Scott. You had no need to jump. I tear down everything as fast as I can, scrunching some pages into balls and throwing them to the floor, ripping others into tiny squares. When it's all gone, I drop to my knees and scoop the remnants into a trash bag. I cart the bag into the kitchen and grab everything I have that was connected to SKIN DEEP—the dummy, the notebooks, the still-unopened envelope the photographer in America sent me, all the files Angela fanned out on the sofa that first day—and shove those in, too. I knot the top and shove the bag under my bed. It jams against the frame and I have to kick it to get it out of sight.

It's only early afternoon, but I crawl under the duvet. I am tired, so, so tired. Whether it's all those months of sleepless nights catching up with me, or a guilt-ridden sense of relief that I can finally let this go, I don't know, but within moments I am gone, pitched headlong into the sleep of the dead.

27

I MEET CONNOR FOR OUR RESCHEDULED DATE AT THE WROUGHT iron entrance to the Isabella Plantation in Richmond Park. I spot him from a distance, waiting out of the way of people coming and going through the gate. He is motionless in a way that reminds me of Scott and the similarity kicks me low down in the belly, but as I get closer he sees me and becomes more animated, lifting a hand and walking down the path, and the feeling passes. After the inquest it took a few days to get my head around things, but now I find myself needing Connor, craving him even.

We leave the treeless plains of the wider park and enter the sheltered oasis of the plantation. Now that the warmer days are here, life is returning: the daffodils are out and the magnolia is in nascent bud. I'm so glad to leave the long, dark winter behind.

As we follow the path, Connor seems lost in thought. I don't particularly mind; it's enough to be in his company. Besides, if he asks me what I've been up to, why I canceled last time, I'm not sure what I'd say. From how quiet he is I get the sense that he's been caught up in something, too. Not another woman—there isn't that vibe—but maybe there are work worries, or money issues. I know how that goes: before Angela's commission every month was a struggle. Over time it wears you down. It'll take a while for me to get used to not having to justify every little thing I want. Money can't guarantee happiness—I certainly know that—but it can take the pressure off.

After we've done a lap of Peg's Pond I lead us out of the top gate and into the grassland, with a vague plan of heading in the direction of Richmond Hill and going somewhere for a drink. We've not long broken free of the clots of walkers when I spot a small group of deer grazing in the park. My heart lifts. I've been in London my whole life and I still can't get over the fact that there are hundreds of deer living only a few miles away from my flat. There have been herds thriving in this piece of preserved countryside since the mid-1600s, quiet and safe in the eye of the city's storm.

I nudge Connor and he sees them, too, and grins. We head a little closer. There are a dozen or so in this herd, females, judging by their distended bellies, and we get near enough to see the motion of a chewing jaw, the twitch of an ear. A crow struts between the legs of one deer like a watchman on patrol.

"Reds," Connor murmurs, quietly to not disturb them. "Like up at . . . like you see around where I'm from."

He told me he grew up in Lanarkshire, south of Glasgow, and that his mother still lives there. In a strange way, his Scottishness brings comfort, given Varaig was where I met Scott and where he died, as if a part of Connor's identity is intertwined with Scott.

As we resume walking, Connor takes my hand. It's the first time he's done this. Up to now I've always been the one to make contact, leaning in to buss his cheek hello or touching him on the shoulder when we say goodbye. His hand is warm, his grip sure. My pulse beats in the center of my palm.

Later, on the high street, as the sun is fading, an older couple come toward us, man and woman, collars turned up against the chill spring evening. Both have had work done, but poor quality, too much filler pumped into cheeks and chin in a bid to win the war against gravity. Their faces look fragile, like dough on its second rise. I wonder whether they've overstretched the skin, if when the filler dissolves they'll be left saggy and wrinkled as deflated balloons. Will I always see what SKIN DEEP taught me to look for?

Once the couple has passed us, Connor mock shudders. We're walking abreast, still holding hands.

"Not your style?" I ask.

"No." A step, two. "You?"

"I've thought about it. Maybe one day."

He turns to me in surprise. "Really?"

"Not like that, though. Something more natural."

"Maybe that's what they said the first time." The way he says it, teasingly, I almost expect him to wink and I'm pleased he's less troubled. Finding the deer seems to have brought him back into himself.

We reach a pedestrian crossing and wait for the buses and cars to brake. On the other side of the road, the window of a men's clothing boutique emits a warm glow. Old-fashioned gold lettering on the window glass reads ARKWRIGHT GENTLEMEN'S OUTFITTERS, ESTD. 1879. When the green man lights up, Connor gives my hand a double squeeze. Time to move.

As we reach the far side, my attention is caught by a sweater on a mannequin in the shop window. Super-fine knit, a high V-neck. Fitted. Classic navy. I stop. Connor, pulled up short, comes back.

I point into the window. "What do you think of that?"

He lets go of me, jamming his hands deep into his jacket pockets and sniffing against the cold. "It's all right, I suppose. If you like that kind of thing."

"It'd suit you."

"You think?" He holds open the bottom of his jacket as if he's drawing apart curtains and looks down at his well-worn Nikes, his lived-in jeans.

The shop is still open—an assistant is tending to a customer. I loop my arm through Connor's and steer him toward the entrance. "Come on."

"Eh? Why?"

I open the door and a bell jangles. "Humor me."

He lets me tug him inside, where the shelves are made of mahogany and it smells of leather and beeswax and the heating is on max. He hovers on the doormat while I locate the rack of sweaters. They hang in a series, arranged with the smallest size at the front. I flick through to the design I want, pull out a large.

I slip it off its hanger. It is soft, cashmere. Holding it by the shoulders, I lay it over Connor's chest, pinning the wool to his frame with my fingers as if his body is a dressmaker's dummy. Looks like the right size, but it's hard to be sure. "Better take your jacket off." I drape the sweater over my arm and hold out a hand for his coat.

Reluctantly he unbuttons and swaps his jacket for the sweater, which he pulls on over his flannel shirt. "Way too small." He looks uncomfortable, his forehead wrinkled, mouth puckered.

"No, it's a fitted style. And your shirt is all caught up." I hang his jacket over a rack and go around him, tugging down the hem of his shirt. I've never been this close to him for this long or touched him this much. He is as rigid as a statue and I wonder whether I should stop. But I'm almost finished now. In front again, I straighten the neck of the sweater around the collar and run my hands across his chest to flatten the creases. "There. Perfect, don't you think?" I smooth once more, even though the wool is lying fine now. My fingertips pause at the outer points of his collarbones, my palms are on his pecs. I get a flashback to doing the same thing to Scott, on the sofa at Varaig. His heart beats, *dum dum*. I look up. His eyes have shifted to gunmetal.

The shop assistant comes over. He is in a full three-piece suit, with tie and pocket kerchief to match. Connor hoicks off the sweater so fast I hear the crick of static.

"What do you think?" the assistant says. "Would you like to take it?"

"I dunno." His cheeks have taken on high spots of color. I'm hot myself. It's furnace-like in here. Connor catches hold of the price tag hanging from the bottom. Whistles, from up to down. "Maybe if I win the lottery."

I return the sweater, warm with body heat, to the assistant. "Not this time. But thank you."

As we step outside, Connor shudders again, a real shiver this time, the kind that drains the color from his face and makes him retreat into his leather and sheepskin.

"Come on," I say. "Let's get out of this cold."

The next day I go back and buy the sweater for him. The same assistant is working. He remembers us and I get him to help me find trousers to match.

"And shoes?" he says.

He's right—the battered Nikes Connor wears wouldn't work with this. I go to the rack of leather lace-ups. I don't know his size, but he's the same height as Scott, and I think of Scott's shoes lined up next to mine in the mudroom, the number twelve printed inside still legible. I ask for the same.

"Any issues, you can bring them back," the assistant says as he wraps everything in layers of tissue paper.

When I take the Tube across town to meet Connor after his shift to go for Vietnamese food—he suggested burgers, but I'd decided something lighter would be better for our waistlines—I take the Arkwright bag with me.

"What's this?" he says when I hand it to him across the restaurant table.

"Couldn't help myself. Go on, open it."

Layers of tissue paper form a cloud over the menus. Sweater, trousers, and shoes nestle on top. He sits quietly, frowning, and I think he's going to say it's too much.

"They had a sale on," I lie. "Half off. No returns, unfortunately. So I hope it all fits." I loved lifting him out of his funk at the park yesterday—and if his gloom was to do with money worries, then that's something I can help with in this little way, thanks to Angela.

He packs everything carefully back into the bag and puts it on the floor. He seems to think, swallows. I wonder if he'll be too proud to accept. Perhaps he's never had someone try to take care of him. Finally he reaches across the table and threads his fingers through mine. "Thank you, Maddy, that's very thoughtful." There's disappointment in his face, as if I've failed him somehow. I look away—because what you can't see can't hurt you.

The atmosphere continues as we eat, a strange tension between us that hasn't been there before, and I decide I've blown it. But then, as we're back outside, dawdling over our good nights, I sense a shift in him and it makes me wonder whether I've been misreading what I sensed, if it wasn't tension but apprehension.

"My flatmate's away," he says, holding my eye.

Not even apprehension; anticipation. This time I'm the one who takes his hand.

It's not far from the restaurant to his street. The house is Edwardian, divided, like many in London, into two flats. Half the grandeur of a hundred years ago for fifty times the price. The front yard, overgrown with bushes, smells earthy. For a moment I stop, transported by the scent to another place.

"Are you okay?" Connor asks.

"Yes," I say, and realize I mean it.

I let him lead me up the garden path and into the house. From an inner hallway, where junk mail is piled high on a shelf, he starts up a wooden staircase that creaks as we climb. At the top, a box yeasty with empty beer bottles blocks the entrance. "Niall." Connor shoves it out of the way and unlocks the door. "Sorry. It's a bit of a mess."

The corridor inside is narrow, tunnel-like. Two bikes leaning against a radiator make it hard to pass. We reach a tiny kitchen. He goes in and picks up the kettle. "Tea?"

You Brits think a cup of tea will solve anything. Just once, I wish he'd suggest wine. "Sure. Thanks."

There isn't enough room for me to join him in the kitchen so I stay by the door. Connor moves in the gymnastic way I'd noticed in the coffee shop, familiar within the limits of his space and sure in his body. He fills the kettle, putting it on to boil, and tosses teabags into mugs. I survey the kitchen, taking in the clean dishes piled up to dry, the pans hanging from the ceiling, a rack of herbs, a bill stuck on the fridge door, urgent demand highlighted in red. Either he or Niall likes to cook; either he or Niall is not so good with money. *Everyone judges.*

"Ach, I forgot, there's no milk," he says. "How about lemon and honey instead?"

"If that's what you're having."

He pulls a lemon from a fruit bowl. "The living room's at the end on the left. Take a seat. I'll bring them through."

The living room is medium-sized, painted fashionably dark, with stripped floorboards and a cast-iron fireplace. The curtains are open, and a streetlight right outside bathes everything orange. That, plus fairy lights, bunched and glowing in the grate, make the room feel cozy, almost as if a fire is burning.

The mantelpiece is being used to display a collection of photos book-ended by bottles of whiskey. One picture is a recent snap of Connor and Niall, the guy he co-owns the coffee shop and rents the flat with, the guy

I'd seen the day I tracked Connor down from the taxi receipt. They have their arms around each other's shoulders. I haven't met Niall yet, but I know they're close. Then there's a younger Niall with, judging by the resemblance, his parents and sisters, looking relaxed somewhere sunny. In a third photo a small boy in Wellingtons and a huge dog grin in front of a farmhouse. The boy has a thatch of hair, a heart-shaped face.

A chink of china, and Connor comes in. "Oh, sorry, we need light."

"It's all right," I say. "I like it like this." I pick up the third photo. "Is this you?"

"Oh. Yeah."

"Big dog. Bigger than you."

"Aye. When we . . ." He puts the drinks on a coffee table and goes to a bookshelf in the far corner. "When we rescued him we had no idea how big he'd grow. Good thing we had plenty of space." While talking, he flips another photo frame face down, one I missed. He tries for nonchalance, but his movements are too fast. What is it—a picture of an ex he'd forgotten to remove?

He indicates a pair of pre-loved sofas. "Why don't you, ah, why don't you have a seat?"

He's nervous again. He watches me replace the photo of him as a kid on the mantelpiece. It's intense, his gaze, almost too much. Once more I feel tugged by a sense of inevitability, but there's still that struggle inside me between want and resistance. I think I'm afraid of moving things forward because of what I would have to leave behind. Suddenly, I need a drink. I lift a bottle of whiskey from the mantel. "Do you mind?"

"Go ahead."

I add a good measure to my tea. "Want some?"

"No thanks."

I take a swallow, realizing as the boozy sweetness scalds my throat that I've made myself a hot toddy. I push away the memory. It's bound to be like this, moving on, the past rearing up uninvited. I need to focus on the present.

I sit on one of the sofas. Connor comes to perch on the edge of the coffee table in front of me. Absently he scratches the inside of his wrist.

I reach for his hand and turn it palm up, exposing the tattoo. I haven't seen it properly before; it's usually covered by his sleeve. It's a black feather, curved as if coming to rest after floating through the air. I run the tip of my finger along its vane, halfway up his forearm. His skin is uniform; I can't feel the ink at all. "It's beautiful. Does it mean something?"

"It's for family." He starts to pull down his cuff, as if he's embarrassed. "For my brother."

"I didn't know you have a brother."

"Had."

God, to lose a brother. It's awful enough with a parent, but for some-one who should have a long, full life ahead of them to die . . . well, I un-derstand that, too.

Connor is struggling to do up the button on his sleeve. I place my fingers over his to still them. He lets me part the cuff opening. The detail on the feather is extraordinary. It must have taken a long time. I imagine him gritting his teeth against the pain. "How old was he?"

"Not old enough. But he was ill for a long time and we knew it was coming."

Even worse, if he was just a child. Connor is looking at me in a way I can't interpret, almost a challenge. Unsure of how to respond, I finish the drink. He takes the empty mug from me, places it to one side, cups my knees.

"Maddy," he says. "I know we haven't known each other long . . ."

We're close enough that I can make out the flecks in his irises. His shirt is open at the neck, exposing a smooth hollow between his collarbones. I bring a hand to his cheek. Bristles prickle my palm. He starts, as if he hadn't expected me to do that, then half smiles, and I stroke the clear skin above with my thumb. He mirrors the tiny movement against my thighs. "It feels a lot longer," I say.

His hands still. His cheek flattens. His eyes grow serious. He looks at my lips and my insides flip, reacting with the intoxicating mix of dread and delight I've been feeling all night and every time I've been near him, ever since I walked up to the counter in his coffee shop—longer, even: ever since I first saw him.

The atmosphere changes, as if a door has opened. Things coalesce. He leans in and kisses me.

In his room, the shock of discovering a new body is like stepping onto unmapped land: the unfamiliar roughness of his beard against the skin of my neck and around my mouth; the unexpected bunch of muscle above the waistband of his jeans. Hair, thick in my hands, falls onto my face. I try telling myself I'm noticing the differences because it's someone new, yet still it stalls me.

"It's okay," he says when I draw away. "We don't have to."

I stay the night and when I wake in the morning the thin light is coming in at the same angle it had at Angela's house. Connor is lying on his side with his back to me, long ridges of muscle framing the valley of his spine. In sleep I've moved close, so that my mouth is almost touching the space between his shoulder blades. For a moment, in the familiar light and the white sheets, I think I'm there, then, with Scott. He even smells the same. Then I realize.

I flip onto my other side. The Arkwright bag stands on the floor by the wardrobe, sides bulging, the clothes still inside, unworn. I flip again onto my back and stare at the ceiling. He isn't Scott, much as I want him to be, and it isn't fair to keep comparing them.

I roll to face him. There's only a foot or so of sheet between us now. I drape an arm over his waist. He doesn't stir. I shuffle closer, close enough to feel the warmth emanating from him, yet keep my distance. I focus on the weave of the thread on the pillow fabric, the weft going in one direction and the warp the other, opposing tensions pulling the fragile threads into shape, forming them into purpose. I close my eyes. Only once they are firmly shut do I nuzzle up to his skin.

28

"YOU LOOK DIFFERENT," SACHA SAYS WHEN I MEET HER FOR lunch in a restaurant in Soho a couple of days later.

"So do you." The pink hair is gone, back to black, cut neat. She's wearing glasses with thick frames, a silk shirt, and culottes—pretty sharp for a weekend.

"Oh, this," she says, with a dismissive shrug. "Promotion coming up. It's me against four men. Thought I ought to start toeing the line, dress the part."

She, Angela, Singh in his perfect tailoring. They're all dressing the part—maybe that's why they're so successful. "It suits you," I say. She looks professional. More than that—she looks powerful. Nevertheless, for a moment I miss the pink hair, the days when we'd go out in our matching sweatshirts.

"Let's not talk about me, let's talk about you. What's changed?" She pulls me into the light. "Don't tell me . . ." She gasps. "You went for the needle!"

I laugh. "No!"

Her eyes go even wider. "The guy you asked out? That's still on?"

My neck and cheeks heat at the realization that I've been so caught up I haven't seen her, haven't filled her in properly on Connor. "Yep."

She unhooks her glasses and pretends to appraise me. "Well, that's some postcoital glow."

Fancy outfit aside, she's the same as ever—straight to the point. But Sacha has it so together, with her job, with Monique, that I don't want to admit that Connor and I haven't got to that stage yet. I need a moment to edit my version of the story.

I look down. The restaurant table is covered in paperwork.

"Sorry." Sacha starts tidying. "Work's mad."

I help, picking up a stack of pages and aligning them by tapping the edges against the wooden tabletop. For some reason I think about trees, how both the table and the paper come from the same source but couldn't be more different, one solid and substantial, the other flimsy, fragile. Although, being Sacha's work, these pages are far from lightweight; they're freighted with money, power, influence. It doesn't pay to mistake slightness for insignificance. And me, too—I've built a career, a life, around pieces of printed paper.

Two names on a page catch my eye: Scott De Luca and Angela Reynolds. The room shifts. "You never said you were still working for Angela."

She takes the paper from my fingers, slots it into a folder, and closes the cover before I can read any more. "Yeah. There's been a lot to sort out. After, you know . . ."

"After Scott's suicide."

She sighs, relieved I can say it. I suppose that's why she hasn't talked about work with me since. "Yeah. We had to redo a lot of what we did before. Although—and I feel like such a cow thinking this—it has made things easier."

"What do you mean?"

"Well, he wasn't exactly supportive of the Singh merger, was he?"

She says this as if I already know, as if Scott and I spent hours talking business. We talked anything but business; I knew almost nothing about the merger, other than the fact there was going to be one, until the launch— and it was Sacha who told me that. God, maybe I should have asked him about it. If he was worrying and we'd talked things through, perhaps I could have released the pressure valve.

"She asks after you, you know," Sacha says. "Angela." Clocking my expression, she hastens to add, "Don't worry, I haven't said anything to her about you and him. I think she just feels responsible for putting you in that situation, sending you up there when he wasn't well."

Sacha never knew Scott had a drinking problem. I asked her after he died. Another example of Angela's discretion. "What do you tell her?"

"That you're fine. Because you are, aren't you? Now."

First Angela calls me, now this. It's odd, like she's keeping tabs. If she is, her concern is a bit too late. Because yes, I am basically fine. "I threw away the chart," I tell Sacha.

She presses her lips together in a smile and nods. *I knew you'd get there*, it means. The last of the papers get crammed into her briefcase. "Anyway, let's talk about something else. I want to hear more about you and this new man." She locks the case and calls over a waiter. "Let's eat. I'm starving, aren't you?"

"Where are you headed?" I ask her once lunch is over and we're outside.

"Mayfair. Reynolds office." She's able to be straightforward because she knows she doesn't have to be careful around me anymore.

"On a Saturday?"

"You know Angela."

That explains the work gear. "I hope you're billing her double."

"As if. More."

I link my arm through hers. "Come on, I'll walk partway with you."

At the corner near the RRX office, about where the recycling sacks stood waiting for collection, we unloop arms and hug goodbye. She is wearing the perfume she's worn every day since she was twenty-two. I breathe in her familiar scent. "Say hi to Monique for me."

"I will."

"Don't work too hard."

"I will." Sacha wouldn't be Sacha if she didn't. She heads for the black door.

I'm setting off for Green Park Tube when I see a person sitting on the doorstep of the next building, a young woman, knapsack on her knees. Her mustard-colored cap sends a shock through me before I register the long hair beneath isn't dark red but a white blond. Probably a thousand girls own that same hat. Then we lock eyes and recognition passes between us.

She's on her feet in a flash, slinging the knapsack over her shoulder and hurrying to the road.

"Hey, wait!" I check for Sacha, for confirmation that this girl really is here, that she can see her, too, but she's already inside.

In that moment, the girl has got ten or so yards ahead. I start after her. She glances over her shoulder and increases her pace to a jog, then a run.

I speed up. "Wait!" Should I be chasing her? Is it even the same person? We're attracting attention, but no one cares enough to interfere. She's quick but, conditioned by all the gym training, I'm faster.

I catch hold of her arm and she wheels around, all pumped up and ready to fight. Her eyes are wide open, a shockingly iridescent green, her nostrils flared. And I almost let go because she *is* the girl from Varaig, from the launch—the hair has changed color and her mouth is different, lips plumped with fillers, but she's the one, I know from the skittishness—and for a moment I think, what if I was right all along, what if she killed him, what will she do to me? But a drive stronger than fear makes me maintain my grip. And then something in her seems to give in.

"What do you want?" American accent.

"Answers. Who are you? Why are you here?" She doesn't reply. Here, Varaig, the launch—that's too many coincidences. "You were at the house." A movement in the mist, handprints on the glass. "You were watching us. Why?" She averts her face. "I saw you! I know you were there. Are you watching me now?" I'm almost shouting, but she continues to cower. I shake her arm. "For God's sake, tell me."

She stares at where my fingers are clutching her sleeve. I'm hurting her. A pedestrian, an older woman, looks at me sharply and the admonishment pulls me back into myself. She's just a girl. She's not the reason Scott jumped. I release her arm, fully accepting she will make a break for it, but she stays. She rubs the spot where I gripped her.

"Sorry," I say. "I didn't mean to—"

"It's all right. I shouldn't have run. And I wasn't watching you. Or him. Although it was kinda hard to miss you, in that house. It was her I wanted."

"Who?"

She rubs her arm again. "Dr. Reynolds."

There's spite in the way she says the name. I consider her altered lips, her eyes, her hair. A groupie, camping out for an appointment? I take in her clothes. Athleisure and a too-thin jacket. Her shoes are canvas, the rubber soles grimy, the laces frayed. She doesn't seem a likely candidate for Reynolds RX. She doesn't seem like she could afford it.

It starts to rain, hard, almost as hard as it did that day in Varaig. Her shoulders freckle with raindrops, and quickly the freckles swell and merge. She slides the strap of her knapsack off her shoulder. Made of hemp, it is not waterproof. Opening her jacket, she tucks the bag inside, trying to keep the contents dry.

I don't know what's going on here. But I do know that she's connected to Varaig. She may have seen things I didn't; she might be able to help me understand what I missed. A glance at the sky tells me the rain is not going to stop anytime soon. Across the street is a café. "Look, we can't stay out here. Will you come with me, over there?"

There's every chance she'll say no. She stands, thinking, while rain runs down her face. Finally she nods, tiny. I take her elbow—gently this time—and lead her across the road.

"I only wanted to talk to her," she says after we've peeled off our wet coats and slung them like hides around the backs of our chairs.

Now that I know it wasn't me she was watching, my anger has dissipated a little, replaced by curiosity. I move the salt and pepper shakers and the napkin dispenser out of the way, so there's clear space between us. Nothing to hide behind.

"Do you know her? Are you a client or a friend or . . . ?" I trail off. If she was either she wouldn't have been loitering outside Angela's country house and office. "Are you . . ." There's no easy way to ask someone if they're a stalker.

She's saved from answering by the interruption of a waiter. I order coffee; she wants tea.

"Do you have herbal?" she asks, and I'm struck by the way she pronounces it: "er-boll," no *h*. A simple word, in a common language, yet it sounds so different. When she places her order—"Peppermint, please"—I remember how polite she was when I'd seen her up at Varaig.

We wait in awkward silence until the drinks come, each pretending to be fascinated by the rain. It is a proper April shower; on the street, pedestrians huddle under umbrellas or pull the yokes of their coats up over their heads like capes. I try to get a good look at the girl without being too obvious. Now that the shock of spotting her has worn off a little, I don't consider her a threat, and from the way she agreed to come in here, I suppose she doesn't view me as one, either. She's taken off her cap and on the top of her head there's an inch-wide demarcation line in her hair: before bleach and after bleach. I'd hazard her natural color was mousy blond. Under the café lights, her eyes are vivid, luminous. I didn't get particularly close to her in Scotland, but I don't remember them looking like this. They seem larger than life, doll-like, Disneyfied. Oversized colored contacts, I'd guess. Her skin is clear and she carries the vestiges of baby fat in her cheeks. Her makeup is heavy, all brows and contouring. It's an attempt to appear more grown-up but it has the opposite effect because it looks like she's trying too hard to be someone she is yet to grow into.

Once the waiter has come and gone again, I say, "Why were you watching Angela?"

"Waiting for."

"Waiting, then."

She dunks her teabag by its string, lifting and lowering, and tannins leach out of the leaves, swirling dark in the water.

I try again. "How long were you *waiting* for Angela in Scotland? What do you want to talk to her about?"

A set silence. This is a waste of time. She's not going to tell me anything. I push away my cup and stand, preparing to leave.

But maybe she wants me to stay longer, because she says, "I'm sorry he died."

The old fear rises. "What do mean you're sorry?" I am so sharp that other customers in the café look over.

"No reason."

"Did you have something to do with it?"

"No!" Her eyes bloom. "I didn't mean anything by it. I heard, at that fancy party. I didn't know him, but it's always sad to hear a stranger has passed, makes me sorry for the people they've left behind. And for me—it makes me think about my gramma. She passed when I was twelve. Like, you hear a person you literally never even met has died and some of your feelings from when someone you loved passed come back. That's the worst part of it, don't you think? Of dying?"

Her emotional acuity knocks me off my feet and back into my chair. Scott, Mum. Compounding, compacting. This girl is not connected to his death. I'm looking for someone to blame—someone else. "Look . . ." I don't know her name.

"Evie."

"Help me out here, Evie. Because I sure as hell have no idea what's going on, why you were hanging around Angela's house for . . ."

"Three weeks."

"You're kidding me."

"Who are you, anyway?" she asks. "Do you work for her?"

"I did. I was writing a book."

"That's why you were at the computer all those times." When she sees my face, she has the good sense to look ashamed. "Just so you know, I did feel guilty at first, seeing you guys, but it was so quiet out there and I was lonely. It was kinda like TV, you moving from room to room."

That nasty skin-creeping exposed feeling comes back. What was worth making me feel that way? "Then why do it?"

"I told you."

"Right. You wanted to talk to Angela. Most people would call, send an email, go to her office and knock on the door." Most *normal* people.

"You don't think I tried that? I couldn't get past her assistant." She fidgets with the label stapled to the string of her teabag. "So I went through the recycling outside her office. I lucked out—found a bunch of grocery receipts for an address in Varaig. I took a bus to Scotland, then a couple more. I thought I might stand a better chance of getting to her there."

This is making little sense. Why would a groupie, or fan, or whatever she is, go to such effort? "But Angela was barely in Scotland. She was overseas."

"She was there. I saw her car, two or three times, down by the lake."

She must be thinking of Raphaela coming to collect the dogs. And what did she mean by "getting to"? Does she mean Angela harm? I take out my phone. "How about we call Angela now?"

She shrinks back. "No!"

"Why not?"

"I'm not ready."

"What do you need to be ready for? You say you want to talk, so talk.

What exactly is it you want from her?" I'm not sure why I'm being protective of Angela. She doesn't need my protection. And certainly not from a kid.

Evie doesn't answer because she's distracted by her knapsack, as if only now remembering how wet it had got. She lifts it from the floor onto her lap and levers back the flap, easing a drawstring on top. She inhales audibly, panicky, and pulls out a small notebook. It's a cheap type, bound in cardboard, and the cover has absorbed water like shredded wheat. When she sees the damage she practically dives into the bag, frantically searching. Her hand stills. She closes her eyes in thankful prayer. Clearly something she feared ruined by the rain is okay.

Slowly, she draws out an object wrapped in a plastic bag. She peels off the wrapping. Inside is a tube, the kind used for sending posters in the mail. She pops the lid and slides out a scroll, which she lays gently in her lap before moving our drinks to one side of the table and taking a few paper napkins from the holder to wipe the melamine dry.

Carefully, she unfurls the scroll, stretching both arms long to stop the paper from springing back. As soon as I see a narrow strip of watery paint, I know what it is she's showing me, but I stay quiet until the whole thing has been unrolled. A farmhouse, a winding path, gentle hills.

She was the intruder. I'm not even surprised—I think I knew that from when I saw her on the street. Yet the mind-movie doesn't start playing. It hasn't since the inquest.

"Why did you take it?"

She slides a palm across the scene and extends a finger until the tip of her nail is pointing at the signature. "Angela Reynolds isn't who she says she is." She taps her finger, drawing my attention. It's a scrawl and from this angle all I can make out is an *L*. She looks at me expectantly, as if she's asked a question I'm supposed to already know the answer to. "This farm is where I grew up. This is where she left me."

"Left you? Sorry, Evie, I'm not following here."

Again she taps the signature, but I don't know what it is she wants me to see.

Her eyes, when I look up, are frightening in their intensity. "Angela Reynolds is my mother." She breaks away to tap at the farm. "This is where she abandoned me. And now I want her to pay for what she did."

29

THIS IS NONSENSE. "ANGELA DOESN'T HAVE ANY KIDS."

"Doesn't have or says she doesn't have?" Evie sounds like Sacha, or even like Angela herself. "Just because she tells people so doesn't make it the truth."

Is she playing me? She lets go of the painting and meets my scrutiny straight on. Innocent? Or good at acting innocent? I don't know. With the contacts, the puffy lips, and the way the makeup redraws the lines of her face, it's hard to find a resemblance. Possibly, in the point of the chin. But that's hardly proof. In the silence that has fallen between us, I can hear the scuffing sound the paper makes as it tries to re-form its rolled shape. How quickly things adapt when forced into new circumstances.

"Why should I believe the word of a thief?"

Her face darkens. "I'm not a thief."

I indicate the painting. "I beg to differ."

"This isn't stolen. It belongs to me, to my family. My grampa painted it. This is the farm where I grew up, where she abandoned me. My house, my dog—well, her dog. And it isn't valuable."

She's telling the truth about that, at least. And something about the way she references the farm feels real, natural. Still . . . "I'm not sure I should trust anything you say."

"Why not? Don't you normally believe what people tell you? You don't seem like the suspicious type. And you believed Angela about not having a kid."

"Yes, but why wouldn't I?"

One groomed eyebrow lifts in a silent *Exactly.*

Point taken. She's clever. "How old are you, anyway?"

"Twenty."

The right age to be Angela's daughter. But that doesn't mean much in itself—it's the right age to be anyone's daughter. Even mine. She pulls the landscape toward her across the table. It clearly means a lot to her; I sense she was happy there. If she ever was there. Lord, this is confusing.

"Look," she says. "I'll give you the short version. If you don't believe me after, that's your problem."

Not really. But at the same time I'm also understanding that somehow, in a way that isn't yet fully clear, it *is* my problem. I nod to say go ahead.

The way she pauses, casting around as if trying to find the best way into her story, reminds me of Scott. In the end, her eyes settle on her bag. She produces a contact lens case and a bottle of solution. She unscrews the two lids of the case, squirts in solution, and brings her thumb and finger to her eye without using a mirror. I try not to flinch. A slide, a pinch, and a disc of green is floating in the case. Once removed, the lens loses all context. No longer an eye, it is merely a striated green plastic disc with a hole at the center. A window to the soul, easily faked.

When she's removed the other lens she makes eye contact, and I understand why she took them out. Her natural irises are extremely, unusually pale.

"She keeps it quiet, *me* quiet," Evie says, switching her attention to the sleeves of her sweater, which she tugs down over her hands. "Maybe she's ashamed of me because she was kicked out of college when she got knocked up. A mistake, dumped with her parents to raise. I was, like, three?" She phrases this as a question, as if checking, but all this is news to me. She carries on. "My memories of her, they're faded, but she didn't seem like some cruel monster, like someone who could ditch her daughter. She seemed loving."

Anger, righteousness, empathy, nostalgia: her emotions and moods are changing too quickly for me to keep up. I indicate the painting. "You grew up there?"

She unrolls it again. Fingertips, the nails chewed right down, emerge from a cuff to stroke the farmhouse. The brush marks are soft, rendering the walls and roof timeworn. "Not at the beginning. At the beginning, I was with her. We were in a city. Portland, Gramps said. In this tiny apartment. Me, her, and the dog Gramma gave her for her sweet sixteenth, Mikey. There was a woman downstairs—she used to babysit me all the time. I can't remember her name, but I do remember her curly hair, her tickly sweaters. Her breath always smelled of Juicy Fruit. I'd try to catch the bubble when she popped her gum."

Portland tallies with what I know of Angela's past, of her studies in Oregon. But it's a pretty big city—in no way a cincher. "Hang on, you say she got kicked out of college when she was pregnant with you?"

She senses my mistrust and becomes defensive. "Yeah. Her financial aid was withdrawn the semester of her finals."

"But Angela's finals were in 2001. And if you're twenty, that would make you born in, what, 1998?"

"Ninety-nine. January fifteenth." She doesn't like my implying that she's lying. Her brows lower in a scowl. Her swollen lips, unable to pucker, pout out. "You want to see my driver's license?"

Before I can say no, she's popping the license out of the back of her phone case and slapping it on top of the painting, turned the right way for me to read the lettering. Evelyn Juliane Reynolds. DOB 1/15/99.

She scrabbles to pick it up. "Look, maybe I have some of the details wrong. All this is what Gramps told me. What I do know is that she abandoned me to move to the far side of the country to be a doctor again."

"Abandoned" is pretty harsh. "What exactly do you mean," I say, "by abandoned?"

She jerks back, releasing the painting. "What do *you* mean what do I mean? *Abandoned*—you know, as in she left and never came back. As in I never saw her again."

Her teeth are bared, defensive. This is nothing like the nervous young woman I came across in Scotland. I raise my palms in surrender. "Look, you have to see it from my point of view. I knew none of this. What about your dad?"

Another glare, a tilt back on her chair until it is balanced on two legs. She is the epitome of a defensive suspect. "Didn't have one."

"Me neither."

That disarms her. She returns her chair to horizontal. "But I bet your mom didn't abandon you."

"No. At least not until the end. And that did feel like an abandoning."

"End?"

"She died."

"Oh." She's guileless; her eyes are immediately huge with sorrow. "I'm sorry."

There they are again, those empty words. Nonetheless, a lump has formed in my throat. I was twenty-five—only a few years older than she is now. So young for that to have happened. I reach for my coffee, but it's cold.

"Do you miss her?" Evie's voice is small.

"Every single day."

"Yeah." She scratches the side of her nose. "Can I ask you something?"

Don't let it be about Mum's cancer. "Okay."

"Can you . . . can you see her in me?" Her voice rises in hope. For the first time since she started her story, she seems unsure of herself.

"I don't know . . ." If she wants to resemble Angela, why has she done all this to herself? It's not easy to tell what she might look like without all the artifice. Or who. "Maybe."

She drops into herself, shoulders sinking, corners of her overfilled mouth turning down. "You still don't believe me."

I don't know what to believe, but I don't entirely disbelieve her. Trying to stop me from unearthing an unwanted child could explain why Angela was so sketchy about her past when I was researching SKIN DEEP. But it's not like Evie would have made it into the book against Angela's will. She could have cut her out.

Evie snatches up the watercolor and rolls it. "I'm not making this up. My whole life I've been waiting for her, asking about her, looking for her. Gramma and Gramps told me there was no point, she wasn't coming back, but I couldn't help it. I wish I couldn't remember her, but I can, although it's like shadow memories, real vague. Nothing I can grasp hold of, but it's like the memories left holes in me, these Mom-shaped holes and worries, like what if I was such a bratty kid that she couldn't handle it? What if it was my fault that she left? And never came back? I mean, she took Mikey with her."

"Mikey?"

"The goddamn dog." She tries to push the painting inside its tube, but it's not rolled tightly enough. "That's just dumb kid thoughts, right? Whatever." The scroll has slipped and loosened into a cone shape. There's no way it'll go back in now. Frustrated, she throws both picture and container onto the table.

"Here," I say. "Let me." I reroll the paper, making sure it can't spring loose.

Evie looks out the window at the rain. "When I was ten I found a letter she sent to my grandparents. I hid it in my room and every so often I'd take it out and read it. I read that letter so many times it was transparent along the seams where it was folded. I knew the address by heart. In London. London! She had to put five thousand miles between us." Not wanting to say anything to disturb her flow, I hold out my free hand for the tube. She passes it to me. "When we got a computer, I looked for her online. There wasn't much on her."

I slot the painting into its holder. "I know."

"Every year on my birthday I emailed her at her company. She never replied. When I was old enough, when I'd saved enough for the flight, I went to London. There was someone else living at the address by then. They'd never heard of her."

The poor girl. She hasn't had a lot of luck. I hand her the painting.

"Thanks." She considers the tube. "You nearly caught me, you know. With this. He closed the kitchen window and then you came back and I had to hide in a bedroom."

So when Scott and I were kissing and we heard the front door beep, that was Evie, sneaking out. God, I was so scared. I remember the footprints in the kitchen. "You were in the house more than once?"

She drops her eyes to the floor. "Only a couple times. I was hungry—my hostel was so far away, and sometimes I was waiting all day. And . . ."

The missing food. "You weren't staying in the bothy?"

"The what?"

"The cottage down by the loch."

"No. I tried to get in, but the door was locked so I couldn't. And there was a guy there anyway."

"What guy?"

"I don't know, some janitor or whatever. You know. I saw him up at your house a couple times."

She must mean the grocery delivery men—maybe they got the address wrong again. She considers her wet shoes, sticking a foot out from beneath the table. Damp tidemarks are creeping along the canvas. "At home I hike all the time. I didn't know it would be so much harder in Scotland."

Suddenly I join two dots. "You stole the boots as well, didn't you?"

"Borrowed, is all. I couldn't get back in the house so I left them where you'd find them." Her cheeks are pink. She angles her face away from me, in the same way she had when I confronted her in the street. "It was so wet up there, and slippery, and these were the only shoes I had."

I know from my chart research that the nearest hostel is twelve miles away. She would have had to take a long bus ride every day, walk for at least an hour each way. She must have been committed. Or desperate.

"What will you say to Angela?" I ask. "When you see her?"

"I don't know. I got close to her a couple times here in London last month but I chickened out and hid. I wasn't ready. And I don't think I'll be sure what to say until I am ready."

She is hugging the painting tube to her chest, holding it tight like a protective totem or a talisman. I nod at it. "Could the painting be your opening? Email her and tell her you have it and you want to give it back?"

"Then she'll know I stole it." She says this small, almost scared, doe-like again.

"I think she already does."

"How?"

"I think she must have recognized you on CCTV." Maybe that's why Angela never contacted the police. Somehow, without Evie having actively convinced me, I've started to accept her story. There's been no one big revelation, but it's as if multiple tiny truths are worth more. Like she said, why wouldn't you trust what someone tells you if there's con-viction in their words?

She is quiet, daydreaming, I sense, about a reunion. Things must not play out well, because she snaps to and stands hurriedly. She unhooks her jacket from the back of her chair, swinging it out so she can thread her arms inside.

There's one final thing I want to know before she leaves. "Evie?"

"Yeah?"

"When you were watching the house, did you ever see anything? To do with Scott, I mean? His state of mind?"

"I came back to London while you guys were both still there, if that's what you mean." I notice she's diplomatic, doesn't say "while he was still alive."

"But before that. You ever see him drinking? Like while I was working?"

"No." She slips on the knapsack straps and tucks her thumbs under them. The mustard cap goes back on her head. She pulls the ends of her hair to lie neatly, if damply, forward. "He seemed like a regular guy to me. Real goofy around those dogs. He used to play with them so much. They were the same kind as Mikey. And real goofy around you, too."

She's trying to be kind, but it still hurts, hearing this. Even so, it is a release, knowing that I wasn't the only one who couldn't see his struggle.

After Evie has headed out into the damp Westminster afternoon, having agreed to swap numbers, I stay a while in the café, staring at my phone. I pull up Scott's Instagram account, examining the tiles for signs of . . . I'm not sure what. Social media is only ever full of half-truths, the lives on display edited to reveal only part of the whole, to keep the grubby, boring, or less palatable things firmly off camera. It is like putting your eye to a telescope, blacking out everything except for that small, bright circle someone has preordained you may see. As I look at Scott's grid—coffee cup, tide lines on a beach, leaves on a tree—I'm reminded of the children's puzzle, the one where you slide plastic tiles in a frame, trying to complete the picture. The thing is, even when you finish, it's never whole. There is always a tile missing—has to be, in order to allow the other pieces of the jigsaw to move around. Without that missing piece, you wouldn't be able to play.

I call Angela. I don't want to be caught in the middle of a family drama that has nothing to do with me. I won't take sides, I'll let her know what's happened and step away. She and Evie can solve it between themselves.

"Madeleine. What can I do for you?" I'm Maddy no longer. Her careful formality is far removed from the upbeat quality of her last call to me.

I give her an edited version, telling her someone has contacted me, claiming to be her daughter. I wonder if she'll take the opportunity to be honest at last. Maybe I'll even be able to play a part in bringing them together again.

She laughs, loosely, musically. "Oh, I'm sorry you've been caught up in that. She's a young woman with issues—self-esteem, identity, mental health, you know." She puts emphasis on "mental health." "I'm not sure quite what it is she wants. I've never met her, but I've spoken to her guardian and they reassured me she means no harm. There's nothing to be concerned about, but if she contacts you again, do let me know."

"Right." It's a story that might make sense—if I hadn't already spent so much time talking to Evie.

"Is there anything else I can help you with?"

I could challenge her lie, but it's not my business if she wants to disown her kid. Cruel, but nothing to do with me. "No."

"Okay, then, if that's all."

Maybe it was Evie mentioning the recycling, but as Angela winds up the call, my mind jumps to the copies of SKIN DEEP ready for pulping. "Actually yes, there is something else. I was curious why the book was never launched. I mean, we hit the printer deadline, didn't we?"

"Yes, we did. But then . . ." She pauses. "Well, you must understand, with all the changes to the company, and after Scott's death, it wasn't appropriate."

"No, I can see that." A sliding, in my brain; a connecting. "But you knew the company changes were coming and you didn't ask me to factor them in. And you pulled it before the launch."

"Sorry?"

"You must have decided to pull the book before the launch, because there weren't any copies at the hotel. But you didn't get the call about Scott's death until during the party."

"Yes." Another pause. "Yes, that's right. And I'm glad you asked me that, Madeleine, because it gives me the opportunity to tell you that you were absolutely correct. It *did* need another draft. I realized that when

I saw the printed copies. And I must apologize for not listening to you earlier. But sometimes you don't realize things until you see them with your own eyes, do you?"

Another half-formed thought pulls at me, like Connor squeezing my hand, one, two, let's go. "By the way, Angela, did the police ever find that stolen painting?"

She hesitates. "Do you know, they did. When they were there, after you left, after Scott died. They found it in his room. Some strange prank apparently. I mean, he wasn't quite in his right mind, was he? You know— you saw." With that, she says goodbye.

Somehow it all keeps circling back to this: what I saw; what I didn't see. Two sides of a tossed coin. Not long ago, probably even earlier today, her bringing it back on me like this would have hit home. Yet Evie's last assertion is protecting me like armor. More than that—it's making me think.

Angela's making up a cover story about Evie I can understand; pulling the book I can't prove. But the painting turning up was an outright fabrication. Why lie about that? Most all of it makes me wonder—what else has she lied about? And what does she have to hide?

30

"HI," CONNOR SAYS, OPENING HIS FRONT DOOR. "SORRY, I'M ONLY just back and I need to shower."

"Go ahead," I say. "I can wait." This party, a fortieth for one of his friends, will be the first time a date's extended beyond the two of us and I'm not yet sure how I feel about going official, emerging from our private cocoon. He kisses me on the cheek. He smells of coffee and hard work.

I wait for him in his bedroom, sitting on his bed, listening to him whistling in the bathroom. He's a good whistler, tuneful. To kill time, I flick through Instagram. Sacha has posted a photo of herself on a set of stone steps, a candid shot taken, I presume, by Monique, who is tagged. Her face is tilted up and lit with happiness, the kind that radiates from within, no filter needed.

I heart the image and comment: You are glooow-ing.

She replies in a message. That's what happens when you're in love. She adds a brown heart.

Next in my feed is a beauty influencer called Zara demoing the SRX Elixir. She is gorgeous and sleek, of indeterminate ethnicity, her face angled yet soft, hair pulled back with not a strand out of place, bare skin poreless and blemish-free. She is what every woman wishes she saw when she looked in the mirror. Zara shows the vial to her camera and wiggles it, then pipettes a couple of drops and rubs her palms together. A pop-up captions reads "Warm to activate." She applies the serum to her cheeks in long strokes from mouth to temple, like a soldier applying war paint, then blends with her fingertips, lifting upward and outward. Finished, she angles one side of her face to the camera, then the other. Another caption pops up: "Perfection." The reel ends with her best side to the lens.

Zara looks amazing, but she must be twenty-seven at most and who knows how much laser resurfacing or moisturizing Profhilo injections she's had. I'd like to see the Elixir used on a normal person my age or more, maybe trialed on only one side of their face for a full six months for a real comparison. But I guess that wouldn't sell. Skin care is a market in which people are as willing to buy into the promise as into the results.

I'm not sure when I became so cynical. When Angela gave me her speech about youth and beauty and death, I believed it. But so much has changed since then. And even though Angela's got nothing to do with me now, meeting Evie has made the old itch come back and I can't shake the feeling that I'm missing something.

I log out of Instagram and plug Angela Reynolds into Google, adding the usual clarifiers. On LinkedIn a new line has appeared above Reynolds RX: "Co-CEO, SRX (Singh-Reynolds) Cosmeceuticals and Clinics, 2018–present." On the doctors' register, SRX hasn't been added to Angela's entry yet—I suppose because the merger is still to be legally completed. I'm about to click out when "Primary medical qualification" catches my eye: 1993–2001, the University of Beaverbrook, Oregon. Evie told me Angela was kicked out in 1998, that that was her final year. I think about what Jon Prosser said, about inconsistencies. Is this what he meant? Maybe I could call him again.

Connor comes through from the shower, a towel around his hips, wet hair raked roughly back with his fingers. He gives me a quick damp kiss, then goes to his wardrobe. A triple, it takes up the whole wall. The doors are mirrored and I watch his reflection as he rootles through the low drawers, taking out underwear. With his hair back from his face like that he's more like Scott. My heart misfires. I sit up.

He opens the wardrobe door and the reflection is gone. The back of his waist tapers as he leans forward. Higher up, his back muscles flash, appearing under the skin, fading, reappearing as he flicks through the shirts, deciding what to wear to the party. He gets to the end of the rod and goes through it again. Half closing the door, he bends to his laundry basket.

He's lost weight recently and the skin above his towel creases as he digs around. I like him leaner, like the way it makes his body more familiar. He pulls out a shirt, sniffs it, sighs, chucks it back in.

He senses me looking. "Sorry," he says over his shoulder. "I promise I won't be much longer." Hangers squeak as he goes through his shirts a third time. I'd had him down as an effortless dresser. Maybe he's also a bit stressed about introducing me to his friends.

The Arkwright bag is on the chair next to the bed. Ditching my phone, I lean over and lift out the sweater. "How about this?"

He glances over. "Bit formal for tonight." He rubs an eyebrow and delves into a shelf of folded T-shirts.

I sit back on my haunches. He's never going to wear it. Or the trousers, or the shoes. I stroke a sleeve. It's classic, not formal, the kind of thing you can dress up or down. An idea comes. While his back is still to me I pull off my shirt and put on the sweater. The cashmere lies soft against my bare skin. The V-neck is wide, and I let it slip down one shoulder.

"How about now? Still too formal?"

He turns and his eyes widen. He comes to me. Slides both hands up my back, inside the sweater. Pulls it off. "It's what's inside that counts." His hair, starting to dry, is falling to one side. I reach up and get it under control, parting it on the left. His gaze flits to the underside of my wrist. "It needs a cut."

"You should wear it like this," I say. "Maybe a bit off here"—I scissor my fingers below his temple—"and here. It'd suit you."

He looks at me for a long time, eyes flicking left to right, slightly hesitant, as if he's trying to get the measure of me. Maybe he's unused to being complimented. Who knows what looks good on someone better than a lover? I kiss him and he kisses me back, hard enough that I know he wants to progress things.

Although the wall inside me is subsiding, the base resistance is still there. I don't want to ruin the lighthearted mood, though, so I use the fact that the skin above my mouth has become sore as an excuse to gently extricate myself.

I touch it gingerly. "Am I red?"

"No. You look great."

I don't want to hurt his feelings. Maybe later, after a couple of drinks, I'll get over myself and it'll come easier. But for now, since I've started this charade about beard rash, I'm going to have to continue with it. I hop off the bed, go to the mirror. My skin is definitely pinked.

"Sorry," he says. "I didn't mean to hurt you."

I dig in my bag for some salve, dab it on. "Ever thought about shaving it off?"

He busies himself in the wardrobe, hidden by the door, so all I can see of him is his lower legs. I can't tell whether he's pissed off. "Sometimes. But I'd have to get another job because it's a prerequisite for owning a hipster coffee shop." His voice is muffled as he dresses. "They won't give you a license if you don't have a man bun or a beard."

If he's joking, we're okay. I watch him feed his feet into jeans. His feet have high arches, neat nails. "Even the women?"

"Aye." The sound of a zip, of fabric being shaken out as he puts on another layer. "Nah—they've got to have a thick fringe. NHS specs at a push. Both and you're a shoo-in."

He closes the wardrobe. The hair is mussed in its usual way, but he's wearing the sweater.

"Looks great," I say. I can't help touching him, running my fingers along his chest. I get a heady flash of déjà vu.

He pulls at the neck. "Well," he says, almost shyly, "I had a good model." He takes my hand, my reticence definitely forgiven. "Right, let's go."

The party is walking distance from Connor's place. The plan is to stop in somewhere for a bite to eat and get there about nine. On the way, we pass a row of shops, one of which is a mini-mart.

"Two seconds," Connor says, pushing open the door, which chimes. "I want to get Andre a bottle of something."

Inside it's small, the aisle too tight for both of us, and unbearably overheated. I tap his bicep. "I'll wait outside."

Next door is a Turkish barbershop, still open, its windows filled with soft yellow light. There seems to be a barber on every third street these days; grooming must be a booming business.

A heavyset man stands outside, holding a tray of little bread rings dusted with sesame seeds. "You want to try some simit?"

I love sesame. I take a ring. My word, it's tasty. Crusty and ultra-savory. "It's good," I tell him. "Thanks."

"Have another." He thrusts the tray at me again. "One is not enough."

I can't keep helping myself to his food without engaging. "What's the occasion?"

"Opening weekend of our new family business." He adjusts the tray so he can hold it in one hand and sweep the other across the expanse of the barbershop's window, as if introducing a play in a theater. Beyond the glass wait three retro swivel seats in a row.

The second simit ring is gone and I'm itching for a third. My appetite is back with a vengeance since I met Connor. "Been busy?"

"Busy enough." The tray comes my way again. I take another. "But always room for more. Special offer today. Half price."

Behind me, a chime sounds. Connor comes out of the mini-mart, bag in hand. He lifts his eyebrows in query, but I can't answer because I've got my mouth full.

"Sir?" The man offers Connor his tray and he takes a simit ring with a thanks. "Half price today," the man says.

"The snacks?"

"No!" The man laughs, a big belly laugh that shakes all the way down his arms. "The barbering."

"What do you think?" I say to Connor, but now he has his mouth full.

"Come inside, take a look," the man says. "No pressure."

I go in and Connor follows. There may be no spoken pressure, but these guys know what they're about, and no sooner has Connor taken up the offer to try one of the seats—"Very comfortable, yes, sir?"—than he is spun around to face a mirror, his coat is pulled off, a towel is draped around his shoulders, and a second man—younger, and carrying some resemblance to the simit bearer, possibly a son or a nephew—is wielding a pair of clippers.

The man from the street brings a new tray: Turkish coffees and sliced pastries, more elaborate ones this time, molded into a boat shape, stuffed with spinach and meat, a plate for each of us.

Connor puts his food on the side and rises from his chair. "You're very kind, but we're on our way out."

"For dinner?" the man asks. He gives Connor's plate back to him. "This can be your dinner. Pide. It's delicious. Try it."

I'm already trying it—it is indeed delicious.

"To a party," Connor says, signaling at me with his eyes that we ought to get going. I'm still chewing and so I can only shrug.

The man puts a hand on his shoulder to encourage him to sit again. "Then you will want to look your best. Yes?"

I make an effort to swallow. "You did say it needs cutting. We have time, right?" I bite into a different flavor of pide, to make the point that if we eat here while he gets his hair cut we'll still make it to the party by nine. This pide is even better: salty and silky.

"See?" the man says. Connor sits again. The young barber approaches with clippers, but the elder takes them from him and, speaking in Turkish, shoos him with a tray back out into the street. "So," he says, "what will it be?"

I sit by the wall while the barber takes scissors and clippers to Connor's head. The barber makes a show of consulting me on the cut and I join in, carried away with the spontaneous fun of it, by our playfulness earlier in Connor's bedroom, and also by the victory of persuading him to wear the sweater.

"The ladies always know best, sir," the barber says, and Connor laughs. I encourage him to take off a little more here, a little more there, and he makes the same joke. Connor merely smiles this time. Then, hovering his comb, the barber consults me on how to part Connor's hair and I indicate a different way from usual, off to the left, like Scott. I notice Connor's jaw muscles tense—but it's only a parting; he can change it as soon as we leave the shop if he wants to. And anyway, I was right, in the way I was right that the sweater would suit him—he looks amazing.

"And a shave?" the barber says, daubing foam onto Connor's cheek.

"Yes," I say, half a beat before Connor says "No."

Our reflections laugh at the disagreement. The barber looks from one of us to the other. "So, yes or no?"

"I don't think so," Connor says politely.

"But you'd look gorgeous." I wink at him in the mirror. "Wouldn't he?" I say to the barber, who is nodding along. "Even more gorgeous," I add.

"Nah, I'm good."

"Come on, Connor." I'm enjoying this game, this evening. I even pout. "Think of my poor skin." I glance in the mirror. The pink tinge from earlier has cleared. "Look, it's still red." The barber is shaking his head somberly, as if this is a travesty that should never be repeated. "Do it for me," I say flippantly, casually, just another part of the play.

Stricken. That's the only word to describe Connor as he looks at me in the mirror. He says to the barber, "Not tonight, thank you." He swipes fiercely at the shaving foam with the towel around his neck, throws the towel onto the shelf, and stands. He's already reaching for his wallet. "How much do I owe you?"

Taken aback by the sudden change, the barber looks uncertainly from Connor to me, but I have no idea what's going on or why Connor is so upset. I put aside my empty plate and fumble for my bag. "I'll pay."

"It's fine." He won't meet my eye. "How much?" he says forthrightly to the barber.

"Twenty."

He pulls a note from his wallet and drops it onto the seat. Then he grabs his coat from where it was hung up and walks out.

I mumble an apology as I dash through the door. He is already a dozen paces along the street. Clearly this is bad. "Connor?" I know from the way he twitches that he heard me, but he doesn't stop. I run after him. "Connor, wait." He's striding so fast that I have to jog and even then I'm lagging behind. "I'm sorry," I say, although he can't know what I was thinking, what I was trying to do; my mistaking him for someone else hasn't come up again since our first date in the pub. "Please slow down. Can't we talk about this?" I grab on to his arm.

He stops suddenly, and I swing out in a semicircle. "What exactly do you want to talk about?"

"I don't know. I . . ." This can't be about a beard. It can't even be about a beard and a sweater. "I'm sorry."

His eyes are ablaze. "Do you know how humiliating that was?"

"I thought it was fun. You seemed to be having fun. It's only hair." I reach up, intending to muss it playfully, flip it back into its usual style, put this behind us, but he knocks my hand away.

"What do you want from me, Maddy?" He's almost hissing. "Buying me clothes, trying to change the way I look. Stop trying to make me into someone else!"

"Scott—" I scrabble to cover myself. "*Got* . . . it's got . . . this has got out of hand." I never meant to be so transparent; I never meant to hurt him. I tug on his arm, but he flings me off.

His eyes are so wide I can see the whites all the way around. "You're bloody right about that."

Just then, the barber appears, trotting up to us. He's carrying the bag with Connor's birthday present for his friend. "You left this."

Connor snatches it back. Cracks open the bottle of Scotch. Takes a deep swig. "You said it yourself, didn't you, pal?" The barber looks at him blankly. He drinks again. "The lady's always right."

He turns his back on me and leaves.

31

THE SHOCK OF THE ARGUMENT KNOCKS ME DUMB, BOTH SILENT and stupid. All I can do is gape at Connor's retreating back, then at the barber, who makes a face like a disapproving fish, lifts his shoulders, and goes into his shop. By then, Connor has disappeared around the corner we came from earlier.

I take a few steps to follow. Then I stop and go in the opposite direction, toward the station, toward home. It was only a suggestion of a haircut, a shave. He didn't have to react so strongly. He has a mind of his own. He can do what he wants. In fact, he's made that perfectly clear. Let him go to hell then.

And yet . . . I slow down. I pushed him into it and I shouldn't have. I also shouldn't have said Scott's name. I've been so careful, ever since the club, after I'd confused him for Scott, not to say it. And I've managed—until now. I make an about-turn so I'm facing the direction of his flat. Take a couple of steps, then wheel toward the station again. To and fro, this way and that, trying to decide what to do.

Eventually, I let my feet lead me back to the flat. Reservations aside, I'm not sure I can walk away from him. I'm not ready to let go.

The downstairs neighbor is leaving as I arrive and I jog to catch the door before it closes. At the top of the stairs the recycling box is taking up all the space, as if Connor has put it there as a barricade. I move it to one side. There's no answer to my knock. I try twice more, then press my ear against the wood. Definitely movement inside.

"Connor?" There's a peephole in the door. I put an eye to it. Because I'm looking down it the wrong way there's a reverse telescopic effect. He's standing in the corridor, rendered tiny but not so small that I can't see he's changed his clothes, put on one of his flannel shirts and well-worn jeans. He's leaning against the wall, arms folded across his chest. "I know you're in there," I say. "I can see you."

"Can you now?" Heavy on the sarcasm.

"Come on, Connor. Open the door, please. Let's talk about it."

He stands there motionless, head hanging, for so long that I begin to worry that it's over between us. I stay where I am, blinking and breathing, waiting and hoping. Eventually he pushes himself off the wall and comes toward me, growing larger and larger. He reaches the door and everything darkens. Then there's a flicker of light and his eye appears against the other end of the peephole. That's all I can see of him, and all he can see of me, and we're just two eyes and I know I don't want to lose him.

"Connor, please open up."

Silence. He blinks. I blink. He pulls his eye away from the peephole. I move away too. More silence. I lean my forehead against the door. I say, in a small voice, "Are you there?"

Nothing. Then I hear, "Sometimes it frightens me, how strongly I feel for you."

I don't know how I know, maybe by the angle his voice comes from and the semi-constricted sound of it, as if his chin is tucked all the way in, but I'm absolutely sure that he's leaning his head against the other side in exactly the same spot as I am. "Frightened? What is there to be frightened of?"

The door practically vibrates with the strength of his sigh. "That you'll see me for who I really am and you won't like it. That . . ." A muted thud of a palm slapping wood. "Maddy. Do you get what I'm saying? Do you understand what I'm trying to tell you?"

I know what he means—I've felt that way before. That point you reach in a relationship when you decide to stop trying to pretend to be someone you're not. When you let yourself be vulnerable, flaws and battle-won scars and all. That point when you let them see the real you and you either sink or swim. "Yes, yes, I think so."

He opens the door.

He's cautious, backing along the corridor as I close the door and lean against it.

"I owe you an apology," I start. "An apology and an explanation." His arms cross over his body again, although there's less defiance in it this time, more of a signal that he's listening. I take a breath. "There was someone before you." It sounds so anodyne out loud—of course there was someone. He will have had a someone, too. "I didn't know him long, but I felt . . ." Connor flinches—perhaps it hurts him to hear I loved another man. "And he . . . well . . . he . . ." My voice is starting to waver. I fight to keep it level. "He died. And it was my fault."

"Maddy—"

"No, I know what you're going to say. How could it have been my fault?" I dab at my eyes. "But you see, it was . . ." Angela's words, on the video call, in the text. I'm crying properly now. "I could have done more. I should have helped. I should have been there."

His face falls as if he's hurt by my hurt. He closes the gap and enfolds me in a hug, pulling me right into his chest and letting me sob it out.

It's a while until I calm, and he holds me the whole time. Eventually he says, "Okay?"

I nod numbly. But it isn't and I'm not, not truly. He holds me at arm's length and looks me in the eye for a long time, coming to some sort of decision. Wordlessly he takes my hand and leads me down the corridor to the bathroom. He guides me to the edge of the bathtub. Puts the plug in the sink, turns on the hot tap. Takes off his shirt and the T-shirt he has on underneath. Looks at me via the mirrored cabinet above with an urgency that conveys an instruction: Don't say anything, just watch.

The tears have left me heavy, too weary to do anything but comply. I slip off my coat and drape it over the side of the bathtub. He's still tracking me via the mirror. When the sink is full, he opens the cabinet and takes out a can of shaving foam and a razor. He shakes the can, squirts foam into his hand, and pastes it onto his face, section by section.

Throughout all this, I say nothing, sticking to our unuttered pact.

Eventually, when his beard is covered, he picks up the razor. He brings it to the base of the foam at his neck. Swallows audibly.

I break the silence. "You don't have to do this."

He looks at me, but again only through the mirror. "I do."

"It was a stupid fight, that's all."

"I think that already you understand, deep down. But I have to show you."

His words make little sense. All the humor, the playfulness of earlier, before the fight, before I broke down, has gone and this feels deadly serious. A drip from the tap echoes in the harsh acoustics. His foot shuffles on the tile. My breathing is deeper. Fear, or arousal?

Again, he brings the razor toward his neck. His hand is shaking. He'll cut himself.

"Don't." I'm careful to say it gently, to not make this anything to do with what happened in the barbershop earlier. Getting up, I wrap my fingers over his, on the handle of the razor, and ease it away from his throat. "Let me."

He resists me to begin with and then he relinquishes control. He lifts his chin, exposing the most vulnerable part of his body to me.

Carefully I bring the blades to his neck, to the clean skin below the foam. Then I slide the razor, oh so slowly, up toward his jaw. The blades scratch wetly. I was expecting to leave a strip of clear skin behind, but I've only taken some of the hair away. The razor is clogged with foam and bristles. The foam smells of the outdoors, of moss and ozone, of a valley view and a low bank of cloud, of a brackeny hill and a path down to a loch. I rinse off the razor in the sink, bring the blades back to his throat. I retrace the same patch, pressing slightly more firmly, and this time I'm rewarded with a flash of clear skin. In the immediate aftermath of the passage of the blades, before the circulation can return, the skin is scored a ghostly yellow-white.

"Okay?" I ask as I rinse off again. He nods, eyes averted as if in shame.

Shaving a face takes more time than I would have thought. I manage to clear most of his throat without cutting him, but when I start on his jawline I slip on the foam and a drop of blood wells, beading red-black on his damp skin.

"Oh my God, I'm so sorry." I bring a finger to the nick. "Did I hurt you?"

He takes the razor from me. "I can finish." He hasn't looked at me since we started. I sit on the side of the bathtub again, but when he doesn't continue shaving I realize he wants me to leave.

"I . . ." I pick up my coat. "I'll wait out there."

He pushes the door, not shut, but closed enough that I can't see. I hover in the corridor for a while, listening to the scrape and splash, to the sound of the plug being pulled and another sinkful of water being run. I was only half-serious when I said I wanted him to shave off his beard. It wasn't a deal-breaker. Somehow things have grown out of proportion and now his beard, shaving off his beard, has taken on this huge significance that's almost ritualistic and I don't understand why.

Standing alone in the dark corridor, with only the intermittent splash of water for company, I become self-conscious, so I go to his room and sit on the bed. Then I lie back. Crying always makes me feel washed out. Watercolor-thin. I close my eyes. Just for a second.

"Maddy?"

I wake in the dark. I didn't mean to fall asleep. I rub my eyes.

He's in the doorway, a sketch against the dim light from the bathroom beyond. Bare-chested, in his jeans. He has a towel around his neck, is dabbing at his face with the end of it, but it's a slow, deliberate movement, nothing like the angry swipe in the barbershop; he's blotting gently, like someone trying not to smudge freshly laid ink.

I fumble for the bedside lamp switch. He stills my hand with his. Kneels in the near-dark by the side of the bed. Brings my hand to his cheek. I stroke it. So smooth. So soft. Sitting up, I lift my other hand to his other cheek. Holding his shorn face, I put my mouth to his. The taste of alcohol is a shock—I'd forgotten he'd swigged from that bottle in the street—and then it's not a shock at all, it's wanted. I kiss him more deeply, leading the moment, and he kisses me back.

Urgent now, I get up, pulling him to his feet. He unbuttons my shirt, unzips my jeans. *That*, I think, *that* was what was holding me back—a beard and the taste of booze? It seems so silly, so insignificant that it makes me smile, and I'm smiling as I kiss him, holding his face again, and that makes him smile, too. In the darkness I feel the edges of his mouth lift up, the skin across his lips tighten in, I guess, relief. In joy.

I want to see his smile, his reaction to me. I move away momentarily to switch on the lamp.

And finally I see.

Scott. Alive.

My back hits the wall. It can't be. It's a trick of the light, an uncanny resemblance. That need in me to see him everywhere. A transference. A dream.

I drive my nails into my palm. It smarts. Not a dream. A tectonic shift, a shunt in reality. A warping, as if I stepped through that looking glass into an alternative world.

Holding my gaze, Connor stands there, hands balled at his sides, chin up, jaw working. The aversion, the shame of earlier is gone. Now he's defiant.

I try blinking—that's worked in the past, to dispel the illusion when my attention has been caught by strangers. Yet nothing changes.

All I can say is, "How?"

He remains perfectly still as I go up to him, an echo of previous times. I can see him breathing deeply, see his stomach caving in and pushing out. His breath, and the creak of the floorboards, are the only sounds as I circle, examining him like a sculpture in a gallery. I start at his feet, drawing up my gaze to the waistband of his jeans and higher, along the more defined line of his abs, his chest, his shaven neck, to the hinge of his jaw. Where the beard had softened it, now his jawline is sharp, and bleeding where I cut. I pass behind him. Because he's shirtless, I can see what a precise job the barber did of leveling off the hair at the nape of his neck, revealing paler, vulnerable skin and a distinctive clutch of moles. I brush them with my index finger. Completing my loop, I stop square to him. Only then do I allow my eyes to travel fully, slowly, over his face. The haircut and shave have changed him inexplicably, altered the balance of his features. My attention lands on the eyebrow ring. He sees where I'm looking and takes it out. He puts the ring on the bedside table. I touch the tiny hole left behind in his skin. This, now, is the face that I knew. Not a passing, sought-after resemblance, not a doppelgänger, not even an identical twin.

The face. The exact same features. This freckle by his mouth. This small scar. This look in his eyes. Haunted.

"You see?" he whispers, and in whispering even his accent is changed. I touch the freckle. The scar. The dimple. "I see."

I don't, not really, not in the way that "to see" is to understand. I don't know how this is possible. Magic. Reincarnation. Resurrection, the greatest miracle of them all. But I choose to accept what is in front of me, the evidence of my own eyes.

My beautiful Scott. Come back to me.

He opens his mouth to speak and I lay a finger over his lips. Don't speak, don't break the spell. I mute him with my own mouth.

This time, all the little differences are gone. I let go completely.

32

ALTHOUGH A LARGE PART OF ME WOULD BE HAPPY TO NEVER
know, to sweep the explanation under the magic carpet and keep the illusion going, as we lie there afterward on his bed, my cheek on his chest, his fingers in my hair, my leg hooked over his hip, reality and my unanswered "How?" begin to press down.

"You knew," he says by way of beginning. Speaking, he is Connor; Connor in Scott's body. "Somehow. I could see it in your eyes when you saw me at that club."

Recognition. To identify, to recall and remember. To see the one you love and know that it is them. But also to perceive, to understand a truth. So did I, somehow, deep down, understand a truth, that they must be the same man? Was I able to look past the smoke and mirrors; is that why I was compelled to track him down?

"Why? Who . . . ?" Pierced by the enormity of the questions, I stop. I get up and wrap myself in his dressing gown. He stays lying on his back, lit sideways by the low lamp, which colors in his body like contours on a map, or like photos sent back from the familiar-strange surface of Mars: golden highlights for his brow bone, the mound of his shoulder, the tip of his nose; dark, unknown hollows for the sockets of his eyes, the underside of his hand. Without the beard he's not Connor, but neither is he Scott. He's caught in between, a revenant.

I start again. "Which one are you?"

He shuffles back against the headboard, where he draws the covers over his lap and bends his knees up to his chest. "I want you to know it all, Maddy. But it's going to take time to explain properly. Will you, I mean, is it okay to ask if you can just listen to begin with and save your questions for after? I'll answer them all, I promise. I . . . I need to get this out." It's almost dawn and he speaks fast, as if he wants to say everything he has in him before the light comes, as if he needs the protection of the night. I feel it, too, that desire for the dark, for the world to stop turning. I sit halfway down the bed and prepare to listen.

Connor begins. "I'm the younger of two brothers. Dad met my mum in Glasgow. They weren't technically married, but my dad had been married before, and he'd left his ex-wife and son in America. We have different surnames because my mum gave me hers."

He opens his bedside drawer and hands me a picture. I recognize the frame as the one from the living room he'd put face down so I couldn't see. The photo is not of him and a previous girlfriend, but of two young men, their heads together, beer bottles in hand, eyes red in the flash. It's clear they're related from the shape of their jaws, the slant of their brows.

"Scott."

"Aye." The significance of that mushrooms outward, like a shock wave. The Scott in the photo is a stranger to me.

Connor drops his nose to his bent-up knees and watches me, trying to work out what I'm thinking, how I'm going to react. It's odd how calm I am, almost numb. I need to know everything before I can decide what I think, how I feel. I need all the pieces. I put the photo in the drawer. "Keep going."

He breaks eye contact, looking at the bedcovers instead of at me. "That was taken when I was eighteen and he was twenty-three. He turned up out of the blue on our doorstep. He took me on a crazy night out, totally mad, these pubs, clubs, and then an after-party at some stranger's flat. There was cocaine. First time I'd seen it, and I couldn't believe how open they were. I wasn't brave enough to take any but he did. He was in medical school and I thought how nuts it was that this guy was going to be a doctor. But I was a broke kid right out of Highers; I didn't want to be the killjoy wagging a finger. He asked if he could crash at mine. We must have got home about four in the morning, passed out on the sofas. I woke up when Mum came down, and he'd already gone. She was furious—we'd left the kitchen in a state, trying to cook chips and make tea."

He's putting in too much detail, things I don't need to know. It's what people do when they're building up to something big.

"From then on, it was always like that with him. He'd pop up unexpectedly. Even after I'd moved out of Mum's and down to London and he was doing his MBA in the States he'd, say, appear at a bar I was working in, all 'Hey, bro!' and wanting to party big-time, and then he'd be gone again, for months, sometimes years. I found out later he was pretty much wasted the whole time through the early 2000s. Just like our dad. That's what killed him, the drink. And it seemed Scott was going the same way. Then something changed. He emailed, told me he'd met a 'chick,' as he put it."

Angela.

Seeing I've made the connection, Connor nods. "I thought he meant he was settling down, but he was going into business. They moved to London. They were sleeping together, too, in the beginning. And she seemed good for him. She has this mega work ethic, and it must have rubbed off. They were doing well—really well. We went out for dinner sometimes, the three of us, and there was no bar after, no club, no party. As far as I knew it, no drugs. It was as if he'd decided to put all that behind him and I was pleased for him, relieved he'd ironed himself out.

"Then he called me one night, drunk, slurring, crying, a proper mess. Said Angela was a liar, a fake. They'd split a while back, so I presumed he meant she was seeing someone else and he'd found out there'd been an overlap. Said he was going to hurt himself. He wouldn't tell me where he was, so I called her and she said she'd sort it. The next time we spoke I tried to bring it up but he shut me down. Said everything was fine. It wasn't, though—his drinking got so bad she put him through rehab. It wasn't partying anymore; it was like he wanted to distance himself from his life. There were a few more cycles over the years. He'd pull himself out, then get dragged back down."

The language Connor is using is so similar to what Angela said that there's a confluence as two realities merge.

"He did a second lot of rehab and that was it, for a long time. He threw himself into work and the business took off. He was flying here, there, everywhere, and so was I. I did a lot of traveling; I'd work for a few months, save like crazy, then take off. Ecuador, Peru, Laos, Vietnam. Anywhere I could be outside, see the sky after months of cooped-up city living."

"Then?"

"Then last year, October, Scott hit another low patch. He called me late one night. He was slurring badly and pretty much all I could make out was 'We're so fucked' and when I asked why he just kept asking me to sing him a song. Kept saying it, over and over. I thought he was having a breakdown. Obviously I called Angela. She called me back a day or so later, told me he was still in a bad way. I asked where he was, if I could see him, talk to him, but she said she'd checked him into the clinic again. 'The thing is, Connor,' she said, 'he needs your help. We both do.' I'd always liked Angela. Truth be told, I was a little envious of what they had. Not that I fancied her; I admired how they'd built something up together. They started from nothing and, well, you've seen. He was driving a flash car, living in this swish apartment. It's not that I wanted to be rich—I'm not sure money interests me, but . . . do you know what I mean? It's like you're doing fine and then someone comes along with more—someone not that different from you—and in comparison it makes you feel like less. Even if they didn't intend it that way, even if you were perfectly content before. A Tesla, a penthouse—they're signifiers. They mean 'I'm successful, I'm worth more' both in terms of money and position."

I can't blame him for being seduced by all that. Hadn't I been, too? "Is that why you were pretending to be him in Varaig?" I know that this must be wishful thinking. The truth is far more complicated than sibling rivalry. For one, Angela was also letting me believe he was Scott.

"No. I did it because she said they needed me. Angela told me their business was at a critical point but Scott's downturn was putting it in jeopardy. Something about a merger that was going to take them to the next level. He'd worked so hard for years to get them to this stage, she said, but the pressure had sent him spiraling and it was awful because it wasn't Scott's fault, he had an addiction, a disease. She told me it was drugs as well as alcohol, prescription sedatives and antidepressants."

I picture that empty pill bottle in the kitchen bin but then think no, it wasn't Scott who put that there, it was Connor. It's taking a lot of unpicking to reframe the fact that the Scott I thought I knew is not this Scott I'm hearing about.

"I said I'd help any way I could—did she want him to come and stay with me? She said no, he was doing well in rehab. I asked if I could call him. She said they weren't allowed phones. I didn't understand what she wanted, why she'd called me. And then she told me."

He rubs his hand down his face, drawing down a grimace, and I know that I'm about to enter the story. I tug the edges of the robe closer together as if to protect myself from what's coming.

"She said she knew it was awkward, but could I step into my brother's shoes for a few weeks, pretend to be him. I said there was no way—I wasn't medically trained; I knew nothing about their business, I couldn't fool any investors. She said I wouldn't have to meet any investors. Just one person, a writer working on a book—that's who I'd have to fool."

Fool. The truth jabs me.

Instantly, he's apologizing. "Oh God, Maddy, I swear that was her word, not mine!"

I have been a fool. And might it have been better to have remained one, for Connor to have stayed the stranger he pretended to be, for me to continue in blind ignorance? No, that's no real way to live.

I ward off his regret and he continues, although he hangs his head lower. "I . . . She said it was to make everything seem normal, get them over this hump, until Scott could come out of rehab. She said she'd tell the other staff he was working up in Varaig so word wouldn't get out. I was thankful she was helping him but I told her it was too weird, that I didn't want to do it. She said: 'You owe him, Connor.' And I did owe him. He'd paid my rent a few times when I got back from traveling, lent me the money to start up with Niall. Two, three weeks, she said. Was that too much to ask to help my brother?

"What could I do? I said okay. She sent over clothes, told me to get a haircut, go on a diet." I flinch—I did all those things, too—but he keeps going. "She even gave me a couple of treatments for free, ironed out the bump here"—he fingers the bridge of his nose—"that I'd had for years, that I got playing soccer, and gave me a few injections to my jawline—to sharpen my profile, she said. They're only temporary, but well, you know, she's one of the best cosmetic surgeons in the world." He flushes, ashamed of his vanity, then clears his throat. "And I have to admit, when I put on those clothes I looked better than I ever have done. Scott grew up with money, on his mum's side. Dad never had any. I dunno, when I dressed like him, put on his accent, it was as if I even stood straighter, as if I'd moved on up. She didn't let me take his car, though—I drove up in mine."

That's why he hid the Golf. God, I've been a dupe. No—duped. My growing anger must be showing, because he pauses and wipes his lips on his hand, as if trying to rid himself of a bad taste. "It was so intense, you being there. When I met you that first time, in the mudroom, I was sure you'd seen right through me—picked up the fake accent, knew I wasn't the kind of guy who wore clothes like that. When I got to my room I felt dreadful. I called her and she said to keep my distance. And I tried. At first, when you were in your room working, it was okay. I shut off the Wi-Fi a couple of times. Thought if you couldn't work there you'd go home. Pathetic, I know." He pulls the bedsheets higher. "And then, well, we started spending time together. I should have left, but Scott . . ."

"You hid from Raphaela."

"I had to. Angela had told her Scott was working up there but she would have known I wasn't him."

"Who else knew what you were doing? Sacha?"

"No. No one." He's getting agitated now, rubbing his cheek as if he's itchy with guilt. "Then when that painting went missing and Angela showed up, I presumed she'd call the whole thing off, send me home. But she didn't, and you and I were already getting closer and, Maddy, I felt such a bastard lying to you like that, but what could I do? If I'd told you, you'd have hated me anyway. I didn't want that. I couldn't stand that."

He reaches down the bed for me. I resist. "Go on."

He blinks hard. "The whole time I was telling myself I was doing this for Scott, that it was worth it because it was helping him. And it seemed that that was the case—Angela would call and tell me he was doing well in rehab, she promised that when you left Varaig I could go home and see him." The phone call, when he asked me to walk the dogs. "And the fucking thing is, it didn't help him at all. That's why I don't drink anymore. She said he checked himself out of rehab, must have got a train up there after you and I left. Told her he'd go cold turkey, but obviously that didn't work. It hardly ever does. And so . . ."

He clamps a hand around his feather tattoo, as if trying to restrain his brother, stop him from doing what he did. I close my eyes against his pain.

"I . . ." Connor's voice cracks. "This is all messed up, I know, and I'm so, so sorry. I almost came clean to you in Varaig so many times. Then you got sent back to London early. That was the worst part of it, when you asked if we'd see each other at the launch—wanting to say yes but knowing there was no way I could. Putting you into that taxi and waving you off, knowing it was goodbye forever."

His hand at my back, helping me into the cab. His outline growing smaller as it pulled away.

"But it wasn't, Maddy. You found me. I don't know how, but it's like, if anything good can come out of this . . ."

A spark, low down in my gut, ignites. I open my eyes. "Stop!" A sham, the whole thing's a sham. Days and weeks and months of lies. In Varaig and since the club.

I lean right over and poke a finger into his mouth. I slide it along and part his lips, hooking the upper one high, searching for the crooked canine, as if the truth of who he is lies in that one tooth. The canine is straight. I let go.

He is watching me closely, his eyes on mine. "I had it straightened."

I get off the bed and pace the small space between there and the door. "And what about in the café? When I turned up and asked you to dinner, you went into the back room to make a phone call—you were calling Angela, weren't you? You were asking what you should do." My God, has all this been another layer of pretense, another game of lies? "Did she tell you to sleep with me?"

"No, of course not! She told me to stay away from you but I couldn't. Maddy, you have to believe this was real."

"Don't tell me what to believe! How much of it was you?"

"What do you mean?"

"How much of *you* was you?"

He flinches. "All of it. Of me."

"That can't be true."

He tents his hands over his face and breathes against them, thinking hard. "Okay, okay." He gets out of the bed, too distracted to cover up. "It's probably easier if I tell you what wasn't me. The name. The clothes. The accent, obviously."

"Huck? Your dad dying?" Small things, individually, but they meant a lot. They made up who he was, the man I fell for, at least I thought they did. And the other things, things it would be too mortifying to say out loud: the secret smile when he wouldn't tell me his initial impression of me; the times he looked, really looked at me; the way he made me feel about myself. The way he made me feel about him. Were they faked, too?

Pacing has brought me to the wardrobe. More closed doors, more secrets. I fling them open, one, two, three. Behind the third is a rack of clothes I recognize from before. The sweater he was wearing when I first came across him in the mudroom, the jacket I'd last seen when he put me into the taxi at Varaig. In the main wardrobe, among his normal Connor clothes, is that out-of-place orange kaffiyeh scarf I'd found in his room. I bet that was the only piece of himself he took to the house.

I whip it off the shelf and chuck it at him, then I lift out all the Scott clothes in one go and throw those as well. Hangers clatter to the floor, the clothes flop. "And what about now? What about the last four weeks? What's real now, what's the truth now, Connor?" It's caustic, the way I say his name, Connor; conner. "Is that even your name?"

"Yes! I'll show you my passport if you want." Passports, driver's licenses— people seem intent on proving who they are to me with these pieces of paper. "It's all real now," he says. "It's all the truth. I promise you. My dad died when I was a kid, like I told you."

"And your brother? You said he died years ago."

"I didn't, I was careful not to lie to you. I said he'd been ill for a long time." He's standing in the same spot, tumbled clothes mounded halfway up his shins, arms by his sides but rotated forward, so his hands are supplicant, like that manikin, wrist veins cording out. His nakedness infuriates me, because how can you help but believe a man when he's laid so literally bare? Those frank eyes, so clear, so sharp; they're quarrying away at my defenses. I step forward and pound the front of his shoulder with the side of my fist. He rocks back on his heels but doesn't retaliate, not even to catch my arm. He stands there, taking it, while I pummel at him.

Eventually I move away. "Why'd you do it?"

"I told you—"

"No, not that. Why'd you show me? Last night?"

"Because I couldn't keep lying to you, manipulating you. That's not who I want to be. And . . ." He inhales, long and slow, exhales through his nose. "And because I don't want to be second-best—"

Ridiculous. "You're not second-best."

"Are you sure about that? Because even now I can't believe you're seeing me for me. The way you're always trying to change me. I tell myself it's all just wrapping and it doesn't matter in the scheme of things, that it is me you want. That *I* was who you fell for in Varaig. On good days, I can believe that. But then you do this thing, looking through me, like there's someone you want to see on the other side. It makes me feel like a ghost."

"Ghost!" I march past him to the wardrobe and yank out a T-shirt and a pair of sweatpants and press them on him. He takes them and huffs a knowing laugh. It incenses me. "What? They're your clothes, aren't they? Yours—Connor's. I'm in *your* flat, I spent the night in *your* bed. So come on, put them on. Be you." I kick at the expensive clothes on the floor. "Forget all this 'wrapping' and be you."

Resignedly, he lifts the T-shirt over his head and feeds through his arms. He pulls the sweatpants up his legs. Dressed, he stands before me. He looks already brokenhearted.

And then I realize my mistake. The clothes I picked are the ones Scott wore on the rainy afternoon. No, not Scott, Connor. I can't keep up with all the shifts; every time I think I've got the measure of him I have to redraw the blueprint, but I don't know how because there are so many blanks, so many gaps in my knowledge about who he really is.

For so many months, I spent sleepless nights fixated on what I was doing at the moment Scott launched himself off the cliff. I was making a cup of tea at home in London while he staggered down the moorland; I was flicking through the morning headlines on my phone while he was crashing down; I was taking a shower when he died on the cold, hard rocks, his skull smashed open. The visualizations were so real. Now, strangely, I can't pull these images to mind. It's as if Connor is layering himself over the imagined memories, like a double-exposed photograph, covering up what was originally burnt onto the film.

"Why did you make me think you—he—you—were depressed? Drunk?"

"I didn't."

"You did—raiding the wine cabinet; downing whiskey in the middle of the night."

"No, that never happened."

"It did!"

So much is changing so fast. One thing I can be sure of, though: a web of lies was spun and a man died, and somehow everything between Connor and me is tied up with that.

Years ago, working on one of my first books, I had an often insomniac client who put a lot of stock in the meaning of dreams and quality of sleep. That's when I learned the word for that shock feeling when you dream you're falling and you wake suddenly, covered in sweat, heart pounding, legs kicking out: hypnagogic jerk. That's exactly what I experience now, except I'm not asleep, I'm plummeting into the pit wide awake.

I scramble into my clothes.

"Maddy, can't we talk about this?"

Rubber squeaks as I ram my feet into my shoes. I grab my bag.

"Maddy—"

He catches my arm, but I shake him off. "No. I can't."

I'm out of the flat before he can stop me.

33

OUTSIDE I RUN AT A BONE-JARRING, LUNG-BURNING SPEED
from Connor's flat to the bus stop, from the bus stop to the Tube, from
Tooting Bec all the way back to my place. I need distance from Connor, from what he's told me. He said he was only trying to help Angela
and his brother, but why go along with the deception in the first place?
Unless . . . my feet slam into the pavement and logic punches, horrific.
Unless he was getting something out of it. A counterargument strikes,
fast as a hook: no, Scott was his brother; Connor wouldn't do anything
to harm him. He's torn up over it. He wasn't to know Scott would go up
there after, that he would kill himself. But why all the pretense and lies,
so many lies, then and now, him and her? What was the point of them?
What did they lead to?

As I run, my phone keeps ringing: Connor. I cut off every call. Texts
come through: Please answer. I'm sorry I lied to you. I shut those down, too.
All I want is to be home. To find the chart.

By the time I get to my front door, I'm gasping for breath and my throat
burns with acid. My hand shakes so much that my key skids against the
lock. Inside, I dump my bag on the floor and shed my coat. Dialing Sacha,
I go straight to my bedroom. I drop to my knees and grab at the plastic
bag under my bed. It takes three calls before Sacha picks up.

"Maddy. Now's not a good ti—"

I cut her off. "Did you know?" I yank at the bag, but it's jammed against
the bed frame and won't come out.

"About what?"

"Scott. Connor."

"Connor? Mate, I'm sorry, but I'm on my way to a meeting and I can't talk about relationship stuff right now. I'll call you after, oka—"

"Switch to video."

"I told you, I'm—"

"*Now*, Sacha." I need to see her face, to tell whether she's lying to me, too. My forcefulness works—I get the notification that Sacha is moving to video. While it loads I claw at the trapped bag until it bursts and the contents spill out onto the carpet like entrails. I rake them toward me.

The video connects and Sacha's face fills the frame. I don't give her a chance to speak. "Did you know it was a setup?"

She zips her head back. "What was a setup?"

"Did you know what Angela was doing?"

"About what?"

Can I trust her? She's changed recently. But no one can remain the same forever. I hate that all these lies and tricks are making me doubt the person I'm closest to, have known for more than half my life.

She unhooks her glasses, every inch the concerned friend. "Maddy, what's happened?"

It's almost as if I can see two versions of her at once, the 2019 lawyer who's got it together layered over the 1999 student who survived on hangovers, Pringles, and *Friends*. All the other Sachas she has been in between are there, too. I know her. I've always trusted Sacha in the past, I can't not trust her now.

"I'm not sure Scott De Luca's death was suicide." I'm saying it before I understand that this truly is what I believe.

"Mate, not this again."

"Just hear me out." I speak super fast so she can't interrupt, telling her that Connor is Scott's brother, that Angela got him to pretend to be Scott while I was in Varaig and led me to believe that that was the case. A flash of shoulder in a hotel room, the back of a head, a glimpse via a low-res camera—that's all it took to convince me. I bet she wasn't even in Saudi Arabia, or Cape Town. "She's been lying all along," I tell Sacha, "and I think it's because she's hiding something." I fill her in on Evie, about the painting and Evie being Angela's daughter. I even tell her what Jon Prosser told me, about there being inconsistencies in her story, although I stop short of mentioning I know about the injunction.

"Fuck," Sacha says. "I said something happened to you up there."

"Exactly! It did!"

"No, Maddy, that's not what I mean." Someone is trying to get her attention. She glances behind her and holds up a finger to them to indicate she'll be one second. The screen goes dark. "Look," she says. I can hear tapping as she types. "I told you I know this excellent therapist. I'm sending you his number now."

My phone vibrates with a message. I ignore it. "I'm not imagining this. She's covering something up."

"What, exactly?" Sacha comes back on-screen. Her eyes are full of sadness, as if I've let her down.

Damn it. I shouldn't have said "covering something up"; I sound paranoid. I should have thought it all through more before I called. There's a fog in my brain stopping me from seeing all the connections, from working it out. "I don't know yet. But why else would she arrange all that?"

"Maybe for the reasons she told Connor. Pride? Protection?"

"That's not it."

"Then why? Scott De Luca died and that's a real tragedy. But it had nothing to do with you. Or her. Just a horrible irony that he went up there to do it after you left." She brings her free hand to her chin in half a prayer sign. "Please, please call the therapist. Please."

I'm too worn-out to argue. All I have are negatives, things I know are not the case, vacuums where the truth should be—but I can't use absences to persuade Sacha. She's someone who deals in hard facts. I concede, just to get her off my back.

"Good," she says. "I'm really sorry, I do have to go now, but I'll call you later, all right?" I nod. "Love you," she adds.

After she ends the call, I stare into nothing. Outside, rush-hour buses hiss. I'm not mad; I can't be mad. It's only that I can't see the whole picture. My phone buzzes—another text from Connor. Don't you think I feel shite, too? I lost my brother. A moment later, another: Going to the mountains to clear my head.

I realize now that when I called him on the inquest day and he said he'd had a rough morning, that was because he'd heard the suicide verdict, that what was affecting me was affecting him, too, even more so. That's why he was so quiet in Richmond Park and so set on not wanting to try on that sweater. It wasn't only that I was trying to change him, it was also that the person I was trying to re-create was a semblance of a brother he'd so recently lost. All the way through our relationship he was dealing with the doubleness of that, the twisted result of his own duplicity. Oh God, it's all such a mess.

I rub my eyes, which are smarting from lack of sleep, and consider the papers all over the floor, the pieces of the chart intermingled with notes from SKIN DEEP. The key to all this is in there somewhere. I pick up the nearest document, a map of the Varaig area—I'll find no answers in that. My contract—also a no. I create a pile of things that aren't relevant, adding my notes on the "intruder," now that I know it was Evie. Prosser's original manuscript I file to one side as a "maybe." It'll take ages to go through it so I'll read it later. I continue in this way until I find the list of things Angela said to me about "Scott's" depression—*He's been really low in the past, he's good at hiding it, I'm worried for him.* With that I start a third pile, a pile of substantiation. Because if Angela wanted Connor to pretend to be Scott so that I didn't know about his rehab and it looked as if it was business as usual, then why tell me about his addiction? Worse—why let me believe I had failed him? She could have left me out of it.

Next is an envelope, still sealed, addressed to me care of Angela's office. The sender is Rex Harris, Sandy, OR. That photographer. I remember Raphaela giving me this the day of the launch. I never opened it because it was no longer relevant. I tear the flap and upend the envelope. Onto my jeans tumbles a note and a contact sheet of images. The note is from Harris: *Alternatives, as requested—all I have of Beaverbrook.* The contact sheet has eight miniature black-and-white photos, laid out like tiles in two rows of four with a list of corresponding captions beneath. The first picture is the one I saw online when I searched the libraries for Angela Reynolds. The caption is as before: "Beaverbrook University Med Soc Valentine social, February 13, 1994. Students GiGi Libcewicz and Angela Reynolds." But this time there's no agency watermark. I already know the girl on the right is a different med student, Angela Rodriguez, née Reynolds. I glance at the girl on the left.

When I was working on SKIN DEEP, I spent a lot of time scrolling through pre- and postsurgery images online and on social. In most cases, a black bar had been pasted over the patient's eyes, redacting their identity. It's surprising how effective covering up that one feature can be. Now, with the watermark gone, recognition jolts.

Quickly, I skim over the next six photos, but they're all images of guys at the university medics' party. At the final picture, I stall. It is the one I saw from 1991 of GiGi Libcewicz and three young men at a different event, the one I disregarded because 1991 was two years before Angela started med school.

In the 1994 photo, GiGi is a little blurred, her eyes almost all the way closed. But in this earlier picture she is in focus. She has striking eyes, the irises so pale that in a black-and-white print they gleam eerily near-translucent. I mentally photoshop out the fringe, thin the face, update the outfit. Angela.

I jump to the caption for the first picture. "L to R: Students GiGi Libcewicz and Angela Reynolds." But the girl on the left is the Angela Reynolds I know.

First, a perception: me last year, considering this photograph as being "not not" Angela, a double negative making a positive. Next, a memory: Scott—no, Connor-as-Scott—goofing around on the sofa at Varaig, calling her Angie, and the affricative sound of the second syllable, -gie. Last, a realization: my own name, Madeleine, and its diminutive, Maddy. Both me.

I dash off a message to Dr. Rodriguez. And then I call Evie.

"Hello?" Her voice is thick, dense with sleep.

"It's Maddy."

"Who?"

"Madeleine Wight. Angela's—"

"Oh yeah." She yawns. "What time is it?"

"Eight thirty."

"Jeez."

I skip the niceties. "Evie, what's your surname?"

"What?" A pause, as if she isn't fully awake yet. "Why?"

"Just tell me, please. Your last name."

"Is this . . . Am I in trouble?"

"For Chrissake!" I stop, breathe. "Evie, what is your last name?"

"You know that. Reynolds."

Her driver's license on the table. "And your mum is Reynolds?"

"Um, yeah." Dumbass, her inflection says.

I grip my fist hard. My nails bite into my palm. I'm so close, but I can't quite break through. "Your dad's name was Reynolds?"

She yawns again and merges it with an uh-huh. "I guess. But it's not like they were married."

"Your mum changed her name?"

"Yeah."

"When?"

"When I was, like, two or three or something."

"Why?"

She sniffs. "When I was little, I used to think it was because of me, so we were the same. When I got older, I had this friend at school whose grandparents had changed their name. It was one of those with a ton of consonants, hard for people to know how to pronounce, to spell—"

"Evie . . ."

"I'm telling you!" Rustling, as if she's sitting up in bed. "So when she met my dad and had me, I think she used that as an opportunity to make things easier."

"And originally she was . . . ?"

"Libcewicz. L-I-B-C-E-W . . ."

I stare at the contact sheet, at GiGi Libcewicz in 1991. In the café, Evie said that her mother was in her final year in 1998, which means she would have started college in fall semester 1990. Yet Angela told me she was in Beaverbrook's integrated program from 1993 to 2001, that she'd verified the dates in the notes herself, and that's what I wrote in the book. LinkedIn had 1993–2001, so did the GMC.

"Hang on," I say to Evie. I put the phone on the bed, grab Prosser's manuscript, and flick through it until I find the Beaverbrook dates. He has 1993 to 2001. So that's what she told him, too.

I check the 1994 image, of GiGi Libcewicz, later known as Angela

Reynolds, standing next to Angela Reynolds. Both this and the 1991 photo disappeared from the agency website not long after I told Angela I'd been doing research. *Digging?* she'd asked. She must have got them taken down, exercised the mandate she'd given Sacha to remove any online content RRX wasn't in control of. And I bet privacy wasn't her main concern.

My phone vibrates. Messenger notification. I snatch it up and open the app. A reply already from Angela Rodriguez, even though it's nighttime for her in the States. An insomniac? My own hasty message, bubbled in blue: I'm sorry to bother you again, but may I quickly ask: are you still a doctor? Beneath it, a longer response than my question warranted.

Well, she writes, even though I don't know you from Adam, I'm going to confess something to you anyway. See, I only went to medical school because my daddy was a doctor and his daddy before him, and I had no brothers, only sisters, so my daddy set his heart on at least one of us taking over the family practice. I didn't have any other clear idea of what I wanted to be at that age and my grades were good, so I applied to med school. Tell the truth, I was always near bottom of my class and my heart was never in it. I realized that when I met my husband. I was never driven like him, or like GiGi, who aced all her exams. Jorge and I met that Valentine's, like I told you, and I just knew, first sight! Bam! And he was the same. We married the week after we graduated and I got pregnant with our first immediately and so Jorge took my place in the family practice and Daddy, once he got used to the idea, was happy with that. Hoo! That's a roundabout way of answering your question! In short, I got my MD in 2001 but I never practiced as a doctor. I'm mom to four boys instead.

Rodriguez, then Reynolds, finished her medical degree at Beaverbrook in 2001—that's too much of a coincidence to accept. I type furiously: And your friend Angela Libcewicz, GiGi? Did she graduate at the same time as you?

It seems an age before I get her response, and I start to worry that I've got Mrs. Rodriguez wrong in pegging her as a blabbermouth. But then a reply pops up. I wouldn't call her a friend exactly. We roomed together my first year because of an admin error, but she was two years ahead of me and I was a freshman, so we didn't mix particularly after that first year.

And she graduated when?

Oh, that's the sad thing. She didn't. She was supposed to in '98, but she lost her scholarship. Officially we never heard why, but it's a conservative college,

Beaverbrook, and you can't hide a bump forever. I should know, after four! Such a waste. She did all the training and she was so talented. Last I heard she had some cleaning job. She looked me up, way back, and we met once when her girl was little and my son was a babe in arms, but I haven't heard from her since. I always thought it was such a shame that she didn't get to be a doctor.

Except she did. Bright, ambitious Angela "GiGi" Libcewicz never finished med school but an Angela Reynolds did. How she must have hated that, being the best in her class, a scholarship winner, and losing it all because of a mistake that had nothing to do with her ability. I can totally see it: she has her daughter and then works odd jobs to pay the rent. Maybe she asks the college to let her retake her exams and graduate and they refuse. She's furious—she's done all the work, has eight years' worth of experience under her belt; it isn't fair. She can't get a job in medicine without a degree . . . but what if she could get her hands on one? Her old roommate won't care; she's happy being a mom. Still, maybe best to engineer a meeting to check. Three years after GiGi drops out, Angela Reynolds turns up doing rotations on the other side of the country, where she starts to carve a reputation, having left her daughter with her parents. I don't know how she managed to get the paperwork past the authorities, but often people don't see what's right in front of them. I didn't, even though I had all those questions about her background, her date of birth, where she grew up, her parents' names. She would have been expecting me to ask these things, but even so, they must have needled. Sharp little jabs, pins pricking a hole in her story. In Boston she bumps into Michael Madrigal from Beaverbrook. She tells him she married, took her husband's name. He notices she's doing good work. But she realizes the more distance she puts between herself and her past the better. An opportunity comes up. London—perfect. She cuts all ties with her family and jets off to the UK. She makes sure she keeps her face off the internet. Her life's work becomes helping people keep their identities, while suppressing her own.

My heart is fluttering like it does when I'm writing and a book is coming together. Yes! It all fits. But how does Scott slot into this? And therefore Connor? And how do I? And why commission a book, go public, if privacy was paramount to keeping her secret?

My name is being called. A tinny, faraway voice. It's Evie, coming from the phone in my hand.

"Where are you?" I ask when I lift it to my ear.

"Some dive of a hostel. Central. Why?"

I've got to see Angela; I need to prove to myself that I'm right. All this time I've wanted answers about what happened in Varaig and why, and now I'm so close. "Meet me. At Angela's office."

"Why?"

I pick up the contact sheet. Angela and Angela, similar but different. GiGi is a master liar. But will she be able to keep it up if I show this to her and have Evie with me, if she sees her daughter face-to-face?

"I'll get you in. You'll be able to talk to her." There's silence at the other end. "Evie?"

"Oh God, oh God." Noises of movement. "When?"

"As soon as you can make it. I'm heading over now."

"I'll be there."

In the living room I snatch up my bag and coat. I'm out the front door before I've even got both arms into the sleeves. I haven't figured out all the details yet, but there's enough to know instinctively that it makes sense. Two Angelas. Two Scotts. I am not going mad.

Nearly twenty years ago, she got what she wanted by impersonation. And it worked. So she did it again. The question is, what did she want this time?

34

EVIE IS WAITING FOR ME OUTSIDE ANGELA'S OFFICE BUILDING.
Her face is clear of makeup, and without her contacts and with her hair parted
in the middle and tied back low she looks both younger and more like Angela.
She says hello in response to my taut nod and follows me up the steps to the
main door. As I ring the bell for the video camera I wonder whether Raphaela
will refuse us entry because Evie is with me. Probably not if she's in on the GiGi
charade. But she buzzes us through. Evie is tentative as she crosses the threshold.

"You haven't been inside before?"

"No." She does what I did that first time—looks around the foyer, peers
at where the stairs sweep up to the next story.

Raphaela is in her own office on the ground floor. She's casually dressed
in jeans and a stained sweater, and her hair is roughly scraped into a pony-
tail. Her desk is covered in archive boxes. She can barely muster a smile as
she stuffs a plastic bag with paperwork. "Angela isn't here. You'll have to
excuse me. I have a lot to do." She sounds tired, even more tired than when
she drove through the night to collect Rudy and Massimo.

"Are you moving offices?" I ask.

"I'm being let go."

"Why?"

From a corner of the room comes a croaking cry. Parked behind a sofa,
obscured by boxes, is a pram. Raphaela goes to it and lifts a baby to her
shoulder. "Apparently I'm a casualty of the merger."

"But surely you're indispensable?"

The baby, a boy, sits up in her arms, rigid in his sleeping bag, so amazed by the room around him that he makes little jerks of surprise. "I thought so. And yet here I am, being dispensed with." Raphaela smooths down her son's hair. "My partner's a nurse. We have our childcare schedule planned out in advance, but then I got fired and I have to clear out my office immediately, so . . ." She catches a waving fist in her hand.

"I'm sorry, Raphaela." She did mention a baby before, in Varaig, but I'm ashamed to admit I hadn't pictured her as a mother. Women are so good at parceling themselves out into their different roles. Parent, professional, partner, carer. Different wardrobes and personalities for each, like an actor stepping into character. How immaculate she looked every time we met before, how capable she seemed. Unbreakable. Now, in her jeans, in her panic, she's brittle, shattered by the hammer blow of Angela's decision. Sometimes loyalty gets you nowhere. "If there's anything I can do . . ." I trail off. She presses her lips together as if to stop herself from crying. I hope she manages to find a job soon. It's tough enough surviving in this city, let alone bringing up a child on one wage.

"We won't keep you," I say. "I'm looking for Angela. It's, well, it's rather urgent. Is she here?"

"She's at Varaig."

Shit. I try to play it cool. "Do you know when she'll be back?"

"No idea." She shows zero sign of wondering what I want Angela for, and it makes me believe what Connor said about nobody else knowing about the pretense.

The baby begins to fuss, wanting her attention. Over his grizzling, she says, "Have you tried calling her?"

"It's not something I can talk about with her over the phone."

The baby kicks. His mouth contorts in a grimace. Raphaela jigs him up and down. "And you are . . . ?" she says to Evie.

Evie hesitates, perhaps remembering their confrontation at the launch. Before she can answer, I jump in. "A friend of mine. Evie. Evie Libcewicz." Evie's eyebrows shoot up. I give a tiny shake of my head. From the cursory half-smile Raphaela gives, she has no idea that Evie is Angela's daughter, or that Libcewicz is Angela's original name. She's not in on that deception either. Not surprisingly, Angela has kept her cards close.

As I glance upward in relief, I catch sight of a black glass sphere bolted to the ceiling. A giant eye, watching, recording. A light pings on in my head, like the exit sign in a cinema showing the way out of the dark. If I can get the footage of Evie taking the painting, that'll be something else I can confront Angela with to prove she's been lying.

"Look," I say to Raphaela. "I realize this is nonstandard and you've got no reason to, but I'm hoping maybe you'll help me. I want to take a look at the CCTV recordings from the time I was at Varaig."

"Why?"

"Nothing illegal, I promise." I look pointedly at her son. "But it's probably best you don't know." Telling her about Connor and about Angela's double-dealing would involve her more than she either deserves or needs.

"Right." She holds my gaze. The old Raphaela, loyal to a fault, would have blocked me as efficiently as she did Evie at the launch. But I'm counting on this tired, worn-out Raphaela perhaps wanting to stick it to her ex-boss.

She sits at her computer, one hand holding her son securely against her body as she types with the other. "There," she says. "But it wasn't me who got you in."

"Understood." I replace her at the desk. Evie comes to watch what I'm doing. An enormous list of files fills the screen, ordered by date. They are named according to a system: Ldn (London) one to five, Sdi (Saudi) one and two, CT (Cape Town) one, Vg (Varaig) one to three. I click on Vg1 and get a black-and-white view down into the empty barn clinic. That's not what I want. I come out and select Vg2. A bird's-eye shot of the atrium and part of the kitchen, up to the window. Bingo. I scroll back to last year and pick Vg2 for the day I arrived at the house. I drag the slider to around the time I landed in the helicopter, then hit play. The house is empty. I choose x32 mode. Here's the top of my head as I come in through the mudroom, followed by Raphaela. Neither of us looks at the camera. I hadn't even been aware then that there was one. We talk, silent and quick, in the atrium, then I dash off in skittery fast-forward on a tour of the house, disappear up the stairs, and come rapidly, raggedly down again like a badly animated puppet. I select another file from Vg2, a day after Scott—*Connor*—arrived. Four figures, two human, two canine, loop from atrium to kitchen, trailing the same paths as if on tracks, tiny and regular as cuckoo clock figurines. Good—it looks like everything is here.

Then there's a flash of black screen, a jump on the clock. Connor, Massimo, and Rudy exit the kitchen; I come through a few moments later and head upstairs. That was after Connor reset the Wi-Fi for me. When he shut it down the recording must have stopped. Exiting the video, I go back to the folder.

"What are you looking for?" Evie asks.

"Confirmation."

Counting the days to when the painting went missing, I locate the correct file and skip through the hours. How much of this has Evie already seen, watching through the glass while waiting for her opportunity to get into the house? The clock advances to midday. I get my phone ready, angling the camera at the screen. Ah, here we go: there I am, sliding open the kitchen window, stepping out through it. I hit record on my phone.

Suddenly there's another blackout. The footage kicks back in but there's been a big jump in time to Connor closing the window while toweling his hair. No recording of Evie entering the kitchen.

Dropping my phone, I pause, rewind, and play at standard speed. Window opens. Jump. Window closes, Connor towels his hair. Rewind. Play. Window, jump, window, towel. In the atrium, the watercolor is hanging as I open the window. After the skip, it is gone. Dammit.

"Whoa, whoa, whoa!" Evie says, backing away, both hands lifted to ward off trouble. "If you're looking for evidence to report me to the cops . . ."

"But there is no evidence. Look." I replay the sequence again. Painting there; painting gone. No footage of the actual theft. And no proof for me of Angela's lies. This time it wouldn't have been Connor shutting the router off—there was no need, seeing as though I'd already left the house, and he'd given up that trick by then anyway. Just a terrible time for the Wi-Fi to actually go down.

"Oh my God," Evie says. "She deleted it." There's astonishment in her voice, and wonder and hope, and instantly I know she's right. I remember Angela when she came to Varaig that day, tapping at her phone.

"She saw you on camera," I say. "But she never told the police." I call over to Raphaela, who is bouncing the baby while pulling Tupperware and muslin cloths out of her bag. "Raphaela, did any of this footage ever go to the police?"

"For the inquest, you mean?"

"Or for anything else."

She gives me a brief funny look, but then lets her curiosity go, as if she's remembered it's best to stay out of it. "No. They never asked. I think they told Angela they had enough from the statements."

Evie reaches for the mouse and replays the section again. I watch, but this time it's not the missing theft that I notice, it's Connor's towel, his wet hair.

I stay Evie's hand. "Wait. Let it run a minute."

Connor leaves the kitchen. He goes into the atrium and disappears through the door leading to the bedrooms at the back of the house. The atrium is still for ages and I indicate to Evie to nudge it on until there's movement again. This time it's me, coming in from the mudroom, soaked through. Connor appears in the corridor, stops in his tracks. There's no sound, but I almost hear it: *Jeez.* A slip into his real voice. The screen version of me shakes her sodden sleeves, makes a bad joke. *Och, aye.*

"Rewind," I instruct Evie. "To the window." Dry me goes out. I check the time stamp. "Forward." Soaked me comes in twenty minutes later, confused about how he could have overtaken me, wondering about another path. But in between, Connor definitely doesn't leave the house. So how could I have seen him outside?

I take back the mouse and skip forward to the point where Angela arrived after I called her about the painting. Another jump on the clock, a really long one this time, and no footage of Angela in the house. I find the file for the same day but a few minutes earlier, on the Vg1 camera. The empty clinic, another jump, the empty clinic again. Rewind, pause. The damp patch on the floor, where the umbrella was tossed, is visible, but very faint. You wouldn't see it if you didn't know it was there. She's excised herself from the narrative. Why?

I think back. I went into the clinic; she was standing by a cupboard. She was startled, on edge. She had something in her hand—what was it? A phone—no, two phones. And . . . come on, Maddy, think. I picture her turning away from the cupboard. It had a phone-activated lock on it; a medicine cabinet. Yes, that's what was in her hand, vials of medication. They rattled. Not unusual for a doctor. She put them in her bag, shoved both phones into her pocket. What's so significant about that that she didn't want a recording of it to be seen?

With a growing sense of unease, I search through the files for the night when we took the dogs to the vet. Here's Connor, coming in fast-forward out of the kitchen, going to bed. He shuts the corridor door behind him. Shortly after here I am, stopping in front of the manikin. That was the night I noticed it had been engineered into a scream.

Behind me, Evie coughs sheepishly.

I twist in my seat. "That was you?"

She blushes. "Yeah. I saw you do it and it gave me an idea. I wanted . . . it was . . . for her."

I think of the theft night, the fetal position. They were messages for Angela. That's why Connor didn't know anything about them, why he denied it in front of Angela. "God, Evie, you freaked me out."

She blushes more deeply. "Sorry, I'm really sorry. I didn't think."

The way she apologizes reminds me she's little more than a kid. A hurt kid. And in the grand scheme of things, it hardly matters. "Never mind."

I return to the computer. Mini-me has already gone up to bed. I expect the next movement to be me coming down the stairs and Raphaela arriving. But earlier than that the mudroom door opens and Connor comes in wearing his Scott coat. He takes a bottle of whiskey and a glass from a kitchen cupboard and wanders off-screen, toward the living room. As he passes the camera, I see a pale slash at his shoulder. His damaged sleeve.

Something's wrong here. I do what I did with the painting: pause, rewind, play. There is no skip on the clock to indicate footage is missing from either a break in the Wi-Fi or from being deleted. Connor goes to bed; Connor enters the house. In between, the door to the corridor stays firmly closed. I pause on the man crossing the atrium. From this angle all I can see is the crown of his head, his coat, his long stride. But I know Connor didn't leave his room because the only way is via the corridor, and he would have been caught on camera. The bedrooms back there all had high skylights, not windows or doors, and the corridor was a dead end.

Evie says, "He looks kinda familiar." I hit play and let him walk across the room. "Oh," she says. "He's that guy, the janitor."

I don't correct her, but it isn't a janitor. There never was a janitor. This is who I saw the night in the mudroom when I heard noises; this is who I talked to in the living room when I smelled whiskey. This is Scott. The real Scott.

I can't believe I mistook him for Connor. The height, the clothes—yes, there's a familial likeness there. But now I know what I'm looking at—*who*—I can clearly see the differences. This man is a stranger. This stoop, this weariness that seems to weigh down his entire body—Connor was never this listless. There is always life to his body, vitality even in his moments of statue-stillness.

The video is still playing. I watch Raphaela arrive and leave; mini-me disappears out of range, going to the living room. A few minutes later Scott stalks out, across the kitchen and atrium and into the mudroom, to exit via the front door. He must have let himself into the house those times, presumably using his phone. But he was supposed to be in rehab down in Hertfordshire. So how and why was he in Varaig?

Evie, bored with all the silent to-ing and fro-ing, wanders off to see Raphaela's baby.

I use the moment alone to click back to the file menu. There's one camera I haven't looked at yet: Vg3. I'm presuming it's in the living room. I'm glad Evie's not looking over my shoulder as I find the day of the painting theft, because that was the night Connor and I were on the sofa. If it caught us, I want to delete it. Angela's not the only one who gets to keep things private.

But when I click on the Vg3 folder, a log-in window pops up, the name SEQUR across the top. The box for the username is filled: angelareynolds. The password is already populated, showing as a series of bullets. I hit enter, but the pane shakes.

I stand and call over the top of the machine. "Raphaela, I'm locked out. What's the password?"

"It should remember it," she says.

"It's not working."

Giving the baby to Evie, she comes back over to the computer, where she clears the field and types again, slowly, deliberately. It shakes. Incorrect password.

"No can do," she says. "Angela must have changed it." Her son begins grizzling. She rolls the chair away from the desk. "Sorry, he's hungry."

I indicate the computer. "Mind if I try?"

She gives me a one-shouldered shrug that says whatever, I don't care, fat lot of good it'll do anyway, and goes back to her son.

Sitting at the machine, I acknowledge the sheer unlikelihood of guessing a password. I try a few combinations, variations on "Varaig," "Skin Deep," "doctor," "Beaverbrook," "Elixir," and experiment with adding "2020" for the year of the product launch, but every time the pane shakes me off. My taps on the delete key become increasingly heavy-handed. I pause. I don't know how many tries it'll allow me before I'm locked out.

Evie is meandering around the office, taking in the plushness. She picks up a glass trophy from a shelf, the kind given out at industry awards, examines it, puts it back. I watch her stroke a pale green hydrangea, checking whether or not it's real.

I try "hydrangea," in case it's Angela's favorite flower. No joy. Passwords are designed to be secrets, not puzzles to be solved. If you want to protect something, you choose the unknown. Oh.

"When's your birthday again?" I ask Evie.

"January fifteenth."

"Nineteen ninety-nine?"

"Yeah. Why?" She comes around the back of the desk.

There's every chance that Angela's password is a randomly generated combination of numbers, letters, and symbols. But I type "Evelyn150199." Nothing. Then I switch the date to American style: "Evelyn011599."

A rotating wheel. Evie's breath hitches. The program loads.

What appears is not the living room, nor anywhere in the house or barn, but a completely new space. A bird's-eye angle again and grayscale: a small room I've never seen before. It's a combined kitchen-living area, distorted to a curve by the fish-eye lens. In frame is a countertop, littered with boxes and bottles, a fridge, a doorway, a sofa on one side of the room and an armchair on the other, separated by a small table with more mess on top. There is something heaped in the corner, but I can't make out what it is. Next to the armchair is a shuttered window; on the wall opposite is a closed exterior door. All is still.

I'm about to click out of the file when the heap in the corner moves. Slowly, it uncurls. It's a man, tall. He stands gingerly, using his hands against the wall to lever himself up. He walks to the kitchenette, staggering as if his muscles have locked stiff. Now that he is closer to the camera I can make out short hair, a V-necked sweater over a shirt. Scott—the real Scott. He grabs for a bottle but knocks it over. It rolls across the counter. He picks it up, unscrews the lid, pours liquid into a waiting glass. Taking both, he returns to the living area and collapses into a chair.

I leave the footage running. "Raphaela?"

She looks up from spoon-feeding yogurt. "Yes?"

"Where is Varaig Three?"

The baby dribbles yogurt onto his chin. Gently, Raphaela scrapes his skin with the plastic spoon, pops it back into his mouth. "The bothy. Well, the old gamekeeper's cottage. On the Varaig estate. It's empty. The camera's to keep away squatters."

On-screen, Scott hasn't moved from his chair. I click out and go back, selecting certain days, certain times. On the afternoon of the golden eagle, the front door opens. I presume it's him, coming in, but it's a woman with light hair. Angela—who was supposedly out of the country, who told me she wouldn't have any time to come to Varaig, who assured Connor his brother was getting better in rehab. She retrieves a crate from the doorstep and moves it to the kitchen counter. I know what's in that crate: bottles, bottles, bottles. She unpacks it and goes out of frame, presumably to a bedroom. She doesn't stay long. After she's gone, Scott emerges from the unseen room and tries the front door but it won't open. She's locked him in. On the afternoon of the downpour he puts on his coat. The shoulder is torn—the lining shows light against the dark wool. He tries the door again. Still it won't budge, so he opens the shutters and the window and climbs out. He forgets to close it behind him. The floor darkens with rain. When he comes back, through the window again, he is drenched. He reaches for a bottle, fills his glass, disappears into the bedroom.

I drag the slider forward to not long before Angela arrived at the big house, when she slipped into the barn clinic. Here she is again. He is slumped in his armchair, she is looming over him. It looks like she's shouting at him, pointing at the window. She does something to the shutters. I see her break away, answer her phone. She goes outside. I check the time. That was me on the phone, calling her about the painting. I remember how edgy she was and also hearing background noise—did she sit in her car while talking to me, pretending to be overseas when all the time she was down the valley? Returning, she goes to Scott's chair and holds out her hand, demanding he give her something. He produces an object from his pocket that lights up. His phone. She takes it and goes out again. He tries the door and the shutters but can't open them—she must have locked those, too. Maybe she saw on CCTV that he'd been up to the house and realized he'd let himself in with his phone. He downs another drink. An hour and a half later, she is back. From the way his head lolls on the sofa, I assume he is either asleep or passed out. She clears mess from the kitchenette, takes a box from her bag and puts it on the counter, uncaps a new whiskey bottle. The box and the bottle stay on the counter after she leaves—until he comes to and stumbles over. He must drop the pills when popping them out of their blister pack, because he pincers something up from the counter.

"Was that Angela?" asks Evie after I click out. "What was she doing?" She asks as if we're watching a normal movie together and she's lost track of the story. I, however, knowing how this one is going to end, can't bring myself to answer. Evie wanders off to the window and stares out.

The cursor hovers over the next file name I choose, November 21. Then I think about the discrepancy over the call to the police and intuition makes me go back a day, to the twentieth. An oscillation starts up inside me, a string on vibrato. My hand trembles as I hit select, the mouse skids as I slip through time.

He's there. Alone, in his chair. Then she arrives. It's 8:14 p.m. I grab my phone and film what's playing on the computer. She has papers in her hand. She thrusts them at him, but he smacks them away and they flutter to the floor. They begin to argue. The lack of sound heightens the drama, exaggerating their movements like actors in a silent movie, loudening my own accelerated breathing. She throws up her arms, exasperated. He backs off. She advances. He retreats until he's cornered. She gathers the papers and tries again, her gestures smaller but still animated. His knees give way and he slides to the floor, returning to the crumpled position I'd first seen him in. He buries his face in his hands, shakes his head. She puts the sheaf aside and goes to the counter. She hesitates, as if thinking something through, and then pours whiskey. She slugs some back. Her attention goes to her handbag. She pulls things from it, things that are too small for me to make out. One is a pair of surgical gloves, which she puts on. Another item, when she picks it up, reflects the light. She shows it to him and must say something, because he looks up and makes a swipe for it, even though there's no way he can reach her. She puts the object on the kitchen counter and takes up something else, something in a packet that she tears open. She brings the two objects together, then holds one up to the light and flicks. A needle. She's checking there's no air in it. Squatting before him, she puts the syringe on the floor by his leg, within arm's reach. Then she retreats to the sofa, sits, and waits.

It doesn't take long. Soon his fingers creep forward. I inhale sharply. I want to yell, No, don't touch it! But whatever I do will make no difference now. He must be practiced at injecting himself, because he manages it the first time, even given how drunk he is. He drops the used syringe to the floor. His head flops toward his chest, as if he's falling asleep, then back against the wall. On-screen, Angela watches. Eventually, she goes over. Gently, she takes his arm. Placid now, he lets her help him to his feet. She steadies him as he puts on one shoe, two. When he can't tie the laces, she takes over. She leaves him swaying in the middle of the room to put on her coat and I know from the way his chin is down and how he is gripping his eyes with one hand that he's crying. Did he understand what was about to happen? Did he care? My throat clogs, the lump expands. My vision blurs. I don't want to watch, but neither can I stop.

She leads him to the door. Docile, he follows. He moves clumsily, striking his shin on the table, thrusting out his hands for balance. In that moment, I can see the child he once was, the old man he might have become but now never will. By contrast, her movements are brusque yet controlled. She opens the door to the night, to the dark moorland, to the cliff. I check my phone is still recording. She takes an object from her pocket. It lights up. A phone. She wipes it with a flash of white I presume is a tissue and tosses it onto the sofa. I understand that the second mobile I saw in the clinic was probably his, that she used it to get into the medicine cabinet to make it look like he'd helped himself to drugs. He pays no heed. She stands back to let him go outside first, a strange kind of courtesy. She follows through.

On the film, half an hour later Angela comes in alone. She closes the door behind her and sags against it. She remains there for some time. Eventually she straightens. At the sink, a flame flares and quickly dies. She has burned the paperwork. She runs the tap. Once satisfied the cinders have gone, she takes a glass from the cupboard. She pours whiskey and keeps the bottle in her hand as she downs it. No sooner has she swallowed than she pours again. The second dram disappears only a little more slowly than the first. Fortified, she rinses the glass, dries it on a dish towel, puts it back in the cupboard. She picks up her bag and takes one last look around the cottage. She holds the door open with the back of her heel as she pulls off the gloves and drops them into her bag, and then she slips out.

The room is utterly still. Lifeless.

35

I STOP RECORDING AND REMAIN SILENT FOR A LONG TIME, digesting what I've witnessed. The tiles are all slotted into place, the full design revealed. Angela lied to Connor in the same way she lied to me and everyone else. There was no rehab that time, no ensuring Scott got the very best care until he was back on his feet. There was just preying on a vulnerable man's weakness to try to get what she wanted, then destroying him when he resisted.

The papers she burned must have been the contract for the merger with Singh that Sacha couldn't get Scott's signature on, because I can't think what else would be so important to her. It makes sense now, what Scott told Connor about Angela being a liar and a fake. He wasn't talking about her ending their romantic relationship; he was freaking out because he'd discovered Angela had stolen someone's identity and was practicing illegally. Perhaps he blocked Sacha's attempts to process the merger because he was scared the fraud would be exposed. *We're so fucked*, he told Connor. *Singh, Singh*. The stress of keeping a secret like that would break anyone, let alone someone prone to addiction. And who handed him that first drink and kept providing more? Who not only encouraged him to embrace his demons but locked him in a cottage so he couldn't escape them? Who, as Connor told me, likes to hide the ugly things away?

I think of the statement she made after his death, thanking the doctors for everything they tried to do, and of Connor telling me his brother had been ill for a long time. To the outside world it might have seemed Angela was helping Scott, but she wasn't his rescuer, his new start. She was the cause, his end. There was zero chance she'd hire someone else to do her dirty work because she always wants control—she's built her entire life on it, controlling herself, the people around her, even the aging process. She used Scott for years, happy to take his investment to get her where she wanted, but when he began to pull away, became a threat, she wouldn't have it. She was able to lead him to the cliff at night because she knew the paths well—didn't she tell me she loved walking there with Rudy and Massimo? Naturally, she made mistakes. Scott got out of the cottage despite the locked door. Overconfident in the lack of signal, she didn't initially take away his phone, meaning he could access the main house. And when she called police to report a "jumper"—she will have been that nameless dog walker—she neglected to account for sunrise. Some oversights she could fix herself—she made sure to imprison Scott properly, sped up her plan in order to prevent things from spiraling again, and eventually took his phone—while for others she held her nerve with the kind of trust only a narcissist can have in her own immunity, and her arrogance paid off. As far as I know the police never tried to trace the caller, perhaps because the story seemed to fit. Sickeningly, the biggest piece of luck for her was that Scott must have taken hours to die, because his date of death was recorded as November 21, which fitted with the alibi she'd set up—the meeting with me. Although, knowing Angela and her medical knowledge, maybe Scott's tortuous end was no convenient twist of fate but something she'd planned for in giving him drugs and alcohol. It's too awful to contemplate.

And me? A pawn right from the beginning, oblivious—in a way that Jon Prosser never was—to Angela's lies and corruption. She needed a witness to Scott's demise, but she couldn't risk having the real Scott stay at the house because she couldn't manage him, couldn't trust that he wouldn't reveal her secret, or know for sure that he'd deteriorate so far he'd jump of his own volition. So she set up a facsimile, inventing a book project, even getting it printed to make it look legit, and brought in someone to feed stories to about her partner's struggles, stories she made sure were recorded and ready to pass on to the police after his death, so that suicide would be the only conclusion to draw. Someone discreet, who'd keep the knowledge to herself; someone who didn't know him, so wouldn't realize she wasn't seeing the real person; someone whose attention would be elsewhere, focused on the vainglorious goal of getting her name on the cover of a book. Me, her puppet. If there's anything Angela excels at, it's exploiting the weaknesses in vanity.

What I can't work out is why she didn't delete the cottage videos. An oversight because she was so caught up in the merger or managing this awful scheme? Arrogance because she'd already doctored the "evidence" from the main house in case the police asked for it, or because she presumed no one would ever guess the password? Or perhaps, in some weird, twisted way, she wants someone to see it, to confront her. Well, I have the proof now, here in my hand. No more looking on—it's time to act.

"I need to get to Varaig." Somehow my voice comes out clear and steady.

Evie, Raphaela, and the baby all turn. Raphaela's face forms a question. Then she catches herself and nods. Baby on hip, she comes to the desk, where her handbag is open. She rummages one-handed and pulls a small object from the bag. "Here."

Hanging from the tip of her finger is a car key. The Mercedes symbol is upside down, like a peace sign gone wrong. She hands it to me. "It's parked outside. I'm supposed to take it back to the dealership, so you'd be saving me a job. Drop it off when you get back to London. The paperwork's in the glove box. The address is on it." Mistaking my shaky anxiety over what I've seen on Angela's computer for reluctance, she adds, "I'll call the insurance people, get you added. Don't worry about the cost—it's on the firm." She grins widely at the baby and lifts him in the air above her head, so he's flying. She blows a raspberry against his pudgy tummy. "The pricier, the better."

A tiny victory for Raphaela, but you take your revenge any way you can. I look at Evie. Her shoulders lift in encouragement.

Outside, as I beep the car to unlock it, Evie opens the passenger door.

"What are you doing?" I say.

"Coming with you."

"You're not. It's too . . ." I was going to say "dangerous."

She takes advantage of my pause to get into the car. "Too what? Too far? She's my mom, Maddy. And I'm finally ready to talk to her." She twists around to grab the seat belt. "If you won't take me, I'll go there myself anyway. You know I will."

I don't doubt her. I hover on the pavement. I got her to come to the office because I wanted her with me when I found Angela. And is it actually dangerous? Surely not for Evie. Angela has protected her so far, shielded Evie from the police; she's not going to hurt her. Besides, Evie doesn't even know what happened with Scott, and as I don't intend to tell her, she's further shielded by her ignorance.

It might, however, be dangerous for me. But everything I've seen of Angela tells me she's the cold, calculating type; crimes of passion are not her style. And what, realistically, is Angela going to do with her own daughter looking on? I think of a windy day on heathery ground and of two crows, seeing off an eagle. Of strength in numbers. Evie's seat belt fastens with a click. I slide into my seat and start the engine.

Connor once told me that it would take at least eight hours to drive from London to Scotland. I do it in a little more than seven. Evie is silent, leaning against the blacked-out window, lost in her own head, presumably preparing what to say to Angela when we get to Varaig.

I try to focus only on driving, but bigger thoughts intrude. She pushed him. She can't have done. I know she did. I don't. I saw it with my own eyes. I didn't—and I've been deceived that way before. She set things up. She set *me* up. But she couldn't have known for sure how it would play out. She lied, she lied, she lied.

When we stop south of Glasgow to refuel for the final leg I try to call Connor. It doesn't even ring, as if he's out of signal range. We push on. Night falls. Mist builds around us. The dashboard instruments glow. Five miles, three miles, two.

Finally, I turn off the road. The gravel driveway crunches beneath the tires. No stealth arrival for us. As we round the bend, the headlights illuminate the side of the house. Parked in front is Angela's four-by-four. And next to that a beaten-up old Golf, one door panel a different color from the rest.

36

MY STOMACH GRIPES AND I FEEL NAUSEOUS. CONNOR BETRAYED me, twice over. Why else would he be here now?

Evie has undone her seat belt and picked up her knapsack, ready to get out.

"Hang on," I say.

"Why?"

I aim for my normal voice. "Just." Connor being here changes things. Perhaps I should call the police. I check my phone. No signal. I try connecting to the house Wi-Fi. Locked out. I could turn the car around, head to the nearest town and a police station. But after Nabil, will they listen? I can only try. I'm reaching for the ignition when the door to the house opens, a slash of gold light widening in the gloom. I need to decide: act, or run?

Angela herself steps out, and a security lamp—a new feature—clicks on. Wrapped in layers of fine wool, she smiles the forced smile of someone caught unawares and quickly rethinking a scenario. The breach in her usual self-possession bolsters me. I assess her. She doesn't look like a threat. Okay then, let's put this to rest.

But it's best Evie stays in the car. "Wait here. Just for a minute. Let me speak to her first, okay?"

Pale, nervous, she's easy to convince. "Okay."

I reach for the handle and get out.

The cold air is as serene and fresh as it was when I was last in Varaig.

Mist is creeping in. The concrete of the house is stained with damp and a ragged fringe of water leaches down from the flat roof, rendering the brutalist architecture sullen and foreboding. Not such a sanctuary now.

Angela hasn't moved. From behind her comes frenzied barking and out streaks a double dash of browny-black: Massimo and Rudy. They nose my legs urgently. I don't bend to pet them, but I'm relieved they're still okay.

"Madeleine. What a surprise." Angela is poise-perfect. Her eyebrows don't even lift when she registers the Mercedes. The windows are tinted and the interior light is off; I don't think she can see Evie inside. I glance to check. She can't.

Although she doesn't verbally invite me in, from the way she turns into the house the invitation is implicit. I follow through the mudroom. The atrium looks much as I remember, although it feels changed, charged. The enormous expanse of glass, black now that it's dark, is streaked with recent rain. Where the watercolor had hung a new work takes pride of place, a black-on-white painting of the Elixir logo, the same quarter-profile of a woman's face that appeared on the now-pulped copies of that goddamn book, the start of all this.

Angela stops in front of the photograph of the freckled girl. "Rudy, Massimo," she croons. She clicks her fingers and points into the kitchen to send the dogs to their beds. I think of her walking away from her little girl but taking her dog and that painting with her. Are animals she can train to her every command the only things she can allow herself to love?

When they've gone she wheels around. The hem of her cardigan, a long waterfall style, swirls out. She clasps her hands in front of her and looks as brightly at me as if she's hosting a cocktail party. "So. How can I help?"

I'm tired of that mask. I want to rip it off. "By dropping the act. Telling the truth."

"And what truth would that be?"

Footsteps. Connor emerges from the kitchen, shocked as hell to see me. "Maddy! What are you doing here?"

Forewarned by the presence of his car, I get to be cooler. "I'd ask you the same thing, but I'd say that's fucking evident."

Connor looks at me like he's never seen me before. "Angela invited me.

To talk about the business." The dogs, unwilling to miss the pack reunion, ignore orders and come back through. They nuzzle Connor's jeans. "I was on my way up here anyway—I told you."

I'm sick of all the pretense. "I've seen the video," I tell Angela. "Videos."

Her facial features elongate in the very picture of polite inquiry. "Of?"

"What's going on?" Connor asks.

"Of you." I address this to her but keep half an eye on him, watching for his response. "Killing a man."

Angela scoffs. "No, you didn't. Utter nonsense."

I expected denial and more lies, but this over-the-top faux ignorance is maddening. "Well then, of you leading a man to his death. By the hand!"

"Maddy," Connor says, his head jerking back. "What are you talking about?"

"Your brother—as if you didn't know!" On my phone I open the recording I took in Angela's office. I shove it at him.

He resists taking it, acting like I'm the one who's out of order, but then he must recognize Scott on the screen, because he snatches up the phone. His eyes widen. A hand comes to cover his mouth. So he didn't know. Some of the tension leaves my muscles.

He starts shaking his head, as if he can't believe what he's seeing. "What is this?" he asks. "Angela?"

I correct him. "Her name's GiGi."

He looks confused, but her smugness has vanished. She takes hold of the edges of her cardigan and wraps them taut across her body. It's an out-of-character gesture, insecure. "You know he was up here, Connor. You heard, at the inquest, remember? Yes! He made his way to Varaig—he let himself into the bothy."

"You shut him in, you mean," I say. "Connor, there was no rehab. She locked him in a cottage down there." I point out at the valley toward the loch. "With a shit ton of booze and drugs and no way out."

"What rubbish! Of course I didn—"

She stops. Connor is holding out the phone. On the screen is a crow's-nest image: Angela, in the cottage with Scott. Setting out bottles on the kitchenette counter. "Angela?" he says again.

His eyes are filling, his brows are knotted low with unease. I place my fingers over his. "You don't need to see any more. Trust me." He lets me take the phone.

He shifts his focus to her. "Why?"

She doesn't answer, so I do. In a way, I've known since the launch. "She wanted the Singh merger to go through. And she wanted to protect what she started; to protect herself." Scott was becoming a liability; if he'd told someone what she'd done, Singh would have dropped her instantly. The GMC would have stripped her of her license—a license that isn't even hers—and she'd have lost her reputation, and to Angela reputation, and what that brings, is everything. Without the wealth, the success, who is Angela Reynolds? She had another identity, once, as a daughter, a mother. But in erasing GiGi Libcewicz she gave those up. Take away Dr. Angela Reynolds, the wealth, the success, and she is nothing. "She's exactly what Scott told you she was," I add. "A liar and a fake."

She fastens on me. "What—I shouldn't be allowed to do what I do just because I don't have the right pieces of paper?"

"It's not just pieces of paper, it's fraud! It goes against everything doctors believe."

"I would have aced those goddamn exams if they'd let me take them. I know it, you know it, they knew it. I wouldn't have gotten this far if I wasn't excellent at what I do. He should have held himself together." How the hell can she blame Scott? I begin to interrupt, but she cuts me off. "Spare me the righteousness. Like you've never stepped off the moral high ground. Look at what you've done to Connor."

Fury propels me forward. She shrinks away. Performed, like her whole life has been a performance? Or actual worry? She circles around to the console table under the stairs. I follow, bearing down on her. It feels good to be the one in charge for once. "But why involve us, GiGi? Him or me?"

She is trapped now, backed up against the wall, gripping the table. She attempts a sneer, trying to gain the upper hand. "Why not you?"

The photo of the freckled girl is on the edge of my vision. That photo— she pointed out six months ago that I didn't know what I was looking at. My eagerness to please, my blind naivete. That's why me. Well, I can see it all now. The blinkers are off, the smoke gone, the mirrors shattered. Scott's blood is partly on my hands, and it's all because of her and her fucking fakery. I move right in. She cringes away, hair falling out of her chignon, spine arched, skin mottled.

All of a sudden, as I loom over her like she loomed over him, I'm not sure if her fear of me is phony at all. Her eyes flick to the side and I see I've raised my fist. I wasn't aware of doing so, but there it is, fingers balled, knuckles white, poised to strike. It seems to me that the fist isn't mine, that it is either somebody else's or that an outside force has taken over part of my body, knotted my hand with rage, angled it to violence. What am I doing? Who even am I anymore? In that split second I understand how easily I've lost control of myself, not only right now but ever since I met her: swelling with ambition, manipulating Connor, turning to violence. It terrifies me and I freeze. I can't be like her. I won't.

Immediately she's on the offensive, twisting out from under me, grabbing the heavy bronze manikin. And there's such fury in her face, such pure red rage, that I know she's going to kill me with it; I can already feel the blow, the skin tearing, the bone shattering. Connor is coming toward us and he's yelling, but there isn't enough time because already she's lifting it right up to the top of its arc, wielding it like a weapon, a club. I can feel the tightening of the air, like the upward tug of a string, and I know there's nothing I can say that will make her stop. I squeeze my eyes shut.

Movement, above. A bang, across the room. A gasp, in front.

I open my eyes. Angela has both arms raised above her head, clutching the manikin, but she's not bringing it down. Something has shocked her rigid. Connor has almost reached her, but he's not the reason. She is staring past both of us, toward the kitchen. I duck away and as I do so I see what has paralyzed her.

Evie is pressed up against the glass, hands and face spectral against the black of outside. Her expression reveals she saw exactly what Angela was about to do. She slams the glass again.

The dogs start barking. They sprint to the window and scrabble against it. The change in Angela is extraordinary. She replaces the manikin, tucks loose strands of hair behind her ears. Warily, as if she's the one with something to be afraid of, she moves across the floor toward the window. The whole way she doesn't take her eyes off Evie, drinking in every detail, as though she is measuring the young woman here against the toddler she'd once been. The height of her, the new length of her skinny limbs. The worn shoes and baggy-knee sweatpants. The inadequate jacket hanging open. The vulnerability in her frightened face.

Evie swallows so hard I can see it. She backs off from the glass, drawing the two sides of her coat tightly across her body, overlapping them protectively, unknowingly aping her mother's earlier gesture. She is shaking her head, unsure. When Angela is an arm's length away from the glass, Evie turns and runs off into the night.

Angela is at the window, hauling it open. "Evie, wait!" A blast of cold air and she's out, onto the terrace and disappearing into the dark. The dogs give chase.

My heart kicks. "Quick!" I say to Connor. "We've got to stop her." Evie is proof of what Angela has done. I'm outside, Connor fast behind me. He doesn't know who Evie is but he understands the danger. Angela is capable of anything.

Beyond the terrace, visibility is worse than I've ever seen, fifteen, twenty yards max. The moor, valley, loch, and mountains are vanished, all perspective lost in thick fog. We slow.

I try switching on the flashlight on my phone and pointing it dead ahead. The fog only seems to jump closer. I shut off the beam. "Evie?" I call. My breath billows. "Evie, come back!"

Somewhere ahead the dogs bark. I step off the terrace onto the lawn.

"Stay close," Connor says. As we move the fog recedes, but only by as much as we've advanced, as if marking us in an unsettling game. I switch on my phone flashlight once more and try angling its light at the ground a few feet in front instead of at head height. That's better. We go forward; tufts of grass and rocks appear. More grass, heather, a bigger rock, rimed and glinting with frost.

"Evie?" I shout.

No reply. I arc the beam, hoping to land on a face. Again it seems the fog closes in, but now I know it's a trick and it'll drop back if I lower my phone. I pick up the pace. Connor switches on his phone's light, too. I strain my ears for the slightest sound over the push and pull of my breath, the scratch of my arms against the body of my coat, the swish of Connor's jeans. The heather thins. Every few seconds we call Evie's name and

Connor whistles for Rudy and Massimo, up-down-up, "Scott's" distinctive call. I lift the phone light and the fog closes in. I tilt it down. Bracken. This must be where the bracken field starts. I know where we are. Evie knows this land, too—but Angela knows it better. I twist around. Over my shoulder the house is visible, the yellow of its fog-diffused lights acting as a beacon. It seems closer than expected. We must not have walked as far as I thought we had.

A bark, nearby. The sound of scurrying, then Rudy and Massimo bound out of the mist. Connor dives and grabs their collars. "I'll run them back," he says. "It's not safe for them to be out in the dark—and someone could trip. Stay here."

"Okay. Be quick."

At first I do as promised. I stay put, calling Evie's name. My throat becomes tight from shouting. "Can you hear me? Can you follow my voice?"

No reply, not even a dog bark. The fog is deadening everything. Am I too late? We really need help, the police. I check my phone. No signal. I've got to go further. I press on.

The fog thickens. Beneath my feet, under the sodden, spongy shroud of grass and earth, the ground is uneven. My breath is coming hard. I think of Connor teaching me about this wild place he so loves, explaining about forces deep within the earth powerful enough to smash and force and rupture. "Evie?"

My foot skids. I bring the phone's beam to where I've stopped. Grit, scree. There shouldn't be scree here. I move my light ahead. Slippery, treacherous stone, fog obscuring what lies beyond. My heart rebounds. I'm not where I thought I was at all. I'm much farther from the house, already in the hidden dip, almost at the cliff. Connor, on that last day: *What are you doing here, Maddy? It's dangerous.* Warning me off from more than just the drop.

Noise, nearby. Muffled shuffles. "Evie?" I creep forward. More slippery rock, more fog. I think of her flimsy canvas shoes, the worn tread. "Please be careful."

The shuffling noises stop. Then, close, a strangled sob. I move the light. Over there, just a few feet away, to the right: Evie, near the cliff edge. And Angela, rushing toward her.

"No!" I yell. The light beam skitters off. I flail it around and it comes down on the pair of them. Dazzled, they stop dead. In the aftermath of my scream there descends a museum-like hush, an anticipatory thickening that seems to slow everything down—movement, breath, thought. Both squint in the light. Then Angela begins to move again, ever so gradually, as if approaching a restive animal she doesn't want to frighten. When she reaches Evie, she cups her face and tilts it gently in the light from my phone, all traces of violence gone. Evie doesn't flinch. As she had done with me in the barn, Angela scans Evie's features, but this time her expression is one of wonderment. Evie has kept her eyes angled down, but now she raises them and meets her mother's gaze, and I'm close enough to hear her take a deep breath. The two of them are side-on to me, each standing parallel to the cliff edge, and I'm struck by how similar their profiles are: the swept-back, light hair, held at the nape of the neck, the curve of the forehead, the slope of the jaw. I can see how Angela would have looked twenty years ago, and I can tell what Evie will look like twenty years from now. Angela's face has softened while holding Evie, which adds to the family resemblance. Her attention falls on her daughter's mouth. She traces a finger across the plumped-up lips.

"You didn't need to do that," she says.

Evie, feeling the shift, the judgment, wrenches her face out of Angela's hands.

The sudden movement shoots my heart into my throat. "Evie, please come away from the edge."

She doesn't reply, but she does at least sidestep toward me. "You left me," she says to Angela, her voice sorrowful as a child's.

Angela covers her own mouth. "I came back for you, you know."

"No."

"Yeah, I did." She nods vehemently, all the conscious held-in quality gone. "You were still small. You don't remember." Her accent has slipped, become more like Evie's. She's GiGi again. "You clung to Gramma's leg and wouldn't let go. You were hysterical. You screamed and screamed as if you didn't recognize me. You worked yourself into such a state you could barely breathe."

"So it's my fault?"

"No! You were a kid, you were confused. You were frightened, I was crying, Gramma was crying. And I couldn't do it, couldn't take you away like that. You were happy there, settled. Before, when you were with me, you were sick a lot. I was cleaning at a hospital then. I tried taking you into work with me, I took time off to care for you. I got fired. I couldn't make the rent. I called my mom, and she said, come here, let us take care of you while you build yourself back up."

"Because that's what family do! They take care of one another."

Angela keeps talking, intent on justifying her actions. "They wanted me to do well. You have to remember, they went to that country with no money, but with a need to succeed."

I can't help myself—I blow a sarcastic laugh through my nose.

Evie, glad of the support, raises her chin. "And what?" she asks Angela. "You inherited that need? That's your justification?"

Angela takes a placatory half-step toward her. Evie backs away. With every shift of a foot my heart jolts. I can't see for sure how far they are from the edge because I'm keeping the light trained on their faces. Angela seems calm now, but I don't trust her and I can't try to call the police because I daren't risk moving my phone. Where's Connor?

"I told myself wait a little longer," Angela says. "You can fetch her soon. At first I needed money for the plane ticket. And then I needed to go back a winner. I needed to show them, and the people who judged me, and you, that it was worth it, the choice I'd made to be away from you, the sacrifice."

"You chose you! You chose all this!" Evie flings her arms wide so fiercely I think she's going to spin herself off balance. Even though she's beyond my reach I shoot out a hand to grab her but she stays firmly on her feet, anchored in place by the ferocity of her anger. "You could have sent for me anytime. You chose yourself and money and—"

"I sent money."

"I didn't want your money! I wanted you!"

Angela pulls her cardigan around herself again, tight as a bandage. "And I wanted you, too, but I couldn't come back."

Evie seizes on that. "You could come home now. Look . . ." She shrugs off her knapsack.

The movement makes me nervous. "Please, Evie, come this way."

I don't think she hears me, preoccupied as she is with extracting the watercolor. She offers it to Angela. "You remember how beautiful it is there. Like here. Gramps said you loved it when you were little." I allow the phone to lower the tiniest bit, to illuminate the farmhouse, the fields. If Evie can appeal to Angela's remaining sentimentality, I might be able to get her away from here, from that drop.

Angela shakes her head. "I can't, Evie. One day you'll understand why. Not after . . . I can't."

"One day? Like, one day when I'm older?" Defiant again. "Well, I'm older now. I understand now."

But she doesn't really. Although she watched Connor and me through the windows of the house, caught glimpses of the video in Raphaela's office, she didn't comprehend what she saw. I, though, do understand. And maybe, if I goad Angela in the right way, she'll come after me again, away from Evie.

"The reason you couldn't go back," I say to Angela, "is because you stole someone else's life. You stole a life and then you took one."

Sharp, Evie turns on her. "Taken a life?"

A new idea comes to me. Connor lost his brother; I almost lost my mind. This is one way I can make Angela pay—tell Evie everything, make her daughter see the real her. "She—"

"Don't!" Grit skids as Angela lunges toward me.

I stall, not because of her, but because a memory flashes into my head, of Mum in our car, driving on that summer outing to a place like this, smiling at me, still healthy, full of life. Of love. In the moment of being stalled it's as if I'm teetering on an edge, and it would be so easy to keep going, but I know that if I do there will be no way back, no way of unsaying what I say, no way of undoing what I've done, of changing who I'll become. Evie is just a girl who wants her mother, who misses her. Every single day. I swallow down the truth.

But Evie has seen Angela's guilt; she's perceived more than I gave her credit for. "Who did you hurt?"

Angela narrows her eyes against my light. The cords of her neck strain. "He fell. He *fell*."

"Tell that to the police," I say.

She blocks both ears with her hands and shakes her head over and over, as if she can't stop. "I'll lose everything."

Evie flings the painting across the gap between them. "You already did."

Maybe it's that sudden movement that does it. Or the way, startled at the noise behind me, I jump and the light jumps with me, plunging what was illuminated into darkness just as a face emerges from the mist, lit from underneath; a ghoul, ghostly white. Maybe it's the setting, all the memories crowding in. The shorn hair, the shaven cheeks, the haunted expression. For a split second it seems he has returned. Scott.

From the cliff comes a strangled sob, a repeated "No, no, no!" Scuttling, scree rolling underfoot. A scream. Short, snapped.

"Evie!" I shoot the phone light around, searching for her. It finds only empty ground. I swing it wildly from side to side. It slices into the dark. I can't see anyone.

And then I do. The beam lands on light hair, pulled back, tied low. She's in a squat, right at the cliff edge, the tips of her toes jutting out into empty air. She has both hands over her face. At my approach she lets them drop. Eyes blink in the sudden glare, pale eyes, GiGi's eyes. Her features are distorted, demented by fear, horror, the kick start of grief.

Evie turns her face to the void.

LATER

THE BOOKSHOP IS QUIET, THE "CLOSED" SIGN HUNG IN THE
window to allow us the chance to get ready before the door opens. There's
not much left to do: the hardbacks are already arranged on a side table,
the drinks are on ice. The shop owner has finished the window display
and popped upstairs to do some admin; Sacha and Monique have run
out, ostensibly to get another bottle of champagne but really to give me
a minute to myself before people arrive.

This is a small independent store and there are a few hundred books on
the shelves, spanning every kind of genre, each one maybe ninety thousand
words long and probably years in the making. The air has that ligninic smell
I love, of ink and press and freshly cut paper, the smell of tens of millions
of letters and words and thoughts, of creativity and craft, the smell of late
nights, self-doubt, and sheer bloody tenacity.

I pick up a copy from the table—ironically, I forgot to bring my own
for the reading. My publisher chose the title *Beauty and the Beast*, copying the headline on the long read I successfully pitched last year to the
Times, the feature that led to other newspaper commissions and, ulti-
mately, to this book. But privately I still think of it as SKIN DEEP because
who better epitomizes the idea of there being little of worth under the
polished veneer than Angela?

I turn to the author photo on the inside of the jacket. I told the photographer not to retouch it. He couldn't believe it, asked was I sure, all
his clients usually did. In this photograph Sacha says I'm more like my

mother than ever. In this photograph I am forty-one and I look it; I have forty-one years of life written across my face, forty-one years of laughing, crying, exploring, succeeding, failing, loving. When I look at this photo I don't worry, like Angela said, about there being more time behind me than ahead. These lines, scars, marks, and moles are the script of my life, and I choose for them to be read. It is a true photo, honest. It is me.

Evie sent a text earlier, wishing me luck. She is in Varaig meeting an estate appraiser, seeing whether there's anything in the art collection that can be donated to a museum before the house is sold, but I suspect she wants to keep out of the limelight. I couldn't see a way to write truthfully about Angela and what she did without including Evie and me and Scott and Connor. I only began to put down on paper what had happened after it became clear the police weren't going to charge Evie over Angela's death. She read both the feature and the manuscript before I submitted them and gave me her blessing. So did Connor, replying in an email from a small town in the Spanish Pyrenees that he trusted me. True to form, he went to the mountains to clear his head. Me, I wrote.

That was nearly a year ago and we haven't been in touch since. Not long after Angela died we decided it would be best to not see each other for a bit, while we came to terms with everything that had happened. At first it was meant to be temporary, but then the gap got longer and I heard from Sacha that he had gone traveling again and I assumed he'd made a decision, that it was all too painful, too twisted. I understand, of course I do, although that hardly makes it any easier.

I dedicated the book to Scott De Luca. I sent a finished copy to Connor at the coffee shop, thinking maybe he'll open it when, or if, he returns. On the flyleaf, above my signature, I wrote: "You only get to experience a feeling like that once." I wanted to put something meaningful, something from Varaig, from before. I don't know whether he'll ever see it, or if he'll want to act on it if he does, but that was my message in a bottle, my leap of faith.

I close the book's jacket and turn it over. There, finally, definitively, on the cover, on the spine, and on the title page is my name. I'm a ghost no more.

An hour or so later, when the small shop is full, the dreaded speeches and reading are done, and my signature has been scribbled enough times that it's no longer legible, the bell over the door tinkles and, after a couple of seconds, something pushes against my calves. I glance down. Wagging tails, hopeful eyes, a double dose of brotherly love. I look up and scan the crowd and there, on the threshold, he is, head tilted to one side in a movement I'd recognize anywhere. Connor, looking at me.

ACKNOWLEDGMENTS

TWENTY-SIX YEARS AGO I WATCHED ALFRED HITCHCOCK'S 1958 masterpiece *Vertigo* for the first time and I've been haunted by what I saw ever since. A print of Saul Bass's iconic film poster has moved home with me countless times, while the English language translation of Pierre Boileau and Thomas Narcejac's novel *D'entre les morts (The Living and the Dead)*, on which Hitchcock's film was based, has an established slot on my bookshelves.

More than sixty years on, *Eye of the Beholder* is my tribute to that movie, a kind of twisted reverse adaptation, because it seems to me that *Vertigo*'s themes of looking and being looked at, of surfaces and depth and the natural versus the man-made are just as if not even more relevant today. For anyone else who finds this stuff equally fascinating, the lecture by the late philosopher Denis Dutton, "A Darwinian Theory of Beauty," referred to in the novel, is on the TED Talks website and well worth a watch.

I'd like to thank the following people: my American editors Alison Callahan and Taylor Rondestvedt for their inspired ideas and astute guidance, Danielle Mazzella di Bosco for a breathtaking cover, Jessica Roth and Bianca Salvant for spreading the word, John Paul Jones and Stacey Sakal for exacting copyediting, and everyone else at Scout Press; my British editors Suzanne Baboneau and Judith Long for their precision and constant cheerleading, Sabah Khan, Richard Vlietstra, Hannah Paget and team at Simon & Schuster UK; and my sterling agent Camilla Bolton, Jade Kavanagh, Mary

Darby, Georgia Fuller, Sheila David and Rosanna Bellingham at Darley Anderson Agency and Associates. Thank you so much for everything you do.

Also huge thanks to the team at Moniack Mhor for looking after me so well on a writing retreat, and to early-, middle- and late-stage readers and consultants Julianne Pachico, Liv Matthews, Nicola Rayner, Ellen MacDonald-Kramer, Julia Rampen, Joanne Rush, Bobbie Darbyshire, Bob Boyton, Karen Wallace, Sharon Brennan, Nina Landmark Lie, Margaret Meyer, Nathan Hamilton, Sean Garnett, Nigel Kellow and, most importantly, Giles Foden—writers all, and the very best of sounding boards. All advice was listened to and most gratefully received, even if not taken, and therefore all bloopers are entirely my own.

ABOUT THE AUTHOR

EMMA BAMFORD is an author and journalist who has worked for *The Independent*, the *Daily Express*, the *Sunday Mirror*, *Sailing Today*, and *Boat International*. She is the author of the psychological suspense novels *Deep Water* and *Eye of the Beholder* and the sailing memoirs *Casting Off* and *Untie the Lines*. A graduate of the University of East Anglia's Prose Fiction MA, she lives in Norwich in the UK.

Visit emmabamford.com.